Kate Eberlen is the author of *Miss You* which was a Radio 2 Book Club choice 2016 and a Richard and Judy Book Club choice 2017, and *Only You*. Her novels have been published in 30 languages worldwide. She lives in London.

ever
after

Kate Eberlen

ORION

An Orion paperback

First published in Great Britain in 2023
by Orion Fiction, an imprint of The Orion Publishing Group Ltd
Carmelite House, 50 Victoria Embankment
London EC4Y 0DZ

An Hachette UK Company

1 3 5 7 9 10 8 6 4 2

A CIP catalogue record for this book is
available from the British Library.

ISBN (Trade Paperback) 978 1 3987 1212 6
ISBN (Mass Market Paperback) 978 1 3987 1213 3
ISBN (eBook) 978 1 3987 1214 0

Typeset at The Spartan Press Ltd,
Lymington, Hants

Printed in Great Britain by Clays Ltd,
Elcograf S.p.A.

www.orionbooks.co.uk

In memory of Kath, my marvellous mum

Prologue

Gus

Spring 2020

I miss you, Tess.

After nightshifts, stepping out of the fug of the hospital into this gorgeous weather, drinking in the early morning air like draughts of iced water, I look up at the blue sky beyond the sparkling silver spikes of the City and your absence feels so overwhelming, it slows the pace of my walking and my thinking. I find myself standing on the pavement in sunlight so bright it should illuminate everything, unable to remember where I'm going, or who I am.

There isn't much left on the shelves in Tesco Express. A lone box of eggs because two are smashed, their fractured shells glued to the porous cardboard; an onion dusty with mould abandoned in the corner of a green pallet; a wrinkled red pepper.

'Vegetables?' I can almost hear you saying. 'For breakfast?'

No amount of Tabasco or toothpaste seems to clear the sour taste of my own coffee breath.

Mid-morning, as I try to doze, the temperature outside is more Italian than English.

We could probably count on our fingers and toes the days we spent together in Italy, Tess, but it is where my imagination always takes me when I think of you. Your face surrounded by lapis lazuli sky, one moment as serenely caring as a Raphael Madonna, the next as mischievous as a cherub, your expression zipping between concern and excitement, faith and doubt, your radiant aura like a blessing, even to a non-believer like me.

I must try to sleep, but I can almost hear you saying it's a shame to waste such a beautiful day.

I never knew how precious time was, until I met you.

The first time I saw you, really saw you, your face was haloed by the gold of a Byzantine mosaic in the church of San Miniato al Monte on a hill overlooking Florence. I was on holiday alone, and so were you. We were both thirty-four. It turned out that our lives had brushed past each other several times before crossing again here, in the very same place we'd first glimpsed each other when we were eighteen. When we discovered that, it felt like we had wasted sixteen years already.

The first time you smiled at me, on the gravel terrace outside the basilica, I felt as if my life was opening up to endless possibility. The first time I touched you was an instinctive grab to stop you falling down the steep stone steps. You were wearing flip flops and had some convoluted explanation about forgetting to pack shoes and your feet being too big for Italian womenswear. All I could think about was how fragile your hand felt in mine and how you were blushing, as if you had never been touched by a man before. At the bottom, you let go, embarrassed. And as we walked down through olive groves towards the *centro storico*, with invisible cicadas clacking around us, my brain was battling to respond sensibly to your questions while all the time trying to think of an excuse to hold your hand again.

When I picture us that afternoon wandering around the narrow streets of Florence, I do not see crowds of summer-school teenagers with identical backpacks, nor tour parties led by guides with umbrellas held aloft, nor queues outside the Uffizi, nor diners sitting at pavement tables in Piazza Signoria, though they must have been there because it was the end of August. In my memory, it is just the two of us, walking side by side but with a carefully maintained distance, both aware and a little scared of the magnetic pull that might make us inseparable were we to move a millimetre closer.

You said things as they occurred to you, offering your life up for examination, giving opinions, sometimes changing your mind mid-sentence. I was astonished by you. Your transparency coaxed admissions I hadn't made before, even to myself, loosening knots of anxiety and leaving me strangely, pleasantly, unravelled.

With my chequered history of relationships, I don't think I'd known what it was like to feel at ease before that day. Yet I felt a slightly off balance light-headedness too, as if from a gulp of champagne on an empty stomach, as my mind attempted to formulate questions I wasn't brave enough to ask.

Is something happening here? Are you feeling it too?

It was only much later that evening that I got my answer.

The restaurants were closed, the shops shuttered, and we were alone, our footsteps echoing, our words softly murmured as if to respect the city's slumber. Pausing on the Ponte Vecchio, we stared down at the river made slick and black by the moonlight, neither of us bold enough to suggest what might happen next.

In my usual way of deferring intimacy, I mentioned something I had read that I thought would sound profound, about the random interconnectedness of the world. Apparently, the flap of a butterfly's wing could cause a thunderstorm thousands of miles away.

You turned, looked into my eyes, your smile all innocence and certainty.

'Or a rainbow,' you said. 'It doesn't have to be something bad.'

Suddenly there was no space between us. My hands were on your waist, touching the warmth of your skin beneath the flimsy fabric of your summer dress, your body so delicate yet so determined that I wanted to treat you with infinite care, like the most precious porcelain, then break you with my passion. Our first kiss was an exquisite alchemy of desire and restraint. We drew back a moment, looked at each other, then it was all urgency.

The first time we made love, under a ceiling painted with ribbons and cherubs in the villa where we were both staying, it felt like an obliterating union of bodies and souls. The intensity of sensation made me cry out then left me feeling both vulnerable and protected, like being lost and found at the same time.

I wake up, roll over, still half in my dream, expecting to find you looking at me, your angelic face on a snowy cloud of pillow like that first morning. But now, in this City bachelor pad, there is only the masculine navy of borrowed bedlinen.

It occurs to me that I may never wake up beside you again.

In the emptiness of this unfamiliar space, I hear myself choking with stifled despair.

Why did this happen to us? Why now?

The sun is low in the sky, washing a coral glow over the bedroom walls.

I must get up and shower then eat something before I get back to the wards.

I miss you, Tess. I long to be with you. But this is how you have decided it must be.

Tess

Chapter One

Summer 2013

That first night, as I lay gazing up at our celestial ceiling listening to the soft rhythm of his sleep, I remembered the feeling of enchantment that used to envelop me as a child when my mother read to me at bedtime.

I can't have been more than four because I could read by myself at five, devouring so many books each week that the nice librarian knew my name and offered me all the new releases.

'Once upon a time...' As I closed my eyes, I would become drowsily aware of Mum's voice fading as images flooded my mind, of turreted palaces and princesses so dainty they could wear shoes made of glass or feel a pea through a dozen mattresses.

The story of Gus and me sounded like a fairytale. As we talked that first night in Florence we worked out that our paths must have crossed on many occasions. We'd been on the same plane, at the same gig and now we lived at different ends of the same London street. There were so many other just-missed opportunities that our encounter, in the very church where we'd first set eyes on each other, felt like fate rather than chance. It was as if we'd had to overcome many obstacles before finally meeting properly. Like the Prince hacking through the overgrown forest to get to Sleeping Beauty, or Cinderella doing all that bloody housework before going to the ball.

'Maybe people miss each other all the time, though,' Gus said, as we sat at a pavement table in the Oltrarno. 'I mean, when you think of all these lives intersecting with ours now for just a second . . .'

He waved in the direction of the locals taking their evening *passeggiata* in the square.

'Or all the people you've ever stood next to queuing for coffee, or passed on the escalator going down to the Tube? Maybe we've just got lucky today?'

Gazing up at the darkening sky I decided that serendipity was just as romantic as destiny, because it meant there was hope for everyone.

In the morning, I was awake before him. I kept as still as I could, feeling a little clandestine as I stared at his face. In repose, he looked younger than thirty-four, more boyish than princely, with reddish brown hair and the sort of freckly, fair complexion that doesn't need a shave every day. Just as I was wondering whether I dared kiss him awake, he stirred, his breath a bit garlicky from the pizza we'd shared the previous evening. I was trying to work out if I could tiptoe to the bathroom to brush my teeth without disturbing him when he opened his eyes, looked at me warily for a second, before remembering, smiling and pulling me on top of him. When we kissed my body was suffused with a rush of affection and sensuality so intense it felt like forever.

The night before, our love-making had been frantic, as if we were trying to clamber right to the core of each other. Now it was exquisitely slow and delicious. I'd never thought of myself as good at sex before. Lying next to previous lovers, I always seemed to have a surplus arm or leg I didn't quite know where

10

to put. Being naked just seemed to emphasise how long and imperfect my body was, and I never knew if I was making enough noise, or too much. But with Gus it felt totally natural and mind-blowingly perfect.

Eventually, he volunteered to find us breakfast, returning with strawberries and tiny pastries. We made love again, his lips dusted with icing sugar, then we dozed until the splinters of sunlight through the shutters were blinding. I threw back the white cotton sheet decisively.

'We can't waste such a beautiful day . . .'

'Waste?' He grinned at me.

'You know what I mean . . .'

Some places in the world are so like the images you have seen on postcards they actually seem unreal when you are there. In Pisa, where we went on our first day, the sky was so blue, the clipped lawns so green, and the lacy marble carving of the cathedral and bell tower so white, it was almost like ambling through a computer-generated landscape. The cobbled medieval streets and squares of San Gimignano on our second felt like a movie set for Romeo and Juliet. And I had stumbled onto it with a stranger who was just as lovestruck as me.

There was this constant dialogue going on in my head. *Is this really happening? Is it love or just lust? Why does love even exist?* Lust alone would do the evolutionary job, so why did god or nature have to add all that emotion whose exquisite joy seems to anticipate anguish?

Don't say that out loud, for heaven's sake!

To the adjectives boyish, charming, sexy, which I'd initially ascribed to Gus, I had rapidly added troubled. As we talked about our backstories, it became apparent that, while he was materially better off than me, he was much less contented.

11

We'd both suffered profound grief in our lives. My mother died when I was eighteen. Around the same age, Gus's elder brother Ross had been killed in a skiing accident. The course of my life had been fundamentally altered, and I missed Mum every single day, but I'd always tried make the best of things as she had done. Gus and his family appeared to have been poleaxed. Unable to move on, his parents divorced and Gus's life had been haunted by the tragedy. He had even ended up marrying his brother's girlfriend, which had been doomed to failure from the start. Sometimes, he would go quiet, as if his mind was somewhere else completely. It made it all the more satisfying when I managed to make him smile. As Jane Eyre discovered, there's nothing more compelling than making a sad man happy.

Which is not to say that he wasn't good company. His sense of humour was so dry I sometimes didn't realise he was teasing, but he was never mean. Gus was a gentle man.

When my best friend Doll and I were at that teenage stage of falling in love with a different member of Take That each week, Mum always used to warn us that good looks weren't everything. What you wanted was a kind man, she'd told us.

Not that Gus wasn't good-looking too. And interesting. He knew all about art and architecture and showed me details I never would have noticed, like the different designs of lamp-posts in each Tuscan town, and the pale horizons of Piero della Francesca's skies. He was generous, always offering to buy me kitsch trinkets as we passed market stalls, so in the end I stopped pointing. He had an appetite for gelato as endless as mine.

There are some couples where one, usually the woman, operates in the shadow of the other. Mum and Dad were like that. And maybe I'd picked that up from her because no man in my life had ever been interested in my opinions. Leo, my most recent partner, had only pretended to be when he wanted sex.

When I'd finally figured that out, I'd felt like a prostitute paid in nods of the head and utterances of 'that's a fascinating idea'.

But it wasn't like that with Gus. He listened to everything I said, never interrupting or looking at his watch. He made me feel equal.

Our third morning together was the first when I hadn't pinched myself hard upon waking. I had become used to Gus's shape, his weight and warmth on the luxurious mattress. I loved lying there in the slight chill of dawn with the sheet pulled up to my chin, gazing up at the heavenly canopy above and rerunning moments from the day before.

In the trattoria full of Italians having their lunch, he'd taught me how to wind spaghetti like a native, using only a fork. His gently guiding hand and the intent in his eyes felt almost as intimate as foreplay.

Over coffee, he'd remarked that I seemed to imagine lives for all the other diners, so I'd confided that my dream was to be a writer and he'd just nodded and said, 'That makes a lot of sense.'

Now, I watched his face as he slept, wondering what he was dreaming about. He stirred, opened his eyes, smiled.

'Is there anywhere you'd particularly like to go before you leave?'

It was the first time my departure had been mentioned. Gus was booked to stay another week. My mind suddenly flooded with doubts.

Was our relationship an illusion unsustainable outside the magical landscape of Italy? Was it just a holiday romance? I'd never had one before. I didn't know how they went.

'What?' he asked.

'Our last day!'

The words came out sounding as if I was being strangled.

13

'We live on the same street, Tess. I walk past the salon where you work almost every single day. I'm not going to be able to get away from you now!' He smiled, reached for my hand. 'It's our last day in Italy. When I'm back, it will be our first day in London.'

Which was lovely. Except if it had been the other way round and I'd been the one booked in for another week, would I have stayed on by myself?

I told myself that if we were going to be together, we'd inevitably have to spend time apart, wouldn't we? And if we weren't, then I'd better make sure we lived this day like it really was our last.

'How far is Assisi?'

Turned out it was much further than I'd anticipated, but Gus was happy to drive.

'Why Assisi?' he asked, once we were sure we were on the right road.

'It was the first place in Italy I heard about. My mum had a photo of the town rising up out of fields of sunflowers. St Francis is everyone's favourite saint, isn't he?'

The postcard had been sent by one of Mum's church friends who'd been on a package tour with Pilgrim Air. It was propped up on the knick-knack shelf in our kitchen behind her other precious souvenirs, like the snowglobe my brother Kevin sent from New York, and the painted plate from Tenerife with the motto: *Today is the first day of the rest of your life.*

I remembered Mum telling me about how St Francis spoke to the animals and how, one Sunday afternoon, watching *Doctor Doolittle*, I'd shouted that St Francis was on the telly, and that became one of the anecdotes she relayed to Auntie Catriona when we went to Ireland for our holidays.

'Are you a practising Catholic?' Gus asked.

It was weird because in some ways we knew each other inside out, in others we were still total strangers.

'I lapsed when I was twelve and refused to be confirmed,' I told him. 'It broke Mum's heart . . . I don't know why I couldn't have just gone along with it to please her. I suppose I wasn't lapsed enough to think that wouldn't be a sin . . .'

Gus turned his head from the road towards me for a second, with a puzzled look that I was becoming used to.

'Is your family religious?' I asked Gus.

'My mother would say she's Church of England, although she never goes. My father thinks of himself as a scientist, so if there's no proof of god, that means he can't exist.'

We exited one motorway for another.

'We should be there in time for lunch,' he said. 'I'm starving, aren't you?'

I noticed that he changed the subject quickly whenever his family was mentioned. Perhaps it was repressed emotion? Gus had been to public school where he said that showing feelings made you vulnerable. I didn't know him well enough to ask for elaboration.

'What about you?' I pushed. 'Religion-wise?'

'I love churches. You meet amazing people there.' He smiled at me. Then, perhaps seeing from my frown that he wasn't going to get away with another deflection, he added, 'I'm in awe of the devotion that made people strive so incredibly hard to create such beauty. But I don't really understand it.'

'My mum used to say that faith is a step you have to take and then it becomes clear. But it never did to me.'

The sunflowers on the Umbrian plain were beginning to turn from golden to brown, making the view a more autumnal shade than the bright yellow on my mother's postcard. I was quite glad that the harvest had not started, as I knew I would have been disappointed if the fields had been stripped to bare brown earth.

As if tapping into my line of thought, Gus said, 'I've always thought Van Gogh's *Sunflowers* in the National Gallery was a rather mournful painting about the transience of life, not the vibrant vase of flowers that other people seem to see.'

That was Gus all over. At first, I thought he was more profound than me, but actually *Van Gogh's Sunflowers: alive or dead?* was only a middle-class way of saying glass half full or half empty.

In a restaurant near the main square, Gus ordered pasta filled with pumpkin, with a sauce of melted butter and a fried leaf on top that he said was sage.

'What do you think?' he asked, as I tasted it hesitantly.

Gus was a bit of a foodie. I never paid much attention to what I ate. There wasn't a lot of money in our family and our most exotic treat was the chicken tikka masala my dad brought back on Saturdays if he'd had a good afternoon at the bookies. The only person I'd had to cook for was my little sister Hope, who rejected anything outside our usual routine. If it was Monday, it was bangers and mash; Tuesday macaroni cheese, which was the only type of pasta I'd had before visiting Italy, apart from tins of spaghetti hoops on toast, which we sometimes ate as an alternative to beans on Thursdays.

I tried to concentrate on the delicate flavours in my mouth, putting on a thoughtful face like one of the restaurant critics on Masterchef.

'It's earthy, with slightly sweet floral notes. Almost like eating a garden.'

Gus laughed, but I don't think he realised I was joking.

I recalled the games that my best friend Doll and I used to

16

play on long train journeys. If you had one last meal, what would it be? Doll changed her mind according to the party food mentioned in *Hello*, often including things like cocktail blinis and mini pavlovas that she'd never eaten and wasn't even sure how to pronounce. Mine was invariably dippy egg and chips. I could imagine Gus putting a lot of serious deliberation and organically sourced ingredients into his choices.

The basilica of San Francesco was on a different scale from the rest of Assisi, like the cathedral of a capital city plonked outside a little hilltop town. Inside, it was flooded with light from the high windows. The colours of the frescoes by Giotto depicting the life of the saint were so bright they looked as if the paint had only just dried.

A sombre atmosphere of reverence was maintained by a priest, dressed in the rough brown robes of the Franciscan order, who intoned 'Silenzio!' in a deep voice whenever Gus's commentary became too audible.

We stared at the panel with St Francis exorcising demons from a little walled town, which was clearly recognisable as the one we'd just walked through. The devils were evil-looking creatures, part human, part bat.

'I wonder if St Francis was schizophrenic,' Gus whispered. 'I mean, he clearly experienced hallucinations and heard voices . . .'

I'd never heard anyone speak like that about stories I'd been taught as facts. With a shiver of fear for the consequences of such heresy, I looked over my shoulder to check we were out of earshot of the priest.

'People didn't know about mental illness then,' Gus went on. 'So what better way to explain weird things than believing that they came from an external source, rather than a misfiring neuron?'

I'd never thought of a medical explanation for miracles before.

'If that is the case, though,' I whispered. 'I'm glad they didn't know.'

'Why?'

'Because if people just thought he was crazy, they wouldn't have been inspired to make these transcendent works of art, would they?'

Outside, we sat on a warm wall in the sunshine, neither of us speaking, as if we needed time to reflect on the emotions that the place had stirred. Below us on an overgrown ledge, a single white butterfly flitted between yellow wildflowers. In the sunflower valley below, occasional planes drifted in to land at Perugia airport. I wondered if pilots made the sign of the cross as they spotted the huge basilica, like a lighthouse guiding them to safety.

I wished Mum could see me in this holy place. When she died, I found it wasn't life's difficulties that I missed sharing with her so much as all the lovely things. I'd never realised how much her enjoyment, when I recounted my little achievements or the beautiful things I'd seen, had enhanced mine. Part of the thrill of a new experience had been the anticipation of telling her.

I felt Gus's hand reach for mine, the touch of his fingers still so unfamiliar it quickened my pulse.

'Tess . . .'

He said my name often, as if he was about to ask me something, and I'd wait and no question would come.

Just at that moment, the strict priest came out of the church and walked past us with a ringtone coming from the voluminous folds of his habit, growing louder until he eventually managed to retrieve it.

'Pronto?'

'Silenzio!' Gus said.

The priest looked at us sharply, then shrugged as if to say fair enough.

'Tess?' Gus began again.

'Yes?'

'You make me feel I'm engaging with the world, not just observing it from a distance.'

'I hope that's OK?' I responded, ridiculously, the breeze blowing my hair across my eyes.

'It's a fucking miracle!'

He took my face in his hands and kissed me so passionately it felt like my whole being was exploding with joy, then he pulled away, his wonderfully expressive eyes flickering from anxiety to happiness as he gathered me into his arms and held me close.

Look at me, Mum, in this beautiful place with this lovely kind man! I shouted silently up to her.

As we walked back to the car, the main street was quiet, half of it in shadow, the other still bleached white by the sunlight. Thinking of all the pilgrims whose footsteps had trodden these warm paving stones, I enjoyed that giddy, privileged feeling that I've only ever experienced in Italy, of being part of the past and the present at the same time.

'Do you think if we had met properly when we were eighteen our lives would have been different?' Gus asked.

'Yes.'

'I wish we had.'

'No point in regretting what might have been. We can only make the most of what's next,' I said. It sounded like one of Mum's mottos.

'Look!' Gus pointed at a sign on a house saying *Vendesi*. He

19

stopped walking, grabbed both my hands. 'Why don't we come and live here? You could write . . .'

For a moment, I allowed myself to picture a rooftop room beneath the terracotta tiles, a wooden desk where I could gaze out over a sea of golden sunflowers and be inspired.

'What would you do here?' I asked him.

He looked a little sheepish. 'I've always wanted to paint. I was going to go to art school . . .'

'How did you end up studying medicine then?'

'It was almost like a genetic condition in our family. Ross was at medical school when he . . . so I . . .'

I hadn't quite been able to see him as a doctor. He was so much less sure of himself than the doctors I had encountered, although maybe they weren't all like that off duty. Snippets of information were gradually forming my picture of his life, like pieces of a jigsaw. Now I knew he had studied medicine to try to make up for his parents' loss, it made more sense.

In my imaginary room, I placed an easel next to the desk and put Gus in front of it, mixing different shades of ochre on his palette.

In the evenings, as the sun began to sink in the sky, he would put down his paintbrush and I would close my laptop. We would go for our *passeggiata*, strolling up to the main square to buy ice cream cones, greeting our neighbours in fluent Italian.

'What's to stop us?' he said.

As if in answer to the question his phone rang, the ringtone as jangly and incongruous on this ancient street as the priest's had been. Gus crossed to the dark side of the street to see the screen. I started walking again, to give him privacy, but in the stillness of the afternoon I could hear every word.

'Bella? What's the matter, poppet? No, of course you don't have to do anything you don't want to . . . Italy . . . Wish you were here too . . .'

'Is everything OK?' I asked, when he caught me up.

'My youngest.' He looked flustered.

'She doesn't like her summer camp. I hope she's not being bullied . . .'

I knew better than to express an opinion. This was new territory and we'd entered it much sooner than I was prepared for.

'Do you want to call . . . ?'

I wasn't sure how to finish the sentence. Your wife? Your ex-wife? He'd told me her name was Charlotte, but that might sound overfamiliar.

He hesitated.

'No, it's fine. I'm sure it's fine.'

His two daughters now lived with their mother in Geneva. I knew he missed them but it hadn't really registered how difficult it must be to have all those little everyday worries and not be able to do anything from such a distance.

He was smiling at me, but I could tell that the focus of his thoughts had shifted back to the real world.

Darkness falls early on Italian summer days and we were still on the road back to Florence when the blood red sunset faded to black. Speeding along the unlit motorway felt like being in a tunnel. The inside of the car was so full of Gus's anxiety that I didn't want to disturb his concentration with words. The atmosphere was so different from that morning, and I couldn't think how to take us back to that carefree breeziness. It was like starting all over again with a different person. And there wasn't enough time for that because my plane was leaving in less than twelve hours.

Trying to calm myself down, I found myself remembering another anecdote my mother had told her sister when we were on our summer holidays. Us kids were meant to play outside while the grown-ups sipped tea from Auntie Catriona's best china, but I used to listen at the door as they competed with smart things their children had said or done. My mum told the story of how, once, she had thought I'd drifted off after my bedtime story, so she had ever so softly closed the book, ever so carefully stood up and ever so quietly tiptoed across the room. And suddenly I'd sat bolt upright in bed and demanded, 'How do you know?'

She'd sighed. 'Know what, Tess?'

'That the Prince and Princess lived happily ever after?'

'Because that's how fairy stories always end, Tess.'

'But they've only just met!'

Auntie Catriona's usually stern face had softened at that, and her eyes had caught Mum's, almost like they had a shared secret. With a strange little laugh that sounded not happy but sad, she'd said, 'Well now, isn't that the truth of it, Mary? Falling in love is only the beginning of the story.'

Chapter Two

It was raining when I arrived back in London, which didn't feel like a good omen for what I had come back to face that afternoon. I had to push hard on the street door because of all the leaflets stacked behind it. Scooping them up, I marched up the staircase and let myself in.

The flyers were mostly adverts for takeaway, livid circles of pizza dotted with crimson pepperoni, which looked nothing like the one we had eaten beside the floodlit façade of Santo Spirito on our first evening.

There was a bank statement, an electricity bill and a greetings card with bunting on the front spelling out 'Welcome Home!', and a message in Doll's loopy handwriting.

'Call me as soon as you're back. Longing to hear all about it.'

I noticed that she had started the first word of the second sentence with a 'D' then crossed it out. I suspected she'd been about to put 'Dying' but thought better of it in the light of my appointment.

I gazed out of the sash window onto the street. Coloured umbrellas were the only contrast to the grey of tarmac and sky. Market traders huddled with cups of tea at the back of their dripping stalls.

I pictured Gus drinking an espresso in the shade of a yellow parasol with bright blue sky above.

He'd told me to let him know when I was safely home, but I didn't know what an appropriate text would be.

Safely home. Hope you're having fun! Might sound a touch resentful.

We had said the words to each other several times, but *I love you!* looked a little presumptuous written down for the first time.

He'd driven me to the airport and stood on tiptoe, waving until the very last moment before I disappeared behind security, but I thought that he'd probably called his ex-wife about his daughter before I'd taken off. The truth was that Gus and I were in very different places, not just geographically. After the opulence of our Tuscan room my studio flat, with its homemade bookshelves, looked very shabby.

After composing then deleting several messages, I finally pressed send with *Safely home. Miss you!* Then I spent the next hour while I was unpacking wondering if that was too intense, until my phone pinged with *Miss you too!*, which sent a wave of happiness crashing through my chest.

I took a shower and dressed in a navy blue shirtdress with white polka dots. As I fastened the belt and smoothed the fabric over my hips, every inch of my skin felt imprinted by his touch. A daft smile spread across my face, until I noticed the state of my toenails after a week in flip flops, which would not do for work. I found some shoes with a covered toe. They were difficult to walk in but that didn't really matter as the salon I managed was on the ground floor of the building where I lived.

Just as I was leaving, my phone rang. I was so eager to answer, it leapt out of my hands and fell to the floor. Grabbing it and stabbing at the screen, I was disappointed to see it was only Doll calling.

'So who is he?' she demanded, before I'd even said hello.

'Who?'

'You send me a selfie of you and a mystery man, then nothing for four days?'

I'd completely forgotten the photo I'd taken on the Ponte Vecchio on our first evening together.

'He's tall enough for you, at least.'

'His name is Gus and I love him!' I said, before she could offer any more of her opinions.

'Fuck's sake. Does he love you back?'

'I think so.'

'You only think so?'

'He says so . . .'

'What's he like then?'

'He's very intelligent . . .'

'Not another academic?' Doll interrupted, alarmed.

My former lover Leo had been my tutor on a creative writing evening class I took when I still lived in Kent.

'He's a doctor.'

'Get you! Is he married?'

'No!' It wasn't like I made a habit of having affairs with married men. 'Divorced.'

'I suppose that's better than not being married at his age.'

'I'm his age and I'm not married.'

'You know what I mean though? Kids?'

'Two daughters, six and nine.'

'That's a lot of baggage, Tess.'

'I've got a lot of baggage too, though, haven't I?'

'I suppose you have with Hope.'

I wasn't referring to my sister, but Doll and Hope had never really got on.

'Where does he live?'

'This you won't believe, in one of those painted houses at the top of this actual street.'

'The ones you've always fantasised about?'

When Doll and I were teenagers we used to escape to London at weekends and wander round posh areas with pretty names, like Belsize Park and Notting Hill, dreaming of spending our lives like the wealthy people who owned those houses. It was probably why she had chosen Portobello Road as the site of her first London branch.

'Well, that's proof if you ever needed it,' said Doll.

'Of what?'

'If you want something, you have to visualise it and it will come to you.'

One of the few books Doll had ever read was called *The Secret* and she swore by its philosophy.

'It worked for me,' she said.

'You didn't get your business just by visualising it and I've visualised lots of things, not just living in one of those houses. That's if this is a thing anyway . . .'

The more I talked out loud about it, the more I wondered whether I'd dreamed the whole thing with Gus, it seemed so unlikely.

'Oh ye of little faith!' Doll said, which was a bit rich coming from someone who'd only started going to Mass again in order to get her kid into the local Catholic primary school.

'Can't wait to meet him . . .'

Would they get on? A frisson of panic went through me when I pictured introducing them and her taking his slightly old-school charm the wrong way.

'I was just going down to work,' I said.

'No need,' Doll said. 'I've told Aggie to cover you all day.'

It was always a tiny bit awkward when Doll spoke to me as

my boss, which she had been for a year, rather than the best friend who'd known me since I was four.

'It will take my mind off things.'

'Do you want me to come with you this afternoon?'

I knew that if I said yes, she'd be there, but she was pregnant with her second child and I didn't want her trekking up to London.

It's always nerve-wracking getting test results because you're hoping for the best at the same time as preparing for the worst. You only get a few minutes with the doctor so you have to be ready to ask sensible questions without choking up. With another person there, it can be more difficult because there's the added dynamic of trying to make it easier for them too.

'I'll be fine,' I said.

'Promise you'll call me straight after?'

'Promise.'

A nail bar was about the last place I'd expected to end up working. I'd never even had a manicure before I took the job, except for the GCSE prom when Doll had insisted on giving me a full makeover. She had known even at St Cuthbert's primary school that she wanted to be a beautician, and often used me to practise on.

We made an unlikely pair. I always had my head in a book. Doll was the life and soul of the party. She was petite, pretty and groomed. I grew tall very young and had unruly curly hair that didn't know one end of straighteners from the other. At school discos Doll had boys swarming round her, while I used to shrink against a wall observing the action on the dance floor like some maiden aunt chaperone out of a Georgette Heyer novel. I stayed on for A-Levels and by the time I won a place to read English at University College London, Doll was already working. That summer we went backpacking round Europe together. Doll hated all the things I loved, long train journeys, sleeping under the skies in a tent, visiting museums and, worst of all, churches. We'd still somehow managed to have fun, but it had felt like a last holiday we'd spend together because our lives were already on different paths.

But everything changed when we got back, with Mum dying and me having to look after my sister Hope. She was only five at the time. I'd promised Mum I would. We both knew Dad was far too unreliable. So that meant giving up university.

While Hope was growing up and I was doing part-time jobs, Doll had gone from setting up one tiny nail bar in our hometown of Margate to owning outlets all over the country. That success was entirely due to her instinct, guts and skill, but I was the one who'd come up with the name 'The Dolls House'.

When Hope was eighteen she left home and moved in with Martin. I had the disastrous affair with Leo. When that finished, I lost confidence in myself and didn't know where to turn until Doll offered me a job managing her first London branch and living in the flat upstairs. She insisted that I had 'transferable skills', which, amazingly, turned out to be true. My work as a teaching assistant had made me good at organisation. As supervisor in a supermarket, I'd dealt with all sorts of tricky customers. It wasn't what I'd envisaged for myself, but Mum used to say that if you do something with a happy heart, it will bring you joy.

'Holiday romance put a spring in your step!' said Aggie, who was manning the reception desk.

Was it so obvious, or had Doll shown her the photo?

The atmosphere in The Dolls House was part hen night, part confessional, especially when there was free prosecco on offer for important dates like Valentine's and Mother's Day. It never ceased to amaze me how much the clients were prepared to reveal to almost total strangers. I avoided speaking about my private life, mainly because I didn't have much of one. Since moving to London I hadn't even been on a date.

'Any problems?' I asked Aggie.

'The card machine went on the blink again. We're out of fuchsia gel so I've re-ordered.'

The millionaire hedge fund manager who never tipped had asked whether we could open at six thirty in the morning as it was increasingly difficult to fit us into her schedule.

'And what did you say?'

'I said, "You are joking, lady!"' Aggie smiled.

'And what did she say?' I asked, a little nervous, because she was a regular customer with a lot of influential friends.

'She managed to find a slot for me after all.'

Aggie was a legend in the nail world and she was booked up weeks in advance. I liked the fact she'd given the financier a lesson in supply and demand.

I told her to take the rest of the morning off, then slightly regretted it as, without her irresistible wheezing laughter, the room was just a quiet hive of industry.

I opened the box of cantuccini I had bought at Duty Free and rang Luis in the café next door to order cappuccinos all round. I tidied the glossy magazines, plumped up the cushions, and filled the dog bowl with water. So many clients brought their dogs in with them these days, it crossed my mind that Doll should set up a kind of grooming creche for pooches. We could call it The Dog House.

I was never sure whether Doll's reaction to my ideas would be, 'That's genius, Tess!' or 'What are you like?'

Since I'd been working for her, I'd offered a few suggestions she referred to as 'blue sky thinking' because she had all the jargon down. She'd even said I should join her as Innovations

Director at Head Office, which was situated in an industrial estate on the outskirts of our hometown. But we both knew my heart wasn't really in Margate or the beauty business. At thirty-four I was still desperately hoping that a fascinating future would present itself.

In Italy, I'd allowed myself to think that might finally be happening. It turned out that if I had gone to university, Gus and I would have been in the same hall of residence, possibly even next to each other on the corridor, because his friend Nash, whom he'd met on the first day, had got the adjacent room as a last minute cancellation. In a weird way, meeting him at this point in my life felt like it might be the chance to start my adulthood over again.

I checked my phone, hoping that he was thinking about me when I was thinking about him, but there were no messages.

I decided to walk to the hospital. The rain had given way to a silvery sunshine and the stallholders were calling out bargain offers for fruit and veg. Further along the street I could never resist pausing to look in the windows of antique shops.

Near the top of Portobello Road I stood for a moment outside the house I now knew to be Gus's. It seemed far too grown-up for him. As strangers abroad we had been equals. Back in London, was he way out of my league?

I imagined his ex-wife peering down at me from behind the curtain.

I started walking again, checking my phone for about the hundredth time. Nothing. If he really loved me, surely he would have texted *Good luck!* at the very least? Unless he was one of those people who think it's bad luck to say good luck? In which case, why had he said it at the airport eight – was it only eight? – hours ago? Perhaps, like most men, he thought that if you said something once, that was enough, because generally they don't seem to need as much reassurance as women do.

Perhaps I was being needy? Though if you couldn't be a bit needy when you were going for test results, when could you?

I tried to distract myself as I stood at the traffic lights. Was the man in sunglasses in the convertible white Audi, revving impatiently as I crossed, on his way to an important meeting or just showing off? And who was sitting behind the tinted glass of the black limousine? A film star or, this close to Kensington Palace, could it even be a royal? I wondered if they were looking at me wondering who I was and where I was going in my polka dot dress and trainers. If so, what were they thinking? Manager? Writer? Cancer patient?

The BRCA mutation runs in our family. My mum was cured of breast cancer but then she got ovarian, which is one of those that hide, so once you get the symptoms it's nearly always too late. So when I got breast cancer just after arriving in London, I'd decided to go for the radical treatment of double mastectomy and ovary removal. I was recovering well but just recently I'd fainted a couple of times, so that's why they'd given me a scan. And that's why Doll had booked me a week in Tuscany, to take my mind off it, or maybe she thought of it as my version of swimming with dolphins, which a lot of people seem to want to do when they don't have long to live.

As I approached Oncology Outpatients, I found myself bargaining with god. *I won't even mind if the cancer is back, if you can just let me be with Gus for a year or two*. Because you do that, don't you, hoping that if you are prepared to accept the worst then you'll somehow trick it out of happening? Then, as I stepped through the entrance, it dawned on me that it was entirely possible both for the cancer to be back and for the thing with Gus to have been a fling without a future.

*

31

Everyone is nice to you in Oncology. It can make you more worried, to be honest.

'Probably all the pasta and ice cream!' I said to the nurse as I stepped off the scales.

'That's wonderful!'

With cancer, they think it's a good thing if you've put on weight.

Back in the waiting area, I checked my phone again. Nothing. I was getting a little bit annoyed with Gus now for preoccupying me when I should be thinking about my questions. He could at least have waited for me to get my results before ghosting me.

Finally, my name was called. I stood up and smoothed down my dress. As I walked towards the consulting room, I could feel my heart rate accelerating, knowing that when I came out in a few minutes' time, my life would be different.

The weird thing about cancer was that I never felt ill before having the treatment so, sometimes, I wondered what would have happened if I hadn't found the lump. How long could I have gone on living a normal life? Now, half of me wanted to turn and walk away in blissful ignorance. But the rational side of me knew that not knowing wouldn't be blissful, because I'd be wondering all the time. Better to face up to it. I took a deep breath.

The doctor wasn't one I'd seen before. In Outpatients you never get any clues about their backstory. No family photos on the desk, no favourite coffee mug. I always found it a bit unbalancing to be in a relationship where they could literally see inside me but I knew nothing about them. He was tapping at his keyboard. I noticed a ring on his wedding finger. He was probably in his thirties. Perhaps he'd been a contemporary of Gus at med school? He looked up and smiled, but there was nothing going on in his eyes. I couldn't tell if it was a good-news smile or an I'm-sorry-to-have-to-tell-you smile.

'Have a seat.'

I obeyed.

'How are you?' he asked.

'Aren't you supposed to be telling me that?'

He looked at his screen again. I wondered if there was some code for irritating patient.

'We've found no evidence of recurrence of malignancy.'

'What does that mean?'

'It means there are no macroscopic signs of disease on your scan . . .'

'What about microscopic?' I asked.

'The scan can't pick up microscopic signs. We will keep monitoring you for five years.'

'So, you're saying I'm not clear?'

'We can't say you're clear until we've monitored you for five years.'

'Oh.'

'Any questions?'

All the questions I had thought of were irrelevant now. I'd prepared myself for the worst and for the best, but not this kind of limbo.

'What can I tell people? Because my friends and family won't know whether to worry or celebrate, will they?'

He looked surprised. However much doctors know about the disease, they seem unaware about the narrative you and everyone around you has to deal with when you've had a cancer diagnosis.

'You could say you are in remission.'

'Am I though? In remission?'

He looked perplexed.

'I mean I *could* say I was clear, couldn't I? But it wouldn't be true.'

I knew if Doll was here she'd tell him to ignore me because I'd always been a bit pedantic.

'But you are in remission.'

Mum was 'in remission' for five years. So it was better than I'd bargained for.

'Right. Good. I suppose?' I wanted him to say, yes, very good. But he didn't.

'And I had the radical surgery, so there's less of me for it to pop up in, presumably?' I tried again to push for a little more optimism.

'That's the general idea.'

I felt like saying, 'The general idea? Bloody hell, I thought that it was more scientific than that.'

Instead I said, 'Thank you very much.'

I had pictured myself leaving the hospital crying. I had pictured myself with fingers tightly crossed, skipping out happily. Now, as I walked into the sunny courtyard, there was still a faint drumbeat of fear inside me, as if a terrifying attacker had run off but might still be lurking round the corner. Mostly, I felt drained. Emotionally and physically.

I realised that I hadn't eaten all day and decided that I deserved a treat. A caramel latte, I thought, would be both nourishing and indulgent. It wasn't champagne, but it wasn't chemotherapy either. It was a good half-celebration kind of drink. As I stepped out on to the street, trying to work out where I would find the nearest coffee shop, I heard footsteps behind me.

'Tess?'

I spun round.

'What are you doing here?' Shock made the words come out a bit aggressively.

He looked just the same as when I'd last seen him. T-shirt,

shorts, trainers, hair unbrushed after a hurried shower before we left for the airport.

'I wanted to be with you.'

'Where's your suitcase?'

'There wasn't time to go all the way back ... I had my passport and wallet, so I just stayed at the airport.'

'Why didn't you text me?'

'I didn't know if I'd get here in time to surprise you ...'

'Why didn't you just fly back with me?'

'I'm an idiot,' he said with a shrug of his shoulders

'You're not an idiot!'

'Don't let's argue,' he said, grinning.

All the hours I'd spent doubting and worrying collapsed to nothing as I realised this was more romantic than any reunion my imagination could have conjured up.

'What did they say?' Gus asked anxiously.

'I'm in remission!'

Suddenly there was no distance between us. I could feel all the buttons on my dress pressing into my chest as he hugged me tightly, then drew away, holding my face in his hands and kissing me so fervently I felt fireworks go off in my head.

'You don't think I'm a fraud, do you?' I whispered, when we finally stopped for breath.

'I'm sorry?'

'Like it was a swimming with dolphins kind of thing ...'

The puzzled look.

'Like you thought we only had a short time together ...'

'That couldn't be further from what I'm thinking.'

Chapter Three

We ambled back to Notting Hill through St James's Park where deep herbaceous borders shimmered with butterflies and bees, then along the avenue of huge London plane trees on Constitution Hill that offered their cool green shade, like the nave of a natural cathedral. In Hyde Park we sat for a while breathing the heady perfume of pink roses strung in garlands around the Rose Garden. By the Serpentine he asked if I'd ever been in one of the rowing boats and, when I said I hadn't, suggested hiring one at the weekend. We started making a list of things we'd never done in London. It felt like being on holiday again. Occasionally, we'd stop for no reason except to kiss.

Gus bought food in an Italian deli, then an entire tray of tomatoes for a fiver at a market stall which was packing up for the day.

'How will you ever get through all those?'

'They make a great pasta sauce roasted with a bit of chilli and olive oil.'

Who knew?

As he put his key in the door, I hovered on the street remembering all the times Doll and I had stood outside this pretty terrace of houses, speculating about who might be lucky enough to live there.

'Aren't you coming in?'

'OK then,' I said, trying to sound nonchalant, but with my heart pounding so hard I feared he would see my polka dots pulsating.

The ground floor was open plan, with French doors leading out into a small courtyard at the back. My first thought was that it was incredibly tidy and clean, almost as if it was ready to be photographed by *World of Interiors*. The kitchen area at the back had matching units in a putty grey colour, and a large wooden table. There were stripped floorboards throughout, but the soft furnishings in the living area were opulent. A huge sofa covered in turquoise velvet, a fireplace with a surround of Iznik tiles, an antique rug with birds and flowers like the ones that hang like works of art in posh shop windows on Piccadilly. Spotting my reflection in the large gold-framed mantel mirror, I thought, *You don't belong here.*

'Make yourself at home!' Gus went into the kitchen area.

'Are these your girls?' I asked, pointing at the framed sketches on either side of the chimney breast.

'They're a lot bigger than when I did those.'

'You drew them? They're brilliant.'

He looked embarrassed and I felt like a fool. How could I possibly know they were, never having seen his children?

'I bet they loved flying on this?' I said, pointing at the rug.

A puzzled look.

'It's what I've always imagined a magic carpet would look like . . .'

'How about a glass of wine?'

'Lovely!'

'Red or white?'

'Whatever you're having.'

'There's a bottle of Sancerre,' he said, opening the door of

37

one of those huge American-style fridges that make ice cubes whenever you need them.

'Perfect!' I said, as if I had the slightest idea.

'Salute!'

'Salute!'

Our glasses clinked together but there was a chasm between us, as if we were meeting for the first time at a cocktail party. Did he feel as nervous as I did? Was that why he suddenly sounded even more middle class?

'Are you hungry?'

'Absolutely starving,' I said, then laughed as he put on an apron.

'What?'

'Nothing.'

The sip of wine appeared to have bypassed my stomach and gone straight to my head.

Everything was in its proper place. A block of Japanese knives, a glass-fronted cupboard full of Le Creuset in a duck-egg shade of green. I pictured the dirty crockery in my sink, the used teabag on my draining board, and thanked god that we'd stopped at his place not mine.

He washed tomatoes under one of those taps that gives you boiling or sparkling or whatever kind of water you want. Then, carefully selecting the ripest, he sliced them thinly and arranged them on a large ceramic plate around a ball of mozzarella.

We sat on opposite sides of a large wooden table. He offered me a piece of bread from a paper bag that had turned translucent from oil.

'Wow!' I said, my mouth full. 'This is the most delicious bread I've ever tasted.'

'Fuck at ya.'

'Beg pardon?'

So he spelled it for me.

38

'You've got a lovely place here!'

'Charlotte's taste mainly.'

'Oh.' I never knew what to say when he mentioned his ex-wife.

'It's still half hers. She'd like to sell it, but I think something in the girls' lives should stay the same, don't you? It is their home as well.'

The catch in his voice showed he was still hurting.

'Was your daughter's summer camp OK?'

'She's fine. Apparently she just didn't like the food.'

I knew I shouldn't hate the fact that he had talked to his ex-wife about their child. But jealousy isn't a very rational emotion.

I got up, took my plate to the sink.

'What are you doing?'

'Washing up.'

'There's a dishwasher . . .'

'There's not much . . .'

Somehow I contrived to wave the plate I was holding straight into the luxury tap. It split right down the middle, one half falling into the sink and shattering.

'Oh my god! I'm so sorry. I will replace it . . .'

I couldn't look at him as he stood up and removed the other half from my hand.

'It's only a plate.'

I suddenly got a glimpse of how he must be as a doctor. Gentle and calm, but quite firm. Then we were kissing, he was undoing my buttons and I was pulling off his ridiculous apron, and we were making love in the warm stripes of evening sunshine that fell across the floorboards.

Afterwards, we just lay there gazing at each other, with the gentle babble of laughter and indistinct chatter wafting in from some nearby garden, along with the scent of barbecue and the occasional blast of a distant siren.

'I'd better go,' I said when it got dark.

'Please stay.'

'I've got work tomorrow . . .'

'But you're only five minutes away . . .'

'I haven't got a toothbrush.'

'I always keep a supply in case.'

He kept a stash of spare toothbrushes? In case of what, I wondered as he ran upstairs.

My view of him kept changing. Was he in the habit of having women back? Was I just another in a long line of post-divorce flings? I put on my dress, even more determined to leave now, as he clattered down the stairs again, brandishing a plastic packet in each hand.

'Beauty or Buzz Lightyear?' he offered. 'Bella is a bit of a tomboy . . .'

Funny how a Disney toothbrush can make everything OK again.

Chapter Four

Like all the Dolls Houses, our salon interior was pink with a black trim, a colour scheme based on the Chanel suit Doll had worn when she first went to ask the bank manager for a loan to set up her business. The staff wore pink uniforms with the logo of a tiny dolls house embroidered on the top pocket. The vibe was feminine, professional, indulgent. Our slogan was 'Treat yourself!'

When I'd pointed out that people weren't actually treating themselves, they were coming to be treated, Doll said nobody except a pedant like me would think of that. In any case, it was manicures and pedicures we were offering, not podiatry.

The shop window was painted pink to look like the symmetrical façade of a real dolls house with four rectangular, Georgian-style window frames left transparent to allow natural light in while maintaining the exclusive feeling inside. For most passers-by the 'upstairs' panes were too high and the 'downstairs' too low to casually gawp through, so my heart missed a beat when I saw Gus waving at me through one of the upper windows. It wasn't that men weren't allowed inside. A lot of men in London like their nails to look nice and several of our regulars were drag queens. I just wasn't ready to handle the speculation his lanky presence would generate, although my frantic gesticulating to Luis's café next door made several of the technicians turn round and spot him anyway.

The café was busy with yummy mummies and their infants.

'You didn't say goodbye,' Gus said, as I joined him at a cramped table at the back.

I'd crept out of his house in the early hours, having lain awake for ages on the side his wife must have slept in the huge double bed.

'I can't be long,' I said, as our cappuccinos and his breakfast arrived. 'Do you always eat a full English?'

'As often as I can.'

It didn't seem very healthy for a doctor, but he was thin as a rake, so he probably had a good metabolism.

'Can I have a dip?' I asked, as he seemed too polite to start eating without me.

The toast was buttery and the egg runny just how I like it.

I felt much more comfortable with him on neutral territory again, until I looked up and saw Doll zigzagging her way through the buggies towards our table. She wasn't due in today, I was sure. I felt as if I'd been caught truanting.

'You've dripped a bit,' she said, pointing to a tiny globule of yolk on my dress before leaning over and removing it with a very long and beautifully polished fingernail. 'Aggie said you were with a fella.'

I was hoping that Gus wouldn't stand up, but of course he did. He would have towered over her even if she'd been in heels, but she was wearing pale pink trainers and her hot pink Juicy Couture tracksuit, so it was like she was looking up at a tall building.

'Doll, this is Gus! Gus, Doll.'

'It's a pleasure to meet you,' he said, holding out his hand, which she shook, still maintaining her suspicious glare. 'Can I get you something?'

'I could murder a cup of tea.'

'Please take my seat,' said Gus.

'I'll just squeeze in next to Tess.'

Her baby bump only just fitted between our table and the next.

We watched Gus negotiating his way back to the counter.

'Very nice manners,' said Doll, making it sound more like a criticism than a compliment.

'I assumed you take milk?' Gus said when he returned with a steaming mug, carefully wiping the bottom with a paper serviette before putting it down in front of her.

'You assumed correct.'

'When's the baby due?'

'Christmas Eve. You've got kids, I understand?'

She sounded as if she was conducting a job interview.

'Two girls, Flora and Bella.'

'Flora and Bella,' she repeated, as if that was exactly what she would have expected them to be called. 'We've got an Elsie and this one will be a Holly if it's a girl. We haven't decided a name if it's a boy.'

'You didn't want to know?' he asked.

'Did you?' she fired back.

'My wife did. Ex-wife.'

'Shame for the kids, divorce. Isn't it?' said Doll.

'Noel,' I interrupted. 'Is a Christmassy name for a boy.'

'No one wants to be called Noel, do they?' Doll snapped at me.

'Nicholas?' Gus suggested.

'What's Christmassy about that?' Doll demanded.

'St Nicholas,' I said. 'You know, Santa.'

'I'm not calling my baby after an old man with a beard.'

Why was she being so arsey?

'Well, I'd better be getting back to work,' I said.

43

Gus stood up again. We hovered between a hug and a kiss, finally opting for nothing.

'Supper?' he whispered, as we brushed past him.

'Isn't it your creative writing class tonight, Tess?' Doll asked.

'Well, yes, but . . .'

'*Ci vediamo*,' Gus said.

'*Si!*' I giggled.

'What was that about?' Doll said when we were out on the street.

'It just means see you later in Italian.'

Doll rolled her eyes. 'Once you meet a man, nobody else gets a look in.'

'What the fuck?'

'You didn't even call me to tell me how you got on yesterday.'

Then I understood. 'God, Doll, I'm so sorry. I'm in remission!'

Then we were hugging and she was crying. She'd supported me the whole way through cancer, even paying for my holiday in Tuscany. She should have been the first person I told.

'I was thinking the worst and I didn't know whether to call, so . . .' Doll sniffed.

'It's just that Gus came back. He was there outside the hospital, waiting for me. So, what do you think?'

'What can I tell you? He's a divorced public schoolboy with two kids.'

'But he's nice, right?'

'There's a reason people get divorced, just saying.'

'His wife had an affair.'

'But have you asked yourself why? That's what I'm talking about. Women always think it's going to be different for them. Hold a bit back. That's my advice. You always give yourself so cheaply.'

The unexpected assault on my character knocked me sideways. I hadn't asked for her advice and 'always' was a bit unfair

44

when I'd only had two serious boyfriends in my life. Leo and before that, Dave, who went on to be Doll's husband, but I wasn't going to bring that up as we'd got over it a long time ago.

I couldn't work out what was going on with her. Perhaps she was being protective, or maybe even a tiny bit jealous? In a long friendship, you have your role. Doll was the petite seductive one who knew the ways of men. I was the tall gawky one who didn't. Now I was embarking on a hot romance and she was nearly ten years married to the same bloke. I wasn't going to spoil my happy mood by retaliating.

My creative writing class was at City Lit in Bloomsbury, where the leafy Georgian squares were dotted with blue plaques commemorating famous writers who had lived there, so it felt like walking in their footsteps.

I was enrolled on the Life Writing course because there hadn't been any spaces in Getting Started on a Novel and, anyway, you're always told to write what you know, even if it's fiction.

At the evening class I'd taken in Kent, back in the day, my tutor and subsequent lover Leo had been the author of a now out-of-print novel about a university lecturer who has affairs with his students. I'd found a second-hand copy on Amazon Marketplace for 1p plus postage, and read it before he even made a move, so I really should have known. Perhaps I had and Doll was right. I'd thought it would be different with me. Why does love make you think you're the exception?

I was working on a memoir about my relationship with my sister Hope. *Living with Hope* was a good title, and I thought it might be helpful for her to have a record of her life if anything happened to me. The other students were always positive when I read my chapters out, which didn't really mean a lot because we had signed up to critique each other's work with sensitivity. Sometimes I thought the most creative thing about the class was finding different words of encouragement for every student whatever they wrote. Just before I went on holiday, the teacher had kept me back at the end of class and urged me to keep going, because a publisher friend had told her there was currently a bit of a vogue for books about neurodivergent people.

I felt a little guilty, because I hadn't written a word since. The events of the past week seemed to have reversed my focus, directing me forwards, not backwards into my past.

That's not the excuse I gave, obviously. I made something up about being overwhelmed by all the beauty in Florence, which, turns out, is actually a thing, called Stendhal Syndrome, according to the teacher. Who knew?

The lights were on downstairs as I passed Gus's house on the way home. Recalling Doll's advice about holding back, I told myself not to, then couldn't resist knocking on the door. It was opened by an attractive woman wearing bright red lipstick. She looked somehow familiar, but I couldn't place her. Was she a Doll's House client? What was she doing here?

'Is this Gus's house?'

'It certainly is.' She held my gaze.

'Oh!'

'Don't worry, I'm used to it,' she said.

'I'm sorry?'

'People thinking they know me. You must be Tess. I'm Nash.' She stood back to let me in.

'Gus didn't say you were Nash Villiers!'

I'd thought Nash was an unusual name, but I hadn't made the connection with the actress who had played Dr Sue, the feisty female doctor in a world dominated by alpha males, in the medical drama *High Dependency*. She was smaller than I imagined and her trademark bob of bright crimson hair was now brown and shoulder length.

'Gus has just nipped out to get fish and chips,' she said. 'My final real meal before the regime of organic alfalfa sprouts begins. I've just landed a new job in LA.'

'Congratulations,' I said, unsure whether I was allowed to ask what it was. I'd never talked to anyone I'd seen on television before. Unless you counted Doll, who was once on the local news when she was voted Thanet Entrepreneur of the Year.

'I thought you were brilliant as Dr Sue. It's not nearly as good since you left.'

Not cool. *Stop it!* I told myself.

'It's what always happens to ballsy female leads. They get tamed or they die,' said Nash. 'Barolo?'

She picked up a half-full bottle, went to the kitchen cupboard for a glass.

The room was full of cigarette smoke. I noticed that there were several butts in the ashtray, some with the imprint of red lipstick, one or two without.

'Does Gus smoke?' I asked.

'Only other people's cigarettes. Have a seat!'

I sat down cautiously, terrified of dripping wine on the velvet.

'Gus tells me that I took your room at university, so I suppose I should say thanks. He says that you've worked out that there were lots of times where your lives just missed each other. You were at the same wedding.'

'On the same flight to New York,' I said. 'At the same Rolling Stones gig . . .'

'You know what it sounds like?'

Destiny or serendipity? I didn't know which word to choose.

'A rom com!' she said, then putting on a serious, film trailer voice: '*Two lives, ten chances to be together. Can you fall in love with someone you've never met?*'

I laughed.

47

'Honestly, Netflix would love it! Course, there would have to be a role for me as the fairy godmother who brought the two of you together by sending Gus to Tuscany. I always wanted to be the fairy godmother in the school play, but I was only ever cast as the principal boy.'

'I wanted to be Mary. But they said I was too tall.'

'What were you?'

'Usually a shepherd, which was better than one of the lowing cattle, I suppose.'

'The only female roles in the nativity, virgin or cow,' said Nash.

I laughed.

I could feel her looking at me curiously, as if she was trying to work me out.

'Gus's description was spot on,' she said, finally.

'Oh?'

'Unsophisticated in a good way.'

She seemed to think it was a compliment and I couldn't really object as I saw my wine glass had left a purple circle on the thigh of my jeans.

'If it had been you instead of me in the room next door,' she said. 'I wonder if you'd have become his best friend, or whether you'd have hooked up then?'

She sounded a little wistful. I wondered if she'd wanted them to be more than friends.

I tried to picture Gus and me meeting on a student corridor aged eighteen. He would have been even more of a public schoolboy then and I would have been even more chippy, so I probably wouldn't even have become his friend, let alone his lover.

'People don't hook up with the first person they meet at university, do they? Anyway, if we had, we would have split up by now.'

'Gus usually goes for more obvious female stereotypes,' she said. 'Little Miss Perfect or the Vampire Seductress . . .'

I didn't know about a Miss Perfect. I assumed the Vampire Seductress was his ex-wife. I was trying to think of a way of asking without sounding as if I cared, when we both jumped as Gus returned with two large paper carrier bags and a cloud of chip shop smell. The expression on his face flashed from surprised to anxious.

'Nash just popped round to say goodbye. I didn't realise you were coming. I only got two cod. You can have mine.'

He was clearly as nervous about me meeting Nash as I had been about introducing him to Doll.

'Look at him worried I'm telling you all his secrets,' said Nash.

Did Gus have secrets?

'I was on my way home. I'm not really hungry.'

Nash had already unwrapped her meal.

'Hello carbs and fat!' She addressed the hunk of battered fish in her hand. 'I am going to miss you!'

'How was your class?' Gus asked me, opening another bottle of wine.

'Good, thanks,' I lied.

'What class is this?' Nash asked, her mouth full.

'Life writing,' I said.

'Is that like life drawing? Do you all sit around *describing* a naked person in front of you?'

I laughed. 'No, it's just writing about your own life.'

I wished Gus hadn't mentioned it. How could my life possibly be interesting enough to write about compared to hers?

'So, like therapy?' Nash said.

'I suppose.' I'd never thought about it like that.

'Cheaper though,' said Nash. 'How's yours going?' She turned to Gus.

Gus was in therapy? My jigsaw picture of his character was becoming more like a video wall with little stories on each screen, like the end of *Love Actually* but with only one actor.

'It sorted a few things out,' he said, awkwardly. 'I've stopped now.'

'You're not allowed to stop therapy in LA,' Nash said. 'Nor is it permitted to drown your sorrows with alcohol...'

She finished her glass and poured herself another large one.

What sorrows could Nash Villiers possibly have? Was the drink making her melancholy, or was she just a dramatic person by nature?

The dynamic had shifted since Gus returned. It felt less like having a conversation and more like watching a performance. Like most old friends, Gus and Nash probably had a language of their own that I didn't know yet.

'I have to get going,' I said, standing up.

'Stay,' said Gus, catching my hand.

The tiniest flicker of anguish in Nash's eyes confirmed that she had once been in love with him.

'No, honestly,' I said. 'It's been brilliant to meet you, but I've got work in the morning and my mouth goes black when I have a lot of red wine.'

I realised as soon as I said it that I didn't really have to add a second reason.

Nash smiled at me, grateful, I thought, that I'd understood she wanted a last evening in London alone with Gus.

'It was good to meet you, Tess,' she said, kissing me emphatically on both cheeks. 'Take care of him for me.'

'I'll walk you back,' Gus volunteered.

'No need.'

'I'd like to,' he said firmly.

Outside in the cool night air, neither of us spoke for a few minutes. The echo of our footsteps bounced around the empty street.

'Well, we both survived,' he finally said.

'Survived?'

'Interrogation by our best friends. If you locked Doll and Nash in a room together, which one do you think would come out alive?'

'Doll's only being protective.'

Doll was like a sister to me. I was allowed to have mean thoughts about her, but I'd jump straight to her defence at any hint of criticism from anyone else. At least Doll was loyal. I knew she'd never go talking behind my back about my ex, whom she called The Tosser with the Ponytail.

'Were you and Nash ever a thing?' I asked.

'No,' he said. Then, as if that wasn't a complete answer. 'She wanted to be at one point.'

'I thought so.'

He smiled at me.

'Nash liked you.'

'How do you know?'

'Believe me, with Nash, you know.'

She and Charlotte clearly hadn't got on.

What did Gus feel about the Vampire Seductress now? Why did he keep the house just as she left it? I was desperate to ask these questions, but our relationship was still so new and fragile, it felt like being in a giant rainbow soap bubble where the slightest knock might make it vanish.

Gus

Chapter Five

Since my divorce, each day was much like the next. I dragged myself to a job I wasn't much good at. I shopped. I cooked. Occasionally I met a friend. Some days, I made myself go for a run because I knew it would make me feel better, but often my sense of pointlessness was so overwhelming, I couldn't be bothered. My existence was as empty as the house I inhabited.

Then there was Tess and every minute that I spent with her was precious.

It made returning to work even more difficult than before. I had more than my fair share of night shifts, which meant we could only meet for snatched minutes in Luis's café, or the occasional illicit afternoon in her studio flat over the salon, where the faded poster of Botticelli's Primavera Blu-tacked to the wall made me feel like a student again. Tess had accumulated few possessions, except for a rail of dresses – 'I say charity shop, Doll says vintage' – and myriad books on shelves made of bricks and planks she'd nicked from a skip.

My training had been interrupted by the career break I'd taken to look after the children when we couldn't find decent childcare. It had allowed Charlotte to rise up the ladder to become one of the youngest consultants in her field but, ironic-ally, she had then needed a husband befitting her status. Her betrayal wasn't that much of a surprise. Apart from the sex, I'd always wondered what she was doing with me. But losing the kids was devastating. I'd loved being there for each little milestone they passed, making art with them, taking them to the park. Being a stay-at-home dad was much more interesting than any job I'd had. And I was good at it. They were my whole life and I would have fought for custody if I'd any hope of achieving it, but lack of income and gender counted against me. So I had let Charlotte have her way. As usual, Nash said. But it wasn't a competition. I didn't want my girls to be further damaged by an ugly battle.

Ironically, returning to medicine was the only way I had of earning enough money to keep up the home for them in London, but I worked as a locum, never quite prepared to commit to the profession, always hoping I would wake up one morning with a better idea of what I really wanted to do.

Although I'd been at the same A & E department for several months, I didn't feel like part of the team. My superiors couldn't understand my lack of ambition, my peers were suspicious of it, the nurses generally found my deliberations annoying. There were strict targets to adhere to. Delays incurred fines for the hospital. Doctors were paid to make decisions and make them quickly.

The final few hours of any nightshift were entirely fuelled by adrenaline and strong coffee. By the time I stepped out into fresh air, I had powered through exhaustion to the point where I was beyond sleep. A good way of tackling the jittery wakefulness was a game of tennis on courts in Lincoln's Inn Fields with my friend Jonathan who was on his way to work at the same hospital, where he'd recently become a consultant. We had met on the first day of medical school but, unlike me, he was brilliant and dedicated.

I recognised the shape of him in the distance practising his serve. With the days getting noticeably shorter, I thought that it was probably one of the last early morning games we'd play this year.

He looked tired. He'd also been up all night, but taking it in turns with his wife to soothe their youngest children, who had contracted chicken pox.

'Do the sleepless nights ever end?' he said.

'When your children leave home?'

'Sorry. Tactless.'

I hadn't actually been referring to my own situation. I still lost sleep when one of my girls was ill in Geneva. In a way, it was more difficult not being there, always wondering if Charlotte was taking sufficient notice of worsening symptoms. She was one of those blasé doctors who seem immune to worry, which was why she was so much more suited to the profession than I was.

'Warm up, then a couple of sets?'

We were pretty evenly matched, although Jonathan was more willing to chase down every shot. But we ended up a set apiece.

Afterwards, we always went to the same café filled with strangely disparate groups of bleary binmen in high-vis tabards, and barristers wearing black garb impregnated with the sharp reek of stale alcohol. We drank tea. I had a full English breakfast, Jonathan a vegetarian one.

'How was Tuscany?'

'Good.' I hesitated, torn between wanting to share the excitement I felt whenever I thought of Tess, and the additional frisson of keeping her a secret.

'Where were you staying?'

'An *agriturismo* near Vinci.'

'Would you recommend it?'

'Wonderful views, an infinity pool, rooms with the original frescoed ceilings...'

'You'll have to send me a link. Were you on your own?'

'Er... actually, I met someone.'

'An Italian?'

'No... English. Lives near me, as a matter of fact. We're seeing each other...'

'You'll have to bring her over for dinner. How about Friday?'

He and his wife regularly invited me to their house. Often with another single friend of Miriam's. I appreciated their generosity but her attempts at matchmaking had been unsuccessful. I wasn't sure I wanted to subject Tess to an inquisition by Miriam. Jonathan's field of expertise was oncology, which might be awkward too.

I pictured Tess's wafer-slim body silhouetted by the setting sun as we stopped to look at the view of the Eye and the Houses of Parliament on Waterloo Bridge the previous Sunday. She was the most vivacious person I had ever met, possessing not an ounce of world-weariness or self-pity, but whenever I touched the scars from her recent surgery I was reminded of her fragility. She never wanted to talk about cancer.

'Bad enough having it,' she said. 'Worse being defined by it and everyone being nice to you, like it's your birthday or something. Anyway, in some ways cancer's a gift. Because it makes you experience things more thoroughly. Obviously, you can't live every day like it's your last, because you'd never get the washing done, but cancer turns up the colours, somehow.'

With the onset of autumn, the leaves seemed more golden and the crunch of leaves underfoot more satisfying than ever before. Even things I had done many times before like visiting the National Gallery felt fresh and new with her.

'It's about the nearest thing in London to being in a Florentine church,' she said, as we stood for a long time in front of Jacopo di Cione's altarpiece with its gilded image of the adult Christ touching his mother's forehead in a gentle gesture of love.

When I took her for dim sum in Chinatown afterwards, she was initially suspicious of the menu written in Chinese, her face turning to surprise as she dared to sample char siu bao.

'It's really just a jam doughnut with pork in it.'

She saw beauty in things I had stopped noticing. The waft of scent from a florist's open door; a toddler's fascination with ducks in Kensington Gardens; the dappled light on the surface of the Thames.

'Not as grey as when Monet painted it,' she'd remarked on Waterloo Bridge. 'Did you know he stayed over there at the Savoy? I always imagine him eating his breakfast thinking, oh for god's sake, not another foggy one.'

I was suddenly conscious of Jonathan across the table, looking at my inane smile, still expecting a response to his invitation.

'Early days,' I said.

Chapter Six

Towards the end of October, Tess announced that it was her sister Hope's birthday and she was going down to Margate for the family get-together.

'Am I invited?'

She looked flustered. I knew she was nervous about me meeting her father. I wasn't exactly relishing the prospect myself. She didn't speak about him nearly as much as her mother, but I knew that both of her elder brothers had left home as soon as they were old enough on account of his violent temper.

'I'm not sure how Hope would react to a stranger...'

'I'm going to have to meet her some time...'

Sometimes I'd inadvertently say something that elicited a smile so guileless and radiant, it was like a shaft of light when the sun breaks through a cloud. I had never known anyone who showed their feelings as openly. It was one of the things I found incredibly attractive about her.

'I'm not sure it'll be your thing. We always go to the same pub with a carvery, a bottomless ice cream machine and karaoke...'

'Does everyone have to sing?' I asked, a little alarmed.

'Only Hope. And Dad, depending on how much he's had to drink. After a couple of pints, he's charm itself, one more and he gets mawkishly sentimental, after that, you have to watch out. Mum and I were always walking on eggshells...'

'And Hope?'

'Hope doesn't do eggshells. That's one of the reasons I had to be there for her.'

'Why don't we make a weekend of it?' I suggested. 'I'll book a hotel.'

I watched her mentally weighing all the cons before eventually giving me the smile again.

Tess took the Saturday afternoon off so we could drive down in plenty of time.

'What's this?' she asked, opening the passenger door of my battered old Volvo, picking up the carrier bag on the seat.

'I didn't know what to get for Hope, so I baked her a cake. It's still warm.'

'It's a lovely idea,' she said. 'Thing is, Dad's partner Anne does the cake, with candles and stuff.'

'Can't have too much cake on your birthday, can you?'

'Hope's very set in her ways.'

Her sister had been diagnosed with Asperger's at the age of twelve. In a way, Tess told me, it had been a relief to know that Hope's difficulties were not due to any deficiency of care she'd provided in the absence of their mother.

Her account made me acutely aware of the narrow perspective doctors have on the complexity of the lives they change with just a few words.

The diagnosis had allowed Hope to get some official support at school. But it also labelled her as different.

'I mean she is different,' Tess said. 'But why can't we just have a bigger range of normal? What's so great about normal anyway? When you're with Hope you realise that most of us spend our lives saying things that aren't true.'

The boutique hotel I'd booked was on the seafront. Apparently, it had been an unremarkable B & B offering temporary housing for care in the community until recently.

'Just as I was leaving for the big city, all these arty metropolitan types started coming down,' Tess said, as we let ourselves into a room with a large bed and a standalone bathtub.

'I've seen those in magazines,' Tess said. 'I've always wondered how come the floorboards don't go mouldy?'

'Come here,' I said, pulling her towards the bed.

We'd been together for nearly three months but I was always the initiator of sex, with Tess responding to the first touch like a shy convent virgin. I had come to love the moment when her breathing slightly quickened and she lowered her eyes modestly.

'Shouldn't we draw the curtains?' she asked.

'Who's going to see us apart from the seagulls?'

'I've never made love with a view of the sea.'

When we kissed, she gave herself to me so completely all I wanted to do was scoop her up and fuck her senseless.

Tess's family had already made their first trip to the buffet by the time we arrived at the pub.

'We'd almost given up on you,' said her dad.

'It's quarter past seven,' Tess told him.

By the floridity of his complexion I judged they'd already been there a while. When he stood up, he was a bigger man than I'd expected, dressed for the occasion in a dinner suit with a cummerbund. He commanded the space like a boxing promoter. Sitting next to him was a blousy woman in a stretchy black dress with purple panels down each side that might have been slimming if it wasn't at least two sizes too small. Beside her, tucking into a bowl of soft serve ice cream, was a younger woman with short unbrushed hair wearing a sequinned dress bunched up over tracksuit bottoms.

'Hope, this is my friend Gus,' Tess said.

'Happy Birthday!' I said.

'How do you know it's my birthday?'

'A little bird told me.'

'What bird?' said Hope.

'Tess,' I said.

'I wouldn't go calling Tess a bird, if I were you!' Her father chuckled.

'Take no notice of him, Gus.' The blousy woman had come to my rescue. 'I'm Anne. Have you known Tess long?'

Her heavily made-up eyes seemed to be able smile at me and scold Tess at the same time for not telling them she was bringing a plus one.

'Call me Jim,' instructed Tess's father, offering a crushing handshake. 'Your first time in Margate?'

'Yes.'

'It's not all Dreamland nowadays. We've got an organic greengrocer now and an art gallery,' he said, sizing me up with wincing accuracy.

'I'm looking forward to visiting the Turner,' I said.

'I see you've nabbed yourself an intellectual, Tess!'

'Come and sit down next to me, Gus,' said Anne.

'That's where Tree sits,' said Hope.

'What's your poison, Garth?' asked Tess's father.

'Allow me,' I said.

'An intellectual and a gentleman, Tess!'

'It's Gus,' she said.

'Gus, is it?' Jim asked, as if her word wasn't good enough.

'Short for Angus,' I explained.

'Scottish?'

'My father is.'

63

'Well, I won't hold that against you!' He slapped me hard on the back, before sitting down again.

'I'll help carry,' Tess said, hurrying me away.

'They seem very nice,' I said, noticing that she flinched slightly and glanced over her shoulder as I put my arm around her at the bar.

'Hope doesn't do metaphors.'

'No, I'm sorry. I don't know where that came from. I was so nervous about getting it right with her, I somehow got it completely wrong.'

The smile.

'Where's Martin?' Tess asked the others, when we returned to the table.

'He's not satisfied with the quality of the speakers,' said Hope.

'So he brought his own,' said Anne, giving me a wink. 'That's Martin for you!'

On cue, an unsmiling young man arrived at the table carrying a toolbox.

'It's all ready for you now, Hope,' he said.

Hope got up and walked to the small stage. A hush fell around the pub as the other customers noticed who was at the mic. I found myself feeling a little nervous for her. Then the intro to 'Crazy' began and when Hope came in her voice was so powerful and bluesy, it could have been Patsy Cline herself in the room.

I watched in disbelief as this eccentrically dressed little person brought all the country singer's range and catches of emotion to the lyrics.

'She's amazing!' I turned to Tess, but she was totally involved in her sister's performance, holding her breath through each difficult key change, then smiling with all the relief, pride and unabashed love you see in the eyes of parents at their child's nativity play.

When the song finished, the whole pub erupted in applause and cheers. Hope stood expressionless and unmoved until she caught Martin gesticulating at her and took a small bow.

The next number on Hope's playlist was bizarrely 'Pie Jesu', which she sang with the same dispassionate expression. while somehow managing to convey all the reverence in the purity of her voice.

'Do you like my singing, Tree?' Hope asked, returning to the table with a refill of ice cream.

'You are simply amazing!'

'Do you like my singing, Tree?' Hope repeated.

'Yes, I do.'

'Do you like my singing, Dad?'

The big man wiped a tear from his eye.

'Yes, Hope, it was gorgeous.'

'Do you like my singing, Anne?'

'Of course I do, Hope. Yes.'

Hope looked at me.

'You've got four yeses!' I said.

I felt everyone tense up and wondered if I'd made some terrible error of judgement. Then Hope smiled and, for the first time, I saw a family resemblance in the flash of unadulterated joy that changed her face from plain to beautiful for just a second.

She hurried back to the stage.

'Get you, channelling Simon Cowell, you charming bastard!' Tess whispered. 'He's only Hope's favourite person in the world.'

Apparently, Hope's usual repertoire also included favourites by Kylie and Celine Dion, but this year she had also learned Adele's 'Someone Like You', bringing to it all the torch-song emotions of a broken relationship and taking each one of us to our own private place of regret.

'I don't know how you do it, Hope,' Anne said, dabbing at her mascara.

'Martin rehearses me. Where's my cake?'

'Anne?' Tess's father glared at his partner.

'I'll be back in a moment.'

A slightly awkward silence ensued.

'What a beautiful voice, Hope,' I ventured then, getting no response, 'You must be very proud of your daughters, Jim.'

'All my kids have their talents, Garth,' he said. 'Kevin, my oldest, is on the stage and Brendan . . . what's Brendan good at, Tess?'

'Plastering.'

'Which is an art in itself,' I said.

I felt Tess freeze beside me.

'I once made the mistake of trying myself, thinking how hard can it be? I got to the point where there was more plaster than wall until I called in a professional. The whole room was silky smooth in a couple of hours!'

The ensuing silence seemed to go on for hours, until Jim laughed.

'More plaster than wall,' he bellowed. 'How hard can it be?'

Everyone breathed again.

The pub manager dimmed the lights and Anne appeared with an iced cake, twenty-one candles alight. The whole pub sang 'Happy Birthday' except Martin and Hope, who looked as if the tuneless chorus was an affront.

'Make a wish!' Anne said as Hope blew out the candles.

'What wish?'

'That's up to you, Hope.'

'Presents now.'

'Anne!'

'OK Jim, give me a chance. I've just been seeing to the cake.'

'A woman's work is never done!' Jim winked at me.

I slightly regretted my attempt to ingratiate myself into his favour. I didn't want to fall into the trap of ganging up with him in a male way.

Anne handed Hope a wrapped box from Pandora, containing a silver bracelet with a key charm on it.

'Who's got the key to the door?' Jim said.

'What door?' asked Hope, fingering the charm suspiciously.

'Never been twenty-one before!'

'Obviously.'

'There's all sorts of different charms you can add,' said Anne, slightly desperately.

'That's birthdays and Christmas sorted for the foreseeable,' said Jim.

'Shall I help you put it on?' Tess asked.

She fastened it round Hope's chubby wrist.

We all stared at the bracelet for a few moments, then Hope said, 'Can I take it off now?'

'Another Guinness, Jim?' I volunteered. 'Can I get you anything, Martin?'

'I haven't finished this yet,' he said, holding up a half empty glass.

'Where's my present from you, Tree?' Hope asked.

'We left them at the hotel,' Tess told her. 'We thought we'd bring them round tomorrow.'

'Hotel?' Tess's father suddenly stood up, looming over her and stabbing his forefinger close to her face. 'You'd waste your money on a hotel when Anne's cleaned the spare room, put fresh sheets on the bed and everything?'

Tess cowered back against me. I put my arm firmly around her shoulder, making us a unit.

'We didn't want to trouble you,' I said, my voice level and firm. I had to deal with a lot of drunks in A & E.

'It's no trouble at all!' Jim shouted.

Which was rather at odds with what he'd just said. As if hearing his own words, he looked slightly bewildered and, having failed to provoke a reaction, sat down.

'It's much closer to Hope.' Tess was trying to be placatory. 'I'd like to spend some time with you tomorrow, Hope. Maybe go out to lunch?'

'Hope's working tomorrow,' said Martin.

'Everyone needs a coffee break, don't they?' I said.

'I don't like coffee,' said Hope.

We seemed to have come to a bit of an impasse.

'Well, it's been a lovely evening,' said Anne.

'I'll need a hand getting the speakers back,' Martin said.

'We'll help, won't we, Gus?' Tess volunteered immediately.

By the time he'd disconnected them and given me one to carry, Tess's father and Anne had taken a taxi home.

'Did you really try to plaster a room?' Tess asked me, as we lay together in the moonlight, under a snowy white duvet cover.

'Do you think I'd dare lie to your father?'

'I'm sorry about him.'

'I'm sorry I caused a problem by staying here.'

'Oh don't worry, if we hadn't booked it, he'd have accused us of treating Anne's place like a hotel. That's if he'd even tolerate me sharing a room with a man under his roof. So we'd have been in trouble whatever.'

She said it with such equanimity when he'd been so threatening, I gathered her into my arms, kissing the top of her head, wanting to her to know that she was safe now.

*

In the morning, we walked up a cobbled street to Martin's shop and stood listening to Hope practising scales in the flat above.

'How did the two of them meet?' I asked.

'I brought her here when she was a teenager because she loved music and the school suggested getting her a keyboard. It was Martin's dad's shop originally, but he died, so Martin carried on the business. He recommended the best one for her. Hope's the kind of person who can get a tune out of anything, so he let her try out some of the other instruments. They just kind of clicked. They're both a bit 'on the spectrum' although I hate that phrase because we're all on the spectrum, aren't we? Otherwise there wouldn't actually be a spectrum.'

I'd never thought about it like that.

'So, we got into a bit of a habit of coming here on a Saturday afternoon. Then, when Hope had to do work experience at the beginning of year eleven, I had the bright idea of asking Martin if she could do her two weeks in his shop. She was good at remembering where all the bits and pieces like guitar strings and clarinet reeds were kept and, to be honest, she was no worse at dealing with customers than him. It freed him up to get on with repairing instruments in the workshop at the back, which is what he really likes doing. So he ended up offering her a job after her GCSEs. After a couple of years, she announced that she wanted to move in with him . . .'

I expected to see laughter in Tess's eyes, but instead there was sadness.

'All I had ever wanted was for Hope to be able to be an independent person, but it was such a shock. She'd never even had a friend before . . . So, maybe it was actually me who found it difficult being independent?' She smiled. 'Anyway, she was eighteen and there's honestly no stopping Hope when she gets fixated on something.'

'They seem happy together?' I offered.

Tess's face twisted into a frown. It was clearly something that preoccupied her.

'It's hard to tell when Hope's happy, but you'll generally hear when she's not. When she first left home, I used to come here every evening and stand here listening to her singing and Martin playing. They seemed to be getting along.'

I gave her a hug. In the context of her family, she seemed a much more vulnerable person.

'I've never been sure how far it goes,' Tess said. 'Hope doesn't do any of what she calls the huggy kissy stuff.'

Tess had bought Hope's present when we were in Pisa. It was a musical box of the Leaning Tower that played a vaguely recognisable tinkly tune as it rotated. Martin identified it as 'The Chorus of the Hebrew Slaves' from Nabucco and set about finding the best version of it from the racks of CDs, so that we could listen to it as it was intended.

'I can sing opera,' Hope announced, when Martin eventually switched off the CD player.

She launched into the 'Queen of the Night' aria from Mozart's *The Magic Flute*.

'Stop!' said Martin, holding up his hand.

Hope obeyed.

'How many times have I told you about warming up your voice?'

'Thirty-seven.'

I suppressed a laugh.

'It's a pity she came to opera so late,' said Martin. 'If she'd been allowed lessons earlier, who knows?'

'Gus has baked you a cake, Hope,' said Tess, giving me a nudge.

'It doesn't look like a cake,' said Hope.

'It's polenta with orange,' I said.

'Try it. Gus is a very good cook,' Tess said, loyally.

'It's gritty and it's covered with marmalade,' Hope pronounced, carefully spitting the mouthful she'd taken back onto the plate.

'Just as well I didn't go on *Masterchef*!'

'Did you apply for *Masterchef*?' Martin enquired.

'No.'

Martin looked at his watch. It was time for the shop to open and for us to leave.

As Tess tried to embrace her, Hope stood stiff as a board and completely unresponsive. I sensed it would not be wise for me to attempt more than a cheery wave.

As soon as Tess and I were out of sight, we grabbed each other's hands and ran down the street, bursting out laughing as soon as we were out of earshot.

After checking out of the hotel, we drove around the streets of her childhood. Tess pointed out the council house she grew up in, the church where they'd all received their first Holy Communion, except they never quite knew if Hope had because she'd spat the wafer out.

Occasionally, she'd spot someone she knew and lower the window to call out and wave.

'Are you back, Teresa? Just for the weekend? And how are you? In remission? Thank god! Who's this?'

They'd bend to peer through at me from the pavement and I'd smile and wave when she told them my name, wishing that I had a more impressive car or had at least put this one through the wash.

We drove past the primary school where Tess had first met Doll, whose real name was Maria Dolores, and where Tess had later returned as a teaching assistant because Hope needed support. I was beginning to realise that she'd been just as much a parent to Hope as I had been to my girls.

'Thank you for being natural with her,' Tess said. 'Most people patronise her or they talk really loudly because they think she's stupid. But there's nothing wrong with her IQ.'

'She really does have the most extraordinary voice.'

'Yes, it's not just that it's pitch perfect, whatever that means, it's kind of transporting too, isn't it?'

I nodded.

'Like when she sings 'Pie Jesu', I'm back in the kitchen with Mum making tea on Sunday afternoon and Hope is in the living room watching *Songs of Praise*, and suddenly we realise it's not the singer on the telly we're listening to. She takes you to a different place somehow.'

On the way to a beauty spot along the coast that Tess thought I'd like, we drove past Doll's modern clifftop house but, somewhat to my relief, she didn't suggest we call in.

Reculver was a castle by the sea. As we ambled arm in arm down the path towards it, Tess was clearly preoccupied.

'Martin thinks I stopped Hope doing things, but I didn't. We couldn't afford singing lessons. Nobody knew about opera in our house.'

'I don't give a shit what Martin thinks,' I said.

'Dad thought I'd mollycoddled her. So I couldn't win really. But Hope's always the most important thing to me in the whole world.'

Her eyes shone with such an intensity of love I felt a sting of jealousy, which I knew was completely irrational. Love is not finite. I'd discovered that when my second child was born.

I stopped walking, held both her hands.

'Don't take any notice of those bullies,' I told her. 'You were obviously a wonderful sister to Hope.'

'Bullies?'

'I'm sorry, I didn't mean . . .'

'No. It's one of the nicest things you've ever said to me.' She gave me a beaming smile. 'It was so good to have you by my side.'

She linked my arm as we walked on and I felt a destabilising mix of excitement and responsibility rushing though my body.

I stopped walking.

'What?' she said, her hair blowing all over her face from the strong breeze coming off the sea.

'Nothing, It's just . . .' I hugged her so tightly we almost toppled over.

'So, when am I going to meet your girls?' Tess asked, as we finally released each other.

Despite the casualness of her tone, I knew she was as apprehensive about it as I had been about meeting her family.

'They'll be here at Christmas. Bella is a joy. Flora can take a bit of getting used to. She's more like her mother.'

'In what way?'

'Well, she's strikingly beautiful and sophisticated. Charlotte always was way out of my league!'

The startled look on Tess's face told me that what I'd intended as self-deprecation had been received as comparison. Idiot! I couldn't think of any attempt at amelioration that wouldn't risk making the blunder worse. I wished we could just rewind to how we had been before my family had come into the conversation.

'Where shall we go for lunch?' I asked hurriedly. 'How about The Oysterage in Whitstable. We could see if Marcus and Keiko are down . . . ?'

My friend from school, Marcus was a City lawyer who invested most of his vast earnings in property. As well as an old rectory in a village near Oxford – the family home – he and his wife Keiko had a pied-à-terre in the Barbican, and a converted fisherman's hut right on the beach at Whitstable, where they spent most weekends.

'I don't really like oysters,' said Tess, turning to walk back the car ahead of me.

So we found a half-timbered pub in the Kent countryside, which served a decent roast. It was still just about warm enough to sit outside, but as the sun faded there was chill in the air, and less conversation than usual. I felt as if my remark had made a tiny irreparable crack in our relationship, which was barely visible but had somehow put the whole structure at risk.

Chapter Seven

On Christmas Eve, I parked next to my mother's Corsa on the gravel drive and sighed as I switched off the engine.

On the front door was the same wreath that had appeared every December for as long as I could remember, its red tartan ribbon now faded to a dull pink and grey. I wished that I'd followed through on the impulse to buy a fresh one from the local florist, made from twigs twisted with dried kumquats and cinnamon sticks, instead of opting for what I'd thought was the safer choice of a hand-tied bouquet of snowy roses and silvery foliage.

'White flowers,' said my mother when she opened the door wearing one of her festive aprons.

I bent to kiss her cheek, immediately detecting a sour aura of gin.

'What's wrong with white flowers?' I asked.

'It's supposed to be unlucky to bring them into the house.'

'I'll leave them out here then, shall I?' I said, with the sarcasm of the resentful teenager I always seemed to become when I returned home.

She hesitated for a moment before taking them, then stepping back to allow me into the hall.

'You're late, so we didn't wait for you.'

I had stayed in London until The Dolls House closed so Tess and I could do presents together, but they'd been exceptionally busy, so we'd only just had time to exchange wrapped boxes before she had to dash for the train down to Margate.

'Daddy!' Bella hurled herself at me.

She was heavier than the last time I'd picked her up in the summer, but she still had that wonderful smell of newly bathed child in fresh pyjamas.

My nine-year-old, Flora, had never been as demonstrative as her younger sister. The top of her head was now level with my chin. She stood on tiptoe to greet me, in European style, with kisses on each cheek.

Though we Skyped every weekend they changed so quickly. I always felt a stab of sadness at what I had missed and would never get back.

'Charlotte and Robert have jetted off for a much deserved week in Antigua,' my mother informed me.

It was typically efficient of my ex-wife to turn a Christmas visit into a stopover en route to a more exotic destination.

'Daddy, can we open our presents now?' Bella asked.

'Of course not,' said my mother, before I could indulge her. 'We open presents on Christmas morning in this house.'

'Will you read me a story, Daddy?'

'Of course I will,' I replied quickly. 'Did you bring a book with you?'

'She brought about a dozen,' said my mother.

Bella was not an economical packer. Sometimes I wondered if her enormous suitcase meant that she was hoping to stay for ever.

The strange paradox for the divorced parent is that you desperately want your children to miss you, while at the same time not wanting them to miss you at all, because that would indicate they were finding separation as difficult as you were.

We read one of our favourite Paddington stories, as we always used to when we lived on the street where they were set.

'I miss our house in Portobello Road,' Bella said, a little wistfully, when I closed the book.

'Well, we'll be back there in a couple of days,' I said. 'And there's someone I'd like you to meet, who also lives on Portobello Road.'

I had been feeling increasingly awkward not telling them about Tess, who had become such an important part of my life, but it didn't feel right to introduce them through a computer screen.

'Who?' Flora asked immediately.

'She's called Tess. She works in The Dolls House,' I added, hoping to impress her.

Flora always peered longingly through the windows when we went for breakfast at Luis's.

'Is Tess your girlfriend?' Bella asked.

I remembered her asking the same question about Nash the previous summer. Did they want me to have a girlfriend, I wondered, or want me not to?

'Yes, she is.'

I got a calm feeling in my stomach just by saying it, like an antacid cooling heartburn.

'Can we have another story?' asked Bella.

'No,' said Flora, turning over to face the wall with her back to me. 'We have to go to sleep, otherwise Santa won't come.'

I kicked myself for getting the timing wrong.

My mother was asleep in front of a sitcom with a loud laughter track when I came down, an empty tumbler in her hand. I removed it gently. The kitchen was tidy, the dishwasher on. The only way I could contribute was taking the rubbish out. The heavy bag chinked with empty bottles.

It was only just after ten, but I decided to turn in, falling into a dreamless sleep until, in the early hours, I was awoken by the sound of my mother opening the door of the room next to mine and calling, 'Goodnight, my darling boy!'

For a moment, I wondered if she had got the wrong door and was talking to me. But I had never been her darling boy.

Did she say goodnight to Ross every night?

When I went down in the morning, the turkey was in the oven and my daughters were sitting dutifully at the table wearing Christmas jumpers.

'There's been a change of plan,' said my mother.

She was the sort of person who started preparations for Christmas as soon as the first Waitrose advert aired, buying in ludicrous quantities of nuts and boxed dates, dosing the cake every week with brandy, creating a timeline for food preparation on the day.

'Were you aware that Bella has gone vegetarian?'

It was more of an accusation than a question.

'Did you know, Daddy,' Bella chimed, '. . . that duck is actual ducks and pork is really little piggies . . . ?'

'You can see where this is going,' said Flora.

'Salmon is an actual fishy . . .'

'You can have cereal, can't you, Bella?' I interrupted.

'On Christmas Day?' said my mother.

'Shall I open the champagne?' I asked, hoping to appease her.

'Robert lets us have champagne,' said Flora.

I reached for another flute from the cupboard and poured a splash in for her.

'Do you want a little, Bella?'

'No thank you. Champagne is sarp!' she said.

I was gratified to hear her still using the family word for something we didn't quite like the taste of.

Flora took a sip and also pulled a face. 'I prefer Premier Cru.'

I glanced at my mother in the hope of exchanging an adult's knowing smile, but she was gazing admiringly at my elder daughter.

'Such an advantage speaking French from a young age,' she said. 'They're practically bilingual you know.'

Since when had foreign languages mattered to my mother? I remembered wincing with embarrassment when my father had ordered in restaurants in Italy.

'Your finest *steak, per favor* and we'd like *it well done! Capeesh*?'

'Trilingual,' Flora corrected. 'We speak German obviously. And I'm starting Spanish next year. I want to be a diplomat.'

'What's a diplomat?' asked Bella.

'Someone who hosts parties,' said Flora.

'I want to be a cowboy,' said Bella.

'Robert bought her riding lessons for Christmas,' Flora explained.

'What did he get you?' I asked.

Flora pushed her shiny black hair behind her ears to reveal slightly infected piercings with small gold hoops.

'Did Mummy sanction this?'

The previous summer, Flora had pleaded with me to have her ears pierced in The Dolls House. When I'd checked with Charlotte she had categorically forbidden it. I'd managed to placate Flora by taking them to get temporary transfers that looked like tattoos.

I'd since wondered how I didn't notice Tess at the reception desk.

'Your daughters were your invisibility cloak,' she'd said, when we talked about yet another missed opportunity to meet. 'Or maybe I'd just popped for a wee?'

'Robert took you?' I asked Flora.

Generally I tried not to think about their stepfather too much. He was so much older than me, it was impossible to feel competitive. He appeared fond of my daughters, but not inclined to usurp my role as their father. However, encouraging my daughter to disobey her mother was potentially more sinister.

'Of course not!' Flora scoffed. 'I went secretly, with a friend. It was a fait accompli!'

'Fait accompli!' repeated my mother delightedly.

I noticed the champagne bottle was virtually empty.

'Mummy said if I got septicaemia it was my own fault, but Robert insisted that I had to have gold earrings instead of the steel ones they give you.'

'Is it present time?' asked Bella.

We went into the living room where I handed out parcels of books, a soft toy each, which they never seemed to grow out of loving to cuddle, and finally two tiny turquoise carrier bags.

'Tiffany!' cried Flora.

When we'd gone Christmas shopping in Covent Garden, Tess had thought it crazy to think of buying a nine-year-old a necklace with a diamond, even if it was a very tiny diamond.

'Tiffany!' echoed Bella, adding, 'What's Tiffany?' as she unboxed the silver chain with a heart that I'd paid nearly two hundred pounds for, despite Tess assuring me you could get more or less the same thing in Claire's Accessories for a tenner.

'Who are these presents actually for?' she'd asked.

I realised now that I'd chosen them to impress Robert.

I'd bought my mother a scarf from Liberty. Apparently Robert had given her an Hermes one.

'I'll be the envy of the WI,' she said.

'What's WI?' Bella asked.

'It's the Women's Institute. We meet once a week.'

'Is it like Mummy's book group?' Flora asked. 'Really just an excuse to drink wine and bitch about your other halves?'

It was slight thrilling to receive these glimpses of Charlotte's not-quite-so-perfect relationship with her smug Eurocrat.

Christmas lunch always consisted of turkey with all the trimmings including forcemeat balls, bread sauce and gravy served in proper boats. Cauliflower cheese was produced for Bella.

'I had to break into the cheese board. Fortunately, I always keep florets in the freezer.'

I couldn't work out how my mother's tone always seemed to suggest that setbacks were my fault.

We were seated in the cold dining room which was now, as far as I knew, only used on Christmas Day. The reading of terrible cracker jokes brought a momentary glimmer of warmth to the chilly sterility, the pink, yellow and purple paper crowns providing discordant colour in the white, red and green colour scheme.

My mother had a special set of Christmas china with a border of ivy interspersed with poinsettias.

These were white flowers, I thought, and she'd never complained about them. Although, in fairness, to stand out against the white surface of the plate they had a slightly grey tinge to them.

'These plates are so pretty!' said Bella.

My mother brightened. 'Oh, I'm glad you like them. Some of us don't, do we Gus?'

I'd wondered how long it was going to take before the usual story was rolled out.

I must only have been about Bella's age. Always keen to get my mother's approval, I had decided to lay the table myself on Christmas morning. I had set out the large dinner plates, but I'd had to pull a chair across to the dresser to reach for the smaller side plates and tried to take too many at once. I lost my balance and dropped them. Luckily there was a deep carpet, but three had smashed against the dresser on their slow motion descent to the floor.

I'd waited in fear, fully expecting someone to rush in having heard the crash, but Ross and my father were practising rugby tackles on the back lawn and my mother had a noisy extractor fan on in the kitchen.

I remembered the complete service was twelve, so there were plenty of plates left over. I'd been young enough to think that by getting rid of the evidence my crime would not be discovered. And it might not have been had I not, in my panic, hidden the shards in the large vase that was never used for flowers, not realising that my mother always moved it when she did the dusting.

My failure to own up was deemed worse than the accident itself.

'I'm very disappointed in you, Angus,' I remembered her saying.

I'd been disappointing her ever since, I thought, watching the glee with which she regaled my daughters with tales of my incompetence and dishonesty.

'What do you eat at Christmas in Geneva?' I asked Flora, desperate to get off the subject.

'We usually have carp at the chalet. It's traditional.'

I had expressly forbidden Charlotte to take my daughters to Robert's chalet, despite her protests that the social isolation from not skiing would be far worse than the risks involved in the sport. She had clearly taken no notice. I wondered what my mother thought about them skiing or whether she had even made the connection. It was impossible to tell from the glazed expression in her eyes.

*

After lunch, I cleared the table and the kitchen while Flora set up the iPad which had been Robert's gift to my mother, and they FaceTimed the Caribbean.

I was trying not to listen in but Bella's voice was loud.

'Daddy has a girlfriend.'

'She works at the place we got our tattoos,' said Flora.

Standing outside on the drive in the frosty air, I wished I'd had the foresight to leave a sneaky packet of cigarettes in the glove compartment of my car. I'd probably drunk too much wine at lunch to safely drive to a garage.

When Tess answered her phone, I could hear that there was singing at Anne's house. 'Fairytale of New York', with Tess's father doing a gravelly Shane McGowan and Hope with the bell-like clarity of Kirsty MacColl.

'Thank you for my present,' Tess said.

I had bought her a marbled fountain pen with a gold nib.

'For writing your novel,' I'd put on the card.

'It's really beautiful,' she said. 'Although I do normally use a laptop.'

'You can sign copies with it when you're a published author.'

She laughed uncertainly. 'Did you like mine?'

She had bought me an elegant vintage watch with a leather strap that I'd opened by myself, in my childhood bed that morning.

'I'm counting the seconds till I see you again.'

'Cheesy,' she said.

'But true.'

'How are the girls?'

'Really looking forward to meeting you,' I said, managing to get more confidence into my voice than I felt.

*

My mother made cold cuts with bubble and squeak for our Boxing Day lunch, with the rest of the cauliflower cheese for Bella. There was clearly only one vegetarian dish in her repertoire and I wished I'd bought her an Ottolenghi cookbook or something useful. I made a mental note for her next birthday.

'I'm going to help Grandma with the washing up while you pack,' I told the girls.

'It will all go in the dishwasher,' said my mother.

'Yes, but I know you rinse it off first.'

She awarded me a rare smile.

It was somehow easier to talk to her standing side by side, especially now that the end of the visit was within touching distance.

'So you're keeping busy?' I addressed the cupboard over the sink. 'With the WI and everything?'

'I miss the children, of course,' she said. 'They're growing up so fast.'

'Why don't you come up to London for the day. We could go to a museum?'

'Now?' she asked.

I regretted the impulse almost immediately.

'In a couple of days, maybe. They fly on the thirty-first, then I'm straight back to work.'

'You're still working in A & E?'

'Yes.'

A heavy sigh. 'Ross was going to be a surgeon.'

'I know.'

Why was it that people revered surgeons above all others in the medical profession? Perhaps because the confidence you needed to slice open another human showed an impressive kind

84

of steel? All the surgeons I knew were arrogant bastards. Ross had been the perfect candidate.

'I haven't got the temperament for surgery.'

'No,' my mother agreed.

Leaving the house felt like breathing fresh air again.

In the rearview mirror, I watched her, still in an apron with a Christmas pudding on it, waving us down the street. She looked so innocuous I kicked myself for acting so churlishly around her.

'I spy with my little eye, something beginning with D,' Bella immediately started on one of the games we played on car journeys.

'Dog?' Flora guessed, as we passed a man walking a chocolate labrador.

'No.'

'Dashboard?' Flora's voice was already weary.

'No! Daddy!' Bella shouted at the top of her lungs.

Chapter Eight

The following day, Tess arrived at my house bearing goody bags from The Dolls House containing several tiny bottles of nail polish.

'Will you do my nails for me, Tess?' Bella asked.

'I'll have a go. I'm not really an expert.'

'I thought it was your job,' said Flora.

'I'm the manageress,' said Tess.

She took Bella's hand and began applying colour to her tiny nails as Flora scrolled through her iPhone occasionally glancing up at me as if daring me to tell her to put it away.

'How long have you been on holiday?' Tess asked her.

'A couple of weeks. We went to Austria.'

'That must have been very Christmassy,' said Tess.

'Obviously. Do you ski?'

'Me? No!'

'Why?'

'Well, I've never had the opportunity. But if I had I probably wouldn't be much good at it.'

'Why?'

'I've never been much good at whooshing downhill, even on a bike!'

'Is there anything you are good at?' Flora asked.

'Hmm, let me think about that,' said Tess. 'Why don't you tell me what you're good at?'

Flora embarked on a long list of grades, trophies and prizes. I was mortified.

'What about you, Bella?' Tess asked, when Flora eventually ran out of achievements.

'Flora's better at most things.'

I winced at a second child's acceptance of inferiority.

'Bella loves books, don't you?' I said.

'Daddy bought me lots for Christmas,' she told Tess.

'Tess helped me choose them.'

'I've read most of the ones you bought me before,' Flora said. 'They're honestly a bit young for me.'

'I'm sure we can exchange them in Waterstones,' Tess said.

'Tess has a really exciting shopping trip planned for you,' I said, feeling slightly desperate about the stand-off that seemed to be developing. 'I told her how much you like Primark and she said she would take you there, didn't you?'

'I'll give you twenty pounds each and you can spend it how you like,' Tess said.

'Primark!' shouted Bella.

'Sorry, but Mummy said we are not to come back with bags of tat like last time,' said Flora.

I was as shocked by her rudeness as Tess clearly was. She looked at me for help, but I couldn't think of a way of scolding Flora without making the situation worse.

Tess stood up.

'I'll leave you to your supper,' she said.

'Please stay,' I whispered to her at the door. 'She's only nine.'

'Bit tired,' she said.

I watched her walking down the street. As it curved away, she turned and, seeing me there, smiled and waved, and I breathed again.

'I love Tess,' said Bella, when I closed the door.

'You can't love someone when you've only said three words to them,' said Flora.

I remembered the moment I'd seen Tess in the Basilica of San Miniato al Monte with the golden mosaic of a solemn Christ behind her.

'You're the one . . . ' we both said, meaning the same person we'd seen there sixteen years before.

Three words.

Chapter Nine

I didn't know how it was even possible for my mother to be more irritating out than at home. The first thing she said when we picked her up from the station was: 'What are we doing for lunch?'

I'd intended to grab a sandwich from one of the cafés on the South Bank, but as she started complaining about the cold wind blowing along the Thames, the Christmas crowds and the length of the walk, I decided to veer off my planned route to a chain restaurant, where we ate a mediocre meal.

'Fifteen pounds for a pizza! It's really only bread and cheese,' she said, even though I was the one paying.

At the Paul Klee exhibition at Tate Modern, she was surprised to read that the artist was Swiss.

'I didn't think there *were* artists in Switzerland.'

'That's one of the reasons we're here,' I explained. 'Flora's doing a project on him at school.'

My mother's only critique was that the pictures were very small.

'I thought they'd be much bigger,' she said, as if she'd somehow been mis-sold.

I prided myself on my children's willingness to look at art, but knew it was because we never stayed in a gallery for too long. Living in a city where galleries are free, I'd often taken them to see just a couple of paintings, before finding somewhere nice for tea. My mother, who would never voluntarily have gone to see art herself, insisted on reading the captions to every single painting, keeping us there so long that it was dark by the time we emerged.

The crisp frosty air seemed to make the city sparkle and the coloured lights of the Christmas fairground on the South Bank were like a magical lure to the girls.

'Do we have to go to the ballet?' asked Flora.

In previous years, a visit to the ballet was the highlight of their trip, but I was out of touch. Now she wanted cool experiences like the ones she saw on Instagram. She hadn't quite reached double digits, but she was a teenager already. I'd always thought of myself as a young parent. Maybe all parents thought of themselves as young until their children started being embarrassed by them.

My mother was complaining about how crowded the trains would be at this time of day.

'What are we doing now?' she asked.

'I thought we'd see you on to the train, then have an early supper . . .'

'Am I invited?'

'Well, Flora wanted to go to Balthazar. It's back across the river . . . You did say you didn't want to go back too late . . .'

I should have told her there and then that Tess was meeting us. I should probably have texted Tess too, rather than allowing the situation to be awkward from the beginning.

By the time we arrived at the restaurant, she was already seated at the table. I'd never seen her with make-up on before. She looked beautiful but somehow different. She was wearing a dark green velvet dress and long fake emerald earrings. Dolled up, I thought, wondering if her friend had had a hand in the makeover.

'You look very glamorous,' I said, giving her a quick kiss on the cheek.

'You do realise that there isn't a dress code at the Opera House?' said Flora.

I was suddenly acutely aware that the only one of my family not in jeans was my mother. I handed round the menus.

'Is it your first time at the ballet?' my mother asked, after I'd introduced them.

'Yes,' said Tess.

'Charlotte prefers opera, doesn't she Angus? You used to come often, didn't you?'

My mother ordered a large G & T. After one sip, she was flushed. She had drunk most of the bottle of bad red wine we'd had at lunch. Was she drinking more because she was with company, or was this was standard for her?

'I expected you to have more . . .' she waved her hand next to Tess's bare arm.

'What?'

'You know. Tattoos.'

'Beg pardon?'

'In your line of business,' said my mother, somehow making it sound as if Tess was a prostitute.

'I think you've got your wires crossed,' I stepped in. 'Tess manages a beauty salon where the girls just happened to get some temporary tattoos. What are we all having?'

The waiter was waiting to take our order.

'I'll have the *plat du jour*, please,' Tess said.

'You don't pronounce the "t".' Flora rolled her eyes.

'They're practically bilingual,' my mother told Tess proudly. 'Have you ever been abroad?'

'I met Gus in Italy.'

'Charlotte loves Italy, doesn't she, Angus? Portofino, Lucca, Venice . . .'

Happily she hadn't mentioned any of the places I'd visited with Tess.

The waiter continued to hover.

'I think I'll just have another one of these,' said my mother, holding up her empty goblet. 'I really cannot be rushing my food. Not with a walk back to Waterloo.'

'Aren't you coming to the ballet?' Tess asked her.

'I wasn't invited,' said my mother.

'You should take your mother, Gus,' said Tess. 'I really don't mind not going.'

I tried to give her a look to indicate the last thing I wanted to do was take my mother.

'That's very sweet of you, dear,' said my mother. 'But I couldn't go back on the train so late on my own.'

I couldn't quite work out how this chance for her to spend more time with her grandchildren had turned into such a disaster.

The Royal Ballet's production of *The Nutcracker* was a visual treat. The sumptuous set was designed to look like an Edwardian Christmas card, with magic tricks and dancers dressed as dolls jumping out of boxes. When the Christmas tree started growing to fill the entire height of the stage, I turned to see Tess's face. It was as filled with wonder as Bella's.

'I keep thinking how much Hope would love this,' she said as we stood in the Floral Hall during the interval, with Bella pirouetting around and Flora scrolling on her phone.

'We'll have to bring her one day.'

'I'm not sure about that. We took her to a panto once and she sang so loudly the dame got her up on stage. That might not go down so well here.'

'We could get a box,' I said. 'It's much more private, a bit like having a little room all of your own. You can stand up, walk around. You can even have sex if you want,' I whispered across her deliciously bare shoulder.

It was a throwaway comment intended to show how much I'd missed sleeping with her over the past few days.

She frowned.

'Not with Hope there, obviously,' I added quickly.

'Did you and Charlotte get a box?' Tess asked.

The day was slipping away from me.

As the curtain came up for the second act, revealing a fairy-tale palace so sparklingly pretty it got its own round of applause, I glanced at Tess's face, but she was sitting very stiffly beside me as if to prevent any chance of touching.

Chapter Ten

'What's that necklace you're wearing, Flora?' Charlotte asked, when we met in our usual place at the airport.

'It's Tiffany,' she said. 'It's my main Christmas present from Daddy.'

'Daddy's spoiling you,' said Charlotte, raising an eyebrow. 'Unfortunately, darlings, our flight is delayed. Would you like to wait here with Daddy or shall we go through and find Robert?'

'Wait here with Daddy,' said Bella.

The immediacy of the response gave me a momentary fillip of gratification, but we had already said all our it-won't-be-long-till-you're-backs and I-miss-you-all-the-times and make-sure-you-only-go-down-marked-pistes, and we'd given each other our big hugs. So it felt odd trying to find other things to do.

I bought Bella a shrink-wrapped magazine with a plastic bangle. Flora asked for *Elle*. Then Bella and I played a kind of hopscotch in a bit of space behind a coffee concession, while Charlotte sat at a distance scrolling through her emails.

Eventually she strutted across. 'I don't suppose you've given any more thought to selling the house?'

'No.'

'It *is* half mine.'

'You don't need the money, do you?'

The flight was called before she could answer.

I stood on tiptoe waving my daughters through the queues at departures for as long as I could see them, then a little bit longer in case they could still see me. As I walked to the steps down to the Tube, I realised that it was the first time I hadn't cried when they left.

I rang Tess, eager to see her before I went to work, but felt crushed as she spoke to me politely but distantly, as if I were a customer phoning to change an appointment.

'It's our busiest day of the year . . .'

'What will you do tonight?' I asked.

'Doll's gone into labour. I'm going down to Kent to help out.'

I'd been thinking she would be there waiting for me when I returned from work.

'Look, we're really busy . . .'

'Sorry! Happy New Year!'

But she'd already hung up.

You could take either Christmas Day or New Year's Eve as holiday. I wished now that I'd done it the other way round. Generally Christmas was less busy as they discharged as many patients as they could before the day.

New Year's Eve always began with relative calm, but a tsunami of drunks started rolling in when I was at peak tiredness. I knew I should have taken a nap, but restlessness had kept me from sleeping in the afternoon, so I had tidied and cleaned the house; then, when all traces of my daughters' visit were erased, regretted my haste. The house felt empty without the clatter of their footsteps. In the absence of Bella's constant chatter my anxious thoughts screamed through the silence.

Was Tess's coldness on the phone just temporary? Had my family put her off completely? It was clear that our wider lives weren't going to fit together as easily as we did, but surely that didn't have to affect what we had together?

'Are you all right, Dr Macdonald?' One of the nurses broke through my thoughts. I wondered how long I'd been staring at the cold cup of coffee in front of me.

I was about to grab a free screen to write up some notes, when the department was rushed by a cohort of police charging through reception, where a gang had turned up after a stabbing. It was a regular occurrence in any London hospital but I was always impressed by the sangfroid of the staff, who carried on their observations as if nothing unusual was happening.

Though we were all calm, professional and tried everything possible, there was nothing we could do to save the seventeen-year-old who'd lost so much blood he'd gone into cardiac arrest by the time paramedics arrived.

As I left the hospital, the blur in my head was brought sharply into focus as I walked past a group of lanky teenagers in hoodies leaning on each other for support, two of them sitting on the pavement hugging their knees and staring into space. They were boys, not yet men, still as awkward as baby giraffes in their long-limbed bodies. Just as I had been when my brother had died. I felt a surge of grief at lives cut short by competitive masculinity, emotions forever numbed by witnessing how suddenly life can ebb away.

My landline was ringing when I got back. I raced to pick it up, hoping it was Tess, but it was Nash's voice.

'Happy New Year!'

'I've just come in from work.'

I calculated it must only be midnight in LA.

'Bad night?'

'Not the greatest,' I said, wondering why doctors never talked about what happened at work. It was like a code of silence.

'Me neither. I'm drinking a bottle of champagne by myself.'

'No glamorous parties?'

'Getting tanked up beforehand. Nobody drinks here. May not even go. How was your Christmas?'

'It wasn't an unqualified success.' I gave her a brief summary of my family's disastrous encounters with Tess.

'It's *Rebecca*,' she said.

'I'm sorry?'

'I was asked to read for the new movie. When I got there, it turned out they wanted me for Mrs Danvers. Can you believe it?'

'I've been up all night, Nash, I don't see where you're going with this.'

'Daphne du Maurier's *Rebecca*. Innocent young working class woman falls in love with handsome aristo Maxim de Winter, whose glamorous first wife Rebecca has died. Obviously Charlotte hasn't died, but you get the picture? There's this evil housekeeper called Mrs Danvers who keeps telling our heroine how marvellous Rebecca was and so she thinks Max is still in love with her . . .'

'Is my mother Mrs Danvers in this scenario?'

'Yes, but Flora sounds like she's competing for the role.'

'Surely Tess can't believe I'm still in love with Charlotte?'

'You keep Charlotte's house exactly as she left it, do everything she says, tell everyone how beautiful she is . . . No, I'm sure it hasn't even crossed Tess's mind . . .'

'Bugger,' I said. 'Do you think it's too late?'

'Defeatism is one of your least attractive qualities, Gus.'

I wondered what the others were.

'Look, it's New Year. You probably have about twelve hours of goodwill left, unless she's got a massive hangover. Get down to Kent and try not to fuck this one up.'

Tess

Chapter Eleven

'Sounds like he needs to grow a pair,' Doll said.

Her face creased in agony. 'That was a strong one. How long since the last?'

'Just over five minutes.'

Her private room was like a posh hotel but with a hospital bed. There was even a mini bar with a selection of soft drinks and a half bottle of champagne. They admitted you at an earlier stage of labour than a normal hospital, probably because they charged by the hour. The contractions had started soon after I arrived, and I'd volunteered to go with Doll so that Dave could stay at home with Elsie, who was asleep.

'Gus is weak. That's the problem here, Tess. And there's nothing worse than a weak man.'

Surely that wasn't true? Too weak must be better than too strong? Gus was a nice dad with his children. He let them get away with stuff, but that was because he didn't see them very often. There was no aura of danger hanging around him like there was with my dad.

The real problem was there wasn't room for me in his family. Charlotte was the children's mother. Gus's mother was clearly devoted to her, and I suspected that at least part of Gus still was too. I'd been scarred by one affair with a married man. I couldn't allow myself to again become the secret girlfriend who conveniently disappeared when family was around.

Doll groaned.

I checked my watch, it was less than two minutes since the last contraction. I rang the bell to summon the midwife and sent a text to Dave.

It all happened so quickly that it was me there at the birth with Doll squeezing my hand so tightly I thought her nails would cut through my palm. I was shocked how primal it was to see a new human being slither into the world, and how instantly all the groans and pain subsided leaving my friend a serene, if slightly sweaty, Madonna.

'You hold him, Tess,' she said, after the nurses had cleaned him up and done their assessments.

The baby had a squashed little face.

'Hello, little person,' I said, with tears pouring down my cheeks.

Then Dave arrived with Elsie.

It was only an hour into the New Year. In the corridor outside I held Elsie up to the window, saying 'Wooo!' each time we spotted fleeting fountains of fireworks in the sky. She was a little bit whiny from being woken up in the middle of the night, but cheered up instantly when Dave called us in, saying they'd got a present for her.

He lifted her onto the bed so that it would be safe, then very carefully placed the tiny wrapped baby in her arms. They'd decided to call him Tommy.

The four of them were like a portrait of a perfect family. It was rare to see Doll without make-up and, now she'd washed her face and brushed her hair, she looked younger and even prettier than usual. Elsie was a miniature version of her mother, all blonde curls and blue eyes, which contrasted with the baby's improbable shock of dark hair. Watching over them all was

Dave, who had always been a good-looking man with the sort of face you could trust, which is useful in a plumber.

It could have been me...

The thought flashed through my mind along with the memory of him proposing at the top of the London Eye. The pod had been crowded with tourists, who'd taken pictures of him on one knee with the ring. Which made it even worse that I hadn't been able to say yes...

I'd been so surprised, not so much by the proposal, as the imagination he'd put into planning it. Turned out he'd secretly consulted Doll to see what I'd like. The next day when she'd come round to mine for a debrief, she'd been weirdly cross with me for not accepting. It only occurred to me much later that, subconsciously, she must have been dreaming up the ideal proposal for herself. To be fair, I don't think it had crossed either of their minds that they were right for each other at that point. It was months later, when I was away visiting Kevin in New York and Dave was helping Doll install the basins in her first salon that they'd fallen in love.

At the time I'd felt betrayed. I was still Dave's girlfriend even though I hadn't wanted to get engaged. It simply wasn't on for my best friend to sleep with him behind my back. It had reignited the insecurity I'd always felt about my attractiveness compared to Doll's. I'd assumed that Dave must have fancied her all along, but hadn't thought he stood a chance.

That probably wasn't the case. I don't think he could believe his luck when it happened with Doll, but if I'd said yes on the London Eye, I'm sure he would have been loyal to me. He was a guy who wanted to settle down and have a family, so he was the perfect husband material going to waste – a handsome, reliable man – and that was what Doll needed. In her previous relationship with a footballer she'd been arm candy. With Dave by her side she could achieve her own ambitions.

They were made for each other and I was glad they'd made such a success of it.

Tommy started crying.

'Stop that!' Elsie pointed right in his face.

'Why don't you give him back to Mummy now?' said Dave.

'He's my present!' Elsie wailed as he took the baby from her.

'I've got another present for you back at home,' I said quickly.

'What is it?'

'A surprise!' I said.

Dave smiled at me gratefully.

'Shall I give you a lift?' he asked.

'No, you must stay here. We'll get a taxi. That will be exciting, won't it, Elsie?'

It had been a struggle to bring the huge box on the train, but I was glad I'd made the effort. I'd bought her a Playmobil castle, which had golden gates and turrets, a queen and a princess.

We were walking the two tiny dolls through each of their blingy rooms, up and down their many ornate staircases, when the doorbell rang.

'Who's that?'

'Probably a delivery for Mummy,' I said.

'Is it another baby?' Elsie asked.

We opened the door to a large white teddy bear waving his paw at us.

'Happy New Year!'

Everyone has their own teddy bear voice. Mine was always gruff and low. Gus's sounded rather posh.

'Is this another present?' said Elsie excitedly reaching up.

I nodded emphatically at Gus, who bent down to her level to hand it over.

'This is my friend Gus.'

Elsie rocked the bear in her arms.

'He's a very fluffy bear, isn't he?' I said. 'What do you think his name is?'

'Gus,' said Elsie.

'That's my friend's name. What would you like to call your bear?'

'Gus.'

I wasn't sure how well that would go down with her mother.

'Well, I'm honoured,' said Gus.

He was still standing outside.

'Doll and Dave will be back with the baby very soon . . .'

I was a bit panicked how Doll would react to Gus being there when they arrived home from the hospital, especially after agreeing with her only a few hours before that the best thing for me would be to end the relationship.

'Bella chose the bear for the baby in Hamleys,' Gus whispered. 'This was supposed to be for Elsie.' He handed me a gift-wrapped box, which I also gave to her.

She ripped the paper off to find a Playmobil fishing boat with a captain and a haul of small fish.

'Bella's choice again, I'm afraid,' Gus said. 'I told her Elsie lived by the sea.'

His face was full of concern that he'd done the wrong thing, but he knew how important it was to give a present to the sibling so they didn't feel left out. He'd remembered me saying that Playmobil was her favourite thing. He was a kind man. I couldn't seem to keep my expression stern nor my body rigid and distant. All the defences I'd tried to erect were crumbling as Dave's SUV pulled into the drive.

Dave took out the baby seat with Tommy in it.

'Why's everyone standing on the doorstep?' he said, waving us in with his free hand.

Then Doll got out, raising her eyebrows at me, and Elsie hurtled towards her shouting, 'Mummy! The fish man sails his boat to the castle and falls in love with the princess!'

'I think we'll go for a walk while you all settle in,' I said, hurriedly grabbing my coat.

There was a bitter wind blowing against us as we walked along the beach.

'How was your New Year?'

'Busy,' said Gus.

'Funny how we both spent it in a hospital.'

'Were you there for the birth?'

'I was. It's a miracle, isn't it?'

He smiled.

We walked a little further. It felt like there was a herd of invisible elephants lumbering on the beach around us, but I was determined I wasn't going to be the first to mention our last disastrous evening together.

'I'm sorry about Flora,' he said eventually. 'It's probably always a bit difficult when a divorced parent finds a new partner.'

The memory of his daughter still stung. And the fact he had said nothing.

'It's not just her, though, is it?'

'I can't apologise enough for my mother...'

'No, I didn't mean that. I think she was just trying to be polite, in her own way.'

I tried to remember all the reasons Doll and I had rehearsed for why this relationship was never going to work.

'I don't think you're ready for another relationship. And I've been hurt before...'

'I won't hurt you!' He caught my hand then, seeing my expression, 'I already have. I'm so sorry.'

'It's not your fault,' I said. 'It's just bad timing, I suppose.'

He stopped walking. 'Tess, I wish you and I had met when we were eighteen, or twenty-one, or all the other times we managed not to meet. But I can't wish away Flora and Bella because they are very precious to me.'

'I don't want you to wish them away! They're not the problem.'

He said nothing for a long time as we walked.

'Is it Charlotte?' he finally asked. 'Nash has this theory that it's like *Rebecca* . . .'

'You spoke to Nash about me?'

I couldn't decide whether this made me feel better or worse.

'She called this morning. Look, Tess, for the avoidance of doubt, if it's Charlotte you're concerned about, she and I hadn't had sex for at least a year before we split up. We didn't even sleep in the same bed. I really do not love her. In fact, I hate her.'

'Hatred is still a very strong emotion. It would be much better if you were indifferent.'

'Indifferent it is!' he said, clasping my hands.

'You can't just go from hatred to indifference!'

'I'll work on it,' he said, looking straight at me. 'I'm so sorry if I gave the wrong impression, but you have to believe that you are the only woman I have ever really loved. We can make this work, can't we?'

His eyes, a mix of blue and gold, seemed to flicker constantly between compassion and anxiety.

Still lightheaded from lack of sleep, my brain struggled to locate any of the objections that had previously been so obvious.

Suddenly we were hugging. He picked me up and twirled

107

me round and round and, when we stopped to kiss, the world continued spinning.

We walked back with the wind behind us, his hand reaching for mine, putting it into his pocket for warmth.

'Maxim de Winter murdered Rebecca,' I suddenly remembered.

'Well, I don't think I can promise to do that.' And then he laughed.

'Shall we call in on Marcus and Keiko?' Gus asked as we headed out of Margate.

It was the second time he'd suggested meeting his friends. The first time I'd made oysters my excuse, but I couldn't think of a good one now.

I was certain that they must be the same Marcus and Keiko who weekended in the converted fisherman's hut next to the unconverted shack where Leo and I had conducted our trysts. It was yet another of those weird not-quite-meetings. Had Gus visited Marcus when I was with Leo, chances are we'd have greeted each other over the breakwater. I dreaded to think what he would have made of me skivvying around an ageing egotist with a ponytail.

The idea of seeing Leo again did not appeal. It's easy to dream up smart things to say in a scenario but, when you've been in awe of someone, it's hard to throw the habit. I would coolly say as little as possible, I decided as we walked along the boardwalk towards the huts, pretend I barely remembered who he was.

Marcus was tall and very charming in that public school way that holds you off rather than inviting you in. I could tell he knew we had met before but couldn't immediately place me. The children, now seven and three, had been a toddler and babe-in-arms when I last saw them, but Keiko recognised me straightaway, giving me an almost imperceptible smile, signalling that the story was mine to tell.

Next door, Leo's hut no longer existed. Instead there was a building site.

'Owner sold up and retired to Spain,' Marcus said. 'Guy I know at JP Morgan bought it. He's using our architect.'

There was a god!

I followed Keiko inside, amazed at how different the vast, clean space was from the shed-like interior of Leo's, with its lingering smell of creosote. She took a bottle of champagne from the fridge and arranged a tray with four flutes and a bowl of nibbles coated with flecks of seaweed.

Outside the children, wrapped up in thick winter coats, were busy creating a garden out of shells. The men were standing further down the shingle looking out at the estuary. As I walked towards them, carefully balancing the tray, the salty breeze blew snatches of conversation back to me before they could hear the crunch of my footsteps.

'I could never understand what someone so attractive was doing with that dreadful old roué,' Marcus was saying.

'Tess!'

Gus turned and raised his eyebrows, so I was in no doubt I'd been rumbled. We both have regrets about our pasts, his amused smile seemed to say.

'Champagne?' I asked, blushing.

A glimmer of wintry sunlight fell across the water, turning it from pewter to platinum as we clinked glasses and toasted the New Year, our fingers as cold as the champagne.

'Who's up for a game of rounders?' Marcus said. 'That'll warm us up!'

'Me!' shouted Milo.

'Me!' echoed Millie.

Gus picked the little girl up and we all walked along to a flatter bit of beach, where he and Marcus marked bases with small piles of stones, striding out the distances with great seriousness. I remembered my brothers doing the same on the flat white beaches of Ireland's west coast, where we used to go for our summer holidays.

We divided into teams. Gus and Keiko with Milo. Then Marcus, Millie and me.

Being tall, I was a useful netball player at school, but I'd never joined in team sports since, so I saw my role as looking after Millie, making sure she didn't get hit by the ball, and pretending that my fielding throws were hers. When it was her turn to hit I held the bat with her, and together we whacked the ball way past her brother, enabling us to complete a home run with me picking her up for the sprint to the last base.

'Brilliant, Millie!' Marcus called. 'You're in now Tess!'

Gus was pitching. I hoped he would be gentle as he had been with Millie, but his competitive instincts proved stronger and he rocketed the ball towards me. I took a flailing swipe.

'Run!' Marcus shouted, as I stood there not quite believing that I'd hit the ball so hard it was still in the air.

I completed a run and prepared to face Gus once more.

Again, I somehow launched it and made another home run. I managed it six more times until Gus put Milo in to pitch and, having observed the direction I always hit the ball, positioned himself to catch me out. Our team still won ten to six.

'You're a legend, Tess,' Marcus said. 'Do you play tennis?'

'I never learned,' I said.

At my school, tennis was the preserve of the middle-class girls whose parents were members of the local club.

'You should really get Gus to teach you. You'd be an absolute natural.'

I felt ridiculously proud.

Keiko, Millie and I walked back towards the hut while Marcus, Gus and Milo picked up flat stones to skim across the gently breaking waves, just as my brothers used to.

'Do you think boys are genetically programmed to skim stones?' I asked Keiko. 'It's almost like they can't help themselves,'

'I once went to a yoga retreat on a Greek Island. On the last day our teacher asked us all to pick up a pebble, invest it with all our problems, then cast it into the sea.'

'Did it work?' I asked.

'It felt satisfying, somehow.' Keiko smiled at me.

I watched Gus as he made a run up, maintaining his crouched position as he focused on counting the bounces, then leapt up and down, his long arms aloft in victory. He was more carefree than I'd ever seen him. For a moment, I felt I'd glimpsed the boy he had been with his brother before tragedy had left him on his own.

I picked up a stone myself, gave it a short silent lecture about not letting my jealous thoughts about Charlotte get in the way of enjoying the wonderful good fortune of meeting this man, then watched it leap across the water before it disappeared with a satisfying plop.

Chapter Twelve

Spring 2014

Valentine's Day fell on a Friday that year. It was one of our busiest days at the salon with everyone getting ready for romantic dates and possible proposals. We'd decorated the place with helium balloons, which I gave the staff to take home with them after we closed, keeping one for me.

In my pocket was the letter I'd received that morning, confirming that the first round of tests on my six-monthly follow-up had found no evidence of recurrence.

I felt I'd been given a reprieve. When you've had cancer, you're suspicious of every headache and pain and, as you approach the cliff edge of tests, that fear is magnified exponentially.

'They're just routine,' Gus had tried to reassure me.

'Only till they're not. I mean, they wouldn't do tests if there was zero likelihood of finding anything. So what if they do? That's what I'm thinking about.'

'You'd be a terrible doctor. It's stressful enough making decisions about what's in front of you. You'd go mad if you thought about all the what ifs.'

Nevertheless, he'd sounded mightily relieved when I'd called earlier in the day to tell him.

*

It was our first Valentine's Day together. An anonymous card addressed in his handwriting had arrived at my flat that morning. A huge bouquet of long-stemmed red roses had been delivered to the salon, impressing clients and staff alike. I was concerned that my gift to him – a year's membership plus one to the Tate galleries – wouldn't seem romantic enough. I hadn't been sure whether he was one of those men who would do the whole hearts-and-flowers thing, or one who would proclaim that Valentine's Day had become too commercialised. I should have known because Gus was generous, and that's usually just an excuse for meanness.

Our relationship was in a good place. I'd stopped worrying that any wrong move would cause him to suddenly realise he'd made a mistake. He was clearly stressed at work, but seemed to relax when we were together. I'd stay with him most nights and, when he was working, I'd catch up on my sleep and washing back at my flat.

After a few weeks of not doing my homework, I stopped going to my Life Writing class. Truth was, my heart wasn't really in the memoir any more. Novels were what I liked to read, and I had the glimmer of an idea for one, but whenever I tried to concentrate on how it might work, I'd get distracted by a tingling memory of something he'd said, or done, and find myself sitting at my ancient laptop, staring into space with an inane smile on my face. It was almost as if finding joy in my own love story meant I didn't need to imagine one any more. Anyway, I'd tell myself as I switched off the light, willing sleep to come so the hours until I next saw him would quickly pass, I'd only ever written short stories before. How would I ever get to a hundred thousand words? And if I did, who would want to read it?

On weekends, we went for brunch at Luis's, then long walks when the weather was fine, galleries or the cinema when it was cold. I loved just being in his company, watching him cook, chatting as we ate, lying in the bath together staring at each other, soaping his back, feeling the tension release from his shoulders. Sex was no longer a frantic attempt to consume each another. We'd learned the things that turned us on. There was something profoundly intimate about giving pure pleasure, taking each other to a plane of existence where it felt as if we were soaring above the world.

As I walked up Portobello Road, ribbon in hand, a plump red heart-shaped balloon bobbing above me, I got that lift when you realise it's still light and the days are getting longer. Soon the cherry trees would blossom. There was nowhere prettier than London in the spring.

Gus had given me a key, so I let myself in. He was already home, his shoulders hunched with exhaustion, but when he saw me he bounded across the room, hugging me so tightly I let go of the balloon and it shot up to the ceiling.

Gus had booked his favourite restaurant in Primrose Hill and when we arrived the proprietor greeted him like an old friend.

'Ciao Gus! My best ever waiter,' he said.

'Tess, this is Salvatore, my best ever boss! I used to work here when I was a student.'

Salvatore shook my hand. 'Bellissima!'

He showed us to a table in a quiet alcove with a chalky mural of a window with a view of a distant Italian hilltop town.

The menu consisted of lots of small plates, a kind of Italian tapas. I enjoyed the risotto more than the seafood as I've never been one for garlic or shells.

'You're such a cheap date!' Gus said.

When we paused to consider the dessert options, a woman came out of the kitchen dressed in chef's whites. Gus stood up and hugged her warmly.

'Tess, this is Stefania.'

'Lovely to meet you,' I said.

'*Piacere*!' she said, giving me an obvious once over before pronouncing me *bellissima*!

When Gus started asking her where the langoustines were from and how she had cooked them to make them so very delicious, I realised that this was where he must have discovered his love of food and cooking. There was still so much about him that I didn't know, and I loved getting glimpses of what had shaped him as a person.

They discussed each of the recipes, then she turned to me.

'You like the risotto?'

'I had no idea rice could taste so delicious!'

She smiled.

'Tess and I met in Italy,' Gus told her.

'In Firenze,' I said.

'You like Firenze?'

'Oh, I love it so much.'

I found myself telling her how I had first gone there when I was eighteen, at the very same time that Gus had first been there. I'd been camping with my friend Doll, he had been in a posh hotel with his parents. Our paths had crossed then in the basilica San Miniato al Monte, but we had only met properly last summer in that very same place.

'*Come una fiaba*!' she said.

I looked at Gus for a translation.

He shrugged.

'*E vissero felici e contenti*,' she said, pinching my cheek. '*Simpaticissima*!'

'Does that mean very sympathetic?' I asked him after she had disappeared back into the kitchen.

'No, it's more like really lovely,' he said, leaning across the table and taking my hand. 'Stefania is a very good judge of

115

character. She and Salvatore were like family to me . . . let's choose our *dolci*.'

I looked at the menu.

'Has to be gelato, doesn't it?' I said.

'But only two flavours,' he said, remembering the rule I'd told him in Florence. 'Because your mouth is always too cold to taste the third!'

He chose hazelnut ice cream with lemon sorbet, just as he had on the day we first spoke.

Slightly regretting my insistence on imposing a limit of two, I eventually plumped for chocolate and strawberry.

Funny how a taste can take you back to a place and emotion you didn't know you had forgotten. Looking at the fresco of Italy behind him, with the taste of strawberries on my lips, I felt the same giddy euphoria as when I'd thrown open the shutters of that beautiful painted room on our first morning together, and gazed at the distant view.

Gus reached across the table and took both my hands in his.

'Let's go back to Italy,' he said, as if he was thinking the same thoughts.

'Yes let's.'

'I mean to live there,' he said, as he had done in Assisi on the last day of the holiday.

'You can't live on sunshine!'

With no knowledge of the language, whatever skills I had would not be transferable. Any savings wouldn't last very long.

'I've thought about that,' Gus said. 'If I sell the house as Charlotte wants me to we could use some of the money to take time off and decide what we really want to do with our lives.'

'But that would mean me relying on you . . .'

'I know you don't want to do that but, if you had the space to write your novel, couldn't you think of it as an advance on future earnings?'

His belief in my potential was very touching, but not very realistic or practical.

'What about your girls?'

'I don't suppose they'd mind spending their holidays in Italy. When or if we decide to come back, I could always buy somewhere smaller. People are always saying that they want to change their lives, then not doing it, and then . . .' He stopped.

I suddenly saw where this was coming from.

'I thought you didn't do what ifs?' I said.

Chapter Thirteen

'It's a great idea.'

Doll's reaction surprised me when I called her the following day.

'It just seems like a fantasy.'

'Why do women always think anything nice that happens to them isn't real?' Doll said. 'You've had a shit life, Tess, you deserve a break.'

I figured that was about as close as she was going to get to approving of Gus. He'd gone up in her estimation after sending a blue teddy bear as a gift for Tommy after Elsie had seques- tered the original white one.

'What if it doesn't work out?'

'You'll always have a job to come back to, if that's what's bothering you.

'What about Hope?'

'How often do you see Hope these days?'

'But I'm here if she needs me.'

'It's a two-hour flight. I'll miss you, your family will miss you. You might even miss us a bit. I think you should grab the opportunity . . .'

The thing people always forget when they advise you to *carpe diem*, *seize the day*, is that the second line of the poem says *because you might not see another one*. Which can feel more of a threat than wise advice when you've had cancer.

Life felt so good at the moment, I felt edgy about making such a major change. But, as I stood at the desk listening to rich women talk about their cuticles, I realised that my comfort zone was a place where I wasn't really me at all.

'Do you mind taking over for an hour?' I asked Aggie.

I ran all the way up the road to Gus's house, where I knew he'd just be waking up before leaving for his night shift.

'Let's do it!' I shouted, clattering up the stairs and leaping onto the bed beside him.

Afterwards, I couldn't help thinking about the what ifs. What if I hadn't taken so long to agree? If the flap of a butterfly's wing could cause a thunderstorm, then surely there was something I could have done to change things?

Maybe everyone tries to blame themselves irrationally when things go wrong. Perhaps what happened to Gus was like a million-fold magnification of that natural human reaction?

Gus was in the shower and I was still in bed feeling happily sinful. The sex had been even better than usual because I was supposed to be at work.

When his phone rang, I picked it up and saw that it was Charlotte calling.

'Gus?'

He came out with a towel wrapped around his waist, his hair dripping.

I handed him the warbling phone.

I could see the thought process behind his frown. He didn't want to answer the call, but it might be something about the girls. Finally he swiped the screen.

'Charlotte? I was in the shower. No, about to go to work. What is it?'

His voice was impatient.

'No . . .' He sat down on the edge of the bed. 'I am now. '

As he listened for a few moments, I could hear my heart beating in my chest. Something was wrong.

'When? How do you know? Who's Marjorie? Jesus!'

His eyes focused on me suddenly as if he had forgotten I was there.

'Can I call you back?'

The look on his face filled me with dread.

'What's wrong?' I asked.

'My mother's dead. Cerebral haemorrhage, they think.'

Chapter Fourteen

Black has never been a good colour on me. Mum used to say it drained the life from my face. But I knew I wouldn't feel smart enough in navy. I was nervous enough about the funeral without the possibility of people who had never met me thinking I was disrespectful.

The shops were full of their new summer collections so it was difficult to find something suitably formal. I spent a fortune in Selfridges on a chic shift with short sleeves and a matching jacket, the kind of thing Jackie O might have worn. In the changing room I stared at the price tag as if it might somehow magically alter under my scrutiny. It was such a lot to pay for something I would only wear once. It crossed my mind, as I watched the assistant carefully folding it in tissue paper, that maybe it was the outfit I would be buried in. I wondered if everyone divided the cost of an outfit by the number of times worn to make it seem less expensive.

I decided against make-up. I couldn't risk mascara running down my face.

When the hearse drove up with Gus and me in his car following behind, Charlotte was standing outside the crematorium, instantly recognisable as an adult version of Flora. Her skin was subtly glowing, her lips lightly glossed. She was beautiful enough to advertise a skincare range.

'Lovely day for it!' she said.

She and Gus held each other for a long time before he remembered that I was standing next to him.

'This is Tess.'

'You're nothing like I expected,' she said, looking me up and down.

The suit had been worth every penny.

I wanted to say, 'You're exactly as I imagined. Possibly worse.'

Instead I said, 'I'm very sorry for your loss.'

A coffin is always a stark and shocking sight. I couldn't grasp Gus's arm because he had his elbows tight against his body, as if he were literally holding himself together. We walked behind the pallbearers into the chapel where there were several middle-aged couples spaced out in the pews, and a group of whispering women.

Loitering in an empty row at the back was Gus's father. He was shorter than I expected, his hair gingery grey. He was one of those men who didn't seem quite complete without a compliant woman beside him. I wondered if he had chosen to sit alone, or whether he had been actively shunned by these people, some of whom must surely know that he ran off with another woman.

When Gus stopped to greet him, his father's face didn't seem to know whether to be pleased or sorrowful.

I was first into the pew when we got down to the front, then Gus, then Charlotte, who could have chosen to sit on the other side of the aisle. But it was going to be awkward wherever she sat.

'White flowers!' Gus suddenly grabbed my wrist so hard it hurt.

'Aren't they the ones you chose?' I whispered, wondering if there had been a mix-up at the florist and feeling somehow guilty for not helping him more with the funeral arrangements, although he had made it very clear he didn't want my involvement.

'Of course!' he said, looking at me as if I was being stupid.

Who was it who first decided what should go on a coffin, I wondered. My father had chosen a similar spray for my mother's. I remembered thinking how Mum would have hated all those lovely blooms having their stalks cut short to make the stiff, unnatural shape.

Maybe Gus's mother would have liked it? She'd seemed like quite a conventional person to me, apart from the drinking. Did all the people here know about the drinking, I wondered. She was only sixty-six, which was a young age to die unless you had cancer.

When the vicar had rung to ask Gus if he would be saying or reading anything at the service, he'd replied, 'I think not.'

It was a phrase so devoid of emotion it made me think I didn't know him at all.

Now, as I listened to the vicar give a eulogy for someone he had never met, based on the brief biography Gus had provided him with, I felt sorry for the woman in the coffin. Maybe she was repressed, but it seemed a bit weird to have a funeral without emotion. The only person crying was me, and I'd only met her once.

The vicar finished with the bit from Corinthians about Faith, Hope and Love.

'Love is patient, love is kind, it does not envy, it does not boast, it is not proud. It is not rude. It is not easily angered, it keeps no records of wrongs. Love does not delight in evil, but rejoices in truth.'

The truth is, I thought, there is no love here.

Outside, Gus's father was keen to get away, revealing that his second wife was about to give birth to twins.

'Goodness me, you'll have your work cut out,' I said.

I hoped I hadn't implied he was too old for it, even though he was. I felt Gus tense up at my over-familiarity.

They shook hands formally.

'You'll have to come and visit,' he said, looking at my mouth not my eyes, which is probably automatic for a dentist. Fortunately, we've all got good teeth in our family.

The wake was at a nice country house hotel, with finger sandwiches and macarons in pale, sophisticated colours: almond, pistachio, rose.

Gus did his best to go round everyone in the room thanking them for coming. He seemed to know very few people so it was just as easy for me to make polite conversation as it was for him, but I could tell from their glances at Charlotte that some were confused. Was she saying she was the daughter-in-law, I wondered. Obviously she had every right to. I wasn't even sure what my status was now as he never bothered to introduce me. All the affection I had come to expect from him seemed to have been replaced with irritation.

Marjorie, a neighbour of his mother's, was knocking back the white wine at eleven in the morning. 'But Caroline always told me that her son was dead!' she said, sounding both delighted and surprised, as if Gus had been resurrected.

I had felt sorry for Gus's mother not being able to move on from her elder son's death, and I'd never quite believed what Gus said about her not loving him, but here was proof of her neglect. My emotions seesawed back to fierce protectiveness as he shook Marjorie's hand, ever polite but with an empty expression.

One thing about the middle classes is that they know when to leave. My mum's wake had gone on way into the night with everyone having such a good time they forgot why they were there.

After about an hour of suitably subdued conversation, people started putting down their plates and drifting out through the lobby.

When the room was empty, Charlotte sauntered over.

'That seemed to go all right?' Gus said.

'Perfect!' said Charlotte, looking at her watch. 'I made the appointment with the solicitor at two.'

I sat in the car while they went inside, glad that I'd brought a book. When they eventually emerged Gus told me that we were going to give her a lift to the airport.

'Would you like to go in the front?' I asked, not expecting her to say yes.

Sitting in the back seat, I felt like a child listening to my parents having a grown-up conversation I wasn't supposed to understand. From what I could make out, they were joint executors of the will, with everything left in trust for Flora and Bella. So Gus's mother had succeeded in reuniting them.

At the drop off, I stayed in the car to let them have their goodbyes, just able to hear Charlotte saying, 'Well, you know where I am.'

The way she said it seemed to carry a slight innuendo. Maybe as a beautiful woman you expect men to desire you and don't even know you're flirting, but I struggled to give her the benefit of the doubt.

'I'll make some tea,' I said, after the long drive back to Gus's house.

'Why do people think tea is the answer to everything?'

'A drink then?'

'Not now.'

Perhaps that hadn't been an appropriate suggestion. The post-mortem had suggested his mother was in an advanced state of alcoholism.

I was accustomed to tiptoeing around men whose silence carried the threat of a sudden violent outburst. But I'd never thought I'd be doing that with Gus.

He was staring just past me. The room felt airless with pent-up emotion.

'Would it help to talk about it?' I asked gently.

'Talk about what?'

'Your mother . . .'

'She's dead now, so there's not much point.'

Everything he said seemed to carry a subtext of accusation.

I knew that sometimes happened if you were trying not to cry. Perhaps he needed to be alone. It had been a long day.

'I'll leave you to get some sleep,' I said, hesitating at the door because somewhere in the back of my mind there was a tiny squeak of fear, like the noise of a mouse that you try to ignore in the hope you're imagining it.

He didn't even seem to notice I was leaving. At the door, as I turned to smile, I saw that the heart balloon had sunk almost to the floor, its plump shiny surface now crumpled and dull.

The blossom that we hadn't been able to enjoy was almost over, the gutters filled with a fall of pink snow. As I walked down the street, I heard a strange howl that sounded like an animal in pain. I turned, petrified, stranded between wanting to rush back and comfort him and allowing him space.

And then the sobs came and I found myself thanking Our Lady for finally allowing him to express his grief.

Be careful what you wish for.

Gus

Chapter Fifteen

I was staring into the bottom of the large ornamental vase.

'What's this, Angus?'

'Broken china...'

'I know what it is! How did it get there?'

'There are enough plates...'

'You wicked little boy! Hiding the evidence is worse than ruining my special dinner service...'

'Like a murderer!' said Ross.

'Stop it! Stop it! Leave me alone!'

My shouting woke me up. Had I been asleep? I appeared to have come two Tube stops past my usual one. Had I screamed? I looked around the carriage. Everyone was looking at their mobile phones. One man had a paper. Were they deliberately ignoring me?

I got off the train and walked to the other platform. The next train was due in two minutes. I was going to be late. The platform was filling up. I looked at the board. Still two minutes. Would it be quicker to run to work? People were pushing me nearer and nearer to the edge. I looked down. Beneath the rails the ground seemed to be moving as the line began to rattle and sing the thin, high note of the approaching train. I couldn't make out whether the creatures running beneath the rails were mice or rats. Like hell, I thought, as the train shot through the tunnel mouth with a thump of hot, stale air. It crossed my mind how easy it would be to fall, or just take one step over.

The traffic lights had turned green and I was still in the middle of the road outside the hospital. A bus started to roll towards me. A lorry driver slammed his horn.

A delivery scooter on the nearside of the bus shot past inches away from my feet.

I was clinging to my mother's legs beside the open door of our car, my father in the front, revving the engine.

'Don't make me go back to school, please don't make me . . .'

'Pull yourself together, Angus! You're a big boy, now!'

'I'm only eight!'

'What's wrong with you?'

Pull yourself together.

'Espresso, extra shot, please.'

I was trying to buy a coffee from the Costa just inside the entrance to the hospital.

Why was the barista looking at me like that?

How long had the queue been building behind me?

'Are you paying by card?'

'Oh, sorry, yes!'

I stirred a teaspoon of sugar into the hot dark liquid. Drank it in one. Felt the rush.

'Better now!' I said to nobody in particular.

The next person in the queue beside me shifted slightly backwards.

I hesitated to open my locker in case of what I found inside. Ross must have taken a copy of my key because there were often unwanted gifts. Once, a single prawn right at the back so I didn't know what was making all my sports clothes smell disgusting.

It was empty. Hospital locker. Not school. Don't have to go to school any more.

I stripped off and got fresh scrubs from the machine.

In the mirror, my face looked normal.

'Hello! I'm Gus, one of the doctors,' I said to my image.

Fine. I was fine.

'I didn't think you were in today,' said the nurse on reception.

'I didn't expect to see you so soon,' said my mother.

'Well, I'm here now.'

'Where's Ross?'

'Still skiing.'

'Sorry?' said the nurse. 'You've missed handover.'

I looked at the clock. It was half past nine. I was supposed to get in before eight. What had happened to the time?

'I came down in the bubble. I mean the Tube . . .'

'Are you OK, Dr Macdonald?'

'Fine, thanks,' I said, briskly.

'Are you sure?'

'Haven't you got patients you should be worrying about?' I snapped.

She turned and marched off.

I picked up the notes of the next patient.

'Good morning!' I said, pulling back the curtain to the bay. 'I gather you are not feeling very well today. Sore throat . . .'

'Not me,' said the woman. 'My daughter.'

There was a little girl, lying on the bed. I did a quick examination, looking down her throat, feeling her lymph glands, listening to her chest.

'Looks like a nasty bout of tonsillitis. Probably viral. Lots of fluids . . .'

'As I said to your colleague, it's very difficult to get her to drink. She's had a very high temperature for days. She's not herself.'

'Well, she wouldn't be with a throat like that. I'll get the nurse to take a swab...'

'But you're not worried?'

'Tonsillitis can be very painful, but it should clear up in a few days...'

'What's that smell?' said the woman.

The next bay along reeked like the men's toilet of a filthy pub, a pungent combination of stale urine and stale beer. I peered round the curtain. One of the homeless people we saw regularly had taken a fall and smashed his jaw.

'I can fix your teeth, but I can't fix your lungs,' my father said when he caught me smoking.

'We can fix your bones, but we can't fix your liver,' I told the man.

What a ridiculously trite warning for someone whose only pleasure came from a can of Tennent's Extra. Why hadn't I ever said anything to my mother about her drinking?

'I'm very disappointed in you, Angus!'

I returned to the desk.

'What did you say to the patient in bay thirteen?' the nurse asked. 'Because she's taken her little girl home.'

'I asked you to get a swab...'

'You didn't.'

'Sorry, got distracted by the powerful stench of deprivation!'

'Mike would like a word in his office.'

'You've decided to grace us with your presence, have you, Angus?' said my headmaster.

'He's decided to grace us with his presence today, has he?' I asked.

The nurse didn't seem to find our usual banter at all funny today.

'Did you discharge the patient in bay thirteen?' Mike, my consultant, wanted to know.

'I gather she discharged herself . . .'

'After speaking to you. She wasn't your patient. The doctor who was attending to her suspected viral pneumonia and had handed her over to me. I was about to examine . . . now she's gone, so let's hope it wasn't pneumonia. Child that age can deteriorate very quickly. What are you doing here anyway? You're not on the rota . . .'

'Sorry, bit confused.'

'Can't afford to be confused in this department, Gus. What's going on? The nurses say you've been behaving uncharacteristic-ally . . .'

'Who exactly?'

'I'm not about to name names.'

'We've had reports that you've been smoking.'

'Reports from whom, sir?'

'I'm not about to name names.'

'You can search my locker if you like, you won't find any-thing there . . .' I said.

'What?' Mike asked.

'I'm sorry,' I said.

'Look, are you all right? We're all a bit concerned about you.'

'Why?'

'You seem different.'

'How different?'

'Disengaged. Rude.'

'Like someone more senior?'

'What?'

'Nothing.'

'Not your usual self . . .'

133

'That's a diagnosis is it?'

'Probably more accurate than the one you've just made. Problems at home?'

How did he know?

'No.'

'Are you sure?'

'The funeral took more organisation than I'd expected.'

'You've had a bereavement?'

'My mother died three weeks ago.'

'Mother's ready for you now.'

The undertaker had shown me into the chapel of rest. He kept calling her 'Mother' as if he was her son not me.

I could only see her face. The rest of her covered with a purple kind of shroud. Was she naked underneath, or wearing some sort of hospital gown? Or clothes? There was a plastic clip on her mouth to stop it hanging open. It gave her an unnatural half smile that made me wonder for a moment whether it was actually her at all.

'I'm very disappointed in you, Angus.'

'I'm sorry.'

It was all I could think of to say to her.

I bent to kiss her cheek. It was as cold as a raw chicken in the fridge.

'Goodbye then!'

I could see the undertaker was surprised how quickly I came out of the chapel. I almost felt I should go back out of respect for the time it must have taken him to get her out of storage and make her look presentable.

'I'm sorry,' I said.

'There's no right or wrong way to be,' he said, oleaginously reassuring, which made me think there very definitely was.

'I'm sorry to hear that,' my consultant was saying.

'There's no right or wrong way to be.'

'What?' he looked annoyed.

'I'm sorry,' I said.

'I think you should take some compassionate leave.'

'I'm absolutely fine.'

'I'm not asking you, Gus, I'm telling you. You're dangerous like this. Go home.'

Nellie the Elephant . . .

Ross and I were doing a life-saving course at the sailing club on the Isle of Wight where we always went for our summer holidays. There were two strange dolls with open mouths and inflatable bags inside their torsos, for us to practise CPR on.

The last person who'd trained on mine must have eaten a curry beforehand.

The rhythm we were told to keep to was *Nellie the Elephant*. Ross kept singing it in the car all the way back to the cottage we always rented.

'Angus let his doll die!' he told my father.

'It tasted horrible.'

'You can't kill someone because their breath smells. I'd have a lot of dead patients if that were the case!'

Gales of laughter from the two of them. Laughter seemed to bring other families together. In mine, it was used to exclude me.

'Some doctor you'll be,' said Ross.

'I don't want to be a doctor anyway.'

'Just as well!'

'Stop it! Leave me alone!'

'You OK, mate?' the man sitting in the opposite seat on the Tube asked.

In the window behind him, I could see my reflection in Ross's mirror ski goggles.

The snow was falling fast.

'Last one to the bottom gets the drinks in,' he shouted, straight to *Go!* when I was still at *Ready!*, just like every other time we'd competed.

I almost followed, but I did not follow. Instead, I took off my skis and went back down in the bubble, but it was airless. Below me, all I could see was pure white snow rising up to smother me.

I was standing on the pavement outside Lancaster Gate Tube station, two stops away from Notting Hill Gate, not sure what I was doing there.

A walk to clear my thoughts. I decided to go through the park on the other side of the road. A car screeched to a halt as I stepped in front of it.

'For god's sake, pull yourself together, Angus!' my father shouted from the driver's seat.

How did he know I was here?

In the park, a cyclist whizzed past, looking over his shoulder to swear at me. Ross's face glancing back as he hurtled through the whiteness, losing the crucial split second he needed to avoid crashing into the looming tree.

Snow on the ground.

No. Blossom fallen from the trees.

Loveliest of trees, the cherry now, is hung with bloom along the bow.

My mother smiling in the audience at the school Open Day.

'I've forgotten the next bit.'

'And stands about the woodland ride, wearing white for Easter tide . . .'

'What's wrong with white flowers?'

'It's supposed to be unlucky to bring them into the house.'

Why was she following me?

I started running.

I slammed the door behind me, and stood with my back pressed against it.

The floorboards were covered in shards of crockery with white poinsettias but, as I got down on my knees, each of the sharp pieces melted away as I tried frantically to gather them up.

I lay on the sofa.

Ross's body lying on a stretcher being brought down the mountain.

'Why did you let him ski alone?'

My mother's body lying inside her coffin, suffocating under the weight of white flowers.

'Take some compassionate leave before you kill someone! I'm not asking you. Gus, I'm telling you!'

Nellie the elephant . . .

'You can't kill someone because their breath smells!'

My brother dead, my mother dead because of my negligence, now a child with pneumonia dying because of me.

Trump, trump, trump!

The Tube train hurtling towards me, the delivery scooter screeching just inches away.

Someone knocking on the door.

The doorbell ringing.

A key in the lock.

'Gus! What are you *doing*?'

On the kitchen counter between us, blister packets of paracetamol, Ibuprofen, Naproxen left over from a tennis injury, an old bottle of Calpol, toilet cleaner, bleach, an open bottle of Sancerre.

'Leave me alone!'

'No I won't leave you alone! '

The rack of Japanese knives. Very sharp. So obvious. Why hadn't I thought of that? Messy but effective. You have to cut along the vein. Seen enough failed attempts from cutting across it.

'Put the knife down, Gus!'

'Please go, Tess! You can't be here!'

'I'm not going anywhere!'

'I'm dangerous, Tess! Stay away from me!'

Tess

Chapter Sixteen

One Sunday afternoon when I was a little girl, I was in the kitchen at home with Mum making an apple pie. Those were the best times, when the two of us were just together chatting about this and that. She gave me a go at rolling out the pastry and showed me how to crimp the edges between my finger and thumb. The radio might have been on in the background, or it might not. All I can remember is how peaceful it felt. Then suddenly the front door opened and, even before it slammed shut, we could both feel the draught of fury that came in with my dad. We both knew what was coming. The red mist, my mother used to call it.

He'd been drinking at the pub where a chance remark by the barmaid made it clear that not only was Kevin, my oldest brother, gay, but that everyone knew it apart from Dad.

He snatched the rolling pin from Mum's hand, wielding it like a truncheon, then slammed it down on the tabletop, making the mixing bowl jump.

'Go, Tess, go!' my mother whispered.

But I was so frightened he was going to kill her, I leapt onto his back, my arms around his neck, kicking as hard and fast as I could. I can't have been more than nine because I was still wearing Start-Rite shoes and my feet grew several sizes in a year when I was ten. The toes that hammered into the tender backs of his knees were surprisingly rigid, and must have hurt him so much he stopped, wrestled my arms from his neck and brandished the rolling pin at me, before coming to his senses. The red mist subsided, but I don't think he'd ever entirely forgiven me for the humiliation.

Now another man was threatening me with a weapon, but I could somehow tell from Gus's eyes that he didn't want to hurt me. I was still more frightened than I've ever been, because it is terrifying to see the person you love wanting to harm themselves so much they'd attack if you tried to stop them.

I heard myself saying, 'Unless you put that down, I'm calling the police!'

'No!'

'I am.'

I started pressing 9 9 . . .

He dropped the knife and grabbed the phone from my hands.

I picked the knife up and frantically swept all the pill packets onto the floor.

'What are you doing?'

'I'm not letting you do this.'

'I'm dangerous! Killed a child. My mother. Ross. All my fault . . .'

He wasn't making any sense.

His eyes were wildly animated, strobing with terror, as if he was watching a horror film.

'Gus!' I screamed, trying to bring him back from wherever he'd gone.

He'd been behaving strangely since his mother's death, but I'd put it down to grief. This irrationality was different, as if the person he was had fragmented in a way I didn't understand.

142

Yet certain bits of his character remained. The fact he was too polite to do anything horrible while I was there.

'Please give me my phone back, Gus.'

'Only if you promise not to call a doctor.'

'I promise.'

I took the phone with me to the bathroom and locked the door. I called Marcus. As Nash was in Los Angeles, he was the only person I could think of who might make Gus see sense.

It turned out that Gus had not even told him that his mother had died. To my great relief, he offered to leave his office in the City and come straight over.

I left them alone, but Marcus couldn't find a way of getting through to him either and when he gently tried to persuade him to see a doctor, Gus ordered him to leave.

'What shall we do?' I asked Marcus as we both stood outside on the street, like evacuees from a fire alarm.

'I think we should call Charlotte.'

I had never thought of her as a doctor, but she spoke to me with the detached pragmatism of her profession.

'Sounds like depression,' she said. 'It can often be accompanied by psychosis. You need to get him to see his GP quickly as he will only deteriorate.'

'Believe me, I've tried, Marcus has tried . . .'

'Gus is probably still registered with the one we used. Why don't I see if I can get her to do a home visit? Let me know what happens.'

'Gus doesn't know I'm speaking to you. I don't think he'd want . . .'

'He's the father of my daughters,' she interrupted. 'I won't have him ruining their lives by killing himself.'

She was true to her word and managed to persuade the GP to come that evening. The doctor prescribed anti-depressants and said she would get Gus an urgent referral to the psychiatric department of the local hospital.

Everyone was clear that Gus shouldn't be left alone until they found the right combination of drugs, which was a process of trying, watching and waiting.

I'd known that depression was a serious condition, but had still thought it was basically about being sad. Very sad.

That's not how it is at all.

Mental illness has its own vocabulary. The word catastrophising describes a kind of escalation of anxious thoughts that seduces then imprisons the patient. In Gus's case, it seemed to go something like this: being a bad brother and neglectful son made him unfit to be a doctor; making a mistake meant he should never work again, which meant that he would lose his home, his children and me.

'Why don't you understand?' he'd shout at me, whenever I tried to reassure him.

I learned later that reassurance is toxic because it simply reinforces the patient's delusions.

In Gus's mind, his failings were about to be discovered, leading to disgrace and ruin. All his mental energy was devoted to trying to escape the inevitable; although this was never going to happen, because it wasn't true in the first place. This is called rumination.

The first round of meds knocked him out. It was a relief to have some calm after the raving but it made me so sad, because he had disappeared in a different way. It was as if there had been a power cut and all the little video screens of his character had gone blank, leaving only a ghostly trace of him, like the one reflected in the television screen which he stared at all day, even when it wasn't on.

*

Doll was brilliant about letting me take time off, even though I couldn't bring myself to confide in her completely. Doll didn't really get Gus. Everything I'd said about him being reliable, caring and fun was so patently untrue now, it would be like admitting that I didn't get him either.

I still organised the rota, tried to keep up with the restocking, dashing down the road once a day to check the till, bank the cash and make sure that the salon was clean and tidy. After several weeks with no identifiable improvement from Gus, it became clear that I wasn't going to be able to do the job properly any time soon. Doll employed a temporary manager called Ash whom she had lined up to take over from me when the plan was to go to Italy, a plan which seemed to belong to a different universe now. He was a business studies graduate in his early twenties who had impressed when he interned at her head office in Kent.

'It'll do him good to get experience at the sharp end,' she said, making it seem like I was the one doing her the favour.

'Do you want me to clear out of the flat?'

'No, you need somewhere you can to escape to,' Doll said. 'Take your mind off it.'

But I wasn't happy leaving Gus for five minutes, let alone an hour or a whole night. I was too frightened. Charlotte and the other doctors had made it clear the risk of suicide was very real.

The house in Portobello Road I'd fantasised about living in as a teenager was like the gingerbread cottage in Hansel and Gretel. It looked pretty and enticing on the outside but was a cage, trapping Gus and me too.

At night he twisted and turned so much I couldn't sleep next to him. So I decamped to his daughters' room and slept in a small single bed. I was no longer Gus's girlfriend, I was his carer. I hadn't signed up to be that, but when the GP asked who was – as if everyone had a carer designated – I said me, because I thought she might section him if I didn't.

She gave me a leaflet informing me I could get a care assessment, which essentially meant someone from the mental health service ringing me up to check I wasn't going bonkers too. It also gave me details of a carers' support group.

I didn't call the number for a long time but, when I spotted it again on the noticeboard at the GP, I decided I had nothing to lose by giving it a go.

We were different ages, classes and ethnicities. Pet, Toni and Viv cared for parents with varying levels of dementia; Lorna had a partner with early onset Alzheimer's; Leanna had an autistic child. I had never thought of myself as a carer when I was bringing up Hope, but I'd wished someone had told me there were groups like this, because it would have helped.

Until I opened up to this random group of strangers, the situation had felt like a problem unique to me, a problem nobody else could possibly understand. But it turned out we all felt lonely and abandoned. Having a place where it was OK to confess to your frustration or cry, or even to have a bit of a grim laugh, was a lifeline.

The Dolls House was a lifeline too. Just the idea that there was somewhere nearby where life went on with nothing more problematic than damaged cuticles.

I was secretly relieved when the staff did not really take to Ash. He was all for rebranding and refurbishing and including non-surgical interventions on our menu of services. He wasn't nearly as flexible as me about time off. My management strategy had always to keep the women we employed happy. They were all hard-working and they all had family commitments. If you created an atmosphere where it was fine for one person to substitute for another, as long as the hours were covered, I felt you got a lot of overtime free of charge.

Ash had big plans for expansion. He was urging Doll to open a male grooming outlet.

'You could call it The Man Cave,' I suggested, on one of Doll's visits.

'That's brilliant, Tess,' she said, then, turning to Ash. 'See, I told you she was worth every penny.'

I'm sure she didn't mean to make me feel worse, but the remark made me acutely conscious of all the months I'd not worked full time but continued to draw my full salary.

Summer passed without me really noticing. It had been months since I'd been anywhere further than the supermarket, and even then I would anxiously look at my watch.

When my own routine follow-up came round, going to the hospital for a blood test felt almost like a nice afternoon out.

I used to think cancer was the worst possible thing to deal with, but it wasn't nearly as scary as seeing someone you love just disappear.

I was still officially in remission.

'You do need to look after yourself though,' Doll said, when I rang to tell her.

'I'm not even sure what that means.'

'It means, you need proper time off,' she said. 'I'm doing a training day at the salon next week. I can pop up every hour or so and keep an eye on Gus. If it works, we can try doing it on a more regular basis.'

I didn't think Gus would like Doll checking in on him, but part of me thought it might be good to get a reaction, any reaction, from him.

Chapter Seventeen

When I was a teenager, I couldn't wait to leave Margate, but as the train flew through the industrial landscape of the Thames Estuary, I felt the comfort of returning home where things were as they always been, and I knew what I was dealing with.

I arrived at the cemetery where Mum was buried as the sun was beginning to sink behind the branches of the big trees. The newly fallen leaves crunched under the soles of my ankle boots. The air was silent, still and cold, with that hint of smokiness that reminds you bonfire night is on its way. I remembered the firecrackers my brothers used to scare me with, and the fizz of a sparkler in a mittened hand, that magical once-a-year joy as special as birthday candles.

I was surprised to find chrysanthemums on my mother's grave. They had been placed there recently, a few white petals remaining among the ones that had gone brown. I took them to the bin, then replaced them with the bunch of bright yellow pompoms I'd bought, wondering who'd been there. I'd been the only one in the family who visited her grave when I lived in Margate, but I hadn't been since I'd moved to London, which was coming up for four years now.

'Sorry about that, Mum,' I said, crouching down beside the headstone.

I remembered thinking about her in Assisi as I sat with Gus on the warm wall outside the basilica, his eyes sparkling with love. Mum had always said that eyes were windows into the soul.

'It's just . . . now the shutters have come down.'

Gus's illness had made me think a lot about a person's identity. Was the man in front of me the same as the one who behaved normally before? Was depression an add-on, like chicken pox, that disfigures, then goes away? Or was it part of his personality that I hadn't seen, but would now always be there, in the same way the chicken pox virus sometimes re-emerges as cold sores?

And who was I really?

When I'd said I loved him, had I really been promising to stick with him through anything?

Or was I, in truth, someone less committed, who sometimes wanted to howl, *Why me?*

'I know it's worse for him,' I said to my mother. 'I know in a relationship you have to take the ups and downs, but honestly, I'm so tired of looking after people!'

'*It will pass.*'

'How do you know?'

'*You have to have faith.*'

It felt like she was there with me. I could almost feel the weight of her hand on my arm.

I stared at the words on Mum's headstone.

MARY LUCY COSTELLO
DEVOTED WIFE TO JAMES AND BELOVED MOTHER
OF KEVIN, BRENDAN, TERESA AND HOPE

What Mum called faith was optimism really, I thought.

She'd had a baby after her first cancer and she'd named her Hope, which said it all.

She still died.

But we all die, don't we?

Faith was about believing in my own ability to cope, and Gus's ability to get better.

The doctors said people did recover from depression so it must at least be statistically true.

Standing up, shaking the pins and needles from my feet, I felt the blood trickling down through my veins again.

'Why are you crying, Tree?'

I spun round. Hope was holding a bunch of white chrysanthemums and scowling at my yellow pompoms.

'I didn't know you came here, Hope.'

'Martin comes to see his dad, I come to see my mum. It's obvious, isn't it?'

'Shall we put your flowers with mine?'

'Why did you bring yellow ones?' she asked.

'I thought they looked cheerful.'

'Mum has white flowers on top of her when she's dead.'

'Maybe it would be nice this time if she could have both colours?'

'Did Mum like two colours, Tree?'

'Yes, she liked all sorts of colours very much.'

It wasn't often that Hope smiled, but when she did, her eyes crinkled almost closed and her mouth showed all her nice, even teeth, which run in our family. Hope was incapable of insincerity, the concept would be completely alien to her, so receiving a smile always felt special.

She put her flowers on the grave next to mine and then we stood beside each other. Instinctively, I reached out my hand and was surprised to feel her take it, just as I taught her when she was little when we were about to cross a road.

'Mum will never stop loving us,' she said, using the exact words I'd tried to comfort her with the night our mother died.

I'm promised Mum that I would always look after Hope and I'd tried my best but, in her own way, Hope looked after me too. She was my constant, whatever life threw at me.

'How are you, Hope?' I asked, as we walked side by side towards the gate with Martin walking a distance in front of us, giving me the chance to talk to her alone.

'Happy as Larry.'

It was one of Dad's expressions. As a child, I'd wondered who Larry was and whether there was a way of getting in touch with him during my father's mawkish moods. I thought he must be a mate of the carefree Riley, whose life Dad also seemed to admire. I'd pictured the three of them at the races, celebrating a winner they'd all backed.

'We'll be locked in if you don't get a move on,' Martin called.

'Where's Gus?' Hope suddenly asked.

'He couldn't come today,' I said.

'I like Gus.'

It was unusual for her to volunteer an opinion.

'Why do you like him, Hope?'

'He's a smiley man,' she said.

I tried very hard to hold myself together but couldn't.

'Why are you crying, Tree?'

'Gus isn't very smiley at the moment, Hope. He's not very well.'

'Does he have cancer?'

'No.'

'Well, thank the lord for that!'

It sounded like something Anne might say, maybe after hearing about me being in remission.

'Shall I sing him better?' Hope asked.

Dad and Anne had brought my sister up to see me in hospital before I had my surgery.

151

She had sung me 'I Had a Dream' as I drifted into anaesthesia. And afterwards, during my recovery, she had become a hit with the staff, who started looking forward to Abba's greatest hits.

Walking up the steps at Notting Hill Gate Tube, the noise of traffic, the rush of people wearing earphones having loud conversations with the air, was almost overwhelming after the misty silence of the cemetery and the warm limbo of the train. I found myself walking very slowly, not really wanting to return to the house.

'How are we?' I asked Doll, nodding at Gus on the sofa.

'Hard to tell. How did you get on?'

'It really helped. Thank you!'

'No problem. We can do it again.'

I noticed she had done her make-up and was wearing a clingy dress and heels.

'Going out?' I asked.

'What? Oh, just a work thing.'

'Have fun.'

'I will!' she said with a smile, then, as if remembering the evening I had in front of me. 'Not!'

I took off my coat.

'How have you been?' I asked Gus briskly, returning to carer mode.

For the first time in months, he turned to look at me as he spoke.

'I missed you.'

Gus

Chapter Eighteen

Winter 2014

Tess said that Hope was the Christmas angel who changed everything, but we both knew that my recovery was not instant. It was a slow process of getting on the right meds, therapy and Tess's extraordinary patience.

However there was a moment during the carols that seemed to make my brain click into a different gear.

I was sitting in front of the television, not really watching anything, when Tess arrived with Hope. She'd met her at St Pancras and showed her the Christmas lights on the way back. She marched decisively in front of me and switched the screen off.

'Hope wants to sing to you.'

'Little Donkey, Little Donkey . . .'

The purity of her voice seemed to chime through the dimness of the room like an angelic chorister.

I can recall my exact thought as I looked from one sister to the other, Tess's face so radiantly proud as she watched Hope singing, so instantly worried when she turned to see what my reaction would be.

I have to stop making her so sad.

*

The different medication regimes interfered with my cognitive experience of time and memory to the extent that when I first noticed that the sun was shining, it was already spring and I felt as though I had missed a whole year of my life.

There had always been a full length mirror on the wall at the bottom of the staircase but I hadn't noticed my reflection in all that time. I was shocked to see how much weight I had put on.

'What are you doing?' Tess asked, as I sat down on the stairs, tying the laces on my trainers.

'I need to go for a run.'

The frown on her face made me look at myself in the mirror again and observe that I was only wearing boxers and a faded T-shirt.

'I'll just put on some shorts,' I said, walking back upstairs, feeling strange to have shoes on my feet.

When I returned, Tess had put on running shoes too.

I was breathless before we'd even reached the top of the street, grateful for the busy road that made us stop to cross. We got as far as the statue of Peter Pan in Kensington Gardens. As we walked home I could feel the sweat trickling down my temples. I kept stopping, unused to negotiating pavements crowded with people. The smell of kebabs made the street feel as exotic as the first evening of a foreign holiday.

I sensed Tess glancing sideways at me every few seconds.

'I need to get back into shape,' I told her, when we got back. 'Again, tomorrow morning?'

Her face lit with a sudden, delighted smile that gave me a moment of déjà vu.

As a doctor, I'd always known the theory that the release of endorphins produced by exercise will help with depression, even though I hadn't the slightest inkling what clinical depression actually felt like. Now, I began to crave exercise all the time, extending the distance I ran each day until I was regularly leaving Tess struggling to keep up.

One morning, I was already up and dressed in running gear when she woke up. She immediately threw back the duvet.

'You don't have to come with me,' I said.

The alarm on her face gave me the stark realisation that I had become another man in her life who intimidated her, not with the unspoken threat of violence to her, but by the implicit threat of violence to myself.

'Promise I'll be back.'

At the beginning of my illness, I'd been too psychotic to gain any value from talking therapy. Now that I was functioning more normally, I was at the end of a long NHS waiting list.

I'd had some sessions with a cognitive behavioural therapist called Dorothy following my divorce, but I'd stopped going to her when I thought I'd dealt with my issues. Now I wondered if she'd be able to help me again.

It was really hard work admitting to the shame that I'd buried for years, but Dorothy's calm, non-judgmental presence allowed me the time and space. Her wisdom helped me to think about my past in ways that weren't so self-punishing. I began to feel stronger mentally as well as physically.

Tess claimed she only really believed that I was recovering when I said I'd make Sunday lunch one weekend.

'Not mad enough to eat my cooking any more,' she said, with a nervous glance to check that I was able to take the joke.

'Are you better now?' Bella asked on our Skype that evening.

The only times I can remember Tess being anything other than gentle during my recovery were around my obligations to my daughters. Skyping them was non-negotiable, even if it was only to wave for a few seconds.

'Yes, I am feeling much better,' I told her. 'My doctor says I can return to work.'

'Really?'

Charlotte's voice. Had she always been there in the background?

Her face appeared on screen as if to check I was telling the truth and then she smiled.

'That's such good news! Well done you!'

The knowledge that she cared made me tear up.

'Can we come and see you soon?' Bella asked.

'Definitely,' said Tess.

Even though she didn't have children of her own, Tess instinctively knew when a simple answer was all that was required.

My consultant group approved a phased return to work with reduced shifts. There was a vacancy in the Minor Injuries Unit which was only open during the day, so there were few unsociable hours. As it covered mainly fractures, sprains, wounds and burns, there were no acutely unwell patients to deal with. Having suffered a fair few sporting injuries myself, it felt like familiar territory.

Dorothy's flat was only five minutes' walk from the hospital, so I arranged my weekly sessions with her after work. It was reassuring to know she was close by, almost as if she was on call for me, although I never did need her emergency help, probably because I'd put in place a support structure instead of my old way of pretending that I wasn't struggling.

One evening, when spring was turning to summer, I heard my name being called as I was leaving the hospital. The woman, who wasn't in hospital uniform, seemed intent on catching me up.

'Dr Angus?'

'Yes?'

'You treated my son, Josh.'

Had I got something wrong?

'I'm very disappointed in you ...'

'The teenager with the broken leg ...'

A thirteen-year-old had been brought in by ambulance the previous afternoon. He'd been caught by a late tackle and the X-ray was grim.

His mother had arrived in a panic, and I'd seen the way her son tried to calm her down by pretending he was fine, but as he was about to go up to surgical ward, he'd suddenly asked, with eyes lowered, 'Will I be able to play again?

We'd already established we were both Arsenal supporters.

'Remember when Aaron Ramsey broke his leg so badly the television cameras turned away?'

He nodded.

'So, what did he do last season?'

'Scored the winning goal in the FA Cup!' A big smile had broken across his face.

Replaying the conversation in my mind, I couldn't think of a mistake, except possibly over-promising.

'How is he?' I asked as casually as I could with a palpitating heart.

'He's coming out today. Operation went well. I wanted to thank you. You were wonderful.'

I wasn't sure doctors were supposed to be wonderful, but her gratitude felt as exhilarating as passing an exam.

'Lucky he isn't a Tottenham fan,' I said.

Chapter Nineteen

The Saturday I decided to drive down to my mother's house, I didn't tell Tess because I knew she would feel she ought to come with me. I'd had to surrender my driving licence during my illness and this was the first time I'd undertaken a long journey since getting it back. I was confident I'd be fine at the wheel, but I wasn't sure that I would be able to walk through the door. I knew that it was something I had to do alone.

Charlotte had paid my mother's cleaner to pop by every week or so to make sure that there were no problems and she had organised for a gardener to keep things tidy. He clearly took his duties very seriously as the urns on either side of the front door were spilling over with red geraniums, a colour and abundance my mother would have considered far too showy. I parked on the drive, sat for a moment in the sudden silence after a long car journey. Then I took a deep breath and got out of the car.

The house was spotlessly clean and smelled of recent puffs of air freshener. I walked into the hall, then into the kitchen, where I had stood at the sink, washing up next to my mother.

The memory was more poignant then painful. Neither my mother's behaviour nor mine that day had been any different from the usual dynamic between us. Our relationship had never allowed expressions of love. Perhaps she had kept her feelings in check to make it less difficult every time she sent me back to a school I hated. I knew that both my parents thought they were giving us the best start in life they possibly could. Ross had thrived. I had not. No wonder they didn't know what to make of me.

I went into the living room, opened both sets of curtains. Turning to the mantelpiece, I picked up each photo in turn. Ross holding up the rowing cup, proud but, I now saw, also embarrassed by the silliness of his long lycra shorts. Ross all dressed up, about to go out to a party with Charlotte, looking like he couldn't believe his luck. Ross and me standing beside a tent we'd erected in the garden. His arm around my back, both of us grinning at our lopsided achievement. I had always blotted out the good times we had together. Still holding the photo, I sat down on the sofa and cried until I imagined a brotherly thump on my arm and him saying.

'Get a grip, mate!'

I found two different-coloured rolls of bin liners in the hall cupboard where my mother had kept the hoover and enough cleaning products for at least a decade. I went upstairs.

I wasn't sure I'd ever previously entered my parents' bedroom. I supposed its white fitted furniture, complete with rococo-trimmed dressing table and mirror, had been very à la mode when first purchased, but now looked terribly out of date. I swept all the night creams and make-up into a black bin liner, then opened each of the jewellery boxes. It was mostly costume stuff, and I was pretty sure that there was nothing that my girls would want.

My only hesitation was the blue velvet box which contained my mother's engagement and wedding rings.

I knew that Charlotte wouldn't want the rings, she was not a person who formed attachments to possessions. Sometimes I

161

wondered whether she formed attachments to people either. There was something enviable about the way she sashayed through life instead of muddling along as I did.

I didn't want to risk my daughters inheriting the bad luck of another failed relationship.

I made a mental note to point out items of possible value to the charity shop.

Opening the cupboards full of clothes, which retained a stale whiff of my mother, I decided to ask the cleaner if she wanted anything and, if she didn't, to get a house clearer to deal with the lot.

I had dreaded the idea of sorting the place out. Now the buzz of confronting it felt almost addictive, and I wanted to press on to finish.

Everything from the bathroom went straight into a black bin liner.

There was nothing I wanted in my old bedroom.

I hesitated before entering Ross's room, as if he might still be lying on the bed wearing the headphones that didn't quite block out the tinny beat of heavy metal, pointing at the door and shouting, 'Out!'

It had remained a shrine, with his rows of framed sporting certificates, his trophies still gleaming on a special shelf my father had constructed.

I went downstairs and threw open the French doors, gulping thirstily at the fresh spring air.

The cover on the hot tub was bowed with old rainwater, a sludgy green eco-system with turquoise plastic edges.

The shed at the bottom of the garden was locked with a rusty chain and padlock. Through the little window, I could see the wireless that my father used to listen to the cricket on, the rows of shelves neatly stacked with miniature chests of drawers containing screws and washers in all sizes. When he'd left my mother, he'd moved into a flat and enjoyed a bachelor life dating a series of his dental nurses before marrying one half his age. There can't have been room for all his stuff. So this had become another shrine, I thought sadly.

The sun was beginning to lose its intensity. I looked at my watch and saw that Tess might already be on her way home.

I called her.

'Are you OK?' She sounded very anxious when I told her I was standing in my mother's garden.

'I'm fine,' I said. 'In fact, I'm thinking of staying over, getting everything done. If that's all right with you.'

'If you're sure you're OK?'

I wondered if there would ever be a time when she wouldn't worry about my state of mind.

When I woke up, I felt disorientated for a moment, curled up on my old single mattress. The doorbell rang again. I pulled on my jeans and ran downstairs. I should have known my father would be punctual.

'M25 was empty,' he said.

'It is Sunday morning. Come in.'

It felt slightly odd welcoming him into his old domain.

He looked around taking in every detail, like someone who'd come to give a quote for redecoration.

'As I said, I wondered if you wanted anything. Otherwise I'll get all the furniture taken away.'

In the living room he picked up each photo on the mantelpiece for a few seconds before putting it down again.

'You can have them all, if you want.'

'Thank you,' he said, not looking at me, but stretching his hand out behind his back.

Tentatively, I took it, feeling the grasp of an old man. I calculated that though he had the wiry build of someone younger, he must be nearly seventy. Men of my father's age often shook my hand at the hospital, their grip tighter than necessary, as if wanting to show that strength was still there.

Neither of us was able to look at the other's eyes.

Eventually my father let out a little half cough, half laugh, and turned towards the French doors.

'Right,' he said. 'What's next?'

The key to the shed was on a hook in the hall cupboard, where he'd left it, but the padlock was seized with rust.

'There's probably some WD40 in the garage, but I've some in the car, just in case.'

'Of course you have.' I smiled at him, pleased to see he was still the same man he'd always been, as efficient at the diagnosis and treatment of a DIY problem as he was a dental one.

He came back carrying an armful of flattened cardboard boxes and one of those handy little tools that dispenses lengths of packing tape.

Once the door of the shed was open, I helped him carry heavy toolboxes as well as his beloved radio out to his car.

'A man needs his own space,' he said, looking around the emptied shed with fond nostalgia.

If I'd learned anything from the property programmes I'd stared at on afternoon television over the past year, it was that the majority of men desired a 'man cave'. It was one of the many aspects of masculinity that I didn't share or understand.

'Anything else?' my father asked.

'Well, yes, upstairs,' I said.

'Right you are!'

My father was clearly enjoying our joint endeavour. But his bonhomie evaporated when he opened the door to Ross's room, shocked to see it looking exactly the same as it had when he left the house twelve years before.

'She couldn't let him go,' he said, referring to my mother for the first time.

'No.'

'Nowadays, they would say she had mental health issues,' he said. 'People didn't talk so much about that then. It wasn't how we'd been brought up.'

His tone sounded apologetic rather than critical.

'I've had some problems with depression myself recently,' I heard myself saying.

My father frowned at me and I half expected him to tell me to pull myself together. But instead he said, 'I'm sorry to hear that.'

He hesitated.

'You were always more like her. Sensitive. Ross and I were the resilient ones.'

It was strange to hear this man I had always known but barely knew talking about our family.

'Recovered now,' I said, briskly. 'Back at work. I'll never make consultant, but I think I'm becoming a better doctor.'

I could hear myself reverting to my old role of excusing my failure to live up to his ideals.

'That's more than I ever did,' he said.

'You're a very successful dental surgeon,' I said, realising from his frown as soon as I'd said it that I'd slightly overstepped. The boundary between us had relaxed, but not that much.

'I don't do as many hours now. Julie works, so we share the childcare.'

'A new man!' I said.

He laughed.

'How old are the twins now?' I realised I didn't even know their names.

'Fifteen months.'

'Walking?'

'Walking, trying to talk. It's a delightful age.' He paused. 'I think I'm making a better job of it this time round. Perhaps it's easier with girls. You don't expect them to be like you.'

Was this an apology? I'd always thought my father despised me for not being more like him, but it crossed my mind that maybe I had made him nervous. Sometimes I was a little afraid around Flora because she was so unlike me. It didn't mean I didn't love her.

'What shall we do with the trophies?' I asked him.

'Julie wouldn't thank me for bringing them home. And I don't suppose charity shops would want them. They're of no scrap value, mostly silver plate.'

'We can't just bin them, can we?' I said.

Without saying anything more, he swept them into a box and carried them downstairs.

As I stripped the walls of Ross's posters, I glanced out of the window and saw that my father had got a spade from the garage and was digging a hole near the roots of the copper beech at the end of the garden that Ross and I used to climb. He tipped the silverware in, and covered it up again, carefully replacing the turf on top, then stood for a moment, looking up at the sunlight filtering through the leaves. Spotting me watching from the window, he waved and started walking back towards the house.

'One day some boy will be digging and find this shining hoard of treasure and wonder how it came to be there,' Tess said, when I told her that evening.

It was so typical of her to think about the creation of a story in the future, when I had only seen it as closure of the past.

Chapter Twenty
Autumn 2015

I was determined to make the second anniversary of our meeting special as I had been too out-of-it even to remember the first. I booked a surprise weekend in Florence, but we had to cancel it when Tess caught a cold which turned into bronchitis.

At her follow-up, her specialist nurse was concerned enough to order a CT scan.

I tried to maintain a professional calm but, spotting Jonathan one day in the doctors' mess, I sat down opposite him.

His lunch tray was empty.

'Could I ask your advice about something?'

He looked at his watch. 'You've got two minutes.'

'I have a friend with the BRCA mutation . . .'

He raised an eyebrow.

I gave him a brief history.

'She has been clear so far,' I told him. 'I just wondered how realistic it is to think that she'll remain that way.'

'How old is this friend?' Jonathan asked.

'Our age.'

Did I detect an almost invisible grimace?

'It's got a terrible habit of turning up in other places. Presumably she's on a follow-up protocol?'

'Yes.'

'That should flag up any recurrence,' he said, picking up his tray, leaving me wishing I'd never asked.

I obviously wasn't very good at disguising my fear because when I went to her appointment, Tess held both my hands before going into see the consultant by herself, assuring me, 'Whatever happens we will cope.'

A wind whipped around the quad, creating little eddies of fallen leaves. A few papery wisps still clung to the tree. I watched one break away and whirl tantalisingly close to my face, remembering how I used to call out to my children as they chased wind-borne leaves in the park.

'Catch one, Flora! For luck!'

I was unable to provide an answer when she asked, 'Why is it lucky to catch a leaf?'

A couple of nurses walked past, giggling as I managed to snatch one from the air, closing my palm around its brittle skeleton.

I sat on a bench until the coldness permeated the seat of my jeans. Each time the automatic door opened, I jumped up, trying to erase worry from my face and paint on resilience instead. I knew I'd never forgive myself for taking away a year of her life if the cancer was back. Each time it wasn't her, my fear deepened.

'Gus!'

I looked up.

'He says it's nothing sinister!'

Then my whole body was shaking with sobs, my nose was running and there were no tissues in my pockets. Tess finally found a packet at the bottom of her bag.

I took a breath. Tried to think of something sensible to ask.

'Did he say why your cough was so persistent?'

'He thought it was inflammation, like you said. My blood test today was within normal range and the CT scan showed no indications of metastatic disease.'

'That's brilliant!'

'So, I asked him if being cancer free for two years made it more likely that I'd make it to five years.'

'What did he say?'

I wondered what it was like to be her doctor. It was generally easier dealing with intelligent patients who could understand what you were talking about, but the very curious ones who asked questions you hadn't anticipated could be slightly intimidating.

'He said that was a question for a statistician. So then I said, well, I suppose you have to make it to two years to be in with a chance of getting to five, don't you? What are we going to do now?'

My emotions were still so frayed that I thought for a moment she was talking about the long term. For the past few days, I'd felt as if our lives were on hold.

There were few things I'd rather do than spend an afternoon mooching around London with Tess. When we'd left the house that morning, I'd been terrified that when we came back, our lives would have changed irrevocably. Now that they were exactly the same, I felt strangely dissatisfied. This morning, I'd have given my right arm for things to be normal. Now, normal didn't feel like enough.

The City was a maze of scaffolding tunnels and temporary pavements around construction sites, but we discovered unexpected pockets of peace amid the noise and traffic: an ancient graveyard where William Blake was buried; the perfectly preserved Victorian arcades of Leadenhall Market, deserted after the lunchtime rush; a panorama of the Thames at high tide appearing almost magically behind the headquarters of an international bank, the gentle splosh of the river absorbing all but the loudest screams of sirens. As we walked across the Millennium Bridge, the banks lit up with strings of yellow lights.

A busker was playing Ed Sheeran in front of Tate Modern, the melody floating on the air along with the charcoal smoke of a vendor roasting chestnuts.

'I love that smell,' Tess said. 'It's how you know Christmas is coming.'

Chapter Twenty-One

As a Christmas treat, I booked a box at the Royal Opera House. Tess and I met Hope and Martin at the station. He went off to talk to a man about a guitar on Denmark Street, which sounded like a euphemism but, in Martin's case, was probably just talking to a man about a guitar. We took a cab. Tess asked the driver to take us via Regent Street. Hope got right down on the floor so that she could see all the sparkly lights twinkling above us.

Covent Garden Piazza was strung with evergreen garlands and baubles, and the boutiques were rammed with shoppers. There was a heavily made-up woman standing outside the Chanel shop next to a person-sized bottle of No 5, offering a squirt to anyone who wanted it.

Tess held out her wrist and Hope did the same.

'Do you like it?' she asked Hope.

Her sister sniffed.

'No,' she said.

'What would you like to do now?' I asked. 'I've booked at table at six so we've got about an hour.'

'Ssshush!' Hope held up her hand for silence.

We all listened. If you concentrated very hard it was possible to hear someone singing above the hubbub of shoppers.

Suddenly Hope was battling a path through the crowds towards the covered market. She pushed her way to the front row of people watching over a balustrade. In the sunken courtyard below stood a tenor dressed in white tie. There was a speaker on the floor blasting out a backing track, but his voice was strong enough to soar above the full orchestra. An enthusiastic round of applause greeted the end of the famously mournful aria from *Pagliacci*.

It was clear that his slot was over because a string quartet was waiting with instruments unpacked, but as the call for an encore continued, he gave in to temptation and selected the drinking song from *La Traviata*. There was probably a soprano on the backing track but nobody in the audience heard her, because Hope came in on cue, her stunning voice reverberating through the space between them. Startled, the tenor looked up to where we were standing and beckoned her down. At first she seemed not to notice, then Martin nudged her and the crowd parted to allow her down the steps to sing alongside the tenor for the final verse.

Their voices created glorious harmonies but they looked an odd couple, with the tenor dressed for a classical recital and Hope, whose chosen outfit for the day was a lilac and rhinestone ballgown under a denim jacket, and her usual red and black trainers. Apparently Tess had told her there was no dress code which meant you could wear a long dress or jeans if you wanted.

When they finished, to rapturous applause, the tenor went to kiss Hope's hand, but she snatched it away from him and his attempt landed mid-air. This inadvertent comedy act made people clap even more.

A friend of the tenor's went round with a cap soliciting contributions. I put a fiver in. He extended it to Martin.

'You should give her a cut,' Martin said, pointing at Hope. His tone suggested he wasn't joking.

'It was generous of him to let her join in, Martin,' Tess said.

'He's getting more money because of her.'

As the tenor picked up his speaker, Hope kept bowing and the audience kept applauding. Aware that amusement was beginning to take over from appreciation, Tess pushed through to lead Hope back up the steps.

'Did you like my singing, Tree?'

'Yes!'

'Did you like my singing, Gus?'

'Christmas wouldn't be Christmas without a song from Hope,' I said, quickly adding. 'Yes!'

'How many times have I told you to warm up before you sing?' Martin snarled at her.

'One hundred and three.'

'Are you sure it matters so much, Martin?' Tess asked. 'She's never warmed up in her life.'

'You're suddenly an operatic voice coach, are you?' His tone was aggressive.

'Who's hungry?' I stepped in.

'I am,' said Hope.

Martin was one of those men who carried grudges. The longer the silence went on the more Tess chattered, as if trying to jolly him out of his mood.

'What's this?' Hope asked, as our food came to the table.

'It's the pizza you ordered,' said Tess.

'It's on a short plank.'

'That's how they serve it here.'

'Our pizza comes in a box.'

Happily the restaurant catered for deliveries so there was no problem switching.

'Who's going to tell me the story of *La Bohème*?' Tess asked, brightly.

Martin finally relented, assuming the mantle of expert, giving us a scene-by-scene breakdown, with Hope occasionally interrupting him with a snatch of aria, before being silenced by his glare.

'You know you absolutely cannot sing during the performance, don't you, Hope?' Tess said.

'Of course she does,' said Martin.

'How about a pudding?' I asked, picking up the menu.

'Is it on a plate?'

'I think so.'

'Brownie and ice cream,' she said.

'Hope . . .' Martin's voice was laced with threat.

'Is brownie the same as cake? I'm not allowed to eat cake any more.'

'Just ice cream then,' I said.

We let them have the two front seats in the box while Tess and I perched behind.

Tess had never been to an opera before and I enjoyed watching the reaction on her face almost as much as I enjoyed the performance.

'It's just amazing,' she whispered.

Hope turned round and shushed her.

In the interval she said, 'I've always wanted to know what it would feel like to be in the crowd at Glastonbury. I mean, I know there's no banner waving or sitting on your boyfriend's shoulders allowed here, but there's a kind of zing that goes round the audience, isn't there, like we're all really lucky to share in something that will never happen in exactly this way again?'

During the final scene where Mimi is dying of consumption,

I felt her hand grasping for mine and saw that there were tears running down her cheeks.

None of us spoke on the Tube back to St Pancras, as if the emotion might disappear if we broke the silence and we wanted to hold on to it for ever.

I watched Tess running alongside Hope and Martin's train as it pulled away, accelerating as fast as she could, waving at her sister until the train overtook her and the platform ran out. She stared down the empty track, before turning back to me.

'What's going on with Martin, do you think?' she asked.

'I think he's trying to turn Hope into an opera singer.'

'Like Svengali?' she said, alarmed. 'Do you think Hope is OK?'

'You said before that it's hard to tell if Hope is happy, but generally you know when she's not.'

The previous Christmas I vaguely remembered that Tess had bought two festive ready meals from Marks & Spencer. I'd never been a fan of turkey with all the trimmings so I decided to prepare an Italian feast with a first course of burrata, which Tess said tasted more like double cream than cheese. For our main course I roasted Sicilian sausages with potatoes and rosemary.

Always alert to the danger of putting too much pressure on me, Tess had suggested that instead of buying presents, she and I would get each other jokey gifts, like a Secret Santa that wasn't actually secret.

She had bought me a snow dome of the National Gallery, warning if I turned it upside down too often the water would go murky because that's what happened to the one her brother Kevin had sent Hope from New York.

When I handed her a little black velvet box, there was a flash of crossness.

'I already know this must have cost more than ten pounds.'

She hesitated before opening the lid.

I'd spotted the earrings as I was running past a shop that had lumps of amethyst and rose quartz in the window, and smaller stones set in silver with little handwritten labels about the power of crystals.

I didn't believe in any of it, but I was drawn to the rainbow iridescence of the tiny moonstones.

The woman in the shop looked a bit like a fortune teller with her long black hair and nose ring. She had given me a home-printed document in Gothic font, which I handed to Tess, who read: 'As ancient as the moon itself, the meaning of Moonstone lies within its energy. A stone for new beginnings, it promotes inspiration, success and good fortune. It is extremely beneficial for travellers.'

'Do you like them?' I asked, watching her tilt the tiny polished domes to see the different colours.

'They're beautiful!'

'New beginnings,' I said. 'I was thinking about the plan we had to live in Italy.'

I felt so guilty about wasting a whole year of her life, if I couldn't reverse time, then surely this was the next best thing.

'We don't seem to have much luck with that.'

'I'm ready now,' I said.

Tess sighed.

'Thing is, Gus, I don't know if I am.'

Tess

Chapter Twenty-Two

Summer 2016

When Hope was small I lost her in Selfridges one Christmas and, even though she was gone for only ten minutes, that vortex of terror shattered my self-confidence for many months, causing me to hold her so tightly by the hand that she would sit down on the pavement and refuse to move or, worse, shout that I was hurting her.

A similar level of terrified panic had persisted inside me for almost a year now. It never quite subsided after Gus recovered. I tried not to show it because the last thing I wanted to do was send him spiralling down again, but I knew that he sensed something wasn't right because he kept doing things to make me smile.

It was as if we were performing a strange sort of dance, each of us skipping around the other, never quite sure of the steps.

I enjoyed the opera tickets, the earrings and the Valentine's gift, not just one bouquet of red roses, but a whole year of multicoloured roses that came every Monday in a slim cardboard package that went through the letterbox so you could never even miss a delivery.

I appreciated the effort he made to suggest new things to do, like walking the length of the Thames, in sections obviously, on sunny weekends, or getting the train to Brighton or Oxford for the day. But I couldn't seem to lose the strange flatness inside me. Somehow, in my determination to keep strong for both of us, I seemed to have locked the door on my emotions, then lost the key.

During Gus's illness we'd stopped having sex. As he became physically active again his desire returned, but I found it difficult to get past the rejection I'd felt, even though I knew he hadn't intended it. The last thing I wanted to do was upset him again, so I pretended, but I knew he could tell, because he quickly stopped suggesting that we make love. Each night we'd get into bed and give each other an affectionate cuddle and a peck on the lips. Then one of us would yawn in a quite exaggerated fashion as if to signal we were too tired for the subject even to be raised, and then we'd both turn over, and lie at the very edges of the bed pretending to sleep, the air thick with questions neither of us dared to ask. Was this a phase? Did he/she still fancy me? Should we talk about it? What was ever going to happen to make things different?

At work, Ash, who Doll had made Director of Strategy now that I was back as manager, decided that The Dolls House needed a refit and, as the summer holidays were our slowest weeks of the year, we closed for two weeks when most of our clients decamped to their second homes.

It was going to be Gus's first proper long holiday with his daughters since his illness. They wanted to go to Cornwall because several of their friends spent their summers there and said it was cool. He had booked a beautiful contemporary house near Padstow, all slate floors and balconies with bifold doors. The three of them would learn to surf and eat in posh seafood restaurants. I intended to sit on the decking and read. I'd bought the Booker shortlist and two swimsuits from Boden so I would look the part. Aggie had given me a luxury pedicure and painted my toenails navy blue, which she assured me was the colour of the moment, although to me it looked more fungal than glamorous.

As I locked up the shop, I felt a strange kind of pre-nostalgia for The Dolls House window and the pink fittings inside. They would be sleek black and chrome when I next saw them.

The ground floor window of Gus's house was open and I could hear from the street that he was on the phone. It was clear from his clipped tone that he was talking to Charlotte. Their relationship had quickly resumed its normal frosty status after a period of truce. Tempers were clearly rising.

I was about to put my key in the lock when I heard my name being spoken.

'But I can't go away with Tess any time! We've booked these two weeks. I know it's been difficult for the children. Well, I'm sorry, but Flora can't refuse to come! Tell her to call me.'

Funny how mobile phones have changed our lives in all sorts of ways. In the past, Gus would have been able to vent some of his frustration by slamming down the handset. Now, as I pushed the door open, I saw him stabbing almost comically at the screen.

'Problems?'

'Flora seems to have become an impossible teenager already.'

'She doesn't want me on the holiday?'

'I'm going to talk to her.'

'I won't come,' I said, immediately.

'No. It can't be good for Flora to think she can dictate...'

'Honestly, Gus, the last thing any of us need is a fortnight of feuding. She's only twelve. She wants you to herself for a couple of weeks. I can understand that.'

'But what will you do?'

'I'll think of something.' I tried to keep it light. 'Don't worry about me.'

I was a little taken aback by his acquiescence, but also by the relief I felt at not having to spend two weeks with his daughter.

'I hope it bloody rains in Cornwall,' said Doll, when I called her the following day after Gus left to collect his girls from the airport.

'I was wondering about coming down to Margate and building sandcastles with Elsie?'

'Thing is, Dave's taken the kids to Marbella. I'm really busy, but maybe we could fit in a spa day?'

I didn't want to be squeezed into her calendar.

'Too much like work!' I said.

'Why don't you go to Italy?'

'I just might,' I said.

'Hasta la vista!'

'That's Spanish.' I called Hope.

'I'm at work,' she said.

'I was wondering if you'd you like to go on holiday with me?'

'Who would be in the shop?'

'I'm sure Martin wouldn't mind.'

I couldn't imagine that there was a particular rush to buy clarinet reeds or guitar strings on August Bank Holiday.

'He would mind,' Hope said.

She was probably right.

'I just thought it might be nice for us to spend time together.'

'I don't like holidays, Tree!'

I recognised the slight catch of distress in her voice that always used to precede a change to her routine. I hadn't heard it for a very long time, because we hadn't been away together for years. Now I remembered the difficulty of getting her out of the house as we set off for our one foreign holiday in the Canaries,

182

with Mum trying to pacify her and Dad threatening to give her a wallop if we missed the plane. I recalled the fuss at the departure gates when she and I gone to visit our brother Kevin in New York. I wondered if she even had a valid passport now.

'Don't worry, Hope,' I said quickly. 'Maybe I'll come down to see you instead.'

'I'm at work.'

'Yes, I know, but . . .'

'I can't keep chatting all day.'

It was still possible to organise a last-minute getaway. The one I liked the look of was in Sicily, flying to Catania, with all sorts of day trips to historic places included in the price, as well as a hotel with half board. The only downside was that they didn't tell you where exactly you would be staying until you got there. It was a bit of a risk, but it was cheap and, as I'd never been to Sicily, anywhere was going to be new and different. I clicked to confirm payment, suddenly feeling very brave and quite nervous at the same time.

My suitcase and passport were back in my flat. I rarely went there these days. When Gus was ill, I hadn't dared leave him alone very often, and now it was just easier to have all my stuff in the same place.

I was surprised to find no unsolicited mail on the mat behind the street door and that the communal staircase had been recently hoovered. Was there a new tenant in the flat above? I couldn't imagine the man who'd lived there wielding a vacuum cleaner, let alone hiring a professional cleaner.

As I walked up the stairs, I could hear the unmistakable gasps and shrieks of sex. Definitely a new tenant, I thought, as I opened the door.

'What the fuck?'

Doll's head popped out of the bundle of sheets on my bed.

Her hair was all over the place. I was so shocked to see her that I didn't even notice the pair of feet where my pillows normally were. In her confusion, Doll pulled up the sheet to cover her naked breasts, revealing the man's head at the bottom of the bed.

'Awright?' said Ash, carefully removing what I assumed was a pubic hair from his mouth.

'Sorry!' I said, slamming the door behind me and running down the stairs.

Opening the street door, I didn't know which way to turn.

I heard Doll's footsteps coming down the stairs. I started walking, my mind a blizzard.

Was this a one-off? Or had it been going on for ages? Did everyone know apart from me? Was this why the staff viewed Ash with suspicion?

I stopped at the crossing waiting for a green light.

'Tess! Tess!'

I could hear her making up ground behind me. I willed the lights to turn.

'You weren't supposed to find out like that,' Doll said, trying to smooth down her hair at the same time as holding an arm over her chest to disguise the fact that she wasn't wearing a bra under the man's T-shirt she'd thrown on.

'How did you want me to find out, then?'

'Don't be like that.'

Doll's instinct was always to deflect criticism back onto the other person, making them feel it was somehow their fault. It was what made her a good businesswoman. I was wise to it.

'Were you actually in bed with him when I called earlier?'

For a moment, she couldn't look at me.

It occurred to me that her ostensible generosity in allowing me to keep the flat had just been a cover.

I felt such a fool.

The traffic had stopped, the crossing started beeping. I set off across the road.

'Tess?'

At the last second, Doll decided to follow.

'Slow down, will you?' she said, panting behind me. 'It's not what you think.'

'You don't know what I'm thinking.'

'You're thinking it's a much bigger deal than it is.'

'So how big a deal is it?' I stopped and faced her.

'If I was a man, you wouldn't be shocked,' said Doll. 'Women dating younger men are always cougars. Men dating younger women are, well, men.'

'You're married!' I screeched.

'Screwing then,' she said, as if it was the word dating that I was objecting to. 'Anyway, your Leo was married, wasn't he?'

How did she always manage to zero in on my faults when she was the one in the wrong?

'What about Dave? What about Elsie and Tommy?'

I suddenly thought of Tommy's curiously dark hair.

'Oh my god! Ash isn't Tommy's father, is he?'

'Of course not!'

Now Doll was the one looking shocked.

'How am I supposed to look Dave in the eye?' I fired back.

'Dave's no angel,' Doll said. If you'd seen his text messages from a hen he met on a stag night . . .'

Hen, stag, this was all news to me. Why hadn't she told me? We used to tell each other everything. Was I so obsessed with my own problems that I could no longer see what was going on around me?

I found myself imagining Dave and his mates in matching T-shirts leering at a group of scantily dressed women carrying a giant inflatable penis. We used to see them all the time on the promenade, strutting from the station to the pub in their

185

devil's horns headbands, then staggering out at closing time, wedding veil askew, kicking the penis along the promenade like a beach ball.

'So this is revenge, is it?' I asked.

Doll sighed. 'Not really. It's mostly boredom to be honest. You've no idea how routine sex becomes when you've had a couple of kids. I mean, all the pelvic floor exercises in the world ...'

'Stop!' I shouted. 'I do not want to know about your sex life or the size of Ash's dick or any of it!'

'This is why I didn't tell you,' said Doll. 'You're always so black and white about everything.'

Chapter Twenty-Three

'Have you been to Sicily before?'

On the plane, I was in the aisle seat next to a middle-aged couple.

'Never,' I said, opening my book.

'Nor have we!' she said, as if it was the most extraordinary coincidence. 'Are you on the half-board mystery package?'

I nodded.

'Do you know anything about Sicily?'

'Only the sausages,' I said, then realising that perhaps sounded a little rude, added, 'They've got fennel in.'

'Oh,' said the woman, not knowing quite what to make of me. 'Viv, and this is Steve.'

The man waved at me from the window seat.

'It's our first time away just the two of us for twenty-four years,' said Viv. 'Our youngest got her A-level results. Straight off with her boyfriend. We were all in Corfu together this time last year. Funny how you don't know which family holiday will be your last, do you?'

I thought of our family in the Canaries, the first and last time we'd holidayed abroad. I'd done well in my GCSEs and Hope was still a toddler. Mum had just finished her chemo and Dad must have backed a winner because he splashed out on a package to Tenerife. He'd won a trophy singing 'The Wonder of You' at the Elvis karaoke night in Los Cristianos and Mum bought the ceramic plate with the hand-painted motto: *Today is the first day of the rest of your life.*

'No, you don't,' I said.

'Who are you with?' Viv asked, craning her neck as if she might be able to pick out my travelling companion.

'I'm on my own.'

'Don't worry, you can eat with us. Nothing worse than sitting alone at dinner, is there?'

Viv was the talker, Steve a man of few words. His one contribution to the conversation was to point out the largest petrochemical plant in Europe, as the coach raced down the coast to our destination. The industrial plant went on for miles and miles. It didn't feel like the most auspicious beginning.

It was getting dark when we pulled up outside a hotel in a fairly ordinary-looking street in the city of Siracusa. My room was very hot. I made the mistake of opening the window which overlooked a well where the bins were, before noticing that there was an air conditioning unit. Then I went down to dinner.

Viv had changed into a dress and put some lipstick on, although the dingy dining room didn't really merit the effort. There was a buffet of pasta in big steel trays and salad that looked as if it had come out of a prewashed bag several hours before.

Viv chattered on about meals they'd had on holiday, with Steve occasionally contributing phrases such as 'nothing worse than soggy chips,' and 'full-on diarrhea for a week!'

As we all folded our napkins and stood up, I said I was going for a walk. Viv wondered if I would be safe and gave Steve a look that made me think that if I was determined to go, they would have to insist on coming with me. So instead, I yawned and said it would be more sensible to see things in the light, and we all returned to our rooms.

I'd let in a mosquito. I pulled the sheet right over my head, but that only seemed to magnify the buzz of thoughts inside my head as I remembered the tumble of sheets on my bed, Ash's surprised face, Doll standing in the street wearing his T-shirt.

Why did I feel so betrayed and hurt by her infidelity when it was really nothing to do with me? And why had I been so sure that Dave was faithful to her?

I'd always been convinced they would live happily ever after. Was that only because he had left me for her, so I had to tell myself it was destiny rather than a simple choice?

Not that I had wanted to be with him. But why hadn't I? Viv and Steve seemed happy enough in each other's company. Was tolerant affection the best you could hope for after the first bloom of romance had faded? Why was there so much invest-ment in finding The One if all you were ultimately looking for was someone to hold back your hair when you had salmonella poisoning?

I threw back the sheet and reached for my phone.

'Tess?'

Gus sounded as if I'd woken him.

'Where are you?' he asked.

'I'm in a horrible room in a vile hotel just a few miles from the largest petrochemical plant in Europe with only a mosquito for company.'

'You're such a cheap date!'

Then we were both laughing, and I was cradling the phone next to my ear as I told him all about my journey. I felt my body twitching with little pulses of excitement, as if he was lying beside me in the dark.

'I wish I were there with you.'

I imagined his long languid shape spooning me on this lumpy

bed, little kisses on the back of my neck, me turning into his arms, his skin against mine, our lips touching . . .

'I don't know how the mosquito would feel about that,' I said.

'I miss you,' he sighed, as if we'd been apart much longer than forty-eight hours, which, in a way, we had.

'I miss you too.'

The silence was full of longing, and then we said goodnight.

I got out of bed, switched on the light and chased the mosquito round the room for a minute or two before splatting it with a Booker-shortlisted novel. Then I slept a dreamless sleep for the first time in months.

Chapter Twenty-Four

I was woken by Viv banging on my door saying that they were holding the day trip coach for me.

The light around the edge of the blind told me that the sun was shining outside.

'I think I'll give it a miss,' I called.

'Are you OK?'

'Yes.'

'We'll see you at dinner.'

I got a map from the receptionist who circled the things I should see with a biro. Dominating the city was a huge modern cathedral in the shape of a tear, dedicated to the patron saint Santa Lucia. Nearby, there was also a seventh-century church where she was buried. An archaeological park contained one of the largest Greek amphitheatres in the whole of the Mediterranean. The place the receptionist circled several times was Ortigia, emphasising it was *bellissima*.

That seemed unlikely as I set off down a shopping street that seemed much like any thoroughfare in any town in Europe. The only thing that said Italy to me was the heat of the sun and the delicious cappuccino I drank standing at a stainless steel bar while eating a sweet croissant dusted in icing sugar.

It was about a mile to Ortigia, which was a fortified island separated from the main city by a narrow channel of water. As it was a heritage site, vehicular access was restricted. As I walked across the bridge, the noise level dropped and I felt a deep sense of peace spreading through me.

This was the Italy that I recognised and loved, with ochre buildings and terracotta roofs against a cloudless blue sky.

I walked up a narrow, cobbled street, inhaling the delicious aromas of lunch being prepared in still shuttered little restaurants. There were the usual shops selling pretty bottles of olive oil. Others had bright boards of fridge magnets outside, which always made me wonder who it was who'd first looked at their shelves of trinkets and mass-produced ceramics and thought, what people really want is a half a plaster lemon to stick on the door of their freezer?

Suddenly the narrow street opened into a piazza so unexpectedly vast and luminous I stopped in my tracks.

A pale oval stretched before me, paved in smooth stone that gleamed like ice in the flood of sunshine. To my left were several elegant palaces painted in fading pastel colours, to my right the ornate white façade of a baroque cathedral.

The cool interior of the Duomo was plainer than many Italian cathedrals, the original stone columns of the Roman temple on which it was built still visible in the side walls. High above the nave, shafts of sunlight cast perfect replicas of a row of stained-glass windows, making it look as if there were twice as many on the opposite stone wall, the colours of the duplicate images as bright as the glass itself.

I wondered if the artisans who made the windows knew this would happen or whether, the first time the sun shone through, they'd thought it was a miracle.

In the chapel dedicated to Santa Lucia I googled a translation of the plaque on the rail before the altar, discovering that it was a prayer by the citizens asking her to shine light – because that was the origin of the name Lucia – so that they could walk a path free from sin and error.

Emerging again through the dim loggia into the resplendent piazza, I imagined the congregation going into dawn mass then coming out to this, knowing that their prayer had been granted.

Santa Lucia, I suddenly realised, was the Italian for St Lucy, the very saint my mother had been named for.

'Look at me, Mum,' I found myself silently whispering. 'In this heavenly place.'

A few streets away, a market was packing up for the day. I bought a slab of pizza, priced by weight and wrapped in paper that glistened with oil, then spent the afternoon walking around the perimeter of the island, finishing up at a viewing point where I could see the modern city of Siracusa across the water and, in the distance, the snow-capped summit of Mount Etna puffing gentle white clouds, tinged pink by the setting sun.

As darkness fell, I returned to the piazza. The contours of the duomo façade were a sharper white in the floodlights.

I sat in the only café on the square, beneath an awning strung with fairy lights and ordered an Aperol Spritz.

There were a few local families taking their *passeggiata*. On the steps of the cathedral a saxophonist was playing 'Moon River'. A toddler escaped his elder sister's hand to bob about to the music. At a nearby table, an old man scraped back his chair, bowed to his wife and led her in a slow waltz.

The waiter arrived with a plate of *aperitivi* substantial enough for supper.

'You like Ortigia?' he asked.

His name was Francesco.

'I never want to leave,' I told him.

'You stay here?'

My Italian was non-existent and his English not the best.

'I wish.'

Half an hour later, as I was wondering whether to have another drink, his sister Patrizia, a tall, fierce woman about my age arrived and, after we were introduced, insisted on leading me through a maze of ancient alleyways to a large wooden door.

Inside, there was a courtyard. We walked up a very grand staircase, then along a colonnaded gallery to another flight, then up some steep wooden steps where we stopped outside another door. She explained, in slightly better English than her brother's, that the apartment had been a labour of love to renovate due to all the red tape around ancient buildings, but it was now almost finished and she was intending to put it on Airbnb. I could have the first week free on the condition I gave her a five-star review but privately told her about any problems that might need fixing.

'You understand these conditions?' she asked, her demeanour more like a prison officer than a holiday landlord.

The apartment was in the roof space with a pitched ceiling supported by wooden beams. It was like walking into a Sunday magazine spread on dream getaways.

I turned to explain that there had been a misunderstanding. But somehow the words would not come. So I took the key and the following day wheeled my suitcase all the way down from the hotel.

Sometimes I wondered whether Viv and Steve had worried about me. I left a note for them at the hotel, but they probably expected to see me on the plane. Perhaps I became one of Viv's collection of anecdotes from holidays gone by.

I began to explore the city, loving the way that ancient and modern sat side by side, and everyone went about their daily lives as if it was nothing special.

I learned that Siracusa had suffered countless attacks and invasions, from the ancient Greeks to the Moors, Normans, Napoleon and, most recently, the liberating armies of the Allies during the Second World War. Perhaps when you've survived and adapted so often nothing fazes you?

There were images of Santa Lucia everywhere. The idea that this beautiful place, where the sun bleached the ochre of the stone to the paleness of sand, was protected by a saint whose name meant light, resonated with the sense I had of receiving a blessing each morning as I stepped out and tilted my face to the sky.

It was Gus's idea that I stay longer after my week was up.

'You sound like you again,' he said.

'What am I like?' I asked.

We had become quite flirty on our evening calls. There was that old cliché about absence making the heart grow fonder but it seemed to be making our relationship sexier too.

'Excited and curious about everything,' he said. 'Why don't you stay for a a bit longer?'

'You could join me and we could try living in Italy, like we planned?'

'Do you want me to?'

'Yes, please!' I said, suddenly realising that the white noise of dread that he would get depressed again was no longer ringing constantly in the background of my consciousness. I didn't even know when it had stopped.

It was such a wonderful thought that I went to the duomo and lit a candle, tilting the wick to take flame from another of the flickering pools of wax. Then I knelt to say thank you, though I wasn't sure who to.

*

195

When Patrizia came to debrief me, I negotiated a monthly rate. The main season was over. It was less than I thought. I calculated that even with just my own savings, I could stay for several months.

'Did you find anything wrong with the apartment?' she asked.

'If you use more than one appliance at a time it overloads the electricity.'

'This is Italy! What do you expect?'

I didn't mention the lack of a kettle or a toaster.

Gus called to say that he'd talked to Charlotte and they'd decided to pool the money from selling both his mother's place and the house in Portobello Road to buy a flat for the future use of Flora and Bella should they want to come to London for university. In the meantime, it could be rented out and he'd receive half the income. The London market was picking up again so it shouldn't take long and he would come to Sicily as soon as that happened.

'Sicily is it now?' said my father, as if it was yet another on a long list of glamorous destinations my jet-setting life had taken me to. He didn't ask how long I'd be staying and I didn't volunteer because I didn't know.

'I'm in a beautiful town by the sea and the sun is shining,' I told Hope.

'Nowhere better than Margate on a sunny day.'

Oh, but there is, I wanted to tell her. There really is.

The conversation I was dreading was with Doll. I eventually plucked up courage the night before I was supposed to return to work.

'Is it because . . . ?' she asked.

'It's about me, not about you,' I said, brusquely, as if we were a couple breaking up.

There was a lengthy silence. When she spoke again, I could tell she was on the verge of tears.

'I'm pleased for you, Tess, I really am. It's just that you've been here from the start. You're the one who named the business and you're the only person I can talk to honestly about it. I'm scared of what's happening with Brexit and the pound and everything . . .'

'You'll be fine,' I told her. 'You always are.'

There were a few moments silence as she thought about that. Then she said, her voice back to normal, 'I am, aren't I? Good luck, Tess! You deserve it, you really do!'

Which made me slightly regret being unfriendly, but I'd left it too late to apologise.

Chapter Twenty-Five

Turns out you can live on sunshine.

I developed a routine of walking round the island every morning, calling in at a bar on my favourite bay for a cappuccino. Almost every day, my path crossed that of a middle-aged woman walking in the opposite direction. Her hair was unapologetically grey and cut in a sharp bob. She wore well-cut jeans and leather boots with a stylish jacket. I had her down as an academic.

After a few days, we started exchanging a smile. When we both ventured a '*Buongiorno*!', her accent made me think she was American.

Returning to the apartment, I'd try to study Italian grammar on the terrace until lunchtime when I'd buy a panino and some ham or cheese from the deli down the street. In the afternoons, I'd choose an archaeological site or church to explore.

One day I was crossing the Piazza del Duomo when I saw that Ipogeo was open. It was a place I was curious to visit but it had always been closed, even during the limited opening hours posted on the iron gates across its entrance. Now I paid the small fee and made my way down the narrow steps.

Ipogeo came from the Greek word for underground, I read. I had no idea that the civilised serenity of the piazza was built over a labyrinth of ancient quarries and cisterns. Picking my way along a dark tunnel with the sound of dripping water all around me, I felt like a character from a Greek myth descending into the underworld. I reached a vast, cavernous grotto with stalactites suspended from the roof and uneven walls hewn from volcanic tufa.

In these incongruous surroundings, there was a permanent exhibition of black and white photos documenting the night of the Allied invasion in 1943. The liberating army had invaded Sicily and the townsfolk had taken shelter in the Ipogeo. The images were a bit like the ones you see of the London Tube during the Blitz, with dozens of families bunking down, their faces pale with fear. The captions were written in English as well as Italian. Apparently, as dawn broke the guns fell silent and, when the crowd peered anxiously out of the entrance to the cave on the harbour side, they saw that it was teeming with soldiers and landing craft.

Following the tunnel that led to that exit, I became aware that I wasn't alone as I saw the slim silhouette of a woman gazing out at the bay. I wasn't sure whether she had heard me and didn't want to make her jump, so I stopped a few feet back and called, 'Hello?'

As she turned, I saw that it was my American.

'Oh, it's you!' she said.

'Tess,' I said.

'Sandy,' she replied.

'Isn't this an amazing place?'

'Indeed it is.'

'Must have been absolutely terrifying for the townspeople,' I said, pointing back at the exhibition.

'And also, I think, a great relief,' she said. 'My father was a lieutenant in the liberating army.'

We stood side by side, perusing the photos again, making occasional observations as if we were both reluctant to leave.

'You wouldn't fancy getting a hot chocolate, would you?' I asked, tentatively. She was the first person I'd had a proper conversation with for a while. It almost felt like I'd forgotten how.

'Why not?' she said.

It felt good to be back in the piazza with the sunshine on my skin warming away the icy chill of the subterranean world. In the café, Francesco greeted me with kisses on both cheeks.

'It's only because I rent an apartment from his sister.'

'You live here?'

'I've been here almost a month.'

'I've been here for two,' she said. 'But I'm not on kissing terms with any waiters.'

I explained how I came to be there, which seemed to amuse her.

'How very fortunate to find this place by chance!'

'What about you?'

'I first heard the name Siracusa at my father's knee,' she told me.

After a gruelling campaign in North Africa, Sicily had felt like a welcome oasis. Apparently, he had talked about it fondly and often.

'When I was growing up the word Siracusa sounded like a magical place, as distant and unreachable as Narnia.'

'Narnia was actually in the back of a cupboard.'

She looked at me sharply. 'You are quite right,' she said, her stern face softening. 'I see I will have to choose my similes with more care in future.'

We sat sipping molten chocolate through a drift of squirty cream. I had the feeling that instead of offending her, I'd inadvertently won her approval.

*

When our paths crossed again a few days later, we sat side by side on the sea wall. Though we were different ages and nationalities, we quickly discovered that we were voracious readers. Fans of Elena Ferrante, we had both recently finished the final volume of the Neapolitan Quartet, deliberately slowing down for the last hundred pages because we couldn't bear to bid farewell to the protagonists.

Sandy leant me a novel called *Siracusa* by Delia Ephron which I read immediately and admired very much, although it gave a much darker vision of the city than the one I saw.

We fell into a habit of taking our morning cappuccino together, our conversations extending as we relaxed in each other's company.

Turned out I was right about her being an academic. She was writing a paper on fourth-century female saints. Their names were vaguely familiar to me from long-ago confirmation classes. St Catherine of Alexandria had been put on a wheel which had miraculously shattered. Santa Cecilia, the patron saint of musicians, had sung all the way through her unwanted marriage, then converted her husband to Christianity. In her prison cell, she wouldn't stop singing. She'd always reminded me a little of Hope.

Santa Lucia of Siracusa, whom Sandy was researching now, had been influenced by Santa Agata from just up the road in Catania. Both had been subjected to awful torture for refusing to marry Romans. In Santa Agata's case, her breasts were cut off. Apparently, she was the patron saint of breast cancer.

I wondered if Mum had known there was patron saint of breast cancer. I thought how delighted she would be that I was finally taking an interest.

'By the sixth century, accounts of Santa Lucia's martyrdom had spread to Rome and throughout the whole Christian

Church,' Sandy was saying. 'In Sweden, they still celebrate her saint's day, dressing little girls in white dresses with red sashes, with coronets of lit candles on their heads. But what was it that made these stories so appealing that they spread like wildfire?'

I was trying to come up with an answer, when I realised she was about to give me hers.

'All of these women came from wealthy, often noble, families,' Sandy said. 'They had money enough to give away and they decided to give it to the poor. I think that angered the Romans as much as their refusal to marry. Was it really their purity that made the stories so universally appealing? Or was it the fact they stood up to the patriarchy?'

'So, you see them as prototype feminists?' I asked.

'Exactly. Like the suffragettes, they were rich, well-educated women prepared to fight for their beliefs.'

'Ironic that the Catholic Church, who, let's face it, are never big on women's rights, chooses to venerate them,' I said.

'But the Church decided that they should be remembered not for their intelligence or social conscience, but for their virginity and death.'

Her demeanour was how I imagined an old-school Oxford don's. She did not allow loose assertions.

The following morning there was a crisp, wintry wind. We headed into the shelter of one of the narrow streets, stopping outside a bakery so that she could take a photo of the gaudy rows of Sicilian cannoli and cassata drenched with white icing and decorated with candied fruit.

'Do you know what those ones are called?' she pointed at some little round iced buns.

I didn't.

'The eyes of Santa Lucia. Some legends say she gouged out her own eyes, others that the Roman governor ordered it. Why she's depicted with them on a plate, I've never really known. My father had a sweet tooth. He talked about the cakes here as much as the scenery! Apparently, there was a bakery that used up all its precious supplies of sugar baking cakes for the liberating soldiers. Perhaps it was this one?'

Sitting at a table inside with our cappuccinos, Sandy took out her wallet and showed me a photo of her dad in his army uniform. He was very good-looking young man, with the same strong bone structure she had.

'I always promised myself I would bring him back here. But he was diagnosed with pancreatic cancer a few months ago. He died shockingly quickly.'

I suddenly saw that her stiff posture was more about holding herself together than holding back. For a moment, our eyes met, hers blinking back tears.

'I'm an only child. We were very close.'

'I'm so sorry,' I said, reaching across the table to touch her hand.

I decided not to tell her about my history with the disease. People behave differently if you tell them you've had cancer, treating you as if they have to be nice to you all the time.

Sandy looked at her watch. 'I have to go.'

I wondered if there was someone in New York she called each day at this time. A lover, perhaps, before he or she left for work because it would be first thing in the morning there.

As I watched her walk away, I hoped she wouldn't regret revealing her vulnerability, because sometimes that can make it awkward for strong people to be friends, but the following day we met again and walked into the bustling modern part of Siracusa, my role as student resuming as Sandy filled me in on the background to our visit.

Apparently every year on her saint's day, which fell on 13 December, the silver statue of Santa Lucia was taken out and carried all the way to this place, where she was said to have been interred in the honeycomb of catacombs on which the church had later been built, before bits of her body were stolen as relics and dispersed all over the Mediterranean.

'How much of it do you think is true?' I asked as we looked at the tomb.

'There are many different versions, of course, but the facts they all agree on are that Lucia lived in the reign of Diocletian. She was denounced as a Christian by a disappointed suitor, so the Roman governor ordered her to be put in a brothel. But when the guards came to take her away they could not move her, even when they hitched her to a team of oxen . . .'

There was something about a young woman making herself immoveable that again reminded me of Hope, who had always rejected hugs or any attempt to make her do something she didn't want to.

'Who's Hope?' Sandy asked, as we emerged into the square.

'My sister.'

The nice thing about meeting someone new in a place where nobody knows you is that you're not defined by your past. It wasn't that I had hidden my family background from Sandy, but she knew me only as a woman on her own in Sicily, who loved books and churches and art. To Sandy, I was just Tess, not someone's sister, or daughter, or girlfriend. She liked me for who I was, and that was a liberating feeling, a bit like a holiday romance, without the sex, obviously.

'I've always wanted a sister,' Sandy said. 'It's the one relationship where I feel you could never be lonely.'

I'd never thought about it like that before, but I realised it was true. Hope was always with me, even when she wasn't. I rang her every week, but she didn't like chatting on the phone and wasn't interested in Skyping, even when I said it would mean we could see each other. 'Not in real life,' Hope would say.

As we found a bar for coffee, I told Sandy a little bit about Hope and how Asperger's gave her a different approach to social and physical interactions, and how she loved singing and wouldn't stop, and how that had reminded me of Santa Cecilia too.

'Are you are proposing that these female saints may have had Asperger's Syndrome?'

'Not exactly,' I said, a little intimidated by her ferocity.

Was this what it was like to be in a tutorial at university? At eighteen, I'd have been a quivering wreck.

'What then?' Sandy demanded.

'When people didn't know anything about neurodivergence or mental illness, they might have attributed religious reasons to things they couldn't understand. Like St Francis of Assisi. He definitely heard voices, so if he were alive today, he probably would be labelled as schizophrenic.'

There was a long pause.

'That's a fascinating idea,' Sandy finally said.

I felt a little giddy to have said something that interested her.

'The bit about St Francis was Gus's,' I said, not wanting to claim credit that wasn't due.

'Who's Gus?'

So, as we walked back, I found myself telling her about Gus. I recounted how our lives had brushed past each other on many occasions, so that when we finally spoke in the same church where we had first seen each other when we were eighteen, it had somehow felt like destiny.

I told her about our plans to come to Italy, then how he'd been ill, and how I'd found it difficult to adjust when he was better.

Sandy listened carefully and when I finished talking, she sighed and said, 'It's easy to mistake a relationship for a vocation.'

The way she said it, I felt sure she wasn't talking about a theory, but someone in her own life, perhaps the person who was responsible for her departure each day at one o'clock?

We parted outside the duomo.

'See you tomorrow?' I asked.

'Sadly, this is where we say goodbye. It's my last day in Siracusa. I'm wanted back in New York. Or at least I think I am.'

'Oh.' I felt deflated. 'I'll really miss you.'

'I've enjoyed our time together too,' she said, handing me a card. 'Here's my email. Make sure you send me your novel when you've written it.'

'My novel?'

'Don't tell me you're not a writer, Tess. Readers like you are always writers and everything you say is a story.'

That meant so much to me. I looked up at the façade of the cathedral, trying not to cry in front of her.

She put a gentle hand on my arm. 'Santa Lucia is the patron saint of the blind,' said Sandy. 'But did you know she is also the patron saint of writers?'

She smiled, then turned and walked across the piazza.

Her determined march reminded me of someone, but I couldn't think who. I waved meaninglessly at her back as she disappeared round the corner. It crossed my mind that maybe she was a little tearful too, which was why she didn't look around.

The following day, I walked around the island feeling lonely for the first time. I drank a cappuccino and ate a croissant in our usual café. Without company, time seemed to stretch endlessly in front of me.

Mum used to say that sometimes god sends you the person that you need at the time when you most need them. I'd never had any truck with that, especially after Leo, but meeting Sandy and gaining her respect had somehow given my life something it was missing.

I knew she would definitely not approve of me making her absence an excuse to do nothing.

As I wandered back to the apartment, I passed a stationer's shop, its window full of items ready for the return to school. I went inside and bought an exercise book and a biro. When I got back, I sat down and opened the book, smoothing its checked pages flat with the heel of my palm.

I clicked the top of the biro up and down a couple of times then, taking a deep breath, wrote the words:

Today is the first day of the rest of your life.

Gus

Chapter Twenty-Six

Autumn 2016

On my last day at work, the staff all signed a giant card and Mike, my consultant, bought me a coffee.

'You've become a valuable team player,' he said. 'Always welcome back, although god knows why you'd want to when you're off to sunnier climes.'

His words really helped. The longer I'd spent without the energy of Tess's physical presence, the more I'd been troubled by doubt about whether I was doing the right thing. Dorothy had reminded me that moving house was supposed to be the most stressful event in a person's life after bereavement and divorce and I'd had all three, so it was bound to be daunting.

It had taken me longer than I'd anticipated to go through the girls' old toys, each one holding memories as potent as a photograph's. I'd kept a few back, unwilling to make a decision about the bedside light that had lit the ceiling with revolving stars, or the Playmobil recycling lorry that had occupied Bella for hours on end. We'd created a replica street out of shoe boxes for it to drive down.

'You're not seriously suggesting we take these back to Geneva?' Charlotte asked, when she brought the girls to London to say goodbye to the house.

Bella's face fell.

'Other children will have a lot of fun playing with them,' I reassured her, noticing that she slipped one of the Playmobil dustmen into her pocket.

The charity shop box was the last remaining evidence that we'd ever lived there. Neither of the girls seemed particularly bothered. Bella was ten now, Flora thirteen. They'd moved on years before and had probably forgotten all the happy times we'd spent there.

I was almost embarrassed to give them the Halloween chocolates I'd bought as a kind of consolation prize, remembering when they'd dressed as miniature witches and we'd trailed around the streets of Kensington knocking on their friends' doors shouting *trick or treat*?

'Oh, what a shame, they're milk chocolate! You won't be able to eat yours,' Flora told her sister.

'Why not?' I asked.

'Bella's vegan now.'

I saw my little one frown and thought perhaps she would have made an exception had she not been challenged.

'I'll get you some vegan ones, no problem,' I told her.

'In the meantime, can I have hers, Daddy?' Flora asked, awarding me a rare smile.

'No, you cannot!' Charlotte told her, snatching it away. 'But they certainly won't go to waste,' she said, with a conspiratorial wink towards me, producing a Longchamp foldaway tote from her handbag as if prepared for unexpected gifts.

'Goodbye house!' Bella called, in a sing-song voice.

I took one look back as I closed the door. It seemed like the empty shell of a place whose soul had departed, so there was nothing to say goodbye to.

*

We took the Tube across London to the Barbican, then walked the short distance to the warehouse flat in Clerkenwell whose purchase we were about to complete. It was the first time Charlotte would see it in person. I suddenly felt nervous the estate agent's details had made it look more attractive than it was, and that Charlotte would accuse me of misspending her part of the inheritance.

There was a lift to the sixth floor from the foyer. With the keys the estate agent had loaned me for an hour, I opened the door and allowed the three of them to walk in front of me. It was a dull day, but it didn't really matter because the main room was mostly window. It was over thirty feet long with bare brick walls and stripped boards. The kitchen area was all utilitarian steel with a long marble counter, rather like the open service area of a high-end restaurant.

'Well,' said Charlotte, turning to me. 'This is very impressive.'

There was a dryness of tone and an emphasis on the word 'very' that made it difficult to work out whether she was being sarcastic.

'You like it?' I said.

'Who wouldn't like it?'

'Do you like it?' I asked the girls.

'It's amazing, Daddy,' said Bella.

'It's pretty cool,' Flora said.

She took some photos and posted them on Instagram.

'It won't be the easiest place to furnish,' Charlotte said.

I knew there was bound to be a negative.

'The estate agent says that flats in this area are easier to let unfurnished. The sort of tenants you get have their own stuff or they buy what they want. So that won't be a problem. Let me show you the roof terrace.'

When I'd been trying to decide the sort of place my girls

might like when they were students, the images that came to mind were New York-style loft apartments, probably because they both loved watching *Friends*. I'd asked for Marcus's advice and he'd come with me to several of the viewings. From a practical point of view, we'd decided it would be safer for them to be in a building with good security rather than a converted Victorian house in Islington. It was also easier to find two equally sized double bedrooms in a contemporary renovation. I was aware it would be a ludicrously luxurious student pad, if they decided to study in London, but if Charlotte and I could afford to indulge them, then why not? We'd put them through enough. In the meantime, Marcus said that somewhere brand new in this location with all the latest spec was going to attract a very good rental income.

As we stepped onto the roof terrace, the contrast between the noise of traffic and the silence inside demonstrated how well soundproofed it was. The view of glass towers and church spires was spectacular.

'Wow!' said Flora.

'Double wow!' said Bella.

I put an arm round both of them.

With both the girls and Charlotte smiling at me simultaneously, I felt as if I'd grown a couple of inches taller.

'Shall we get some lunch?' I said.

Bella chose pizza with roasted vegetables, specifying no cheese.

'Why did you decide to go vegan?' I asked.

'It's the only logical way to live,' she told me, surprising me with an answer about food production and greenhouse gases rather than her love of animals.

Looking across the table, I saw both a child who was reluctant to let go of a Playmobil toy and a growing person who

214

was developing a conscience. These nuances and contradictions didn't show up in Skype conversations.

'What will you actually do in Sicily?' Charlotte was asking.

'I'll have a bit of a break, then decide.'

'Are you ill again, Daddy?' Bella asked.

'No, I'm absolutely fine now.'

'Phew!' she said.

I'd never forgive myself for alarming, possibly traumatising, my daughters, when what I'd wanted most in life was for them to be happy.

'Are you retired?' Bella asked.

'Daddy's not old, like Robert,' Flora told her. It was the first time they'd mentioned their stepfather's name.

Charlotte shifted a little uncomfortably in her seat.

'Has Robert retired?' I asked.

'Of course not,' Charlotte snapped. 'Investors never really retire, do they?'

'I wouldn't know,'

'Quite.'

'It's really more of a sabbatical for you, isn't it, Daddy?' Flora said, ·

'Exactly.'

I was grateful for her extensive vocabulary coming my rescue.

'I can't believe you're having a gap year at your age!' Charlotte said with a derisive little chuckle.

I should have known there'd be some sort of comeback after the reference to Robert's age. She had always had the ability to laser in on my insecurity.

Was she right? Was this adventure, in truth, a pathetic mid-life crisis that had come a bit early?

'I could always practise medicine in Italy,' I said, to reassure myself, as much as her.

'Well good luck with that!' she said. 'Might not be so easy

with Brexit and you wouldn't believe the red tape I had to go through to practise as a consultant in Switzerland. God knows the bureaucratic hoops the Italians would make a junior doctor jump through. I hope you've got all your certificates?'

'Yes.'

'Translated?'

'Not yet. My priority will be learning the language.'

'But don't they speak some awful dialect in Sicily? In my experience, Italians can be very dismissive of anyone who comes from south of Florence.'

'I'm sure there must be some doctors in the rest of the country, mustn't there?' I said, determined to hold my nerve.

'Thank god it's me paying for their school fees!' Charlotte said, nodding at the girls.

'They were perfectly happy at state schools in London, remember?' I regretted that comment straightaway as her face hardened.

'No time for pudding,' Charlotte said, looking at her watch. 'We have to check in in less than two hours. Do you think it would be quicker to get Tube or taxi at this time of day?'

'Tube, I should think.'

I was going to go to the airport with them, then remembered I had to return the keys to the estate agent, so Bella and I had our goodbye hug on the pavement outside Old Street station, while Flora kissed me formally on both cheeks as her mother did.

I watched them descending. None of them looked round to wave. I wondered how I had managed to go from hero to zero in less than two hours.

Chapter Twenty-Seven

Tess was the first person I saw when the automatic doors opened. She ran behind the line of cab drivers holding boards then rushed into my arms, her body crashing against mine, clinging to me as if her life depended on it. The coconut smell of her hair, the softness of her skin, the press of her lips on mine awakened my senses as if I had been only half living all the time I'd been away from her.

Outside the terminal, the warmth of the Mediterranean air spread relaxation through my body as if I had been holding my breath for days and could finally exhale.

As we loaded my suitcase onto the bus, Tess greeted the driver in Italian and asked him when we were leaving. He replied in Italian, smiling at her as if he knew her, then stood up to shake my hand and welcome me to Sicily.

'I was the only person for the last bit of the journey here,' Tess explained. 'So we had a bit of a chat.'

As the bus trundled along the motorway, she was full of questions about the past week. Was I sad to leave work? Was it a good flight? Was I hungry? Then, nuzzling her face against my shoulder, she said.

'I've got a surprise for you when we get home!'

'Can't wait,' I said.

'Not *that*!' she said. 'Honestly!'

Tess ran up the final flight of wooden steps and put the key in the door.

'Wait!' I said, as I dragged my heavy suitcase up, then put it down and, to her great amusement, carried her across the threshold.

'What do you think?' she asked.

None of the photos she'd pinged me had given any impression of the size and airiness of the place, or the views, so high over the ocean and the rooftops, it felt almost like being in a look out tower.

'It's beautiful!' I said. Then, looking at her, 'You're beautiful.'

When we kissed, it was tentative and tender, almost like the first time. I pulled away to look at her face, eyes closed, as serene and sweet as if she was enjoying a lovely dream. Then she looked straight at me, pushing me back against the wall, as we grappled with each other's clothes, with all the pent-up urgency of the months we had spent apart, as if we were taking possession of each other again. We fucked on the floor, over the kitchen counter, in the bed, until finally flinging ourselves apart, feverish, breathless and satiated. Then we lay watching the sunset turn the sky from rose to orange before darkening to indigo.

Tess put a saucepan of water on the hob and opened a box of Twinings Everyday teabags, which was the only thing she'd asked me to bring. Then she pointed to the large object with a decorator's sheet thrown over it that I had assumed was a step ladder.

'Luigi carried it up the stairs,' she said.

'Who's Luigi?'

'The man from the shop. Look what's underneath!' she said, excited as a child at Christmas.

It was an easel, complete with a box of drawing pencils, a small sketchbook, brushes, and a large box of tubes of acrylic paint.

'I wondered about watercolours, but the colours are so clear and bright here, it made me decide on acrylics, but Luigi was very helpful and said he'd change anything. Do you like it? I mean I know you've always wanted to paint and I just thought that if you had the materials . . .'

'It's the best gift anyone has ever given me.'

'I'm so glad.'

'I've got something for you too,' I said, opening my suitcase to retrieve the very slim new laptop I had bought as a replacement for the ancient one she had asked me to bring.

'Oh my god!' She hugged it to her chest. 'I've been writing in longhand!' She pointed to the table on which I'd already noticed the exercise book with *NOVEL by Tess Costello* scrawled across the front.

At the café in a floodlit piazza, which looked almost like a giant empty ballroom, a waiter she introduced as Francesco kissed her on both cheeks. An old man stood up to say '*Buonasera*!'

Her Italian wasn't grammatically correct, but she was a good communicator. I knew it was ridiculous to feel jealous that she had flourished without me.

When we had met in Florence, my Italian had been better than hers, mostly because I had learned Latin from the age of eight, but now I was slow and stilted in comparison, and people naturally looked to her first.

'What's wrong?' she asked, picking up on my silence.

'Seems like I have a lot of catching up to do.'

'It's not a race, is it?'

It was as if she had grown in confidence, becoming the woman she was supposed to be.

'You don't seem to need me,' I said, trying to make it sound as if I was joking rather than asking for reassurance.

'Of course I need you! It's only because of you that I'm here!'

I knew that I needed to exercise. House clearing had involved humping a lot of boxes up and downstairs, and I'd been on my feet all day at work, but I hadn't had time to go for long runs.

Tess made it clear that she preferred to go for her morning walk alone because that was when she thought about her novel. I learned not to probe. I could tell when she was thinking about it, because there was a distracted look in her eyes. She'd sometimes race to her notebook to write something down, but she refused to talk about it.

In the time it took her to walk once round the island, I ran around it twice, waving as I lapped her.

There was a bathing platform at the end of the street with a ladder leading straight to depths so inkily turquoise, it was difficult to believe that you would emerge dripping clear water. No Italian would dream of going in the sea in October, but it wasn't any colder than Cornwall in the summer. Sometimes Tess would wait for me on the sea wall after her walk, then we'd return to the attic flat and make love with my hair still wet and our skin tasting of the sea.

Every day, I'd go to the market to shop for our lunch while Tess sat on the terrace writing. In the afternoons, she'd show me all the interesting places she'd discovered while I was away, bringing her idiosyncratic brand of tour guide commentary, which combined her thoughts with the bits of history that appealed to her.

The Ancient Greeks must have brought cushions with them to watch plays in the amphitheatre because your backside went numb after five minutes; the Greek mathematician Archimedes, who'd lived in the town, had used his theories to design a weapon made of mirrors that focused the sun's rays on invading ships to set them alight, which, according to Tess, was a bit flawed because what if the attack came on a rainy day?

I thought it must be wonderful to live in her world, looking at everything through stained glass instead of a plain, ordinary window.

It was Tess who gave me the inspiration for the first painting I started. I'd found a tall shutter abandoned outside a house that was being renovated, although she was initially suspicious when I brought it in, dirty and damaged with rusty hinges hanging off.

'Once I've cleaned it up there will be four rectangles to paint on.'

'The four seasons, maybe?'

I'd only thought of sawing it into equal pieces, but now the idea of a linked series of images began to develop, perhaps of the potted lemon tree downstairs now laden with heavy yellow fruit. The spring panel would show blossom, summer tiny green buds that grew larger and yellower for autumn. Perhaps winter would be a still life of lemons in a ceramic bowl.

'Good,' said Tess. 'Now we'll have to stay for a year!'

I started making sketches until I was finally brave enough to open the tubes of paint and apply colour to the first rectangle of my shutter, propping it up against the wall as it was too big to fit on the easel. It took several attempts at mixing green to find the exact shade of the waxy surface of the fruit, then to see that the shine could be conveyed in a simple dab of white. Unlike Tess, who slammed the lid of her laptop shut if ever she caught me peering over her shoulder, I was unable to hide my work in progress.

Once I took the first step of starting to paint, I began to see the world in images I might try to capture. I took my sketchbook everywhere we went, recording little details, like the ornate pediments of the columns that flanked the doorway of the duomo, and the curve of shabby buildings on the bay where I swam.

I began to look for offcuts of hardboard on skips and brought home pieces of driftwood I'd found washed up on the narrow stretch of stony beach. I couldn't tell whether the paintings were good or not, but the more I tried the more I learned. The act of applying paint was so completely absorbing I would sometimes only become aware that hours had passed when it had become too dark to see what I was doing.

In the evenings, we always headed out for our *passeggiata*, sometimes making a single glass of wine and a plate of *aperitivi* last all evening. As the nights became colder we'd huddle in our coats drinking hot chocolate then wander along the main street, peering into the windows of the unlikely collection of shops. High-end boutiques with sophisticated dresses and accessories stood adjacent to souvenir outlets stuffed full of embroidered table napkins and bottles of limoncello in the shape of Michelangelo's David.

There were a couple of workshops where you could watch local artists ply their craft. A woman hand printed silk with designs based on artefacts from the archaeological museum, and displayed her work like washing on a line. Another made ceramics and silver jewellery, incorporating found items like shells and coloured glass smoothed by the sea.

Tess tried on a couple of pairs of earrings before selecting a design with cabochons of translucent brown glass that matched the sparkle in her clear brown eyes.

'They're like amber, aren't they?' she said, turning her head slowly from side to side as she looked in the mirror.

'It is glass from a beer bottle,' the designer said, which made us all laugh.

'I wonder what cheap date is in Italian. *Fidanzato economico*?'

From the look on the shop owner's face, I was pretty sure she'd just accused me of being a cheap partner, so I immediately bought the earrings.

The woman, who Tess quickly established was called Camila, asked us whether we were on holiday. Tess explained that she was writing – or trying to – and that I was painting. Or trying to, I added.

Camila said that she would be interested in seeing my paintings. There was plenty of space on her walls to display the work of a local artist. I thought she was just being friendly and encouraging, as Italians generally seemed to be, but the following day Tess insisted I take a painting to show her.

It was a view from our flat of terracotta rooftops and the top of a single, spindly palm against a blue Siracusa sky. I finally felt I'd got somewhere near to capturing that sky, with a subtle shift of paleness that became almost white on the horizon.

Camila said she liked it very much and wanted to hang it in the shop.

Though I told myself I wouldn't mind whether the painting sold or not, I found myself passing the shop ever more frequently on my morning run, discovering that if I came at it from one direction I could spot whether it was still on the wall before Camila saw me approaching. Then I could run on by, concentrating on the road ahead, as if I had forgotten it was even there.

The shorter days and longer nights made it feel as if the town was going into hibernation. People now closed their windows against the cooler winds and we could no longer smell suppers cooking, nor hear conversations and laughter as we walked the alleyways on our evening *passeggiata*.

Then rain arrived in prolonged and gusty storms that churned up the sea.

'It's like a wild animal, writhing and rearing and spitting froth at us,' Tess said, as we stood clinging to each other on the jetty by the bathing platform.

It was too dangerous to go in the water, too rainy to walk the slippery cobbles with any pleasure. So we spent several days indoors until the sun came out again, with Tess writing and me painting.

'Look at us artists in our garret.' She smiled at me. 'We're just like Rodolfo and Mimi. Without the consumption, obviously...'

She must have seen the flicker of anxiety cross my face. Neither of us had mentioned the follow-up tests she had missed.

'I figure if everything's OK, then it won't matter,' she told me. 'And if I'm not, then it would be straight into treatment and all this would be over, so...'

I squeezed her hand, not knowing what to say. It had to be her decision. I had to respect that.

'When you have cancer, people are always telling you to be positive and that's an extra pressure you don't need,' she tried to explain. 'Because sometimes, you feel like shit, and you worry it's going to be your own fault for not being positive enough if you die. Since I've been here, I have felt very healthy and positive.' She smiled at me, then reached forwards to touch the wooden easel, just in case she'd jinxed things by even saying it.

'You're the most positive person I've ever met. And if it feels right to you, then I totally support that.'

I wanted to tell her that of course everything would be fine. But we both knew that would be an empty reassurance.

Tess

Chapter Twenty-Eight

Winter 2016

The feast day of Santa Lucia fell on 13 December, which used to be the shortest day of the year before the calendars changed.

In Ortigia preparations began ten days beforehand, when a brass band went round the streets then, on 9 December, the statue of the saint was taken out of the locked cupboard where she was kept and displayed in the duomo. The radiant figure, cast entirely in silver with touches of gilding, was Amazonian. With a crown on her head and her eyes intact, she was depicted stepping forward with a plate in one hand, a martyr's palm in the other, looking so strong that it was a shock when you noticed the dagger sticking out of her neck.

When the day itself arrived, the Piazza del Duomo, usually so empty and serene, was thronging with people of all ages, as noisy and boisterous as a football crowd. There were vendors with great bunches of balloons, wearing sleeves of Day-Glo bracelets, hawking cheap toys and lollipops. It felt like a giant carnival.

As three o'clock approached, an almost tangible current of anticipation crackled around the arena but, when the cathedral bell began to toll, everyone fell silent. There was a collective intake of breath as the statue emerged glittering in the sunshine, as if the light was coming from within her.

A huge cheer went up. Some people fell to their knees as the heavy plinth juddered precariously down the steps of the cathedral, held aloft by a team of strong devotees, and slowly began to inch along its route.

Gus and I cut down a side street, hoping to see the procession closer up around the perimeter wall, not realising that we would have to wait over two hours. Darkness had fallen by the time we saw Santa Lucia slowly approaching in the distance, illuminated by hundreds of candles. As she finally passed us, the shining aura of beneficence was so awesome I found myself making the sign of the cross.

'I thought you didn't believe in all that.'

'I believed in you, didn't I?'

It just came out. He looked a little taken aback. Then he bent and kissed my cheek.

'Yes, you did. Thank you.'

As we wandered back up to the piazza, we heard someone call my name and saw that our landlady Patrizia was beckoning us over.

'Come meet my mother,' she said.

An older version of Patrizia stood up. She was tall and quite imposing. I did a double take. Apart from the styling of her grey hair in a chignon, she looked very much like my friend Sandy.

'Alessia,' she said, shaking my hand.

'*Piacere*,' I said.

She didn't speak much English but my Italian was now good enough to engage in basic small talk.

When I told her how thrilled I was to have seen Santa Lucia, she smiled fondly as I'd noticed the locals always did at the mention of their patron's name, as if she were a much loved relative.

She asked if I was enjoying living in Siracusa. I told her I adored it, attempting to explain how much I loved the way the past coexisted with the present here.

Wasn't that true of every city, she asked?

I thought about London. It had nothing as old as an ancient Greek amphitheatre, but there was the Tower of London. I had never visited it because it was a tourist place, fenced off and inaccessible unless you paid. Here it was as if the past was stitched into the present. I mimed the act of sewing, hoping she would supply me with the word.

'Ah, *cucire!*' she said.

'*Per me, il passato e cucito nella fabrica della citta,*' I said.

I felt proud of that, until I remembered that *fabrica* meant factory in Italian.

She asked me if I had visited the Ipogeo, pointing in the direction of the entrance.

'I have.'

Her mother's family had taken refuge down there during the liberation, she told me. Everyone was scared, but the Americans were very kind. Her grandfather, who was a baker, had made the soldiers cakes. He had used up all his precious supplies of sugar on the Americans! She laughed. It was obviously one of those stories families repeat to each other down the generations.

'*He always remembered the cakes . . .*' I heard Sandy's voice inside my head.

Could the cakes her father had enjoyed so much have been made by this woman's grandfather?

'You're uncharacteristically quiet,' Gus said as we wandered back to the apartment.

My mind was full of what ifs. What if Alessia's mother had served Sandy's handsome father over the bakery counter? What if he'd bumped into her on the *passeggiata*, and bought her an

231

ice cream, if there even was ice cream during the war? It was certainly conceivable that their paths could have crossed.

What if they had fallen in love? What if it was a forbidden passion, rather than cake, or even a deliciously sinful combination of the two, that had made him remember Siracusa so fondly?

What if Alessia was Sandy's sister?

She had always wanted a sister.

I abandoned several drafts of the email, eventually realising that the only thing to do was to relay exactly what I had heard and let Sandy draw her own conclusions.

Her response was almost immediate.

Thank you so much, Tess! I can see your novelist's imagination at work. The possibility that I may have a half sister in Siracusa is fascinating. My father's name was Alexander. I was named for him. It occurs to me that Alessia could have been too. It certainly gives me the excuse – if I needed one! – to return to beautiful Siracusa as soon as I can.

I read the bit about being named for him a couple of times before realising, of course, Sandy was an abbreviation of Alexandra.

The email ended with the words: 'Now, back to your own story, Tess! I am longing to read it!'

How did Sandy know me so well? Or did every writer go through a stage of occupying their mind with any distraction to delay returning to their work? I was happy to have written a plan and a few scenes, but I seemed to have come to a standstill.

I remembered Leo saying that there was no such thing as writer's block, just a lack of planning, but the harder I tried to think on my morning walks, the more random my thoughts seemed to become. Most of them were nothing to do with the book at all. I wondered whether the refrigerator needed defrosting and when I would need to send cards in order for them to arrive in time for Christmas at home. My inability to focus was making me wonder whether I was really a writer at all.

For our Christmas dinner Gus roasted Sicilian sausages and potatoes along with fennel bulbs. Their flavour when cooked was not at all like the aniseed they tasted of raw. I loved that he'd created our own tradition, although I did slightly yearn for the ordinary taste of turkey, gravy and the little sausages Hope used to devour by the dozen.

In the first week of 2017 there was a blizzard over the whole of southern Italy and Sicily. The news showed pictures of drifts on beaches that hadn't known snow for generations.

Our huge airy apartment wasn't suited to cold weather. The only method of heating was an old paraffin heater Patrizia brought over, but I didn't trust it because of the fumes it belched out. We didn't have any warm clothes so Gus and I huddled together under blankets on our sofa, or snuggled up in bed, isolation bringing us closer than we'd ever been.

One day, Gus put both our jumpers on under his jacket and ventured out to see what fresh food he could find, but the market was closed. He returned with some pasta, a tin of tomatoes and a pair of gloves for me to cut the fingertips off because my hands got so cold when I was writing.

'*Che gelida manina*!' he said.

As I sat at the desk by the window that looked out towards the concrete grey sea, Gus sketched with a blanket round his shoulders. I tried to respect his privacy in the same way he respected mine, but when I went to put the espresso maker on the hob, or boil a pan of water for tea, I couldn't help glimpsing that he was drawing me.

'I think this is the best work I've ever done. Because of the subject mainly,' he said, looking up and catching my hand.

After five days, the sun finally broke through and we could hear the meltwater dripping from the roof. Gus rushed downstairs to take photographs of the crusts of snow on the lemon tree, so he would be able to complete his four seasons tetraptych.

The apartment felt suddenly empty without him. I stared at the painting with its blank section waiting to be filled, feeling a shiver of presentiment that its completion would signal it was time for us to leave.

Then my phone rang. Anne's name was on the screen. It wasn't very long since I'd spoken to my family at Christmas, so I knew instantly that something must be wrong.

'What's up?' Gus asked, when he returned to the flat to find me packing a bag.

'I'm going to have to go back home for a few days.'

'Why?'

'Seems like Hope has split up with Martin. They came for Christmas and she refused to leave. No explanation. Anne and Dad are going on a cruise . . .'

'Can't they cancel it?'

'How many cruises are they going to get? My father's nearly seventy.' I was repeating what Anne had just said.

Gus clearly wasn't as convinced as I had been.

'Won't Hope be OK on her own?'

'Anne doesn't want to leave her alone, because she's been behaving a bit oddly . . .'

'In what sense?'

'She's stopped singing.'

Chapter Twenty-Nine

Anne's house was a modern detached on one of the newish estates on the outskirts of the town. It had three bedrooms, the smallest used as my father's den, with a giant television where he could watch football to his heart's content. I guessed she'd given it over to him because she didn't like the mess of another person in her pristine lounge.

Apart from a marble effect cocktail bar, with bottles of brightly coloured liqueurs arranged on shelves with mirrors behind them, the room was all cream, from the curtains with plaited tie-backs to the cream velvet three-piece suite, and the deep-pile carpet.

I suspected that one of the reasons I'd been called back was to ensure that Hope kept to the first of the rules underlined several times in red on the list Anne left in the kitchen: *No food in the living room!!!*

I was relieved to find my sister very much as she always was. It was nice to spend time together out of the shadow of Martin's brooding presence. We fell straight back into the routines we'd had when we'd lived together. If it was Monday, it was bangers and mash; Tuesday, macaroni cheese. Hope was clearly more used to living on takeaways, as on a couple of occasions when

I asked her to clear the table, she put all the dirty crockery straight in the bin.

Hope liked watching daytime television. Sometimes I asked her to do it in Dad's room so I could try to write. I was unsettled by the sudden change from Sicily's glorious colours to the monochrome of Anne's living room. But once I started concentrating the writing seemed to flow more easily here, as if, in the absence of much external stimulus, my imagination was creating scenes to entertain me.

I tried to get Hope out for a walk each day but we were far from the sea and the bus services were poor. In the evenings there was more television.

My attempts to ascertain what had happened were short and unproductive.

'Did you and Martin fall out? Have an argument, I mean?'

'He's bossy.'

'He certainly is. Is this a temporary thing? I mean, are you going back?'

'No.'

'Don't you miss him?'

'I miss his piano.'

The jukebox in the kitchen-diner looked a lot like one from the fifties, but it played CDs. It had always been Anne's biggest attraction for Hope, and possibly, I'd occasionally thought, for Dad. His entire collection of Fureys CDs were installed, and there had been many Christmases where he and Hope had sung along to them. If he'd had enough drinks to turn him mawkish, he'd always select his favourite track, 'I Will Love You', and sing it with tears in his eyes, his hand on his heart, just as he'd done at my mother's wake.

'Would you like to listen to some music, Hope?' I asked every mealtime.

'No.'

'Would you like to go down to town for the karaoke?'

'No.'

'Why not?'

'I don't have to do anything I don't want to. I never have to do anything I don't want to!' she said, her voice rising.

Sometimes, I thought Hope was more emotionally intelligent than she let on. I had said that same phrase to her so many times in her life and we both knew it. I could hardly argue with her now.

'What day is it?' Hope asked the second week I was back.

'Wednesday.'

'Wednesdays we go to see Mum.'

It was a nice bright day for a walk, although we were quite far away from the cemetery.

'It's always walking with you,' she said crossly as she puffed along beside me.

At the cemetery, we replaced the withered chrysanthemums she had left on a previous visit with a bunch of yellow tulips from a florist we'd passed on the way.

'Mary Lucy Costello, devoted wife to James, beloved mother of Kevin, Brendan, Teresa and Hope.' Hope read the inscription out loud. 'Why does it say "And I shall have some peace there?"' she asked, as if she had never noticed the quotation before. 'Why doesn't it say "Rest in Peace" like the others do?'

'It's from Mum's favourite poem, "The Lake Isle of Innisfree",' I told her, remembering the row I'd had with Dad to get it inscribed. It turned out he was more worried about the cost of the extra letters than the sentiment. Once the stonemason had said he'd do more words for the same money, Dad had backed off.

Hope and I stood silently with our heads bowed.

I don't quite know what's happening with Hope, Mum, but I promise I'll always look after her, I told her silently.

I wondered if Hope was talking to her too as she was touching the little silver cross Mum had left her. Could she even remember Mum? She had only been five when she died. I didn't even know if I remembered her properly because whenever I thought about her, it was in images very similar to the ones in the photo album I'd found in Dad's den. I could still hear how her voice had sounded, but I could no longer feel what it had been like to give her a cuddle.

Just as we were leaving the cemetery, a bus pulled up beside us and the doors opened with a hydraulic sigh. Martin got off. He ignored us, pretending to be looking at his mobile phone, even when I said, 'Hello, Martin!'

As he marched past, I suddenly felt Hope's hand in mine.

'I *can* do anything without you,' she called at his back. 'Because I've got Tree by my side.'

I think it was the first time that Hope had ever expressed affection towards me and, though it was only a crumb, my heart grabbed at it so eagerly my brain didn't really think about the subtext until later.

'I *can* do anything without you.'

Did that mean that Martin had told her she couldn't do anything without him? I'd never quite known whether their relationship was friendship, love or just an arrangement that suited them both although, if I was honest with myself, there had always been a tiny doubt nagging at the back of my mind.

'Hope, was Martin nasty to you?' I asked her when we were eating our beans on toast.

'No cake, no biscuits, no sweeties . . .' she said.

'Why?'

'He said I'm too fat. Katherine Jenkins doesn't eat cake.'

Katherine Jenkins had always been one of Hope's favourite singers.

I had to stop myself laughing. Had Gus been right? Had

Martin had serious visions of turning Hope into a recording artist?

'No singing until you do your scales!' Hope barked.

I couldn't quite work out whether she had been so brainwashed she had taken this instruction at face value, or whether she had simply gone on strike.

'I don't like scales, Tree.'

'You still like singing though?' I asked, tentatively.

'It's not my happy place any more.'

I suspected she had picked the phrase up from watching reality television. 'Happy place' sounded like a cliché from the mouth of a celebrity, a bit like 'no pressure!' or 'comfort zone' or 'one hundred per cent' when they just meant 'yes'.

But Hope never usually attempted to describe her feelings so the phrase sounded rare and poignant. And it made me very sad.

I knew that I should have probed further into her relationship with Martin before, but Hope didn't really do probing. So I'd convinced myself she was OK with him. Now that made me feel guilty.

'So Martin really was Margate's version of Henry Higgins!' Gus said when we spoke on the phone.

'It's not funny,' I said. 'I think some sort of coercive control's been going on. He's been undermining her, taking away all the joy she got from singing. I'm furious with him.'

'But good on Hope for leaving the miserable sod.'

I hadn't considered her courage until then. In her own way, Hope had broken free. She had left him. Lots of women never find the strength or wherewithal to do that.

'What about you? When are you coming back?' Gus asked.

'Dad and Anne will be here in a couple of days.'

*

There had been an outbreak of norovirus on the cruise, so everyone had been confined to quarters for the last week and, though they'd been given a voucher, Dad said wild horses wouldn't get him back on a boat. Why pay good money to be kept in a cell. Luxury cruise? Prison ship more like!

I'd thought my dad had mellowed under the influence of Anne, who stood up to him more than my mother had, but now I realised that was only because I hadn't spent a lot of time with him. Dad could be a real charmer when he was in a good mood. When he was angry you knew about it. The atmosphere that pervaded any space he was in was felt filled with poison gas. Any wrong move or comment might cause to ignite. The red mist.

Anne and I crept around trying to be as unobtrusive as possible as he sat in the living room fuming, waiting for an excuse to take out his wrath.

I regretted putting Hope in his den to watch television. He stomped upstairs and switched it off. Hope turned it on again as soon as he'd left the room. That did it. We could hear him shouting.

'What's the plan, Hope?'

'What plan?'

'Where are you going to live?'

'Here.'

'Have you asked Anne?'

'No.'

'You'd better ask her then, hadn't you?'

Hope came downstairs and marched into the kitchen with my father following behind her.

'Can I live here, Anne?'

Anne looked at me slightly desperately.

'For the time being, Jim. Just until she gets herself sorted out.'

'Teresa?'

It was never a good sign when he addressed me by my full name.

'I'll be going back to Sicily as soon as possible . . .'

'Going back to Sicily, is it?' He mocked me in a sing-song voice. 'What about your sister? Anne's been very good, Teresa, more than accommodating. But there are limits . . .'

'What am I supposed to do?'

'Hope's made her bed. She can lie in it.'

'I haven't made my bed,' said Hope.

Combustion.

'She hasn't made her bed! She hasn't washed up! She doesn't wipe down the shower!' His fist thumped the dining table with every complaint.

I saw in Anne's frightened eyes that these were little things she had moaned about, so she couldn't really take them back now.

'She's left her house and her job and planted herself here without so much as a by-your-leave . . .'

Hope got up and left the room.

'Come back here! Hope, do you hear me? Come back when I'm talking to you!'

'Calm down now, Jim,' Anne said.

'This is your doing!' Dad rounded on me. 'Always molly-coddling, never saying no . . .'

I remembered the terrible Sunday when he'd gone for my mother. *Bang bang bang!* When he'd struck the tabletop making the mixing bowl jump up and down. Bang bang bang went his fist now and he wasn't even drunk.

How long before it would find a different target from the tabletop?

'What's Martin done wrong anyway?' he shouted in my face.

There was no point in trying to explain to Dad about coercive control. He'd been doing it all his life.

'I'm going to find out what benefits Hope might be able to get, housing associations, that sort of thing. As soon as I've got her sorted out, I'll come straight back.'

I was standing at the bottom of Anne's cul-de-sac in the dark as I didn't want anyone listening in.

Gus's silence seemed to go on for a long time.

'On the plus side, I can have my follow-up tests!' I said, my voice trailing away as I realised that wasn't much of a sweetener for either of us.

'Let me come and help you, Tess.'

'No, please don't! I'll be back in no time. I've got a novel to write. You've got paintings to paint. I don't want to give up on that.'

On the screen I could see the crescent of the rising moon through the window behind him. Glancing up at the sky, the new moon was there above me too. Two different places, the same moon. It felt as if I was inhabiting a surrealist version of my life, where everything had been pulled out of shape.

'I love you,' he said.

'I love you too.'

I've always thought that there should be more than one word for love.

My love for Gus was passionate and exciting, like a miraculous elixir that turned me, when I was with him, into the person I should be.

It felt nothing at all like my love for Hope, which was protective, visceral and embedded in the person I was, like part of my DNA.

When I let myself back into the house, Hope was already asleep in the twin bed guest room we were sharing. Her dark hair, which had always had a mind of its own, however much you damped it down or brushed it, was splayed out on the pillow. Out of habit, I stroked it back from her temple, lightly touching her soft skin. Hope had always had a beautiful complexion. She still used the same toothpaste and shampoo we'd had at home because it wouldn't have occurred to her to try something different, so she smelled just the same when I gave her a little kiss.

It was chilly in the room. As I pulled the blanket up to cover her shoulders, she opened an eye.

'You will always look after me, Tree.'

Gus

Chapter Thirty
Spring 2017

Running had always been my solace. I took it up after Ross's death, stretching the distances further and further as if hoping that one day I would run far enough to escape the pain. I ran all the way through my divorce and after my breakdown.

It was the only sport where I did not feel the urge to compete. I had no wish to count miles or time myself against others. I had to be alone. Running could not replace loss but I knew that if I could raise the initial energy to start then, eventually, and without even being aware of it, a meditative state would come and I would forget myself for a while.

'The loneliness of the long distance runner,' my father used say, whenever he saw me pulling on my trainers.

At the time I'd thought the phrase meaningless, just the title of a film he'd seen in his youth. Now, I wondered if I had underestimated him. Teenagers, as I was becoming all too aware with Flora, assume that their parents know nothing.

With Tess absent, I missed the company of other people too. Chatting to random tourists, making friends of stallholders and shopkeepers, did not come naturally to me as it did to her. Time on my own seemed endless. Sometimes whole days would go by when I realised that I had not interacted with another human being except via the screen of my phone.

So I ran further and further each day, discovering a coastal path that skirted the suburbs leading to the boundary of the petrochemical plant and an incongruous ancient site called Megara Hyblaea, where the remains of a prehistoric settlement were still visible in the shadow of the steel cylinders and chimneys. I ran to the war cemeteries in the west of the town, their lines of identical headstones softened by a dusting of pale pink blossom from nearby orchards of almond trees. I ran through the modern city to the archaeological park, climbing the tiers of seats like giant steps, until stopping for breath at the top and marvelling at the view of the coast stretching south towards a seemingly infinite ocean beyond.

One day as I neared the end of my run, I saw that there was a blank space on the wall in Camila's shop where my painting had hung.

The bell above the door clanged and she appeared from the kitchenette with an espresso pot in one hand and a tiny cup in the other.

'Ah Goos! Always running!' she said, making me acutely aware of my sweaty face and T-shirt as she kissed me on both cheeks like an old friend, which I wasn't quite ready for.

'You have more paintings?' she said. 'This bought by Japanese lady.'

Apparently, she had paid the full price.

It was a strange mixture of feelings knowing that I would never see the work again. Part regret, part astonishment that someone had paid money for something I'd created.

It made me remember my father's reaction long ago when I told him I wanted to go to art school.

'But you can't earn a living as an artist. Van Gogh never sold a painting in his life!'

It was the one fact that people who knew nothing about art always cited.

Would he feel proud of me now? Maybe I should paint a seascape and send it as a gift?

I was filled with a renewed sense of purpose.

The sea was calm enough to swim again; it sparkled irresistibly in the sunlit mornings. Now, there didn't seem to be enough hours in the day to do everything I wanted. I ran, I swam, I painted, experimenting with different sizes and styles. As well as the views of Ortigia that Camila requested, I attempted images of fishing boats, flower stalls, a still life of a cappuccino on the shining stainless steel counter of a bar.

As the cruise liners returned to Siracusa's port, disgorging their cargo of day trippers, Camila demanded smaller paintings, which were proving a successful alternative souvenir to heavier ceramics. I became addicted to popping into her shop to see what had sold. It was my version, I thought, of Flora checking her likes on Instagram.

Sometimes, Camila urged me to sit and take a coffee with her. Sometimes I would stop off at a bakery and buy us both a croissant. We were a similar age, both divorced, although she had no children. I enjoyed having company, although her English was as poor as my Italian, so we never got much beyond superficial discussions about what was in the news.

Tess and I had switched to voice calls mostly. She didn't like talking to me where she could be overheard, and video used too much data if she stood outside. I thought the main reason was that it was easier, when we weren't looking at each other, to keep up the pretence that it would only be days before she returned.

Voice calls were somehow more intimate, almost as if we were there in bed together, chatting in the dark.

Apparently tensions were running high at Anne's house, but Tess was hoping to find somewhere for Hope to live soon.

She was sure she would be back after my daughters' Easter visit.

'Oh, and I got my test results,' she said, in such a bright voice I knew I didn't need to panic. 'Clear. As they were a bit delayed, they've said I only have to go for the final check-up in a year's time . . . if I continue to feel well, obviously.'

Automatically, I reached to touch wood as I knew she would be doing at the other end of the line. It had become a habit that was difficult to give up even without her there to make sure I did it. Tess was such a curious mixture of belief and superstition, but I had ceased challenging after she'd once asked me, 'Why does it matter so much to you if it's irrational, anyway? Lots of nice things aren't rational.'

I couldn't disagree with that.

'Miss you,' she said.

It was how our calls always ended.

'Miss you, too!'

I lay staring out of the window at the pale yellow moon in the extraordinary Prussian blue of the night sky, a colour I had only ever seen in Italy.

Chapter Thirty-One

The automatic doors opening for each new arrival built up the anticipation of seeing my girls again. Each time it wasn't them I felt the slight embarrassment of smiling at a stranger, my face quickly adjusting back to normal. Standing beside the line of limousine drivers, I wish that I'd had the foresight to write 'Flora and Bella' on a card as a joke. It was the first time they'd flown unaccompanied to see me.

When the doors finally revealed them Flora was walking in front of Bella, phone in one hand, suitcase in the other. Hers was cabin size. Bella was struggling to pull along a huge one. Flora ignored me as I waved to attract their attention. She was almost as tall as me now, even wearing the flattest ballet pumps imaginable. Her body was that of an adolescent girl, but it looked as if it had been stretched so that her T-shirt left bare skin above the waistband of her skinny jeans. Her face was longer but still startlingly beautiful, like a painting by Modigliani. I was aware of the eyes of the cab drivers following her as she walked past them, and I felt capable of punching anyone who stepped out of line.

'Daddy! Daddy! Daddy!' Bella hurtled towards me, while her sister held back, concentrating on the screen.

*

I'd booked a villa at the opposite end of the island near the Zingaro national park and rented a car to get there. It took us all day to drive over Sicily's mountainous interior. As I attempted to interest them in the island's history that had been shaped by geology, geography and migration, I had the impression that, as a captive audience, they had decided to indulge me. I only realised when Flora removed an earphone and asked me how much longer the journey was going to take, that neither of them had been listening at all. I was suddenly nervous that we would have nothing to talk about in our two weeks together and they would be as bored with me as I had been with my own parents at that age.

It was dark by the time we arrived. The villa was isolated with no other properties around to lighten the star-stippled sky. After our long day in the car, we all jumped into the swimming pool spontaneously in our T-shirts and shorts.

'It's paradise here,' I told Tess the following day, as I gazed at the turquoise sea framed by yellow and pink wildflowers, just like a view on a postcard, listening to the delighted splashing of my children in the pool which had proved, finally, more compelling than their phones.

The next day we walked up to the medieval village of Scopello to choose fruit and salad for our lunch, but instead discovered a restaurant serving caponata, the local stew of aubergines, celery, tomatoes and sultanas, topped with toasted almonds, which was vegan and so delicious I was sure I would never be able to replicate its complexity of sweet and sour flavours.

Passing a shop selling flippers and snorkels, the girls leapt at my suggestion that we spend our afternoon exploring the blue cove at the bottom of the cliff on which our villa perched, discovering an underwater world as colourful and diverse as the one above.

In these relaxed surroundings, a picture of my daughters'

day-to-day lives began to emerge, which revealed much more about them than firing questions on Skype ever could. Listening to them chat, I learned the funny things their friends had said, the nicknames they gave their teachers, what they ate for lunch. I absorbed insights into their home life. Robert was mostly away at conferences; Charlotte had two secretaries because she was on the board of the hospital where she worked. Recently, she'd modelled in a charity fashion show at their school. The following day Mr Juan Carlos, Flora's Spanish teacher, had said what a beautiful woman her mother was, which had totally grossed her out.

Flora played badminton for the school and was the youngest girl on the debating team. Bella did hip-hop dance classes with a boy called Jonas.

'Not a boyfriend, obviously,' Flora assured me.

'We do hold hands!' Bella revealed.

In the gelateria we decided was the best in the village, I was proud to hear Bella asking in Italian whether the sorbets contained any animal products. Both were unselfconscious about speaking a different language. With a stab of guilt, I remembered my mother's comments that last Christmas we had spent together. She had been right. Growing up in a different country had its advantages.

The school they attended followed the International Baccalaureate Programme, which encouraged more conceptual and interdisciplinary thinking. When I was their age, it had been de rigueur to be bored, but they seemed much more engaged with the world.

Flora was set on being a human rights lawyer. She had her path to this goal mapped out. Oxford University, a masters in the USA or possibly at Sciences Po in France. Her violet eyes were full of conviction that she could change the world.

'What do you want to be, Bella?' I asked.

253

'An activist,' she replied casually.

For now, she was still a little girl who, whenever she saw a patch of grass, felt compelled to do a cartwheel. She could never resist hanging upside down on a railing, part child, part bat.

Flora's sudden growth spurt had made her self-conscious. She wore only black clothes and often walked just behind me, like a shadow. As someone who had also grown very tall suddenly around her age, I recognised the desire to hide.

She was not shy, however, of asking pointed questions.

'What do you actually do in Sicily?' she asked me one day.

'I think he's an artist,' Bella said.

I took my notebook everywhere we went and she had watched me sketching.

'I don't know about that!' I said, quickly changing the subject.

On the long drive back to Siracusa we played *I spy with my little eye*, but in Italian, laughing each time we repeated, '*Io spio con questo mio occhietto.*'

We arrived back in Siracusa as the sun was going down, parked the car outside the pedestrianised zone and walked through the narrow streets to the palace. When I opened the door to our apartment it was filled with amber light from the sunset.

'Oh, I can exactly see why you live here now, Daddy,' Flora said, taking a succession of photos and posting them immediately.

In the morning, we enjoyed a swim together then, while they were showering, I arranged some of my paintings for them to look at.

Bella loved the one I'd recently finished of my bathing platform with a swimmer and a dog in the sea.

'You can take it with you, if you like,' I said, gratified to see her hugging it to her chest like a favoured teddy bear.

'Would you like one, Flora?' I asked her, slightly nervous of her reaction.

I pointed at one that I was quite pleased with. I felt I'd got somewhere near to capturing not just the fiery colours of the setting sun, but the stripes of pink and duck egg blue above.

'Who wouldn't like it?' she said.

On the drive to the airport Bella chattered on about all the things she was going to do when she got back to Geneva. It occurred to me I didn't feel the usual descent into melancholy at our parting. We no longer lived together, but over the fortnight we had become close again, which I'd never been with my parents, even when we were occupying the same house.

My eyes still blurred with tears as I waved them through departures and I headed for the bus stop in a strange kind of limbo, suddenly bereft of the constant chiaroscuro of Bella's noise and Flora's quiet reflection.

The first bus that pulled up said Catania Porto on the front. On impulse, I decided to get on it, guessing there would be a fish market where the stalls would just about be closing for the day after selling their morning catch. Nearby, there would be a trattoria where the fisherman ate their lunch.

The place I found had no menu. The waiter brought me two sea urchins, their creamy flesh quivering like exotic flowers in their half shells. I pictured Bella's horrified expression as I squeezed a little lemon and took an ambrosial spoonful of the sea.

I walked slowly through the city towards the station. It had the edgy feel of a port city, a scent of danger in the dark little streets that led off the main drag, the shadow of the great volcano looming above. Living here must make you constantly aware of the precariousness of life. I wondered if you ever got used to that.

I realised that I'd missed the hustle and bustle of city life, in the protected, pedestrianised enclave of Ortigia. Here, there was the constant noise of lorries reversing, car horns blasting as soon as traffic lights went red, and the occasional ambulance siren, so different from the sound in London. In Italy, a long blast of horn was followed by three rising quavers. To my ears, it was a much gentler, less alarming warning than the sudden whoop-whoop of an English ambulance.

I bought myself an ice cream and sat in the main square watching the world go by, reluctant to go back to the empty apartment.

It was dark by the time I returned to Ortigia and the streets were quiet. The island was principally a day trip destination. Few people stayed overnight.

As I walked past Camila's shop, she was locking up.

She told me that she had sold my view of the bay with Etna in the distance. There had been a group of tourists in the shop at the same time all wanting to buy it. Could I please make her more?

'How many?'

'Ten, twenty, as many as you can. The season start. People like Etna.'

I felt curiously deflated by the offer.

I could still hear Flora's voice in my head. *Who wouldn't like it?*

Whether she had intended it or not, my daughter's critique had been spot on. My paintings were pleasing, nothing more. My art was no more authentic than the souvenirs imported from China and sold by illegal traders on the street.

'Do you want to take some wine?' Camila asked me, as if she sensed my mood of disenchantment.

'Why not?'

The Piazza del Duomo was white in the floodlights.

Tess found an almost spiritual connection with the beauty of this place but I was never going to capture any of the serenity and radiance she experienced here, because I wasn't an artist. It depressed me now to recognise that truth so clearly.

Francesco brought us glasses of white wine.

At the table next to us, there were four middle-aged Americans drinking gaudy cocktails. The loudness of their enjoyment grated on my nerves.

'This is the man,' said Camila pointing to indicate an overweight man behind her. 'The man who bought the painting.'

For an agonising moment, I thought she was going to stand up and introduce me, but I managed to stop her with a slightly manic shaking of my head which made her giggle.

She took out a packet of cigarettes and offered me one. I hesitated, then took it. The first hit of nicotine was always a pleasantly sinful reminder of how much I enjoyed smoking, and how easy it would be to slip back into the habit.

The cool white wine damped down my feeling of distress.

'You are sad?' she asked.

'Maybe a little,' I said, as I flicked ash into the ashtray.

I didn't think I could begin to articulate in Italian the sudden sense of disillusionment I was feeling. She might even be insulted that I was denigrating her business.

'You are lonely all this time,' she said.

I was a little startled by the personal nature of her comments.

'Yes,' I admitted.

Tess had been gone over two months. I had stayed here to keep the dream alive. But without her, I was lost.

257

'Sad to be lonely,' said Camila, with a sigh.

She sounded as if she was talking about herself as much as me.

I looked across the table at her. She was wearing a loose white linen shirt. I couldn't help noticing, in the cool evening air, that there was nothing underneath. The sleeves were rolled up and three buttons open, exposing a triangle of lightly sun-tanned skin beneath the hollow at the base of her throat. The long dark hair she usually wore tied in a ponytail fell across her face. She pushed it back.

'Wait!' she smiled. 'Do you say lonely or alone? This is something my English teacher always correct.'

'I think you mean alone,' I said, taking a long pull on my Marlboro. 'You can also say "on my own".'

'Goos is on my own in Siracusa? Is correct?'

'Gus is on his own,' I corrected, wishing I hadn't complicated it. 'I am on my own.'

She looked puzzled, then asked, with a shy little laugh, 'You like be with me tonight?'

My eyes held hers for a moment. I couldn't be sure whether she was asking me if I was enjoying having a drink with her, but the current of attraction that crackled between us seemed to suggest something more.

Behind her, the two American couples had finished their drinks, paid the bill and were walking away. The café was suddenly quiet. Camila was looking at me, twisting a lock of hair around her finger.

'What are you thinking?' she asked.

I was trying to work out how long it was since a woman had come on to me, and what the language was for saying no without causing offence. I was trying to stop myself wondering whether I could let things run on a little and see where it went. I was alarmed to find myself speculating whether casual sex

258

with an attractive woman would be worth the risk of being found out. How much longer was Tess going be gone?

The Americans were trying to take a selfie against the backdrop of the cathedral façade. The men were brothers, I had gathered from unintentionally eavesdropping their conversation, their banter louder and more irritating because I could understand every banal word of it.

I looked at Camila.

'It's late. I'm tired,' I said.

I noticed one of the men keeling over as if in slow motion, then he was lying motionless on the smooth paving stones.

'Never a good idea that third Martini . . .' his brother joked.

Camila had her back to all of this. There was a flash of hostility across her face as I stood up, to get a better look, pushing my chair over in my haste.

By the time I reached the scene, the man's wife was kneeling beside him, calling his name – Bryan – elongating the syllables in her increasing panic at his failure to respond.

I felt his neck for a pulse. There was none. I had seen him go down. He had not hit his head.

I heard myself saying, 'Call an ambulance! I'm a doctor. I think this man is in cardiac arrest.'

His wife screamed. The other woman started stabbing at her mobile phone.

'Is it 911? What's the emergency number?'

'I don't know. Ask in the café. Please stay calm and give me space.' I could hear my voice as if it was another person speaking. Cool, collected, confident.

His mouth had the stale taste of an old person, combined with gin and some sort of fruit syrup which I tried to block from my mind as I breathed into it twice. Nothing. I started on chest compressions, keeping to a steady rhythm.

Nellie the Elephant . . .

Two more breaths. Nothing.

Come on!

Around me, I was aware of the wife shrieking, the brother shouting at her to calm down. Francesco and the other waiters were leaning over, asking me what was happening, what should they do.

'*Chiama un'ambulanza!*' I said.

'*Viene!*' It's coming.

Come on Bryan!

All I knew was that I had to make Nellie pack her trunk and say goodbye to the circus again and again and again, until finally I became aware of the faint *der di da di der* of the siren, as distant as a memory, then gradually becoming louder and louder, until the ambulance pulled up in the square.

The paramedics were suddenly there, pushing me away, placing the paddles of a defibrillator on Bryan's chest. His heart started pumping independently on the second shock. They stretchered him into the back and hooked him up to monitors. I stood watching until they gave me the thumbs up, then my knees buckled and I sank down onto the paving stones, my arms and back aching from their unaccustomed workout.

Apparently, it had been twenty-one minutes since they received the emergency call.

'Bravo!' they said.

The small crowd that had gathered clapped as I sat up again.

As my brain processed what had just happened, it felt as if I'd woken up after some strange dream in which, for once, I'd been able to save a life.

Camila, who had been translating as best she could, called a cab to take the three remaining Americans to the hospital.

'Bryan should be OK now,' I tried to reassure them.

'I don't know how to thank you.' His wife gave me a tight, desperate hug, before letting go, a little embarrassed.

260

'All in a day's work?' The brother joked, a clumsy male attempt to show me he was strong enough to take over now.

I shook his hand.

'*Sei dottore*?' Camila asked, as I returned to the table and swilled my mouth with the last of my wine.

'*Si. Sono dottore*,' I said. I am a doctor.

Her eyes shone with adoration. 'It late. You walk with me?

Chapter Thirty-Two

It was nearing eight o'clock when I arrived outside Anne's house the following evening.

Hope answered the doorbell. 'I'm not allowed to let anyone in.'

Anne and her father were at the pub. It was quiz night.

'Is Tess with them?'

'No. She is at work.'

I knew that couldn't be right, but wasn't about to argue.

'I think when they said not to let anyone in, they meant people you don't know.'

Hope was not inclined to budge. After a few seconds, she closed the door, and I was still standing outside an hour later when Tess returned.

'Why didn't you tell me you were coming?' she asked, stopping in her tracks.

'I wanted to surprise you!'

'Did something happen?'

I looked at her and wondered how I could have imagined, even for a second, that it would be possible to lie to her.

I'd walked Camila back to her apartment across the water in Siracusa. Outside her door, a friendly kiss turned into something else. For a moment, I was kissing her back, our bodies pressed against the door, when a light came on in a nearby window and I froze.

'I can't do this,' I said, unpeeling Camila's fingers from my shoulders, leaving her bewildered.

I ran all the way back to the apartment and spent the night clearing the flat.

In the morning, I was standing outside Camila's shop when she arrived. As she turned the corner and spotted me her face wavered between a smile and a frown, settling on the latter when she saw the stack of paintings I was delivering.

I insisted that they were a gift. I didn't want any money if she sold them. That seemed to make our parting even more awkward. If she'd had the language to say that I was an arrogant fucker to think she might be looking for a consolation prize, I think she would have done. As it was, we parted with a frosty *ciao*.

Returning to the apartment, I placed the sketches I'd made of Tess at the bottom of my suitcase and packed all our remaining possessions.

I left the almost completed *Quattro Stagioni* panel in the apartment as a gift for Patrizia. She must have liked it because Tess spotted it on the wall in the photos on Airbnb when she checked out the apartment months later.

'Nothing happened,' I told Tess.

I'd been tempted enough to know I had to get out of Siracusa. But it was just a kiss, a mistake in the euphoria of a moment that wasn't going to happen again, so what was the point of making it seem like a much bigger issue?

She looked at me curiously, as if she could tell my answer was a little economical.

'Actually, I saved someone's life,' I said, as she put her key
the front door.

'You what?'

I thought of the blue light flashing against the cathedral
façade, like a contemporary art installation. It seemed almost
unbelievable now, standing in this quiet suburban cul-de-sac
less than twenty-four hours later.

Tess listened intently as I recounted the detail of what had
happened. A sleepless night, my determination to get a flight,
the journey from the airport all began to catch up with me.
Hearing my voice choke up, she hugged me close and we held
each other tightly for a long time. Then, breathing a big sigh,
we separated and smiled at each other.

'Did you tell Bryan's wife you were the person who painted
the picture of Etna?'

'No, I didn't.'

'How amazing that they will put your painting on their wall
and it will be a talking point when they have friends around in
Utah or wherever they live. They will tell them what a beautiful
place Siracusa is, but how Bryan nearly died there and was
saved by a stranger. And all the time you will be there in the
room with them, inextricably linked to their lives.'

I had forgotten how her imagination gave everything a story.

I had forgotten how exhilarating it felt to be in her company.

'It's a miracle, really,' Tess said. 'That you were there and
you knew what to do. Right outside the duomo.'

I knew that, for her, it wasn't a figure of speech. She was
probably thinking Santa Lucia had a hand in it. I wasn't about
to argue with that now.

'And you?' I said, pointing at the supermarket uniform she
was wearing. 'When were you thinking of telling me what
you've been up to?'

Tess

Chapter Thirty-Three

I'd decided to return to the supermarket job I had before leaving Margate for London.

It was only meant to be a temporary thing. It had become clear that Hope wasn't going to get any extra benefits. The past seven years serving in Martin's shop had proved she was capable of working. With an assessment system that seemed designed to ignore the complexity of special needs in order to deny as many candidates as possible, someone who stated unnuanced facts was never going to qualify.

The council's housing list was oversubscribed, priority given to families with small children. Without a job, it was impossible to rent privately. It was easier for me than Hope to find employment quickly, and the manager had always liked me. Once I was in, I thought I might be able to wangle something for Hope too.

Not telling Gus while he was on holiday with his kids made it easier for me to stay in denial about the end of our Italian dream. Then he was back in Margate before I got the chance. I don't think he was as disappointed as I was to leave Siracusa behind. It had always been his idea to live in Italy, but he didn't like it as much as he thought he would.

Can you change your life by changing your location? Kirstie and Phil would say yes. For Gus and me, Sicily had been a place of transition rather than a destination. He had discovered what he wanted to be, which, ironically, was what he was already. A doctor.

It had been a turning point for me too, although now I appeared to have gone into reverse.

'The only place I want to be is with you,' Gus said to me later that night, as we sat in a freestanding roll-top bath looking out at the sea.

We were back in the boutique hotel on the seafront, not so much a romantic reunion, more the first place we thought of after my father returned from the pub.

It was quiz night and their team had lost by one point. Martin still played with them, so Hope refused to go, which was another irritant for my father, as she'd always been useful on the music round.

He was simmering with resentment and looking for an excuse for more drinking, which Gus's unexpected presence provided.

'What's your poison?' Dad asked, taking up his favourite place behind the marble-effect cocktail bar.

I could see the agitation in Anne's eyes. He had already had his usual three pints of Guinness. We both knew that there was a tipping point soon after when capriciousness would flip into rage.

'I'll have a white wine, please,' said Gus, assuming, in his middle-class way, that would be the easy option.

'White wine, is it?'

My father didn't consider white wine a man's drink. I was pretty sure there was none in the house.

'Anne's a great one for prosecco. Any prosecco in the fridge Anne, or have you drunk it all?'

'The last prosecco I had was at New Year.'

'It's a large gin and tonic for her every time it's my round!' said my father, winking at Gus. 'I'll pour myself a whisky, while you make up your mind.'

'Whisky would be great,' Gus said, quickly.

Both Anne and I breathed again.

'I haven't any scotch, if that's what you're after.'

'Whatever you're having,' said Gus.

My father poured two large glasses of Jamesons. Downed his own in one and poured another.

'You would have thought Martin would have known the year Mozart died, wouldn't you?' he said suddenly, looking at each of us as if expecting a response.

'It was a long time ago,' said Anne.

'Martin's supposed to know about music!'

'Have you eaten, Gus?' said Anne, trying to move things on.

'What is this, a restaurant now?' my father shouted.

'He's had a long journey, Jim. Airplane meals. They're not more than a mouthful for a fellow his size.'

'Is that suitcase yours?'

My father pointed at the offending item as though he'd only just noticed it. Sometimes I wondered if the drink was making him soft in the head.

'I just flew in from Sicily,' Gus faltered.

'You just flew in, did you?' Dad banged the counter of the bar with his fist. 'This is not a hotel, you know!'

'I can easily make up a bed in the den,' Anne offered.

'No, please, I wouldn't dream of it,' said Gus, getting out his phone to call a cab.

'You can take Hope with you while you're about it!' shouted Dad.

'Don't be so silly, Jim. Hope's in bed, She's not going any-where tonight,' said Anne.

I noted her emphasis on tonight.

It's amazing what a difference it makes to be male, middle class and in the medical profession. All the estate agents who could barely be bothered to look up from their desks when I'd gone in jumped to attention when Gus enquired in his public school accent about short term rentals. On my day off we were shown five properties, including a spacious two bedroom flat on the Royal Esplanade.

'What do you think?' Gus asked, as we stood on the balcony looking out at the sea. The estate agent was hovering inside pretending to look at his phone.

'It's way beyond our price range.'

'I'm going to be living here too,' said Gus. 'And it's so con-venient for the station.'

I stared at the view, struggling to believe that the sea was made of the same stuff as the inky water that lapped the walls of Ortigia. The sky was cloudy, the water grey, the only indica-tion of a horizon was the wind turbines, their spinning white blades like giant versions of the shiny little windmills I used to buy for Hope to stick in the sand.

'We'll need to show Hope.'

'Really?' Gus was keen to sign as the hotel was costing a fortune.

'Honestly, you've no idea how much she hates change.'

'Would you like to live here, Hope?' I asked when the three of us went back that afternoon.

'Yes,' she said immediately, making me feel a bit of a fool.

'Why?' I asked.

'The television's much bigger than Anne's.'

The first weeks we spent there together were some of the happiest of my life. I woke up each morning realising I didn't have to brace myself for whatever mood my father was in. The certainty that Hope was safe brought me a sense of peace that I hadn't even known I was lacking.

After she moved out of the home we'd shared since Mum died, there had always been an area of my brain taken up with worrying whether she was really all right. There's that saying about parents that you're only as happy as your unhappiest child. The same, I think, applies to big sisters.

Hope also seemed calmer in our new home. When I suggested we go to see Mum on a different day of the week, so we didn't bump into Martin every time, she agreed without the usual fuss.

Before the interview I organised for her at work she allowed me to brush her hair and suggest a different outfit. Occasionally the combinations Hope threw together from her rummages in charity shops looked like something you might see on a fringe catwalk show held under grungy London railway arches. Usually, it was more bag lady.

'Smile, Hope!' I reminded her when she walked into my bedroom for her practice interview.

But she always forgot.

We sat in front of the mirror together.

'What's your favourite thing, Hope?'

'Christmas tree.'

I drew a Christmas tree and flashed it at the mirror. The piece of paper flopped forwards so you couldn't see the tree. That made both of us smile.

'Christmas tree, Hope!' I whispered, when she was called in from the waiting area outside the Human Resources office. I hovered outside trying to hear whether she was responding, standing so close to the door that I had to jump back when it suddenly opened.

'I've got a day's trial on Tuesday,' she announced, stiffening like a board when I tried to hug her.

Hope followed instructions, doing exactly what she was told, and passed with flying colours. The part-time job she was given involved stacking shelves and, as her memory was practically photographic, she quickly learned the location of every single item in the shop.

She became a kind of human signpost, for customers and staff alike, able to direct people to things she'd never eaten in her life.

'Sumac? Third aisle, three shelves up between the saffron and the allspice . . . Hummus? There are five different types. Red pepper, coriander and lemon, organic, virgin olive oil, velvet. They are in the chilled deli section.'

'I'm a legend, Tree,' she told me one morning as we were leaving for work.

I caught a glimpse of the two of us in the full-length mirror in the hall, and couldn't help thinking how Mum would have laughed to see us wearing the same uniform, how she might have taken a photo of us dressed like little girls in the same dresses for a special occasion.

'Mum would be proud of me, wouldn't she, Tree?' Hope said, as if she'd read my thoughts.

Occasionally, I wondered if all our assumptions about her were wrong. Maybe she did feel empathy but just wasn't able to articulate it, except in the emotional purity of a song? But she never sung now.

Gus got a job in the emergency department of a different London teaching hospital. With the train journey into London he was up earlier than us and back late. When he was on nights we didn't see each other at all, but he often cooked something delicious for us in the afternoon, although his efforts did not always receive the reviews they deserved from Hope.

'I don't like rice pudding with peas and bits of bacon,' she said of his risotto.

As he began to explore the possibility of continuing his medical training, he would sometimes go for networking drinks or dinner with colleagues after work, and stay overnight in Marcus's flat in the Barbican. When he was away I spent the evenings writing in our bedroom, as I had done at Anne's house.

The process of constructing the novel felt a bit like colouring little pieces of a jigsaw without really knowing what the finished picture was going to look like. Sometimes, the pieces I had fashioned with great care didn't seem to fit. Other times, I'd get a fleeting glimpse of what the big picture might look like, and the challenge of getting there excited me even though I wasn't sure whether I had the skill to achieve it.

Hope watched the telly. Occasionally, she'd march into where I was working and ask to look at the photo album I'd brought with us from Anne's. Mum had taken most of the photos, so I figured we had just as much right to it as Dad did. Hope never tired of turning over each heavy, yellowing cartridge paper page, hearing the stories my mother had attached to each photo. They were stored in my brain, as clear in my memory as the images.

The first few were formal portraits of my brothers dressed for their first Holy Communions. Hope was born after Kevin had left home and Brendan was already in his teens, so she'd never known them young. Their boyish faces and hair combed flat always fascinated her, as did the school photo of me with long plaits. After that, there were the holiday snaps featuring a windswept beach with a mountain in the background.

'That's Croagh Patrick in County Mayo, where St Patrick banished the snakes...'

Mum had always said it as if it was a fact.

'That's where Mum grew up,' said Hope.

'Yes, and we used to go back every summer. To see Auntie Catriona.'

'Where am I?' Hope asked.

'We didn't go after you were born.'

First, there had been Mum's cancer treatment. After that, Hope got the terrible-twos tantrums that she'd never quite grown out of when she didn't want to do something. And she never wanted to go on a long car journey to the ferry across the Irish sea.

'There is Mum with me!'

Hope loved getting to the page with the only other professionally taken photo, which showed my mother with Hope as a baby, and a bright blue studio curtain behind them. To me, it was as radiant an expression of maternal love as any Renaissance Madonna.

The rest of the album was photos of Hope.

Hope had had her own style from the earliest age. There was one of her in her high chair wearing a bowl as a hat, and one of her in a grey tracksuit and a cardboard donkey mask I'd made for her.

'That's my first nativity play,' Hope said. 'You took the photo, Tree, because Mum wasn't with us any more.'

Little Donkey... I started singing her favourite carol gently in the hope of her joining in, but she wasn't going to fall for that.

It appeared that nothing was going to make her sing again.

'I really miss Hope singing,' I said to Gus on one of the rare evenings when our schedules coincided. We'd retreated to our bedroom to get away from *The Voice* at top volume. 'I'm worried that she's cutting herself off even more from the world.'

'I expect she'll start again when the time's right,' he said.

But I wasn't so sure.

Chapter Thirty-Four

Time apart made the hours Gus and I spent together more special. We went for long walks along the beach with Gus skimming stones to his heart's content.

When you grow up somewhere you don't really notice its beauty. I'd never seen how the sky was reflected in the shallow pools left by the outgoing tide, nor understood why Turner would have chosen to live here. Obviously the Dreamland theme park hadn't existed in his day, nor the sixties tower block that dominated the curve of the bay. Now, even those buildings seemed to have acquired a retro appeal.

Our only problem was sex. Or, rather, the lack of it. The soundproofing wasn't great in the flat, and Hope didn't like it when Gus kissed me on his return from work or gave me a cuddle when we were watching television, so the idea of her overhearing anything was off-putting. Gus found it exciting to do it absolutely soundlessly, but for me the pleasure was muted by the idea that Hope might march in. We should probably have asked the landlord to put a lock on our bedroom door.

As the days became longer and warmer, Gus increasingly wanted to find secluded sand dunes or forests where we could make love. Once, when it started to rain, we rushed back to his car, breathless and giggling and clambered into the back seat, like a pile of spaghetti all wound round each other.

On one occasion, we left Hope watching television and drove along the coast, stopping at Whitstable.

'I've got a surprise for you,' Gus said, as we walked along the boardwalk.

'Are Marcus and Keiko down?' I asked as we neared their hut.

'No, they are not,' he said, producing from his pocket a set of keys. 'We will have the place to ourselves!'

I didn't know how I felt about him discussing our sex life with Marcus. I hadn't quite realised how frustrated Gus had been until we were inside, fucking against the kitchen island, on the quarry-tiled floor and, afterwards, in the guest bed in the attic, with a wall of glass looking straight out to sea.

Afterwards, as he slept beside me, I lay listening to the gentle crash of waves on the shingle outside, the exact same noise I had heard when I'd lain awake only yards away on a damp mattress in the ramshackle shed next door which reeked of lobster pots, with Leo snoring beside me. Funny how this place had been an illicit love nest then, and now it was again, albeit a much more fragrant and luxurious one.

In October, the banker who was renting Gus's London flat relocated to Singapore and moved out two months before the lease was up.

The photos I had seen on the agent's website gave little impression of how vast the living room was, all bare brick and stripped wooden floorboards. The apartment reminded me slightly of the loft my brother Kevin and his husband shared in Tribeca.

The view from the terrace was spectacular. It was like being in a magical forest of glass towers, their angular surfaces sparkling in the sunshine.

'I'm so glad you like your new home,' Gus said, putting his arm around my waist, drawing me close.

'You want to live here?'

'Of course!' he said, as if it were a foregone conclusion.

'I'm not sure,' I said, going back inside.

He followed me in.

'What's not to be sure about? I'm spending three hours a day on a train, that's when they're even running on time. It doesn't make sense.'

'But my wages wouldn't even cover my fares!'

'You can get a job in London. Or even better, take some time off and finish your novel!'

'What about Hope?'

Gus's face fell.

'Now that she's got a job, she'll be able to get her own place, won't she? That flat's a bit big for her . . .'

'She's got a job, she's settled and now you want to uproot her? Gus!'

'What's so unreasonable about that?'

'I can't believe you don't get it. You've lived with her for almost six months . . .'

'Exactly. And I've never complained . . .'

'Gus, you were the one who insisted on getting that enormous flat. I told you we couldn't afford it . . .'

'If it's money that's the problem . . .'

'Do you have any idea how entitled that sounds? Money is a problem. Money's always a problem, but it's not the only one . . .'

I was searching his face for a clue that this was a joke, his dry wit just a little too parched for me this time. But I couldn't see any sign of it.

'I don't think you've understood anything,' I said, dismayed.

'I've understood how she dominates you,' Gus said, gently. 'And me for that matter. I think I've been pretty patient. Surely we both knew it had to be a temporary thing? Tess...' He tried to put his arm round me again, but I stepped away, walked to a window, pretending to look at the view.

There were tears stinging my eyes because it was clear neither of us had really known what the other one was thinking all this time.

'Look, Tess, if you really want, Hope can live here. There are two bedrooms...'

'Gus, she can't even get on an escalator. How would she manage in London?'

'She can learn! You're always saying she's not stupid!'

My heart always started beating faster when confrontation was in the offing, a reaction from my childhood. It had been such a relief to meet Gus. A kind man. A gentle man. But I could see he was now a man losing his patience.

'You're always saying that lots of your patients have mental health issues and they've ended up in A & E because society doesn't understand their particular challenges.'

'Hope is neurodivergent,' he argued. 'I wouldn't necessarily class that as a mental health issue.'

Suddenly he was going all aloof doctor on me.

'How would you even know?' I said, my voice rising in frustration. 'She can't express herself well enough to tell you her needs. I'd say that not singing when singing has been your only pleasure in life is a cry for help, wouldn't you? Now that you're suddenly the great expert on mental health?'

That last sentence just came out. It was below the belt and Gus looked as if he'd been punched.

'If you want to continue caving in, go ahead. I thought you didn't want to be a carer!'

We were both landing blows.

'I didn't want to look after *you*,' I screeched. 'I actually thought you might look after *me*!'

'I'm trying to look after you, but you won't let me! I was prepared to give up everything and come to live in Siracusa...'

Was that how he saw it?

'You were prepared to give up a job you said you hated at the time. Living in Italy was your idea in the first place...'

That was the truth and he had no response to it.

'I thought you'd love to live here!' he shouted, marching up and down the long, empty living area.

'You just assumed that I want to live in your hideously expensive ivory tower like some sort of kept woman!'

He stopped pacing and looked at me. Then he said, with a supercilious blurt of laughter, 'You know who you sound like? Your father, with your ridiculously old-fashioned working class pride...'

'Says the public school boy with the inheritance!'

Gus sighed.

'So what am I supposed to do? Sell this place and buy some mediocre semi halfway between London and Kent so things are fairer?'

'No! I don't know!'

I couldn't work out what I did think. I'd been so happy but all this time he'd just been waiting for everything to change. How could I not have seen that?

'I promised Mum I'd look after Hope. It's easy to say she'll be fine, but you've never seen her when she's not...'

Infuriatingly, he shrugged as if I was making a big deal out of it.

'If Charlotte died, god forbid, and Flora and Bella had to live with you, you'd expect me to fit them in to my life!'

'It's not the same!'

I knew it wasn't, but I couldn't quite think why. Arguing made me panicky. I immediately doubted every statement I made.

'I suspect you need Hope as much as she needs you. There was an acidic quality to his voice now. 'It's a co-dependent relationship.'

He'd got all the lingo from going to therapy. I knew co-dependency was a pejorative term.

'But isn't that what families are all about?' I argued. 'You wouldn't know, of course, because you've never been very good at family, have you?'

I couldn't believe what I'd just said. It was like being in some horrible fairy tale where a spell had been cast on me, so that venomous creatures came out of my mouth instead of words, as if I was spitting scorpions.

'Bloody hell,' said Gus, raking his fingers back through his hair. 'So we can't have children of our own, but we have to have Hope!'

I reeled, a peculiar retching sound issuing from my mouth, as if I'd been punched.

All the time we were supposed to be in love, had he secretly been harbouring that resentment?

We stared at each other as if unable to believe we'd just said things that could never be taken back, because they went to the core of who we were. And they were all true.

Picking up my bag, I walked to the door.

'Goodbye Gus!'

'No, Tess! Don't go!'

Now, I felt wearily resigned, as if I'd always known our parting was inevitable, just not the time or place.

'Let's end it before we make each other even more miserable.'

For a moment, he didn't move, and then as I opened the door, he ran and grabbed my arm.

'Tess . . .'

I waited for him to say something that would miraculously make everything all right.

No words came.

Gus

Chapter Thirty-Five

Autumn 2017

There was a painting, on the wall behind Dorothy's chair, of a dusty Mediterranean village street. One half was sunlit, the other in shadow. A peasant woman carrying a basket on her shoulder was about to step into the light. I always wondered what was in the basket. Bread? Fruit? Or just the burden of her worries?

'Are you telling me that you and Tess have never had a row before?' Dorothy asked.

I thought about the question.

'Not really, no. Sometimes I've said the wrong thing and Tess has been offended. She's been exasperated, exhausted, of course. But she has an enormous capacity for forgiveness...'

'What about you? How's your capacity for forgiveness?'

'She hasn't done anything that warrants forgiving.'

Curiously, some aspects of Tess's character that I'd found endearing in the beginning I now found tiresome, like her convent-girl modesty.

'I'd have liked more sex...' I said with an embarrassed laugh.

It seemed trivial in comparison with what she had had to put up with.

'Did you talk about it?'

'No. It was difficult talking about anything personal when Hope was around. Tess was so concerned about upsetting her.'

We'd always been walking on eggshells. Just as she said she had done as a child.

'It sounds as if you'd have liked her to be less preoccupied with her sister?'

As usual, Dorothy had a way of zooming in on what was really bothering me even if I didn't say it because it didn't seem fair to complain about Tess always putting others first.

'Not just from my selfish point of view . . . I'm not sure it benefits anyone, least of all Tess.'

'Did you ever say this to her?'

'Not until the row. I didn't want to sound like her dad.'

'You've never thought it was important to express your own feelings?'

'Not important enough, in the scheme of things, no.'

'In the scheme of things,' Dorothy echoed.

'Look, I know where you're going with this.'

It was territory we had looked at before. Throughout my life I'd suppressed my emotions because I didn't think that they were significant enough to merit people's attention. Dorothy thought it was a result of being the child who survived. The one who'd been told he was lucky. The one who didn't really deserve to be alive. I'd compounded this by setting myself up for failure with my family, my work, my marriage.

'It's not the same thing with Tess,' I said.

Tess had had a much tougher life than me. She'd lost her mother, she'd had to look after her sister, her father was a bully, she'd had cancer. She'd stuck by me through my illness. I was forever indebted to her. I didn't feel I had the right to criticise her.

'The reasons may not be, but the process,' Dorothy said.

'You say you don't think your feelings are important enough . . . enough for what, do you think?'

'Enough to potentially cause hurt.'

'So you store them up until there isn't enough room to contain them and then . . .'

'I suppose I ended up causing more hurt . . .'

'To yourself, as well as to Tess.'

How stupid I'd been to think it that healing was a process with an end. You could stop seeing a therapist, but you always needed to be alert to the way you were thinking.

'So you and Tess have never had the chance to learn a process of de-escalation?'

'We've had our fair share of misunderstandings, but we've always somehow managed to muddle through and make up.'

'You do realise that in every relationship, people say terrible things to each other. Then they say sorry and they explain what made them say it.'

'What I said was beyond terrible,' I said. 'Tess had cancer at thirty-three because of her genes, so she went through life-changing surgery that would mean never having children of her own. I don't even know why I said it! I've never wanted more children. It's difficult enough trying to be a decent father to the ones I've got . . .'

'Perhaps you chose the thing you knew would hurt her most?'

It was so clear when someone else said it.

'You mean it was gloves off, so I lashed out? Because she had said the thing she knew would hurt me most?'

'When we are cornered, we have an adrenaline response.'

'It's probably the only time in my life I've gone for fight instead of flight. Tess and I never had the best timing!'

'It sounds as if there were quite a few things that you weren't telling each other.'

Dorothy was used to my tendency to try to deflect the conversation with a feeble quip.

'Might it be a good idea to try talking to someone together to try to find a better way of communicating?'

'You mean couples therapy? It might have helped before but it's too late for that now!'

'Are you sure?'

'Tess is very black and white about things. Very insecure. Very defensive.'

Now it sounded as if I had nothing but criticism of her.

'All these are reasons why it might be helpful for her too, even if you don't manage to find a compromise...'

'Food for thought,' I said.

My hour was almost up. I was beginning to feel as if I was lying to Dorothy, because as we talked it had become even clearer to me that I wasn't going to call Tess. I had struck at the two most fundamental elements of her life. The sacrifice of her fertility and Hope. It was low and spiteful of me. I could say sorry a million times but it would always be there. Every time we saw my children, or other people's children. It would be there in every kiss and every fuck. She would see it as her failure. And she'd never failed me. It was I who had failed her and I wasn't worthy of her forgiveness, even if she gave it.

'Let's end this before we make each other even more miserable.'

I loved her for her capacity to find joy in the smallest things. Yet I had only succeeded in making her unhappy.

Chapter Thirty-Six

When I was a student, I used to try to befriend the nurses in the hope that when it came to doing tricky things like putting in a cannula or an NG tube, they would pity me and take over. It had often worked until a staff nurse had cottoned on. After that, several patients had to suffer while I learned that quick and decisive is much better than hesitant and nervous.

Since my first day after qualifying, when I had laughed when the nurse addressed me as Dr Macdonald, I'd never got the register of communication quite right. Nurses didn't want me to ask their opinion. They found my tendency to veer between indecision and caution frustrating. On the terrible day that I had opted for recklessness, I'd been lucky no one had made a formal complaint.

Now I'd decided I wanted to pursue a career in medicine actively, and was working at a hospital where no one knew my history, I seemed to have found the requisite combination of briskness and respect. I no longer happened upon huddles of staff whispering at the desk who jumped apart when they saw me. I felt much more comfortable in my role.

Jonathan and I resumed our regular game of tennis in Lincoln's Inn Fields.

'How's the new job going?' he asked, as breakfasts were delivered to our table in the working men's café.

'I think I'm becoming a better doctor.'

'You seem surprised?'

He speared a slice of meat-free sausage with his fork.

'Experience,' he pronounced. 'It's the most precious commodity when practising medicine, as I imagine it is in almost every profession. Ironically, it's not something we value very highly until we have, well, experience!'

It was the closest I'd ever heard him get to making a joke. Jonathan had always been a very serious person. His principal form of relaxation as a student had been playing chess for the university.

I wondered if it was really experience that had transformed me. Or whether what had happened spontaneously in the square in Siracusa had somehow liberated me from habitual doubt that I was not quite good enough. Confidence, I might have told him, is also a precious commodity. But that would have seemed too much like an admission of weakness. When discussing medical matters with Jonathan, I always felt as if I was sitting at the feet of a revered uncle, rather than a peer.

'How is Tess?' Jonathan asked.

'Er, we've gone our separate ways.'

Despite several invitations to dinner, they had never met in all the time she and I had been together.

'And your friend with the BRCA mutation? How is she faring?'

I was sure he knew it was Tess, but remained scrupulous about confidentiality.

'Yes, she seems to be OK. Almost five years now.'

Out of habit, I crossed my fingers under the table out of view of the most rational person I knew.

'That's good news at least,' said Jonathan, looking at his watch. 'Will you be alone at Christmas?'

I knew that if I were, an invitation to spend it with his family would be forthcoming after he had consulted Miriam. Even though neither of us would ever say it, he kept an eye on my welfare, and I was grateful to him for that.

'Working on the day then going to Geneva to see the girls.'

The girls had exams to revise for and, as the Clerkenwell flat was still mostly unfurnished, I'd agreed to fly over and stay with them. I assumed that Charlotte and Robert would take the opportunity to get away somewhere glamorous for winter sun.

It was quiet in A & E. A concerted effort was always made before Christmas to clear the wards. That made it less time-consuming for us to admit patients, which in turn relaxed the constant tension that pervaded the department when targets were not being met.

All the nurses were wearing angel wings. I was persuaded to don a red headband with antlers. There seemed to be a never-ending supply of mince pies and Celebrations in the staff kitchen. Perversely, I found myself wishing it was busier.

Christmas was one of those benchmark days when you thought about what you were doing the year before. I didn't want to have the time to remember sitting on the terrace in crisp sunlight under a pure blue sky, eating Sicilian sausages with fennel, and Tess saying, 'It doesn't taste nearly as bad when it's baked.'

We'd done our usual not-so-secret Santa. Hers to me a fridge magnet in the shape of a lemon, mine a replica of the silver statue of Santa Lucia. She had put it on her bedside table and kissed it each night before switching off the light, like a child with a favourite doll. I missed the guileless smile that told me she knew it was silly but did it anyway. I missed snuggling under the bedcovers with her, chatting in the dark about everything we had seen and thought that day. I missed her idiosyncratic descriptions of sights and sounds and smells. I missed hearing the stories she made up. I missed having sex with her.

The board behind the reception desk was decorated with Christmas cards. I hadn't received one from her and I hadn't sent her one even though I'd been to the shop at the National Gallery and bought several different designs, including a packet of eight of a detail from the Jacopo di Cione altarpiece. I'd even written several of them, before tearing each up. Christmas cards were what you sent out of duty, to people you only contacted annually, usually with some insincere message about not letting another year going by without seeing them. Even the most dedicated angel was never going to convey a message of how much I missed her.

Every time I heard Christmas songs on the hospital radio, or walked past a Salvation Army band playing carols outside St Paul's, I thought of Hope singing 'Little Donkey'. I wondered if she was singing again.

Christmas wouldn't be Christmas without a song from Hope.

I remembered the perplexed look on her face as she tried to figure out the double negative.

There were the usual burns sustained from wielding oversized turkeys or heavy saucepans of boiling sprouts after several glasses of fizz. A couple of children were brought in howling with broken wrists having fallen off their new scooters. Several objects had got stuck in unexpected orifices, including a candle in the shape of a Christmas tree and a 'Here Comes Santa!' vibrator with its jaunty jingle still playing inside the patient's rectum.

As the end of my shift approached, I was feeling both tired

and buzzy from all the sugary snacks, when one of the F2s asked me to look at a seven-year-old girl who was presenting with pain in her lower abdomen.

'It's probably all the rich food,' the father was saying.

'But she didn't actually eat anything,' said the mother.

I was used to the dynamic of one parent, often the father, apologising for wasting our time. Usually the mother's observations were more reliable.

Left untreated, appendicitis can be extremely dangerous, but operating also carries risk and you don't want to take a patient into surgery, then discover a perfectly healthy appendix. It was Christmas Day. I was about to finish my shift but I decided to stay on until the tests came back. They showed an extremely high white blood count, so I arranged for the child to be admitted for surgery.

Normally, once a patient is admitted, you have to move on. There's enough to do without thinking about cases that are no longer your responsibility. But my shift was over and I was anxious to hear the outcome.

The appendix had ruptured. Left any longer, septicaemia would have taken hold. There was no doubt that we had saved her life.

It felt like the best possible gift.

Dawn was breaking as I left the hospital. The father of the child was outside smoking.

'Nice one, doctor,' he said, as I walked past.

Christmas lights still twinkled on the lamp posts, but the City streets were deserted. Catching my reflection in a shop window, I saw that I was still wearing antlers.

Chapter Thirty-Seven

On landing in Geneva, I was surprised to receive a text from Charlotte saying she'd pick me up outside the airport. Even more so when a Mercedes pulled up with three sets of skis on a roof rack and the girls in the back seat.

Robert had been called away on business. As a last-minute Christmas treat, Charlotte had booked a chalet in the French Alps.

'You know my views about skiing,' I said, as I got in the front seat and fastened my seat belt.

I felt I should at least have been consulted, but there wasn't much I could do other than insisting on getting out of an accelerating car.

'You don't have to ski,' said Charlotte. 'You can do what you want in the day and we can all eat together. It's got a big kitchen.'

'So I'm to be the chalet boy, am I?'

In the back of the car, Bella giggled.

'I thought you liked cooking,' Charlotte said. 'We've been rather depending on it, haven't we, girls?'

I'd forgotten how pretty Alpine villages are in the snow. After Ross's death, I had always avoided this type of landscape, but having just spent twenty hours in a windowless emergency department, the clear, chill air was as refreshing as an ice cold beer.

The apartment had three large bedrooms.

'The girls can share,' Charlotte said, opening each door in turn. 'Unless you want to bunk up with me,' she added, with a little laugh, her eyes flicking up and down my body so quickly I wondered if I'd imagined it.

We ordered in pizzas.

There were three sofas in the vast open plan living space. The girls took one each; Charlotte stretched herself out like a cat along the other. I sat on a long-haired white rug, with the pizza boxes open on the large coffee table between us.

It was a nice feeling being together again, with nothing to do except concentrate on not dripping tomato sauce onto the soft furnishings.

I gave the girls bracelets I had bought for them from a shop in Islington that made jewellery from recycled materials. I seemed to have made good choices.

'No books?' said Bella.

'I wasn't sure what you would be reading now.'

'Tess usually knows.'

'Erm. Tess and I are not together any more.'

Charlotte's eyebrows shot up. Bella burst into tears.

'Don't be so melodramatic!' Flora scolded her. 'It was never going to last.'

'Why do you say that, Flora?' I asked.

She thought about it for a moment.

'You weren't really suitable for each other.'

I wanted to say, of course we were, but the evidence seemed to suggest that she was right.

'God, you're insufferable sometimes, Flora,' Charlotte said.

When the girls decided to turn in, she suggested we open

the other bottle of wine. I declined, not sure it would be a good idea for us to get drunk together, although I'd already had enough not to be able to figure out quite why that was.

In the morning, the three of them left the apartment before I got up. I took a long hot shower to try to wash away the slight muzziness of the booze. Outside, the snow sparkled in the bright sunshine. From the balcony, I could see tiny figures zigzagging down pristine white slopes high above the village. The pull was as strong as that of the sea on a hot day. I went into a shop to buy a pair of sunglasses and found myself enquiring about equipment hire.

That evening, I served up schnitzel with fried potatoes and salad, with grilled portobello mushrooms for Bella.

The three of them were comparing notes on how many times they'd been up and down.

'I'm thinking of joining you tomorrow,' I said.

'Hooray,' Charlotte breathed, making me feel guilty I'd made it such an issue all these years.

The girls said goodnight as soon as they'd finished eating and retreated to their bedroom.

'The mountain air must be making them tired,' I said.

'They've gone to look at their phones,' Charlotte said. 'They're banned at the dinner table.'

Which explained why our evening meals this time had felt quite so companionable. Privately I'd always thought I was the better parent, but now I wondered whether Charlotte's more structured approach had its advantages.

Back in the day, I had been a pretty good skier and I was thrilled to discover that the basic skills didn't go away, which was lucky since I'd been put in Flora's class and I could see that my presence embarrassed her enough without the humiliation of incompetence.

As we queued for the lift, she stood with her friends ignoring me. I managed to stop myself telling her please to be careful not to get separated from the gang, nor to attempt unmarked pistes, but my heart was beating hard as I watched them take off down the slope.

What I'd forgotten was the adrenaline of high velocity, the concentration it demanded, leaving no space in my mind for worry.

When I finally took off my skis, I could almost hear Ross say, *What a total moron you are to miss out on twenty years of this!*

At the bottom of the slope, I noticed the ski instructor was talking to Flora and when she joined me for the walk back to our apartment, her face was flushed. I guessed it wasn't entirely due to the cold air.

'Could I go out tonight?' she asked.

'With Serge?'

'There'll be a whole gang of us.'

'Fine by me,' I said.

'Certainly not' said Charlotte back at the chalet.

'But Daddy said I could.'

'Honestly, are there no limits to what you'd do to get them to adore you?' Charlotte hissed as she passed me in the kitchen on her way to the fridge.

I couldn't think what else I'd done that would fall into that category, except perhaps for turning a blind eye to sugary treats.

'Flora's very sensible. I'm happy for her to go,' I said, digging in my heels.

'He's a fucking ski instructor!'

Was Charlotte a bit jealous, I wondered? Was she the one the ski instructors normally came on to?

'Why don't I go with her?' I suggested.

A look of utter horror flashed across Flora's face.

'Don't worry, I'll wait in the bar over the road,' I said. 'So if you feel uncomfortable you can come out and I'll be there to walk you home.'

'Oh Daddy, would you do that for me?'

'Of course I would,' I said, giving Charlotte a triumphant look.

Charlotte shrugged, poured herself a glass of wine and re-treated with it to her room.

I'd never seen Flora dressed up to go out before. She was wearing a simple white polo neck over her usual skinny black jeans but, with make-up on, she was very striking. Watching her go into the hotel foyer, and be greeted by a crowd of party-goers, felt like witnessing her rite of passage into adulthood.

I bought a beer and sat in a booth by the window in the bar opposite, wishing I had brought a book so it looked like I was doing something more salubrious than watching young people stream into the club but, in less than five minutes, Flora was out and waving urgently across the road at me.

'Just walk,' she said, marching ahead.

'What happened?' I had to run to keep up with her.

'You can't go in unless you're eighteen!'

'Did you tell Serge you were eighteen?'

'Of course not!' she screamed. 'I didn't even know you had to be eighteen! So I seemed like even more of a child than I am!'

I assumed that all teenagers carried fake IDs, but perhaps that came later. Most fourteen-year-olds wouldn't pass for eighteen like Flora. I found her naivete rather refreshing, but I knew it would be the worst possible thing I could say.

When we got back, she marched straight to her room, slam-ming the door behind her.

'What's going on?' Charlotte appeared, wearing a white

towelling dressing gown, her hair piled up loosely on her head, her face bare of make-up. She'd just had a bath. A few droplets of water were clinging to her smooth bare legs.

She found the incident hilarious.

'Serves you right for trying to play the hero,' she said, flopping down on one of the sofas. 'Oh do get over it, Gus, she's like this all the time. She's a teenager. Weren't you annoyed with your parents at her age?'

'Not to their faces.'

'And that's better is it?'

'No, you're right,' I conceded. 'Better not to bottle up resentment.'

Charlotte gave me a little smile

'We didn't do so badly, did we?' she said, waving in the direction of the girls' bedroom.

'They're both strong characters . . . Which is a good thing,' I added hurriedly.

'I know it's been hard for you, Gus.'

It was the first time she'd said anything that sounded remotely like an apology for taking the children with her. But it was so brief, I wondered if I'd misheard.

'Will you have a glass of wine? I bought a lovely Sancerre.'

'OK,' I said, sprawling on the opposite sofa.

She poured a large glass and put it on the table between us, the edge of her dressing gown brushing my face, the exotic sandalwood scent of the bath oil she used so familiar I found it slightly confusing.

'Where is Robert at the moment?'

Charlotte looked sharply at me.

'If you must know, he's at the chalet with his mistress.'

A mean pulse of schadenfreude coursed through my veins.

'And if you must know, we're getting a divorce.'

It explained why there had been no tart remark about my break-up with Tess.

'I mustn't know,' I heard myself saying, then realised that sounded odd. What was the negative of 'If you must know'?

'You don't have to tell me,' I said, but that wasn't quite right either, because it sounded like I wanted to hear, when in fact I now regretted asking. I put down my empty glass and held my hand over it when she offered me more.

'I hadn't actually seen that Robert needs a wife and a mistress like he needs two cars,' Charlotte said, with a heavy sigh. She put her feet up on the sofa, the robe falling open and baring one leg from thigh to painted toenail. 'A little electric for running around the city and a bloody great Beemer for eating up the autostrada.'

'Which are you?'

'What?' Charlotte asked.

'The Nissan Leaf or the BMW?'

'Oh, for god's sake, Gus!'

There was a long silence.

'Shall we have a ciggie?' she asked, sitting up excitedly.

I pointed at the rules of the house on the wall by the door, the first of which was No Smoking.

'Look at your face!' she laughed. 'Promise I won't tell!'

I followed her out onto the balcony. The sky was clear and star speckled, the chalet rooftops and church spire frosted like decorations on a Christmas cake.

Charlotte offered me a cigarette. I waved it away even though I was tempted. She lit it, took a drag, then offered it like a joint. The desire to smoke had never left me. I took it, tasted the sweetness of her lipstick on the filter, inhaled deeply before blowing a cloud into the frozen air, then handed it back, feeling the sinful hit as giddily as I had sharing my first ever Marlboro with Marcus behind the school cricket pavilion.

300

'Women's capacity to fool themselves is quite incredible,' Charlotte was saying, looking out over the village, not at me. She took another drag, exhaling a thin, controlled stream of smoke. 'You meet a man who is quite open about the fact that his first marriage broke up because he had affairs, but you still think you're special enough to buck the trend.'

I felt a tiny stab of anguish for her.

'But you are!' I said. 'I mean, you were.'

'Well thanks a lot!' she said.

'I meant that you're just as stunning as you always were.'

Too far. Shut up. You're drunk. Don't say anything else.

She turned her head towards me, her gimlet stare softening. The impression she gave to the world was steely but, very occasionally, she revealed exquisite softness and vulnerability. It had always been the most intoxicating combination.

I don't even know which one of us made the first move but her lips were on mine and her body was cleaving to me, sinuously firm beneath the soft robe.

Tess

Chapter Thirty-Eight

There are certain places in the world where it's said that everyone you've ever known will pass by if you sit there long enough. One is St Mark's Square in Venice, the wobbly bridge over the Thames is another, I think there's somewhere in the Lake District. For me, that place seemed to be the supermarket tills at Christmas.

The shop was heaving with people filling their trolleys with things they'd never eat at any other time of year. Why is stilton suddenly a treat? Same goes for port. It's not even expensive but nobody chooses to drink it for three hundred and sixty-four days of the year. The queues were so long, I couldn't allow a single checkout to close when staff went on their break, so I took over myself, amazed at the number of Biscuits for Cheese I was bleeping through, wondering how many tons would be thrown out in twelve months' time because they'd passed their sell-by date, only to be replaced with new boxes that nobody was going to eat.

All around me, I could hear cashiers asking, 'Are you ready for Christmas?'

What did that even mean when, in a few days' time, the same people would ask the question *How was your Christmas?*, and the same customers would reply *Good thanks. Quiet. That's what you want, isn't it?*

If a quiet Christmas was what you wanted, why were trolleys piled high with boxes of mini beef wellingtons, goat's cheese tartlettes, smoked salmon parcels on four-for-three with selections of vol-au-vents which, in my experience of nibbles at Anne's, looked tasty then seared the roof of your mouth off with a molten filling.

Our customers were more champagne truffles than the drum of Quality Street that had represented the pinnacle of Christmas luxury in our family, but I wondered if these cocoa-dusted treats tasted as exceptionally delicious as the purple one with the hazelnut in caramel, if you were lucky enough to get first pick.

One of the few advantages of breaking up with Gus was the absence of rich food. No buttery risotto for us any more, no creamy burrata. I had lost my appetite for all that. For everything really. Some evenings I'd realise I hadn't eaten a thing all day, which was a mistake because any food gives you indigestion on an empty stomach, even dippy egg on toast.

Serrano ham, Manchego cheese, salted almonds and two bottles of Rioja. There was something familiar about the items coming down the conveyor even before I heard him.

'Tess?'

There had been a time when I found that voice a major turn-on. Low and melodic, with a hint of Welshness, a bit like Michael Sheen's.

It was six years since I'd last seen Leo. His salt and pepper hair was now just salt, still tied back in a ponytail. I couldn't remember ever seeing it loose. But then I'd never watched him come out of a shower, or slept a whole night with him, or anything that normal couples do. Presumably he must take the band off to wash it? Not that often, by the look of it.

'Are you still here?' he said, as if I'd been sitting at the till waiting for him ever since we last saw each other.

'No,' I said. 'Well, yes, obviously I am here, but I haven't been all this time . . .'

His enquiring look still had the power to fluster me.

What was he doing back in Kent anyway? Had Spain not worked out? Had his wife left him? Was there someone else? I had first tasted Serrano ham and drunk Rioja at his fisherman's hut. Was another seduction in the offing? Not at the hut, obviously, because someone from JP Morgan now owned that. Maybe Leo had got himself a garden shed on an allotment?

I tried to think of all the clever things I'd planned to say to him if I ever saw him again, but couldn't remember any of them.

'Are you still writing, Tess?' I'm starting the classes back up in January.'

'No,' I said, so quickly I hoped he wouldn't guess it was a barefaced lie.

I'd always found it easier to write when there was nothing much going on in my life. Some people say writing is therapy. For the hours I sat at my laptop, while Hope watched telly, it certainly took my mind off my sadness. Sometimes it almost felt as if the romance that had gone from my life was miraculously reappearing on the page.

Not that my novel was autobiographical. Novelists always say that, don't they? Not that it was actually a novel either, but I had now written 21,321 consecutive words.

I wasn't going to share any of this with Leo for fear of jinxing it.

'Are you writing?' I politely returned his question.

'When you're a writer, you never stop.'

'You just stop getting published,' I said.

307

There was a slight tightening of his smile. 'Ultimately, publication's not what it's about, Tess . . .'

Pull the other one. 'Cash or card?'

He handed me his debit card.

'It's nice to see you, Tess,' he said, leaning towards me, his voice lowering to a whisper. 'I was thinking about you only the other day.'

'That's funny because I was talking to someone about you the other day,' I heard myself saying, which was another lie, in timescale terms.

'Really?'

He was so vain, it made it easier to deliver my punchline.

'He said you were a dreadful old roué.'

Funny thing was that I derived only fleeting pleasure from his mortification. In fact, it felt more like a victory for him because he'd made me vindictive and that wasn't really who I was. As soon as he'd got over the sting, he'd console himself with the thought that I was just a woman scorned.

My only true revenge would be to write something that was published, I thought, as I watched him walking off with his two bottles of Rioja clinking in his hessian Bag For Life.

'What do I have to do to get a bit of service?'

I looked up to see Doll smiling at me.

'Bloody hell, it's the ghosts of Christmas Past today,' I said.

'What's a roué?'

'You heard?'

'You were so focused on the tosser with the ponytail, you didn't notice me behind!'

'It means a debauched man, especially an elderly one.'

Then we were both laughing and, as I bleeped her enormous trolley load of shopping over the scanner it felt like we'd gone

308

straight back to how we'd always been together, as if I'd last seen her hours rather than years ago.

'Got a lunch break?' she asked, as I eventually pulled a metre-long receipt from the till.

I looked at the queue behind her.

'Not now. Day off tomorrow though.'

The staff at the country hotel she drove me to all knew Doll. The dining room glittered with tasteful Christmas decorations in white and silver, like an enchanted forest.

'Are you feeling Christmassy yet?' Doll asked.

'What does that even mean?'

'Oh dear,' said Doll. 'Like that, is it?'

'You'd feel the same if your life was an endless conveyor belt of gift wrap on three-for-two and luxury puddings.'

'Which brings me nicely to my first question,' said Doll. 'What the hell are you doing back on the tills?'

So I told her and, for once, she didn't butt in with her opinions. When I had finished there were tears rolling down my face. She waved away the waiter who'd come to take our order, and handed me a tissue.

'I'm sorry, Tess.'

'You were right all along. It was never going to work with Gus.'

'He was a lot better than your other choices...'

'Don't,' I said, thinking of Leo shuffling away. I'd had a lucky escape there. Not that it was really an escape, seeing as he was the one who'd originally dumped me.

'I always thought Leo was like that horrid old professor bloke in *Little Women*,' said Doll.

As far as I knew, *Little Women* was the only novel Doll had read in her life and only because I made her.

'Gus was more like nice Laurie. The one you should be with . . .'

'I thought you didn't like him.'

'I think I might have been jealous. My life was so dull. Yours was so bloody romantic all of a sudden . . .'

Reflection wasn't usually Doll's thing. It sounded almost like an apology.

'All those times you almost met and didn't! It was like you were meant to be . . .'

I sighed.

'Sometimes I wonder whether it was actually our destiny *not* to meet. Maybe it was our meeting that was the blip, not all the other blips. I mean, it makes just as much sense.'

Perhaps the reason our paths had kept missing each other during all those years between our meetings in Florence wasn't chance or bad timing, but our different class backgrounds, his marriage and children, my obligation to Hope, all things that were fundamental to us not being together now.

'He's got a point about Hope, though, hasn't he?' said Doll.

'She's getting on well at work.'

'Yes, but what about you?'

Hope and Doll had never liked each other.

'Isn't any relationship really about negotiation?' said Doll. 'What are you prepared to put up with, what *should* you put up with? In my case very little . . .'

'How's Dave?' I asked, glad for the chance to change the subject.

'He's good. Kids are growing up fast. You must come and see them. Elsie thinks you're far away. I won't tell her you've been living round the corner . . . honestly Tess . . . I can't believe you never called . . .'

'Sorry.'

Now I was with her, I couldn't believe that I hadn't either.

Why did I always have to be so final and absolute about everything?

'I've sold the flat on Portobello,' Doll was saying. 'I was trying to open up in my first European outlet in Marbella, but everything went a bit tits up with Brexit...'

'And Ash?'

One of us had to mention it.

'Had to get rid of him. Turned out he was fucking half my staff. Very unprofessional,' Doll said, looking in every direction but mine. 'He's setting up a chain of barbers' shops. All wet shaves, retro leather chairs and *something for the weekend, sir*? Your idea really. I told him I'd sue him if he uses The Man Cave as a name...'

I knew from the way she was talking nineteen to the dozen and not looking at me, she'd been hurt and embarrassed. I felt sorry for her.

'You're the only person who knows about it,' she said, now holding my eyes.

'About what?' I said, picking up the menu.

The hotel's version of Christmas dinner involved a three bird roast with black pudding bonbons, a madeira damson sauce and duck jus. I opted instead for the fillet of sea bass with steamed vegetables.

'Very Victoria Beckham,' said Doll. 'Are you doing low carb?'

'No, just not that hungry.'

'Whatever you're doing, it's working. Look at you, like a model. You've gone all pale and interesting...'

As she said the words, I saw worry fly across her face.

'You are OK, aren't you?' she asked.

'As far as I know. At my next follow-up, if everything's clear, I'll be declared cancer free.' I crossed my fingers under the napkin on my lap. I was pretty sure she would be doing the same on her side of the table.

Our plates were delivered under silver domes, which were whipped off simultaneously by two waiters. We caught each other's eye but managed to hold in our laughter until they'd gone.

'Have you got plans for Christmas?' Doll asked.

I knew that if I hadn't, she would invite me to hers, maybe even extend the invitation to Hope, because it was Christmas.

'We're going to Australia,' I said. 'Brendan and Tracy are paying for the whole family fly out. It's their twenty-fifth wedding anniversary. He's done really well for himself . . .'

'Brendan?' said Doll.

'I know.'

The great thing about someone who's known you all your life is there's so much you understand without needing to go into the details.

'I'm not really relishing spending thirty-six hours on a plane with Hope. That's even if we can get her to the airport. Nor three weeks with Dad for that matter. God knows how he's going to react to meeting Shaun. But it's not my worry. It's summer there. I shall lie under a parasol and read. Maybe think about what to do with the rest of my life . . .'

My eyes were suddenly brimming with tears again.

Doll threw her napkin onto her plate, the damson sauce seeping into the fabric like blood.

'Nobody said living happily ever after was easy,' she said.

Then, after thinking about it for a moment, 'Actually, they did, didn't they? The whole point of fairy tales was that happily ever after was supposed to solve all the problems!'

Then we were both laughing.

'Is there anything I can do?' Doll asked. 'Seeing as I am your fairy godmother?'

'I don't suppose you could wave your wand and take me back to before Gus and I said unforgiveable things to each other?'

'Why don't you just pick up the phone? Someone's got to go first.'

I wasn't sure that's what a real fairy godmother would say.

And I'd already thought about that option about a million times. We'd probably end up trying again and it would be wonderful for a few weeks but, ultimately, what was the point when I could never give him what he wanted?

Chapter Thirty-Nine

We flew out on Christmas Day because flights were so much cheaper. Brendan had done well for himself, but he wasn't going to shell out thousands of pounds extra for the sake of a day or two. They gave us Christmas dinner on the plane. For me, an airline portion was just about the right amount, although I could see Hope was disappointed, so I handed over my little sausages and roasties and ended up enjoying my two biscuits for cheese with an individually wrapped piece of cheddar.

It was surprisingly comforting to enter the warm embrace of my extended family. Brendan's expertise as a plasterer had led him into the building trade like my father, but he'd gone on into property development. He'd bought and sold homes to fit his growing family, so now he was the proud owner of an eight-bedroom, eight-bathroom house set in several acres, with an annex for his daughter Lizzy and her children, a pool and several guest bungalows, one of which I was staying in, too far away from Hope's bedroom to even hear the television.

'Did you ever in your wildest dreams think Brendan would be the one of us who'd become a millionaire?' I asked Kevin, who'd flown over with his husband Shaun from New York.

'Obviously not.'

I'd meant it as a rhetorical question really, but I saw that

Kevin had taken it personally, because he'd been the most likely candidate before.

The on-stage career of a ballet dancer is very short, and he had never reached the status of principal, so I think he always felt he'd underachieved, even though he was now having some success as a choreographer.

I thought his greatest achievement was to marry Shaun, who was handsome, kind, interesting and always smelled good. I was a little bit in love with him myself.

We were sitting at the long table under the pergola by the pool, at the New Year's Eve barbecue.

When I'd last seen Brendan, at our mother's funeral almost twenty-one years before, he and Tracy had only two children, Lizzy and Jessica. Now they had five and Lizzy had two children of her own, Little Maria, who was three, and Little Jimmy, who was just two, named for great-grandparents they had never met.

I watched Brendan say grace, pulling the teenagers up on their manners, telling Hope not to start before everyone else. My brother was a big man and, in this house, he was king. My father looked rather frail and old beside him. It's weird how things are passed down the generations, not just looks, but little sayings that Brendan had picked up from our parents, and his children had picked up from him. You can feel kinship with people you've never met just because of a shared family language.

After an initially awkward introduction, my father was getting on with Shaun like a house on fire, which made me feel sad because Shaun had never been able to meet my mum and I knew she would have adored him.

I hadn't seen my sister-in-law Tracy since she was the teenager with peroxide hair who had, in my mother's words, 'got herself pregnant'. She was the only person I'd ever witnessed

Mum being mean to, because she thought she was flighty and had led Brendan astray. Now Tracy was a matriarch presiding over a large family, and she also managed a dress shop in the Melbourne suburb where they lived.

Everyone in the family was expected to pull their weight and Tracy didn't tolerate of any signs of laziness in Hope.

'If you're staying in my house, Hope, you abide by my rules. And I don't care if they are your Christmas chocolates, in my house you share and the limit is one per person per day.'

I was half expecting her to add an extra column to the family calendar pinned up in the kitchen with Hope's timetable and duties written on it.

It occurred to me that Brendan was the only child who'd done the whole family thing that Mum had wanted for all of us. He wasn't the cleverest or the best looking, and Kev had teased him relentlessly, but he'd grown up to be a successful man, a good father and now grandfather. Everyone in this household seemed well adjusted and happy. I wondered if Brendan and Tracy had managed that because they were the ones who'd got away from our intimidating dad, and the self-sacrifice Mum had left as her legacy.

Or was it just that I had made all the wrong choices in life? I was the only one at the grown-ups' end of the table not in a couple. Perhaps I should have settled with Dave, back in the day when he'd asked me to marry him, and built something that lived and thrived like the people I saw in front of me? I'd claimed to be frightened of having kids, in case of leaving them, as Mum had left Hope. But if Dave and I had done it then they'd be almost grown up by now. The truth was I hadn't wanted kids with him. So I'd put all my nurturing into Hope, all my imagination into dreaming there was something more out there for me, and only now discovered – too late – the profound joy of creating a happy family.

Had the real reason for my jealousy of Charlotte not been her beauty and success, but the fact that she would always be the mother of Gus's children, which was a more fundamental bond than any I could share with him?

At the other end of the table, I was surprised to see how easily Hope was getting on with Lizzy, who ran the house while Tracy was at work, and Jessy, who was training to be a beautician. Although they were technically Hope's nieces, they weren't very different in age and had no preconceptions about her. They expected Hope to behave like them and weren't afraid to call out her weirder dress decisions, or tell her to shower and pick up the towel after her. Hope had even let Jessy practise make-up on her this evening, just as I remembered Doll doing to me when she was training. Hope's flawless skin didn't need foundation, but she looked pretty with her eyebrows plucked and a bit of lipstick.

All Mum and I had ever wanted was for Hope to live a happy, independent life, but maybe Dad had been right all along. Maybe I'd worried about her too much and held her back?

I suddenly felt nauseous.

'Are you OK, Tess?' Shaun asked.

He'd always been able to tune into how I was feeling.

I found myself explaining how it had all gone wrong with Gus.

I think I was expecting him to agree that it sounded like an impossible situation.

Instead he just said, 'It's a shame you couldn't work something out.'

Which sent me into another paroxysm of doubt.

Was I the inflexible one?

Even Doll had seen it from Gus's perspective.

'Why is everyone on Gus's side?' I asked Shaun.

'Is it helpful to see it in terms of sides? You made a decision that it couldn't work.'

'You're always so reasonable. I don't know how you've put up with Kevin for all these years!' I said, trying to lighten the conversation.

Shaun said nothing.

Perhaps he was thinking that he didn't know how Gus had put up with me?

I looked at my watch. Nine o'clock here meant it would be midday in the UK. I wondered if Gus had chosen to work Christmas Day or New Year's Eve. If the latter, he might just be getting up and having a Full English to see him through the long night ahead.

It had felt odd not wishing him Happy Christmas. Not like me at all. I'd had the excuse of being on the plane. I'd tried to compose a message, but I didn't know what to say. It was like being right back at the beginning, not knowing whether to send him a text in Tuscany and what to write if I did.

It was New Year, the time for resolutions.

May I be excused?' I said, using the formula that Brendan had instilled in his children, that hadn't crossed my lips since childhood Sunday lunches in Margate.

'Of course,' Tracy said.

I saw her and Brendan exchange the briefest of glances and knew they had been talking about me.

I ran to my bungalow, my heart beating fast as I tapped Gus's contact details and waited for the connection. Then it was ringing and I suddenly wished I'd prepared something to say.

'Hello?'

'Hello?' A familiarly languid voice.

'Hello?' I said again, confused. 'Is that Gus's phone?'

'I'll just put him on.'

His face must have been close to the phone, close to her face, because I could hear him whispering.

'Fuck! Fuck's sake, Charlotte, give me the fucking phone!'

And Charlotte laughing, holding it out of his reach, I imagined.

Then his voice, ludicrously bright.

'Tess? How are you?'

'Are you actually in bed with her, Gus?' I asked.

There was enough of a hesitation to know that he was.

'Do not lie to me Gus. Are you sleeping with Charlotte?'

'It's not . . .'

'Goodbye Gus.'

I must have gone back to the party. I must have knocked back several glasses of wine in quick succession or eaten a dodgy burger because the next thing I can remember is being copiously sick in my ensuite with Shaun banging on the door.

'Tess? Are you all right in there?'

Brendan and Tracy were all for taking me to a doctor, but I knew no doctor could prescribe a remedy for existential despair.

I spent most of the next few days in bed. I couldn't seem to keep my eyes open. Everyone said it must be jetlag, but I knew that didn't last this long. Each time I woke, I had a split second of acute anxiety trying to figure out where I was and what I was supposed to be doing, then relaxed as I heard the distant sound of the little ones playing, knowing that Hope was safe and occupied, and I didn't have to worry what the day would bring.

Often I'd drift off again, only getting up when Tracy brought me a cup of tea.

'What you need is a break,' she said. 'You're worn out.'

She smiled and sat down on the edge of the bed, like Mum used to do when she read me a story.

'Brendan and I have been discussing this,' she said. 'We'd like Hope to stay with us for a while, if she wants to. We've got enough room here and Jessy and Lizzy can keep an eye on her. They get on really well. She seems to like it here. Maybe she will want to settle permanently with us . . .'

I was crying again. I couldn't work out whether it was with relief or misery.

Tracy put a comforting hand on my back.

'You've done more than your fair share, Tess. It's time to let someone else take some responsibility.'

'Have you asked Hope?' I said, sniffing loudly.

'Of course we haven't. We wanted to check with you first. If you agree, we think the offer should come from us . . .' she paused, holding her hand up. 'Tess, listen!'

Someone in the house had put on a playlist of seasonal music. I could hear the piano intro to 'Fairytale of New York', my dad doing his growly Shane McGowan impression, then the band coming in with the Irish jig and, suddenly, there was Hope's bell-like voice singing Kirsty MacColl's lyrics.

I didn't trust my ears. I had to see this.

As Tracy and I walked across the lawn, Dad and Hope were on the terrace duetting, with the rest of the family swaying to the music or dancing in couples, Shaun in a waltz hold with Anne, Kevin with Little Maria stood on his feet.

When the song finished, Jessy, who'd been videoing it on her phone, said, 'Wow, Hope what an amazing voice you've got!'

And Hope went round asking everyone individually, 'Do you like my singing?'

There was no stopping her after that. It was as if all the songs she'd been bottling up inside came pouring out. *La Traviata*, with no warming up whatsoever, then 'My Heart Will Go On' from *Titanic* and Kylie's 'Spinning Around', with all the dance moves exactly as in the video first shown on *Top of the Pops*, which she probably should have warmed up for, as she got a bit dizzy and had to sit down.

That gave Dad the opportunity to put on The Fureys. He'd been watching Hope's singing with increasing impatience, telling her to give other people a turn, meaning, of course, himself.

His favourite track was a ballad called 'I Will Love You'.

With the first poignant notes of the banjo intro, I was transported back to my mum's birthday every year of my childhood when, in the flickering light of a single candle, Dad would take her hand and sing her this most beautiful Irish love song. And each year, however unreasonable or violent he had been in the days before, I would always believe that he loved her and that everything would be better from now on.

He'd sung it at her wake and he was singing it now with tears in his eyes and his hand on his heart.

Was this his way of telling Mum, and us, that he still loved her? Or did he just like the sound of his own voice? Perhaps it was both those things. Could you be both a brutish bully and a sentimental soul? If you could, why wouldn't you choose to be the good version of yourself all the time?

I noticed that Anne had gone inside. I wondered if it was painful being the second love of his life. It was difficult enough to quell jealous feelings for a living former partner, and probably worse if your rival were an unimpeachable soul who had passed away.

When the track ended, we were all silent for a few moments, then Hope stood up again, and sang 'Crazy'.

Later that evening Hope knocked on my door, which was a first. Normally she just marched in.

'I want to stay in Australia,' she said.

'Why is that?'

'Tracy makes proper gravy. I like being with my family. Jessy is better at doing make-up than you.'

All of which was unquestionably true.

Shaun held me until I'd cried myself out. And when there were suddenly no more tears, he said, 'Are you eating, Tess? You're so scrawny.'

'Not really,' I sniffed. 'Not good at cooking.'

'You can't go on like this.'

'No, I don't think I can.'

'Why don't you come and chill out with us in New York? I think you need some pampering.'

The prospect of spending time with Shaun in New York felt empowering and very tempting.

'There's honestly nothing I would like more,' I told him. 'But I've got to learn to be by myself'

I was going home, but I didn't know where home was any more. It wasn't the flat in Margate I'd rented with Hope. I gave notice to the landlord and worked until the lease was up, doing as much overtime as I could and trying to work out where I would go next.

Siracusa had been the closest I'd ever felt to being who I wanted to be, but when I looked on Airbnb, Patrizia's loft apartment was booked up from Easter. In a way, it was a relief, because I knew it wouldn't be the same without Gus. I probably could have rented a different apartment, but I didn't feel strong enough to start all over again in Italy on my own. I wanted a place where I could go for long walks and think calmly, where I could get back to my writing.

Clearing out the flat, I found myself leafing through the family photo album at all the pictures of our holidays in Ireland.

I remembered my father driving us down to Connemara for the day and my mother saying, 'Look at that beautiful western sky. Doesn't it make you think the world is full of endless possibility?'

Gus

Chapter Forty

Summer 2018

When my daughters came to visit, they loved to watch *First Dates*. I also found a guilty kind of pleasure in the excruciatingly awkward behaviour of couples put together by television producers for maximum effect. Less so when I was on my own first dates with people I'd been matched with by an app.

It seemed to be how everyone met new people now but each time I gave it another go, I found myself wondering why I'd bothered. You could share interests and values with a woman, you could even like her photograph, but if a spark was not there, time passed agonisingly slowly even if you had just met for a coffee.

I tried experimenting with someone who had very different interests, thinking it might be stimulating to expand my horizons. She'd put her loves as animals and the countryside. What she meant by that was horses, in particular dressage.

I learned about vet bills and grooming, how much it cost to keep the horse at livery, the journey there and back each day, and the perils of driving to shows towing a horsebox. Who knew that the accident the Highways Authorities dread most is a loose horse on the motorway? Not me. Turned out I wasn't interested in finding out about new things after all.

'What's his name?' was the only question I could think of asking, when she finally stopped for a bite of flapjack.

'Anton. Short for Anton du Bit, because he's very good at foxtrot!'

I was clearly supposed to laugh.

'Why the long face?' Marcus asked.

I was telling the story as we ate dinner, as we sometimes did when he was staying in town.

I gave him a grim smile.

'Did it go any further?' he asked.

As a happily married man, I think he found his own guilty pleasure in hearing about my dating adventures.

'She was very attractive,' I said. 'Long black hair . . .'

'In a ponytail, presumably?'

'Ha ha. Loose actually, swish swish.' I waved my head from side to side.

'So you made out?'

All the talk about controlling the horse's movement with her inner thigh muscles had a certain effect so, when she said she'd love to see the view from my apartment, I hadn't hesitated to show her. There was a moment when she'd been on top when I'd felt like a poor substitute for Anton. Neither of us had suggested meeting again.

For Marcus's amusement, I did my best impression of a whinny.

'The joys of being a single man,' he said, with deep sarcasm.

'Didn't plan on being a single man,' I said.

'Don't you think it's worth calling Tess?'

'Not after what happened with Charlotte. Even if we could get over everything else, that was a red line.'

'Charlotte is bloody attractive though.'

'I know.'

'Almost worth it?'

'No. Great sex, but . . . well, you know.'

We'd already ventured too far into personal matters that neither of us felt comfortable discussing.

'Another?' Marcus held up the empty bottle of Beaujolais.

'I won't thanks. I've got homework.'

I had decided to train to become a cognitive behavioural therapist. I was fed up with hearing the same stories from patients who ended up in A & E after botched attempts to take their own lives, knowing that if they'd been given a bit of support at the right time, it could have prevented a whole chain of problems. Mental health services were woefully underfunded. Stress affected not just the patient but all their family, friends and colleagues, not to mention the doctors who treated them, and this gave rise to even more mental and physical illness.

It was Dorothy who suggested that I channel my frustration into doing something useful about it. Initially, I'd assumed I'd be the worst person to advise on other people's mental and emotional problems. She thought the exact opposite, reminding me that cognitive behavioural therapy wasn't about advice, it was about enabling a person to think about their behaviours in different ways. I had been through the process myself. That would be useful for my practice.

I started by volunteering one evening a week at a local crisis centre. People suffering from financial and social deprivation were affected disproportionately by mental illness. When you are living in a box on the streets or in damp, defective accommodation, or wondering how you are going to be able to feed your children, it's not really paranoia if you struggle to see how you can go on coping. A lot of my time was taken up trying to help with accessing the relevant social services, which wasn't easy outside normal working hours and made me angry, because it shouldn't be my job. Government after government had talked about the link between social care and the health service. It wasn't just about finding ways to look after our elderly people, the problem pervaded the whole of society, but no one spoke about it. But that wasn't my job either. What I could do was offer my time and I got a buzz from feeling I was at least contributing something.

I'd decided to apply for high-intensity training to become a therapist which, if I was accepted, would involve two days a week back at university and three days in a clinical environment.

I'd never been a diligent student before. Perhaps I hadn't been mature enough to appreciate how satisfying reading books and case studies could be when the goal you had in mind actually felt important. Studying demanded my full concentration. It filled some of the void of Tess's absence. Sometimes I wished there was a way of letting her know what I was doing because I felt that, despite everything, she would be proud of me.

'You could just pick up the phone,' said Nash, every time she called.

'She wouldn't answer.'

Goodbye Gus.

The words had been final. Not even *Happy New Year*. The connection severed.

'Write to her, then.'

'I've tried to compose a hundred emails. I don't know what to say. *I felt so bad about hurting you that I ended up in bed with Charlotte*? Can't see that working, can you?'

'Hmmm. Here's a thought. Couldn't you go down to Kent and casually wander into the shop where she works?'

'Been there, done that.'

I'd spent a weekend with Marcus and Keiko. We played

rounders on the beach. The kids were old enough now to handle the bat themselves, but Milo still remembered the legendary Tess and all the home runs she had scored. Whichever combination we selected, the teams were uneven now.

I lay alone in the attic guest room, listening to the rhythm of waves dragging shingle up and down the beach.

She wasn't in the supermarket and nor was Hope. After walking the aisles several times, I'd finally charmed the woman at the customer service desk into revealing that Tess and her sister had both left, but she couldn't say where they'd gone because of data protection. Adding, as she saw the crestfallen look on my face, that even if there hadn't been the rules, she didn't know.

I'd stood on the Esplanade outside the flat where we'd all lived. There was a child's buggy on the balcony, and the couple who answered the bell were Portuguese and didn't understand what I was asking.

I'd even plucked up the courage to call in at Anne's house. Unfortunately, it was Jim who answered the door.

'She's fucked off and so can you.'

I knew better than to try Doll.

'Sometimes I wonder if our paths keep on crossing now without us knowing, just like they did before,' I told Nash. 'And whether one day, the timing will be right again and we'll bump into each other . . .'

'Oh god, now you've gone all rom com on me,' she said. 'I think you need a holiday.'

So I didn't tell her that whenever I took the Tube, I stood in the last carriage, so that at every stop I could look out at the people getting on and off the train in case Tess was among them. Every escalator I went on, I stared at all the passengers going in the opposite direction instead of standing in a bubble of anonymity like all other Londoners.

Nor did I mention how recently, when I was walking through

Covent Garden, I heard a soprano and found myself pushing through the crowds. But it wasn't Hope.

Or how, on my last free weekend, I had crossed the Millennium Bridge a dozen times, because I'd woken up that morning remembering Tess saying, *'People say that if you stand here long enough you'll see everyone you ever knew. Or is that somewhere in the Lake District?'*

As the fifth anniversary of our meeting approached, I was even considering getting a flight to Florence and standing in the chancel of San Minato al Monte waiting for her to appear. Even if she didn't come, I reasoned, I would get to experience the sunlight as I stepped out on to the terrace outside the church, and the intensity of joy I had felt when I was with her that day.

I missed her dazzling smile that made the world seem full of fascinating possibility. I missed the forcefield of energy around her that lifted my spirits whenever I saw her. I missed her lithe, amazing body and the way she went all shy when I told her how much I adored her.

I thought that the longing would subside with time, but when I closed my eyes at night I could see her animated face across the table in the pizzeria that first evening, saying, *'I guess serendipity is as romantic as destiny because it means there's hope for everyone.'*

Travelling to Florence would be neither destiny nor serendipity.

Our timing had been wrong all our lives. The simple truth was that, meeting in our thirties, we'd gone too far on our separate journeys to have a realistic chance of continuing on together.

So I survived by keeping busy.

Chapter Forty-One

When working nights, I'd always grab the opportunity go outside for a quick run in the fresh air on my breaks, but it was a night of such torrential downpours that London's Victorian drainage system could not cope. The roads around the hospital had become rivers. The news, which we usually had on silent in the waiting area, showed water gushing down the steps of Tube stations.

As I stood under the ambulance entrance, the air was full of rain and the blare of fire-engine sirens. It was three in the morning, and the department was fairly quiet, but this was the lull before the aftermath of the storm hit us. Inevitably, there would be casualties and we would get busier at exactly the time when my concentration started to wane. I knew I had to exercise to stand any chance of being able to cope.

I started by running up and down the staircase beside the lift several times, then, conscious of the echoing clatter of my footsteps, decided instead to take a brisk walk along the corridors of each floor.

Away from the constant bright light of A & E, hospitals can feel like eerie places at night. The lights were dimmed, the silence seemed profound, though if you stopped and listened, you could hear the rumble of a snorer. I encountered no one except a hospital porter wheeling a middle-aged woman I'd admitted earlier back to the surgical admission ward after a scan.

I think she thought I had come to check how she was doing, so I listened to what she'd been told so far, nodding occasionally and opening the door for the porter and, since there was no one manning the desk, helping him wheel the bed to its allocated place at the far end of the dark ward.

I said goodnight, drew the curtain and was about to follow the porter out, when the murmur of female voices behind the curtain around the neighbouring bed stopped me in my tracks.

The accent was similar but it wasn't her, I realised after a few moments. Of course it wasn't.

Without being able to see them, I guessed that the younger one, who sounded so much like Tess, was a nurse administering pain relief to the occupant of the bed, who was old and frail.

'How would you score the pain now? If ten is the worst you've ever had in your life and zero is no pain at all?'

'Not so bad now,' said the woman. 'I'd say about a five. I had three children, you know.'

I often wondered if there were vast differences in the way people experienced pain. Personality played a part. Some patients tended to minimise the numbers because they wanted to appear brave. Others exaggerated if they thought they'd be seen quicker. But who really knew what it felt like? Did scoring pain from one to ten really give a useful indication unless you knew a bit more about who the patients were?

'I'm just going to check your blood pressure. Any of them live in London?'

'All of them . . . I expect my daughter will visit tomorrow. I've got eleven grandsons.'

'Eleven! All boys? Nice deep breaths.'

334

'I've been lucky really, haven't I?' said the old woman.

Her voice sounded hollow, as if she knew she wasn't going to be lucky much longer.

'I'd say,' said the nurse.

'Where's my phone?'

'Right there next to you.'

'That's the oldest, at his wedding last year.'

'Very good-looking!'

'The one next to him is his brother. He's still available! '

They both laughed quietly.

'Do you think you'll be able to sleep now?'

'Yes, I think I'll be all right.'

Realising that the curtain was about to be pulled back and I might have to explain myself, I tiptoed back out to the corridor.

It was one of a hundred little conversations the nurse would have had that day when an old person, or a younger one, needed a bedpan, or a change of dressing, or simply called out in fear. Doctors didn't often witness such encounters on their rounds. Nurses' work was repetitive, tiring and messy, but their ability to build instant relationships allowed patients to feel human in a place where their autonomy had been stripped away. Sometimes doctors even got annoyed with nurses for wasting time chatting. I had been guilty of impatience myself, but it seemed blindingly clear to me now that these little gifts of kindness were as important to the healing process as any medication.

Tess had known that and perhaps that was why, for a split second, I'd thought it was her voice behind the curtain comforting a person in need.

I looked at the watch she had given me and realised I was due back in my department. As I hurried back along the quiet, dimly lit corridors, I found myself thinking that it was really only the little moments of connection we made with another human being that were important in life.

Pleasure was the ephemeral joy of standing arm in arm watching a sunset, the exchange of a guilty smile before the first lick of a gelato, a kiss on the Ponte Vecchio. Pain was a flash of memory: my mother in the rearview mirror, waving in an apron with a Christmas pudding on it; Tess's face crumpling with disbelief the last time I'd seen her.

Tess and I, of all people, should have known it was moments that counted, after our history of always just missing each other. She seemed to grasp that instinctively, but I had tried to insist on a continuity that was never going to be achievable between two people approaching forty with established lives and obligations. I'd always thought that she was the more insecure, when it had been me all along.

The lift dropped silently to the ground floor, then the doors opened to bright lights and frenetic activity.

The rain had finally stopped when I left work in the morning, the school playground I passed, which was usually filled with shrieking children dashing, now a silent lake. Pavements normally crowded with mothers and buggies were deserted for the summer holidays.

I took a shortcut through the scrubby patch of park behind the council estate. Beside a row of rubbish bins, a shaft of sunlight picked out a single pink rose defiantly blooming on a battered bush that stood in a puddle of petals. It was a tiny pocket of beauty that I never would have noticed before knowing Tess.

The sky was still bulging with ominously dark purply grey clouds. But, as I looked up at the City towers, there was a rainbow reflected on the mirrored surfaces.

I suddenly knew that I had to find her, if only to let her

know that I was trying to be a better person because of her. I could picture telling her, her face lighting up with that beautiful guileless smile. I had to have that moment, whatever happened after.

Tess

Chapter Forty-Two

After flying into Dublin, I took a train west to Galway City and rented a tiny flat in the little seaside suburb of Salthill. On my first night, I sat on a bench eating chips out of paper, watching the spectacular sunset, with a busker nearby playing songs my father had sung to us when we were kids.

When I woke up the next morning I'd slept so soundly it took a moment to realise where I was. I could hear seagulls and see sunshine through the loose weave of the cheap curtains.

I walked into town beside the mouth of the river, stopping to look at the picturesque painted cottages on the other side.

A pair of swans glided past.

People always said that swans mated for life. I wondered whether there was any choice involved. To human beings, one swan looked much the same as another, but did they to each other? Were there leagues of swans with different levels of class, beauty and intelligence? Were some swans more fun than others? Was there a *coup de foudre* between two particular swans when they realised they'd found The One?

The sunny breeze whipped through my hair. I found myself smiling. I crossed the bridge, walked up the main street, and bought myself some milk, teabags and a supermarket sandwich.

The busker I'd seen the previous evening was standing

outside. He was playing that song by The Script about a man who waits on the corner of a street hoping that the lover he first met there will pass by again. I sat on a bench eating my sandwich and, when he finished, put a euro in his guitar case. We smiled at each other. He had dark curly hair and blue eyes that danced with mischief. I felt a blush over my cheeks even though I was probably twice his age.

I walked home and opened my laptop at Chapter One.

I deleted the words: *Today is the first day of the rest of your life.*

Then I wrote: *In the kitchen at home, there was a plate that Mum had bought on holiday in Tenerife with the hand-painted motto: 'Today is the first day of the rest of your life.'*

I got up and made myself a cup of tea. Then I went back to the computer and continued writing: *It had never registered with me any more than Dad's trophy for singing, or the New York snow dome my brother sent over one Christmas but, that last day of the holiday in Florence, I couldn't seem to get it out of my head ...*

At the beginning of the course I did at City Lit, the teacher had asked us to visualise the word inspiration, then draw what we saw. I'd sketched faces and objects floating around a brain with hands reaching out trying to grab them.

They probably got you to draw it again at the end to show how much your ideas had changed. I didn't know, because I'd never finished the course.

The more I wrote, the clearer it became that inspiration didn't come from some external force. Instead there seemed to be a narrative-making process inside my brain that had been silently fashioning the story all along. Almost as if my novel had always been there, and writing simply revealed it.

I felt happy each day when I woke up and went straight to

my computer, sitting in my nightie tapping away until I noticed how cold my bare feet were. I'd shower, make myself a cup of tea and start writing again. There would come a point, usually around midday, when I couldn't write any more.

I decided to rent a bike. The Connemara coastline was an intricate pattern of inlets, where the edges of bog and sea were almost indistinguishable. Inland, a ridge of heather-clad mountains towered; westwards, there was only the vastness of the ocean and the sky.

It felt like a magical place, not quite land and not quite sea, a place where I was suspended between my past and my future.

I remembered Mum saying, *'Nothing between here and America now!'*

That wasn't quite correct because, on a clear day, you could see the dark humps of the Aran Islands like a family of whales on the horizon.

Halfway through, it occurred to me that a novel I had conceived as a romance about two people whose paths kept missing each other's was just as much a love letter to my mother. As if I'd found a way of being with her again, even though I'd probably been trying to find a way of being with Gus.

The day I finished my first draft, the weather turned. The mist was so dense outside my window I could see nothing at all. I decided to go for a walk instead of a bike ride.

It was what my Auntie Catriona would have called 'a fine rain', which made it sound like a blessing instead of a cloud. It crossed my mind that I should probably visit her since I was staying in the adjoining county, but we'd hardly been in touch since Mum died. I didn't know what we'd talk about, and there was no way I would tell her about the writing. She'd seen my mother's love of reading as frivolous.

I walked across the bridge into Galway City.

I don't even know why I was drawn to the jewellery shop on the high street because I'm never normally fussed, but it was a special day and I wanted to mark the occasion by buying myself a present to remind me that, however things turned out, I had achieved what I always wanted to do by writing a novel.

In the window, my eyes fell on a tiny silver butterfly charm dangling from a delicate chain. The shop assistant helped me fasten it around my neck. I continued up the street, passing the busker I'd seen so often now he felt like the only person I knew here, even though we'd never spoken.

He was wearing one of those little umbrellas you can attach to your head and was playing a traditional jig on a banjo. I stopped to listen, then put a euro in his open case.

'Any requests?'

'Do you know 'I Will Love You' by The Fureys?' I asked.

'Ahh, The Fureys!' He smiled, I wasn't sure with pleasure or amusement, as he plucked the first evocative notes and I stood listening, touching the little butterfly charm, tears and the fine rain making my face wet.

'Can I buy you a coffee?'

The song had finished but I was still somewhere in the past. 'Why?' I asked.

The busker shrugged and looked at the sky. It was pouring. We were the only people still out on the street.

'I should probably buy you one,' I said quickly, in case I appeared a bit mad.

The café at the top of the street was rammed. I ordered hot drinks, while he bagged a table beside the steamed up window.

'Niall,' he said, offering his hand after I'd put the mug down in front of him. He'd taken his umbrella hat off. He really was good-looking, in a very Celtic kind of a way.

344

He was from Dublin, he told me, but doing a Masters in Gaelic Studies at the university here and busking to make beer money. When he asked what brought me to Galway, I told him about the holidays with my family when I was little, then heard myself saying:

'I've actually written a novel.'

It felt weird telling a stranger, as if saying it made it real.

He smiled. 'I thought you looked like a writer.'

'Go on! I'm not actually a writer.'

It was the first face-to-face conversation I'd had in weeks. It was almost like I'd forgotten how it worked. I tried to explain that nobody had read my book yet, so it might be crap. He said he knew what I meant.

I raised my eyebrows.

'Only because when I write songs I feel nervous about playing them in front of people for the first time.'

'Well, you shouldn't,' I told him. 'Because you've a lovely voice!'

'Thank you,' he said. 'You have a lovely face.'

He was looking across the table at me in a way I wasn't expecting. It hadn't crossed my mind that our encounter was anything more than a chat. He was funny and smart, and he must be at least ten years younger than me.

I looked away, realising we were the last people in the café. The proprietor was leaning on her mop, waiting for us to finish.

Outside, the rain had stopped and the shops had closed. It was getting dark.

'There's a pub just along there, with live music,' Niall said, pointing.

'I'd better be getting back.'

'Why the rush?' His mischievous eyes held mine.

I was flustered, my cheeks suddenly very hot in the cool air.

*

345

I woke up the following morning with one arm asleep from him lying on it and the other cold because he'd taken all the blanket.

I watched him sleeping, feeling guilty without knowing why because we were both grown-ups, weren't we? Though I was probably a bit of a – what was Doll's word for it? – cougar. I was half tempted to take a photo of him with his handsome face and his curly hair splayed out on the pillow and send it to her. But that would probably be against data protection, and the etiquette of casual sex, if there was one.

I could almost hear Doll saying, 'What are you like?'

I got out of bed and put the kettle on, impatient for him to wake up and go now.

He sat up when I brought him a cup of tea, pulling me towards him when I sat down on the bed, kissing me with beery breath, making it quite clear he wanted to do it again, which was flattering, but I had work to get on with.

'Shall I see you tonight?' he asked.

I'd never slept with anyone I wasn't in love with before. It had all felt a bit silly really. A couple of times I'd found myself trying not to laugh at the seriousness of his expression, like when he was putting on a condom and the moment just before he climaxed. But it was nice to be desired.

'Thing is, I'm spoken for really.'

It seemed the easiest way of letting him down. Even though it wasn't really true, in a way it was, because I'd tried to enjoy it by closing my eyes and imagining Gus. Although that didn't even work because Niall was so much hairier. But I couldn't tell him that.

It took me a week to read through my work, cutting bits along the way. When I had a draft I was satisfied with, I had no idea what to do next. I wanted someone whose opinion I trusted to read it, but I couldn't think who. There was no way I was going to get back in touch with Leo. I could send it to the creative writing tutor at City Lit who'd been encouraging, but she might think it was a bit of a cheek after I'd given up on her class. Shaun was someone whose opinion I trusted, but I didn't want Kevin reading bits over his shoulder and making snide remarks. He liked to think of himself as the creative one of the family.

I knew that you were supposed to get a literary agent, but I didn't have the first idea. I googled a few who said to submit three chapters and an outline. I wasn't sure my first three chapters were the best. I tried to write an outline but it was boring just to describe what happened in each chapter. My confidence draining, I wondered if all writers went through these massive ups and downs.

I rode my bike to a little harbour along the coast and took a boat to the largest of the Aran Islands, Inishmore. There were bikes to hire when you arrived. I was stronger from my daily cycling and managed to pedal along the narrow road that ran between fields the size of blankets enclosed in drystone walls, all the way to the Iron Age fort at its tip. Standing alone, on top of the sheer black cliffs with my hair blowing back from my face, I felt that same exhilarating sensation I had in Siracusa, of being a tiny part of the vast span of human history, which made me feel somehow humbled and liberated at the same time.

When I arrived back at my cottage, I opened my laptop to find an email from Sandy, the person who had first given me the impetus for the novel.

'*Nothing between here and America now,*' I thought.

It was almost like I'd been calling across the ocean to her.

The email had her paper about fourth-century female saints attached. Too tired to read a dense academic text, I skipped to the acknowledgements as she instructed.

There were citings and thanks to many other people, and at

the end of the list, *I am indebted to my friend Tess Costello for shining her own particular light on Santa Lucia.*

'Remember to send me your novel when it's finished,' she'd said. *'Santa Lucia is the patron saint of writers.'*

What did I have to lose?

Chapter Forty-Three

I arrived back in London the evening before my tests and stayed at the Premier Inn next to the hospital. The anonymous room was a transitional place between one part of my life and the next, whatever that was going to be.

I knew that if I called her, Doll would come to the appointment with me, but I did not want to give myself the option of collapsing if it wasn't good news, which is easier to do with another person there.

I tried to ration myself checking my inbox. Nothing.

I got my blood tested in the morning, and opened my inbox as soon as I was out of the phlebotomy department.

Nothing.

I sat in the hospital courtyard waiting for the test to be processed.

There's often a good spell of weather at the beginning of September, just after the schools have gone back, when the air is full of sunshine with just a nip of winter in the air. A few yellow roses were clinging to straggly bushes, a single white butterfly landing on each in turn.

I looked up at the sky. The reflection of the sun in the glass towers of the City made it seem twice as dazzling.

I found myself bargaining with god.

'If Sandy likes my novel, I won't care if the cancer's back.'

Then I went back inside to face my future.

I took a deep breath before pushing open the door. It was the doctor I'd seen five years before, but he was now a consultant. There were a couple of strands of grey in his hair, but otherwise he looked much the same.

'How are you?' he asked.

'Aren't you supposed to be telling me that?'

He smiled as if thinking, 'Oh, it's her again'.

He peered intently at his computer, as if to make absolutely sure he was on the correct screen, then said, 'As far as I'm concerned, you're discharged.'

And then he stood up and held out his hand.

'You're sure?' I said, keeping a firm grip until he answered. 'I'm officially cancer free?'

'As sure as we can ever be.'

'I'll take that.'

Which was a bit odd, because it was what celebrity contestants always said on game shows as though it meant something, when really they didn't have a choice.

For once in my life, I didn't have any questions for him.

'Thank you!'

'My pleasure,' he said. 'Congratulations!'

Which was also odd, because it wasn't anything I'd done. In fact, I thought afterwards, I should probably offer my congratulations to the team for getting the treatment right in the first place, but decided that might sound impertinent.

As soon as I stepped out into the hospital courtyard I wished that I'd asked for confirmation in writing, or that Doll had been there as a witness to repeat his words back.

I had absolutely no idea what happened next.

Then I heard my name being called and footsteps approaching.

'Tess . . .'

'What are you doing here?'

'I had to see you.'

'How did you know it was today?'

'I'm a doctor. I phoned the department and asked when your appointment was.'

'So much for medical confidentiality.'

This wasn't like any of the conversations I'd imagined if we were ever to meet again.

'How was it?' he asked quietly, his face hollow with worry.

'I've been discharged!'

His blue and gold eyes went from concern to delight then filled with tears. I found myself putting my arms around him, smelling his lovely fresh scent, feeling his body collapse against mine, forgetting for a moment that we weren't together any more.

'It's all right, it's all right,' I told him as we sat down on one of the wooden benches, his head against my chest, me stroking his hair, which felt like the wrong way round.

Then he sat up straight and took my hand.

'Tess, I had to find a way of telling you face to face that I'm so sorry I fucked up. What I said was so wrong. I love you and I want you to know that. Even if you never want to see me again and I will totally respect that if you don't . . .'

It was as if he thought he only had one chance and every-thing he wanted to say came out at once.

I couldn't process what was happening.

'What about children?' I said.

'I didn't mean it. I've never wanted more children.'

'Why did you say it then?'

'I'm an idiot?'

I couldn't seem to stop the corners of my mouth twisting into a little smile.

Then I remembered I should be feeling much crosser.

351

'What about Charlotte?'

'I'm so sorry about that . . . you and I had broken up . . .' he said. 'It was just sex. But it won't happen again. I hate . . . no, I don't hate her and I can't really be indifferent to her either . . . But I don't love her, Tess. I didn't even know what love was until I met you.'

I wondered if I should tell him about Niall, but decided not to. It didn't mean anything. I hadn't really understood about sex not meaning anything before.

Both of us looked at each other mystified. Could it really be this simple?

'I've missed you so much,' Gus said.

'I've missed you too.'

Walking through the arch onto the busy London street felt as unreal as the first time we'd stepped out of San Miniato al Monte together five years before, keeping a careful space between us, as if aware of a magnetic pull that might make us inseparable were we to move a millimetre closer. Neither of us were quite sure what to do next.

'How shall we celebrate your news?' Gus asked.

'I didn't dare think that far.'

'How about lunch at the Savoy where Monet used to have his breakfast?'

I couldn't believe he'd remembered from all those years ago.

'I expect you'd have to book,' I said.

'Lucky I did, then,' he said. 'Just in case . . .'

I'd forgotten how good he was at surprises.

The first fleeting soft touch of his lips sent currents of electricity zinging through my body. He pulled away, tilting his head, as if to seek permission, and then we were kissing passionately in the middle of the pavement with people walking past us on each side, until a kid on a skateboard whizzed past shouting, 'Get a room!'

352

Our window table had the view that Monet had painted, but it wasn't foggy like when he was there. The Thames was inky; an occasional vapour trail made a white gash across the blue of the sky.

Gus ordered oysters and champagne, but I knew my tummy wouldn't be able to deal with all the bubbles, so I asked for the shepherd's pie and a cup of tea.

Afterwards, we ambled across Waterloo Bridge and along the South Bank talking, listening, sometimes stopping to kiss. We crossed the river on the Millennium Bridge, pausing at its midpoint to look at the view of all the way down to Tower Bridge.

There was a pair of swans on the flat water near the bank.

'They're supposed to mate for life,' I said.

Gus took my hand and squeezed it.

'Do you think swans sometimes find aspects of their partner difficult after the initial honeymoon period and wonder if they were compatible after all?' I asked. 'Do they sometimes hiss unforgivable things at each other in the heat of the moment when they feel cornered or afraid? Or don't they even think about that, because being together is so much nicer than being apart?'

Gus

Chapter Forty-Four

The exact timing of the email from her friend Sandy was very important to Tess. It must have arrived while we were eating lunch at the Savoy, even though she didn't see it until the following morning when she looked at her phone for the first time after our reunion.

'I was on my way to being independent before I moved in, even though I didn't know it at the time,' she said later.

Tess had always been more bothered than I was about the difference in our finances.

'That's because you're the one with the money,' she said whenever the subject arose.

Sandy wrote that she loved Tess's novel and asked if she could share it with a friend who was an editor at a New York publishing house.

Tess was ecstatic at Sandy's reaction, but after a few days doubts began to creep in that maybe the New York editor hated it.

I felt I was constantly holding my breath, so I can't imagine what it must have been like for Tess. Then things suddenly began to move very quickly. The New York editor read it and said she wanted to make an offer. Tess plucked up the courage to ring up a UK agent, who said she would read it overnight and meet her the next day. A deal was struck in America, before an auction between publishing houses in the UK, one of which offered a six-figure sum for a two-book deal.

'But you've only written one book, haven't you?' I said.

'Yes, but they want to know that I won't go off somewhere else if this one is a success. I can't believe I'm saying this!'

'I'm so so proud of you! Not that I had anything to do with it, obviously . . .'

'I think you can be proud of someone even if it's nothing to do with you,' Tess said. 'There should really be a different word for that kind of proud, because it's like you're happy for someone, and it's even better because you know them too. Mum is the only person who could be properly proud, because she taught me to love books, but if she'd still been here, who knows if I'd have written it?'

She was nervous about letting me read the book, saying that it probably wasn't my kind of thing, but when I was finally allowed, I knew that wasn't really the reason.

'It's like meeting you all over again,' I told her. 'I didn't know so many of these things about you.'

'It's not me, it's a fictional character . . .'

'Well, I have to say the guy seems quite a lot like me. Although far more attractive, of course.'

'Do you really think so?' Tess asked.

'Why does that surprise you?'

'You never really know what's going on in someone else's mind.'

She looked out of the window, unable to look at me as she asked, 'Did you like it?'

There was a childlike innocence about the question that made me think of Hope's *Do you like my singing?*

'I loved it!'

'What did you love, though?'

'Well, you bring the characters to life. It's not too sentimental...'

I could see that I was hovering around a B minus for literary criticism. These were generic comments you could make about lots of books. I tried to pinpoint exactly what it was about her writing that I liked, and it came to me that it was exactly what I liked about her.

'I love the way you make ordinary things miraculous.'

The smile.

'Any criticisms?'

'Well, the only thing is...'

Her frown told me my opinion might not be quite as welcome as she'd suggested.

'The only thing is the title.'

'What's wrong with it?'

'*You're The One* just sounds a bit naff to me.'

'What do you think it should be called then?'

'Perhaps *Miss You*?'

Chapter Forty-Five

Charlotte was in the midst of an acrimonious divorce from Robert. Though he had agreed to give her the Geneva house, she seemed determined to push him further.

'I uprooted everything for him, the girls' education, everything,' she said, when we discussed arrangements for Christmas, as if I was a disinterested party who should share her outrage.

'Well, the girls seem pretty well-adjusted,' I said.

'You wouldn't say that if you ever saw Bella these days,' she said, rejecting conciliation for conflict, as she always did and I always forgot she did.

'Bella refuses to get on a plane and bans me from increasing my carbon footprint by flying to see her just for a couple of days,' I protested. 'Which makes it quite difficult for me to get there, as it's really not possible for me to get extended leave around Christmas.'

'I suppose you've got plans with Tess?'

'Yes.'

There was a long silence, as if she was expecting me to apologise, explain or tell her it was none of her business. For once, I didn't oblige.

'Well, for god's sake, don't buy Bella anything unsustainable.

It's like living with the plastic Gestapo here. She's even de-manding vegan shoes!' she said, and cut the call.

Tess and I didn't actually have plans. She had done so much travelling during the year, she claimed she never wanted to board a plane again. We enjoyed discovering new bits of London, like the towpath of Regent's Canal where it emerges from a tunnel in Islington and you find yourself suddenly in a watery, industrial landscape that feels like a different world from the elegant residential streets above.

Tate Modern was only a fifteen minute walk from the apart-ment, so we sometimes went to look at one or two paintings, then sat on the terrace of the Members Room gazing over the Thames.

In Bermondsey, with its wharves and Victorian slum streets now populated by artisan boutiques. Salvatore and Stefania had opened a second branch of their restaurant Piattini.

'You see, I do like restaurant food when it's delicious!' Tess told me.

One of the only drawbacks of living with her was her lack of interest in food. During the months we'd been apart, she seemed to have become even less adventurous, while I had come to depend on Indian and Thai takeaways after long shifts at work.

'Not enjoying spicy food isn't a character flaw, Gus!' she informed me when I complained her diet was too beige, all mashed potato and toasted cheese sandwiches.

It was the only tiny point of contention in a relationship that made me feel as contented as I'd ever been. Spending the long, cold nights in our warm, empty flat, making love whenever we felt like it, was reminiscent of that special time when snow had come to Sicily.

We were happiest when it was just the two of us at home together with nothing to do. Since she'd come back to me, I'd

noticed Tess always wore a necklace with a tiny silver butterfly charm. It glinted like a diamond when it caught the light.
Her natural animated curiosity sometimes reminded me of a
butterfly flitting around a meadow, landing for a second on
one flower before flying off to another source of nectar. The
last thing I wanted to do was trap her, but sometimes it was
wonderful to see her settle so I had a moment to gaze at her
iridescent beauty.

The thought of Tess's next novel frightened her. Maybe if there
hadn't been so much noise around *You're The One* even before
it was published, she would have felt less pressure.

'Of course it's fine to have a break,' her agent had told her.
'But don't leave it too long. It's really important to keep up the
momentum.'

'I feel as if I put the whole of my life into that novel,' Tess
admitted. 'Maybe that's all I'm capable of.'

'I'm sure it's not,' I said, thinking how peculiar it was that
just as she had achieved her ambition, she seemed more insecure than ever.

As soon as Tess's first publishers' advance was in her bank
account, she allowed herself little extravagances. Her first
thought was to transfer enough money to Brendan to buy Hope
the baby grand piano she had always wanted for Christmas. Her
second was to take Doll on a weekend at a spa hotel.

While she was away, I bought an eight-foot Christmas tree
from Columbia Road Market and spent a small fortune in Heals
on lights and glass baubles. I hadn't dressed a tree since the
girls were little. In those days, I'd had to give pride of place to
cardboard and glitter ornaments, still sticky with glue, that they
brought home from nursery school, resisting my slightly OCD
impulse to rearrange their asymmetric placement of trinkets.

Now I decorated the tree with masses of tiny white lights,

perfectly balanced globes of gold, silver and bronze, with no garish swirls of tinsel adorning the lower branches, only glittering threads of silver lametta dangling like fragile icicles from the pine-scented branches.

Tess was the most rewarding person to surprise because she had never developed the filter for enthusiasm that most adults have.

'It's so magical, Gus. I can't wait to show Hope!'

We opened the Christmas Day Skype to Brendan's family with the webcam pointing at the tree.

'Christmas tree, Hope!' Tess called.

Hope suddenly smiled.

'How was your day?' Tess asked, because it was already evening in Australia.

'Instead of turkey and little sausages we had a barbecue with prawns and big sausages because it's summer here.'

'Well, that sounds nice. Say Happy Christmas to Gus!'

Tess turned the screen so my face appeared too.

'Happy Christmas to Gus!' said Hope. 'Shall I sing to you?'

'Christmas wouldn't be Christmas without a song from Hope.'

'Little Donkey, Little Donkey . . .'

I didn't even know that particular carol until Hope came into my life. In prep school we'd sung 'Once in Royal David's City' and 'Oh Come All Ye Faithful'. At boarding school, one of my pathetic attempts at rebellion was not to sing hymns at all. At my parents' house, Christmas had always felt like a joyless ritual that had to be performed.

Now, enveloped in the crystalline purity of Hope's voice, with the twinkling Christmas tree behind us, I looked at Tess's radiant face on the panel of our screen and, for just a moment, didn't recognise the smiling person beside her.

*

I had to work on New Year's Eve. I think both of us were keen not to be reminded of what had happened the year before. When I got back just after eight in the morning, I tried to make as little noise as possible, assuming Tess would be asleep, only to be greeted with a shower of confetti from a party popper, a glass of ice cold champagne, and the smell of frying bacon.

'You have to admit, my bacon sandwiches are better than yours,' Tess said. 'You see, it's all about the quality of the bread.' She mimicked my foodie seriousness. 'For a really good bacon sandwich, what you need is the most pappy, manufactured bread you can find, the sort that flattens to nothing when you press down on the sandwich to cut it in two. It's almost impossible to buy anything other than organic, stone-baked sourdough in London, but fortunately, I managed to source one rare packet of sliced white in the corner shop.'

I couldn't help noticing that she only ate a mouthful herself.

'Champagne always gives me indigestion,' she said.

Unused to a job that kept her at home alone all day, Tess decided to volunteer at the Early Years after-school club in the school I passed every day. It gave structure to her day, and her experience as a classroom assistant when Hope was little was highly valued. Tess had an easy authority with small children, but it was her laughter and engagement that made them respond so delightedly.

One evening, I passed by on my way home and stood on tiptoe peering through the window. She was sitting in a circle with five little ones singing 'The Wheels on the Bus'. In the version my children had learned in the mother-and-baby group where I'd been the only father, I was pretty sure the babies on the bus had screamed and the mummies on the bus had chattered. But in Tess's version, the babies on the bus went 'sleep sleep sleep', and the mummies went 'read, read, read'.

Spying on her there, I found myself gulping back grief for the children we could never have and, when she spotted me watching, her face transfigured through curiosity to understanding, before turning her attention back to one last chorus.

'If you like, we could look into fostering,' she said, breaking the silence that stretched between us as we walked home, confirming she had read my thoughts. 'There are so many children who need a home. Only, we're probably a bit old ... and ...'

I squeezed her hand, not wanting her to complete that sentence.

'I'm completely happy just the two of us,' I said.

Chapter Forty-Six
Spring 2019

It was the year of our fortieth birthdays and I knew Tess was planning something when she nonchalantly asked me to keep the weekend of hers free.

When I brought her a cup of tea in the spare bedroom, which she used as her office, I caught a glimpse of the iconic dome of Santa Maria dei Fiori in Florence on her screen just before she slammed it shut.

'I'm just checking details for the copy-editing,' she said, never able to look me in the eye if she was telling a fib.

She watched me all the way to the door before turning back to her desk.

It was Wednesday evening before the long weekend and Tess still hadn't revealed her secret.

We were watching television together when Charlotte called.

'The school's threatening to expel Bella,' she said.

'What?' I stood up from the sofa, walked into the kitchen area, my back to Tess.

'Did you know she's been skipping Fridays for the climate change protests?'

Bella had mentioned it. In a way I was proud of her being only twelve and so committed to her ideals.

'Please don't tell Mum,' she'd pleaded.

I'd taken the easy option.

Now I could see that was stupid and disloyal of me. Charlotte had every right to be angry.

'I don't suppose you thought about what she would be doing on Fridays instead of attending class?' she was saying.

'I imagined her sitting outside school with a placard.'

'You didn't actually encourage her to spray graffiti over the gates and lie down in front of the head teacher's car, then?'

'No, of course not!'

'She's been suspended. And now she'd gone on hunger strike.'

'I doubt that will last long, given her appetite for pizza.'

'For god's sake, Gus!' Charlotte screamed down the phone. 'The headteacher has called us in for a meeting tomorrow morning.'

'It's not great timing for me,' I said, glancing at Tess, who was frowning in my direction.

'Funnily enough, it doesn't exactly fit into my plans either,' said Charlotte. 'So I'm not going. I am simply not prepared to face any more humiliation. If you want Bella to remain at a school where she is doing well, has friends, and costs a fortune that you don't even contribute towards, I suggest you get the first flight out in the morning.'

'But the school doesn't even know me,' I protested.

She had already put the phone down.

'Go!' Tess said immediately. 'Better to sort it out quickly, otherwise everyone's position will get entrenched.'

'Are you sure?'

'Only thing is, we're meant to be flying somewhere tomorrow.'

'Really?'

'You knew?'

'Well, you did tell me to take the time off.'

'Guess where we're going?' she said, now eager to share the details.

'Paris?' I guessed, not wanting to spoil another reveal.

'Do you want to go to Paris?' she asked, with a worried look.

'Not especially.'

She smiled.

'It's not Paris. It's somewhere very special to us . . .'

I wondered if I should try another city, or just land on the one I was pretty sure it was since my performance didn't seem that convincing.

'It's not Florence, is it?'

'How did you know?' Now she was a little cross.

'Florence will always be our most special place, won't it?'

'This is Florence like you've never seen it,' she said excitedly. 'You know when I was there that first time with Doll? We got a bus from the station up to the campsite and it went this really long route past all these amazing villas. I remember wondering what sort of people lived there. So, here's the thing, one of those villas happens to be a five-star hotel. Which means that we can be those people, for a weekend anyway. It looks so beautiful. Like being in a palace in the country, but there's a bus stop outside so you can just pop to the city centre in five minutes if you want!'

I grinned, not wanting to point out that a five-star hotel probably had its own car service to the *centro storico*.

'Florence is not that far from Geneva, is it?' Tess asked. 'I mean you could meet up with me there when you've sorted Bella out. It wouldn't be like us to arrive in the same place at the same time anyway.'

I was grateful for her making it so easy.

Before we'd got back together I'd thought for a long time about what it would mean, knowing I couldn't will away the parts of her I wasn't so keen on, like her totally selfless devotion to

368

Hope, or her jealousy of Charlotte. I had to commit to the whole Tess package for as long as she would have me.

I think she felt the same. She still found it difficult when I talked to Charlotte, but we'd both made the decision to accept and trust one another.

Curiously, this felt like liberation rather than constraint.

Chapter Forty-Seven

Bella was in the puppy-fat-and-spots phase of adolescence that Flora had never gone through. Her clothes looked a couple of sizes too small, her shirt buttons stretching across her developing chest. The woman she would be remained hidden in the chrysalis of adolescence, but the child she still was couldn't stop herself bounding into my arms.

As we approached the school, I noticed that there were patches of white paint on the walls not quite masking where she'd daubed the Extinction Rebellion graffiti.

'I'm sorry Mummy made you come.'

'No worries.'

'Yes worries! Think of the carbon!' she said, exasperated.

'How are things going, apart from the protests?' I asked, as we sat side by side on hard chairs outside the headteacher's office.

'That's the trouble with your generation! You think climate change is somehow separate from the rest of life.'

'Fair point.'

I wondered how on earth I was going to mediate with the headteacher since my daughter seemed to have perfectly good arguments.

'Mummy's always cross,' Bella said, answering my question. 'Flora's always with her boyfriend.'

'Flora has a boyfriend?'

'None of them care about the planet. They think I'm boring.' She was staring miserably at the floor.

'I don't think you're boring. I'm proud of you, actually.'

'Are you really, Daddy?'

'I really am. But I don't think going on hunger strike is going to do much for the cause.'

'I only said that because I thought they couldn't expel me if I was starving outside the gates.'

Bella's headteacher was an impressive woman about my age who had clearly tackled much more serious issues than a twelve-year-old eco-warrior.

'This school is committed to promoting young people's awareness of the environment. But via the more orthodox route of teaching the scientists of the future. We cannot support students truanting, defacing property, or endangering themselves and other people.'

'Of course not,' I said.

Bella looked aghast that I would simply agree to her expulsion. I imagined this was exactly the response the headteacher was looking for.

'As it's a first offence, Bella, and I know your intentions are admirable, I am prepared to allow you to protest peacefully at the school gate during your Friday lunchbreak, but only, and I must emphasise this, only when I see a marked improvement in your science grades. Does that sound reasonable?'

Bella, wrongfooted by being taken seriously, burst into tears.

'You can join your class now.'

'Can't I spend the day with Daddy as he's come all the way from London?'

'Why don't I pick you up after school?' I offered quickly, not wanting to push our luck.

The headteacher stood up, shook my hand and thanked me for coming. I told her that I would make sure I attended parents' evenings in the future.

Leaving her office after a meeting that had lasted less than ten minutes, I couldn't help feeling that I'd been dragged to Geneva under false pretences. The stress of divorcing Robert was obviously getting to Charlotte. We needed to discuss ways of sharing responsibility for the girls more equally.

I rang Tess, who had landed safely in Florence, and explained the situation. My flight left the following morning. I'd arrive around lunchtime.

'You are going to love it here,' she said. 'It's got the largest chandeliers I have ever seen, and our room has painted ceilings and a huge vase of scented pink lilies. I don't even need to go out because it's honestly like being in a fairy tale right here.'

The house my daughters called home was surrounded by trees on three sides, with the fourth looking out over a pool towards the lake. On the walls of the vast, open plan living area I recognised a couple of large canvasses by Peter Doig, an artist whose work I knew had recently fetched over ten million pounds at auction. I wondered if these formed part of the divorce negotiations.

Blessing, the housekeeper, shared an annex on the property with her husband, who looked after the garden. She took care of every practical need including cooking us a buffet that Charlotte called a kitchen supper. We helped ourselves from platters arrayed along the island that separated the kitchen from a dining area. Charlotte and I sat at each end of a refectory table, with Bella on one side and Flora and her boyfriend François on the other.

I was fascinated to observe the first man who had captured my elder daughter's heart, in whose presence she lost her sang-froid, becoming alternately giggly or worshipful. I'd expected a playboy with a sharp Italian suit and loafers with no socks, so I was surprised and relieved to encounter a bespectacled seventeen-year-old French boy, his forehead still freckled with acne, who clearly fancied himself an intellectual.

François was the lead in the school debating team and had his sights set on Sciences Po and a career in the European Union. His English was not nearly as good as he thought it was so we all spoke French, Charlotte protesting when he used the formal 'vous' form when addressing her, when she had asked him to 'tutoie' her.

'Please, it makes me feel about a hundred!' she said, with a little laugh that trailed away as François shrugged, as if to say that she was so old she might as well be.

When Bella explained what the headteacher had said, François took it upon himself to explain that change would only be effectively achieved through international accords rather than activism. Bella's veganism was naïve, he pronounced, be-cause there was more Brazilian deforestation for soya production than there was for raising cattle.

'Please don't give her any more reasons not to eat protein,' Charlotte said, with a histrionic yawn.

'So you really might as well eat a Big Mac,' Flora taunted.

'Stop it!' Bella cried. 'This is what I was telling you about, Daddy. Flora and François have set up an anti-bullying commit-tee at school, but they're always ganging up on me!'

'Honestly, can't you take a joke?' said Flora.

'Vegans aren't renowned for their sense of humour,' said Charlotte, winking at François who frowned, clearly unused to flirtatious behaviour from a parent.

Bella stood up and threw down her napkin, her eyes burning with righteous indignation.

Suddenly, I was back in my parents' house. Ross was relentlessly kicking me under the table, belittling everything I said, while my mother gazed adoringly at him and my father warned me that I'd have to do better than *Stop it!* if I wanted to survive in the world.

'Actually, I agree with Bella,' I heard myself saying. 'It is bullying.'

Now they all turned to stare at me.

'It's easy to talk the talk. Bella walks the walk. Also, I think it's true to say that most soya production is for consumption by cattle not vegans, so who's the naïve one here?'

I'd read a few climate change articles so Bella and I would have something to talk about. As far as I could tell, what she believed was incontrovertible. Anyone who didn't at least try to adjust their diet was either lazy or in denial.

'I wish you lived here, Daddy,' Bella said sadly.

Flora said nothing.

Her boyfriend, trying to recover his pride, said, 'That is an interesting perspective, sir.'

'Isn't François a charmless bore?' Charlotte said loudly when the boy left, prompting Flora to dash back to the front door to make sure he'd cycled away without hearing, before storming off to her bedroom.

'Better than some jetsetter with a Porsche and a pocketful of cocaine.'

'You think?' Charlotte was only half joking.

'He's not who I imagined as a first love for Flora, but he seems pretty harmless.'

Charlotte lit a cigarette.

'It is my house,' she said in response to my raised eyebrow, then chucked the packet at me.

I hadn't had a cigarette since the last time I'd seen her. I was about to take one, then remembered where that small transgression had led.

'Who was your first love?' Charlotte asked, exhaling a perfectly formed smoke ring.

An image flew through my mind of Tess at eighteen, gazing at the golden mosaic in the apse of San Miniato al Monte, but I hadn't known she was my first love then.

At Flora's age, my only experience of the opposite sex was a row of girls with bright blue eye shadow huddled together on the other side of the hall at our sister school's post-GCSE dance, with Marcus and me wondering how you moved things on after dancing meaningfully to Toto's 'Africa'.

'I'm not sure,' I replied.

'I thought *I* was!' Charlotte said.

I couldn't quite tell if her tone was mocking or offended.

The first time I set eyes on Charlotte she was in a white bikini on a lounger beside the hot tub my father had just installed in our garden. Ross's incredibly sexy girlfriend.

'I lusted after you. But I never loved you and you never loved me.'

'Didn't I?' she asked, slightly wistful.

She'd always had a way of creating an earthquake beneath my feet whenever I thought I was on safe ground. The atmosphere was suddenly alive with questions I certainly wasn't going to ask.

'Do you remember our first time?' she said.

'I do.'

'I don't suppose—'

'No!' I said immediately.

In the silence that followed, I half expected her to accuse me of inferring something that was not in fact on offer, but instead she just sat staring at the floor.

In this vast space, she looked small and fragile.

'It's not that you're not still very attractive,' I said, as clumsy as a teenager.

'Still?' she repeated. 'God! Now I really do feel about a hundred!'

She threw her head back as if to tip tears swiftly back into her eyes.

'Be honest, Charlotte, the only reason you want me now is because you can't have me.'

'Is it?'

I couldn't answer that and wasn't going to make the mistake of trying.

'You once said you'd do anything to be with me.'

That was true. I'd been desperate at the thought of losing my family. But almost ten years had passed and I had met Tess.

'The girls are almost grown up now,' I said.

'The girls! What about me?'

'Charlotte, you left me,' I said, feeling the need for a reality check.

'And now you're getting your revenge?'

'I'm honestly not. I just love someone else.'

The earthquake subsided, and the ground became more stable under my feet.

'I'm sure you'll find someone,' I said.

'Not as nice as you.' She sniffed.

'You don't want nice, though.'

'You're probably right.'

She looked at me directly and smiled. 'You're very welcome to stay the weekend in the guest suite. The girls would love it.'

'Thank you, but I'm supposed to be in Florence. It's Tess's fortieth birthday weekend.'

'Oh, for god's sake, Gus. You should have said! Now you've made me feel even more of a bitch.'

Chapter Forty-Eight

'*La signora* has gone for a walk,' said the receptionist in the opulent hall of the Villa Cora. 'She said you'd know where to find her.'

I wondered at what age a signorina became a signora in Italy, or was he just assuming that we were married?

The Basilica San Miniato was a thirty-minute hike up a road that wound through the hillside forest, occasionally offering glimpses of Florence's iconic dome through soft green pine trees. As I drew nearer to our rendezvous, my heart began beating faster, my insides trembling, like the sensation I always got when called upon to speak publically. I raced up the three steep flights of stone steps that Tess and I walked down together almost six years before, then paused for a moment trying to compose myself.

There was a party of tourists leaving the church, a clutter of noise as their guide corralled them for a photo in front of the green and white marble façade, before leading them back down to their coach. Then, as the sound of their chatter faded, silence.

I pushed the heavy wooden door, the smell of dust and incense evoking a rush of memory as I entered this vast, dark temple of solemnity.

Once again, I was drawn towards the steps up to the raised chancel, to get a closer look at the huge Byzantine mosaic of Christ in the apse.

As I reached the top, the light you paid a euro for came on, and there was my love, her flimsy lemon dress bleached white by the illumination, her smile as spontaneously delighted as it had been the first time I had seen her there when she was eighteen, and again sixteen years later when we had met and fallen in love.

'Marry me!' I said, stretching out my arms.

'I will!' she said, taking both my hands.

And then the light went out.

On the terrace outside, we stood hand in hand, gazing at the glorious panorama of Florence and the bowl of wooded hills surrounding it.

'It's funny,' said Tess. 'When I first stood here I remember thinking it would be the perfect setting for a wedding, which wasn't like me at all because I was never one of those girls who pictured themselves in a long white dress. But just now, that felt like the perfect marriage, being in the sight of god, but without the need for a priest, which is the bit I don't like about religion.'

There was a way she looked as her thoughts spilled out of her mouth. When we were apart, even for the shortest time, I always forgot how her vivacity seemed to project back on to my face, making me smile too.

Back at the hotel, she insisted on a taking me through all the reception rooms and gardens so that she could point out their luxurious features. When we finally opened the door to the bedroom I was so desperate to make love, we toppled fully clothed on to the four-poster bed, enveloped in the heady, heavenly scent of pink lilies.

*

We were the only guests beside the pool that afternoon, as it was still far too cold for any Italian to venture in. A waiter brought me a bottle of fizzy water and Tess a teapot with a small plate of almond biscuits.

Tess poured water into her cup and swore. 'Why don't Italians ever put the bag in the pot?' she said, getting up from her lounger. 'And it's always lukewarm!'

Sometimes you see people differently in unaccustomed surroundings. As I watched Tess marching towards the poolside bar, teapot in hand, as determined as an aristocratic woman from the thirties about the appropriate way to make tea, I noticed how painfully thin she was in her swimsuit. A whisper of unease rippled through me, like the slight breeze across the flat blue surface of the water.

I knew how much she hated going to the doctor, and I couldn't blame her after everything she'd been through, but when we returned to England, I would insist she went back to the GP about her indigestion. Maybe I would even go with her.

Not now, I told myself, swallowing my impulse to say something, as she sauntered back, triumph on her face and a uniformed waiter with a steaming teapot on a tray behind her. I must not spoil this moment.

The car dropped us beside the Ponte Vecchio which was still thronging with people window shopping and snapping selfies with the sunset. Some of the windows of the little jewellery shops gleamed with gold, others sparkled with silver.

'Do you see anything you like?' I asked Tess, pointing at a padded card of diamond rings.

'Really?' she said, her eyes lighting up for a second, before reason took over. 'You probably pay twice as much for stuff here. I mean, look, no prices on anything. That means it's really expensive, Gus.'

'It probably means that they estimate how much they'll charge by the look of you,' I said.

'But we probably look quite rich.'

I was wearing a grey linen suit with a white shirt, she was in a dress that used to fit her perfectly but now made her waiflike, emphasising the length of her thin limbs and the pallor of her skin.

'It would be appropriate to get you something here,' I said.

'Like coming full circle?'

We were only yards away from the spot where we'd first kissed.

'What about that one?' I pointed to a plain gold ring with a solitaire diamond.

'It's the sort of thing you could get in Bond Street or any-where in the world.'

'What about that, then?' I pointed to one with five stones.

'It's lovely,' she said. 'But it doesn't exactly say Italy, does it?'

I lingered, slightly disappointed, as Tess moved on.

'Hey, come and look at this!'

She'd found the only window full of colour, displaying jewel-lery made of Venetian glass and cameos from Naples. She was pointing at a silver ring set with a flat, oval mosaic of a fleur de lys, inlaid with different shades of marble.

'It's like a beautiful Italian floor,' she said.

I doubted anyone else in the history of the world had chosen their engagement ring for that reason.

The shop was so tiny we had to squeeze into it.

'Would the *signora* like to wear it?' the owner asked.

As we walked towards the restaurant, she occasionally rocked her left hand this way and that, then looked up at me with a secretive smile.

*

I should have known that a giant beefsteak, its crust charred, the inside still bloody, was not as much of a treat for Tess as it was for me. Sitting in the formal restaurant with heavy white tablecloths, and a waiter who decided when my glass should be replenished with Chianti, I rather wished that we'd done as she suggested and eaten pizza al fresco in the Piazza Santo Spirito on the less swanky side of the river.

Tess valiantly struggled with a few little pieces of the more well-done edges of the steak and pronounced the rosemary patatini the best potatoes she'd ever tasted, but as I reached for more rare meat from the platter, she suddenly stood up and said, 'I'm so sorry, I don't feel very well.'

'How?'

She swallowed.

'I'm just going to pop to the loo.'

Time ticked past. I put down my knife and fork, my appetite gone. The waiter tried to refill my glass. I waved him away. I was just about to go and find her when she reappeared, looking pale.

'I'm fine,' she said. 'It must have been the coffee. It always makes my indigestion worse, but the aroma of it at breakfast was just so delicious I couldn't resist.'

'Why do you think it was the coffee?'

At least twelve hours had passed since breakfast, so it seemed a very delayed reaction.

Tess lowered her voice, looking around, making sure our conversation wasn't overheard. 'The sick looked like coffee, if you must know.'

'Your vomit looked like coffee grounds?'

'What's the matter?' she asked as I stood up and hailed the waiter for the bill.

'I'm so sorry, Tess. I think we need to get you to hospital.'

*

Vomit like coffee grounds is one the symptoms that ring alarm bells for medics. It indicates digested blood in the stomach, which can have several causes, some of which require urgent attention.

The doctor in the emergency department admitted her overnight for observation, to await the results of blood tests and to have an endoscopy first thing in the morning.

I wanted to stay with her but it was not permitted.

'Please go and enjoy that beautiful room,' Tess said, letting go of my hand and attempting to shoo me away. 'Honestly, the bed's so comfortable, I don't think you could feel a pea under the mattress even if you were a princess!'

She was trying so hard to make it better for me, I felt cross with myself for not being able to put on more of a game face to cheer her through a night that wasn't going to be very comfortable for her at all.

'I'll be back first thing,' I told her.

'Honestly, don't rush. The breakfast at Villa Cora is to die for! Not literally, I hope!'

She was even able to manage a grim joke.

I grasped her hand again, but she pulled hers away, waving and smiling bravely as I left.

When my children were ill or hurting, I remembered wishing that I could take away their pain and suffer it myself. Now, as I walked alone down the spotless hospital corridor, I felt the same peculiar, overwhelming intensity of love for Tess. She was the light of my life, she was in my blood, she was part of me.

Tess

Chapter Forty-Nine
Spring 2020

I can tell what time it is when I wake up from the light coming through the blinds. They're wooden slats that, like the rest of the apartment, look very simple and utilitarian, but cost a fortune. On the whole, I think I prefer curtains for the warmth, but you couldn't put curtains over warehouse windows.

The slivers of dawn are chill and colourless, a different quality of light from the yellow glow of the streetlamps at night. I reckon it's about seven.

Across the room I can just make out the framed sketch of me that Gus made in Siracusa. Sometimes I wonder if I am really the same person who was lucky enough to be drawn with such love.

Our bed is vast and super comfy, and I enjoy the cocoon of our duvet so much, I always wait until I'm absolutely dying for a wee before getting up. But today the doorbell is buzzing so persistently it means there's a delivery, probably for one of the other residents. It's all delivery now.

I wait for the lift to reach the second floor, then open the door a tiny chink with the chain still on. It's a great big box and it's addressed to me.

The delivery guy is standing two metres away. He takes a photo of it.

'Is it your birthday?' he asks.

'I wish,' I say, opening the door a little further, craving conversation, even with a stranger, then stop. Just because he's the first human being I've spoken to in person for a while doesn't mean he needs to know my life story. 'Thank you!'

The box is so big, it's awkward to pick up, but it's light, so I kick it gently along the wooden floorboards.

When I first started living here, I thought it was like an apartment in a film. All glass and bare brick walls. The living room's open plan and so huge there's a dining area with a wooden table at one end and a sitting area with two sofas at the other, but it still looks empty. In between, the kitchen bit has stainless steel everything and a counter like a high-end restaurant in *MasterChef*, where the contestants work for an exacting chef in the final week. At first, even if it was cheese on toast, I'd call out 'Service!' when I put out the plates.

When Gus was here, it was our home but, on my own, I still sometimes feel like an intruder who's wandered onto the wrong studio lot.

Inside the big cardboard box there's a bunch of pink lilies, the ones with the heady scent, their stalks in a bag of water, the sort you'd carry a goldfish in after winning it at the fair. So no need for a vase, but when I put it down on the counter the bag kind of splurges and the flowers splay out, dangling their gobbets of orange pollen dangerously close to the surface.

Marble absorbs stains. I remember Doll telling me that when she bought her first house off-plan, and had to choose the flooring and stuff herself. It's made me cautious around ketchup all the time I've lived here. Now there's a smattering of orange pollen which I stop myself wiping, just before making it worse. I get the handheld vacuum cleaner and suck up the pollen dust. Disaster averted. It's a tiny victory but it feels like a good omen.

There's a card stuck in the lilies with care instructions, but there's no message to say who it's from.

It must be Gus. When he's on nights he sometimes leaves a paper bag with a croissant outside the door for my breakfast. But today, he probably figured I needed more cheering up.

I take a photo and WhatsApp it with the message:

There's no card, but I assume from you. Thanks so much! See you later.

Then I think, what if it wasn't him that sent them? Will he think I'm trying to make him feel bad?

I doubt it, because if I've learned anything in my forty years, it's that men don't do backstories like women do. Like I do, anyway.

I see that he was last online around midnight. Which is when he texted me:

Goodnight x

The hospital is at breaking point and the PPE's so difficult to get on and off, I don't hear from him during his shifts.

The City has a different rhythm now. Like Christmas every day, but not in a good way. The streets are unnaturally quiet, which is weird because loads of people live round here, but they're all so rich, they've moved out to their second homes.

There are dragons on plinths guarding the entrance to the Square Mile, although they're so small I didn't notice the one at the end of our street for several months. Now I give it a little stroke for luck, then I have to get out the mini hand-sanitiser.

It's less hazardous now to look up and marvel at the unique skyscape of glass towers and church spires, because there are no beeping, reversing trucks, nor harassed workers talking on phones to barge you off the pavement. The Dickensian alleyways are deserted, the only sign that it's not the nineteenth century are the double yellow lines taking up most of the width of the narrow streets.

You can smell Smithfield meat market before you see the building, though I'm not sure whether it's still in operation. Not at capacity anyway, because of all the restaurants closing. These days, there's no aroma of bacon frying in the nearby cafés, for the breakfasts of butchers who've been up all night. That used to mask the tang of blood and sawdust in the air.

My destination is a typical City building, a mix of old and new. You enter through an arch and there are cobblestones underfoot, a little church to your left. Then there's another arch with a courtyard beyond with flowerbeds full of yellow roses. Through another door you find yourself in a vast modern atrium, all glass and air, that's like a high-end airport hotel. A lift takes you the seventh floor.

I'm surprised how few of us there are this time, probably because we're all spaced out now and you're not allowed to bring a companion. It makes it scarier with no one to talk to while you're waiting.

To be honest, the person I would most like here with me is Mum.

I still miss her after twenty years, although I don't think about her all the time, like I used to. It's the extremes mainly. When something lovely happens, I still have that momentary thrill at the prospect of telling her; then, when I remember I can't, the experience feels somehow incomplete.

Like at the party my publishers arranged in Waterstones Piccadilly to celebrate publication of my novel, which I dedicated to: *My inspirational Mum, Mary Lucy Costello.*

I had to keep rushing to the loo to have a little weep, thinking how much she'd have loved it.

If she were here now, she'd hold my hand and be a reassuring presence, not keep trying to jolly me along, like people who've never experienced chemotherapy do.

In the days before she died, when I used to sit by her bed chatting quietly, I once asked her please, if it did turn out there was life after death, could she send me a little sign?

She'd laughed and said, 'I can't give you faith, Tess. It's a step you have to take yourself. And then everything follows.'

But on the day of her funeral, there was a white butterfly in our bathroom, even though it was a bit late in the year for butterflies. After that, every time I needed her, a white butterfly would appear, and now, even though it's over twenty years, I'm looking out of the window, touching the charm on my necklace, hoping to see one.

The view is amazing. Really, it could be some very exclusive City rooftop bar. I suppose, in a way, that's what it is. There's a nice calm atmosphere and very professional staff who attend to your every request and carefully prepare your bespoke cocktail.

I think of my dad standing behind the marble-effect cocktail bar in Anne's living room.

'What's your poison?'

Here it's given intravenously and it's so lethal the nurses have to wear protective gear when they handle it.

Maybe the seventh floor is too high up for butterflies? Normally, they seem to flutter around shrub height, although I once heard a programme on the radio about them migrating from North Africa to the UK. I think they must catch an ultra high airstream, because nobody ever talks about seeing a swarm of butterflies on the Kent coast, which would be a pretty notable event, wouldn't it?

A quick check of Google says butterflies can fly as high as the Empire State Building. Who knew?

Is the collective noun for butterflies a swarm? Google says a flutter or a flight, but they also say that a lot of flamingos is called a flamboyance, so it sounds like you can make up any name you like.

A lone seagull swoops past the window a couple of times, almost as if he's pretending to be a white butterfly, but Mum would never send me a seagull. She didn't trust them after it was in the local newspaper that one had grabbed a chip from a toddler's hand on the promenade.

At the mindfulness class I started going to before all this happened, we learned techniques to relax.

Imagine your favourite place.

Sometimes I can get myself back to the Villa Cora just outside Florence, that heavenly, hedonistic afternoon in our suite with the painted ceilings. The windows are open and a breeze is caressing our naked bodies with the warmth of Italy as we make love on the fairy-tale four-poster bed, and it feels even more miraculous than before because we have just committed our lives to each other.

At least we had that one perfect afternoon.

A lot of my thoughts seem to begin with 'at least . . .' these days.

The endoscopy showed that my life wasn't in immediate danger, so I was allowed out of the hospital in Florence the following day. They promised to forward the results of the biopsies to my GP in London.

We were all smiles as we thanked the hospital staff and tried to pretend that, after an inconvenient blip, our special weekend would continue. But it wasn't the same with Gus constantly asking how I was feeling, and when I told him to stop, the silence filled with so many thoughts that I would suddenly wonder whether a minute or an hour had passed without us speaking.

That afternoon we ambled along quiet roads bordered by

olive groves, and villas with cascades of wisteria. It's amazing how proper Tuscan countryside begins only yards outside the city walls.

In the *centro storico*, we headed to the Gelateria dei Neri to buy cones, both remembering the two-flavour rule because, however tempting it is to get a third, your tastebuds are always too cold to distinguish it. Gus chose *nocciola* and limone, I opted for *fior di latte* and pear, but I think we were both disappointed. Perhaps we had been spoiled by our time in Sicily, or it was too early in the year, or maybe it was seeing the worry on Gus's face each time I swallowed.

'What do you want to do now?' he asked, as we sat on a stone bench in Piazza Santa Croce.

'No more churches and museums!' I remembered Doll saying that in the exact same place over twenty years before. Back then, I couldn't have envisaged a time when I would feel the same way.

Stifled by the humidity and tired of walking on cobblestones, I suddenly wasn't able to bear all my special memories of the city being tarnished, so we took a bus to the hill town of Fiesole, where Gus had never been. The air was fresher up there, and there was a Roman theatre. I remembered standing on the stage when I was eighteen shouting 'Tomorrow and tomorrow and tomorrow' with Doll applauding from one of the stone tiers. Now we just stood at the top agreeing it would be a great place to see a play.

In the small onsite museum, the collection of Greek vases gave us something to focus on. We read all the captions thoroughly, informing ourselves about an art form neither of us had previously studied and weren't especially interested in.

When the museum finally closed we sat in a bar looking at the view of Florence in the distance, like the backdrop of a Renaissance portrait. Then, as darkness began to fall, we took the bus back to the city centre to walk one final time over the Ponte Vecchio, both of us so preoccupied that we didn't remember to take a selfie in our spot until we were hundreds of yards beyond the bridge and neither of us was fussed about going back.

'Where would you like to get married?' Gus asked, linking arms as we quickened our step towards the hotel.

'Let's see,' I said.

I smiled at him to show I knew what he was trying to do and was grateful, but I just couldn't pretend that I wasn't more worried than I'd ever been.

I wasn't a doctor, but I knew they didn't take biopsies if there was nothing there, did they?

Gus's friend Jonathan, who's top of his field, saw me as soon as the results came through. He said I was lucky to have the BRCA gene mutation because that would give me access to more clinical trials.

It's funny how often cancer patients are told they're lucky. The first time, aged just thirty-three, people said it was lucky I'd felt the lump in my breast when it was still small, lucky that it had only spread to a couple of my lymph nodes, lucky I was young and fit enough to recover fairly quickly from the operation.

Now, at forty, I had inoperable stomach cancer, but I was lucky to be in a group of people who'd inherited fascinating killer genes.

'So, are you saying it's terminal?' I asked, because I didn't want Gus to have to do that in an informal conversation between doctor friends afterwards and then have to decide whether to tell me.

'Are you asking for life insurance purposes?' Jonathan enquired.

'No,' I said.

'Well, in that case, I'm saying that it's currently very unlikely we'll be able to get rid of it. But you're young and otherwise fit. So, if we can keep you alive long enough, you never know.'

Which made me wonder what he would have said if my question had been for life insurance purposes.

Sometimes I find myself thinking about the what ifs.

What if I'd pointed out my weight loss when my consultant asked how I was at my final follow-up appointment? But he had all my records and if he wasn't bothered, why would I be?

What if I'd asked the GP if she was sure, given my history, that my indigestion was just a bit of gastritis? You don't, do you, because you're so relieved that the doctor doesn't seem worried and you don't want to appear neurotic.

Jonathan said that it was a cancer that might not have shown up in an earlier endoscopy anyway as it had formed beneath an ulcer and so that's what the diagnosis would have been. Even a PET scan might not have picked it up because there's already so much activity going on in the stomach.

I think that helped Gus a bit with his guilt about not being more insistent.

My own theory about the BRCA gene mutation is that the bastard was going to get me anyway. It did my mum and probably many generations of women in my family before her. So, in some ways, it was better to live life not knowing, because there are other what ifs.

Like what if I'd known it was cancer when I started getting symptoms in Australia? Would I have finished my novel, or got back with Gus, or spent a perfect afternoon in a four-poster bed in a room with painted ceilings in my favourite city in the world?

At least we had a brilliant time before they punched a hole at the top of my chest, just above my heart, to make it easier to pump the chemotherapy cocktail into my veins.

The first few cycles appeared to stabilise things, and I was on a treatment break when my book was published. I decided to go the bandana route rather than get a wig, which was bound to go askew for the photos anyway. Doll did my make-up.

'I always visualised you as a bestselling author,' she told me, as she stuck on false eyelashes and held up a mirror so I could see how natural they looked.

'Have you read it?' I raised the eyebrow she'd just painted on.

'Course I have!' she said. 'It's really good, Tess. It made me want to go back to Italy.'

I was probably happier with this critique than any of the favourable reviews I would read in the papers. Doll had only ever read one other novel the whole way through and only because I made her.

'Doesn't it prove that if you visualise something, then it will happen?' she said.

'You can't visualise things on behalf of other people, surely?'

'You know what I mean, though?'

What she meant was that she'd always had faith in me, but she just had a different way of saying it. Because if it was all about visualisations, it would probably have been better for her to have envisaged a cancer-free life for me. Not that it's her fault, obviously. Doll's been fantastic.

The night before my wedding, the two of us stayed in a twin room at the Ritz, chatting to each other from our separate double beds. In the morning she helped me into my outfit. I'd never pictured myself in a long white dress, but when I'd spotted a nineteen-twenties ivory silk shift overlaid with delicate lace in one of the posh vintage shops you get in North London, I had changed my mind. It had fitted perfectly and solved the question of what to wear on my bald head because it came with a matching lace veil fixed with a silk band round my forehead, like a flapper girl.

'Very *Downton Abbey*,' Doll said, which was about the highest compliment she could pay. But it almost made me want to change back into jeans.

She was my witness, of course, in her latest pink Chanel suit.

Nash flew in to be Gus's witness, turning up in a red-carpet-worthy dress with flounces.

'Probably a bit much,' she said. 'But I did bring you two together and I've always wanted to play fairy godmother.'

'Gus's fairy godmother,' Doll corrected her. 'I'm Tess's. But seeing as you're Dr Sue, no offence taken.'

We were married at Islington Town Hall.

It wasn't meant to be a big thing, but Doll had rung Brendan to tell him, so when we came out onto Upper Street, Hope was standing on the pavement wearing an apricot satin bridesmaid's dress with a hoody and trainers, singing Abba's 'I Do, I Do, I Do, I Do, I Do' to an astonished flash mob of Saturday-morning shoppers.

Gus said he'd organise a pub lunch with a few friends, but when we arrived the place was empty.

'Let's just check if they're outside,' Gus said, putting his finger to his lips so Hope knew to keep quiet, before leading me out into a vine-covered garden strung with bunting and bunches of balloons, where everyone who'd ever been important in our lives was waiting for us.

Gus was always good at surprises.

Hope sat down at the upright piano and struck up the 'Wedding March' as our friends and families formed a guard of honour, throwing rose petal confetti and cheering. Gus took me in his arms and kissed me in the dappled shade of vines with heart-shaped helium balloons glinting above us in the sunshine.

Just about everyone we knew was there, some of them having

travelled long distances. Brendan had come from Australia with the whole family; Kevin from New York with Shaun; Flora from Geneva with her very serious French boyfriend François. Bella was having a very animated conversation with Milo, Marcus and Keiko's son, whom she had played with as a child.

There was a buffet of delicious Italian food laid on by Stefania and Salvatore, but the main sensibility was Irish, with a lot of singing from my side of the family. After a few glasses, Dad sang The Fureys' 'I Will Love You' with Hope harmonising, and all I could think was how much Mum would have loved it.

'Thank you so much,' I said to Gus as we took a break from dancing to sit and watch our families and friends united for the first time, and somehow all getting on.

'Oh, this arrived,' Gus said, taking an envelope out of the inside pocket of his jacket.

It was one of those cards you can generate on the internet from a photo on your phone. The message said 'Congratulations!' and the image was of Sandy in front of the beautiful baroque façade of the duomo in Ortigia, with a copy of the Italian edition of my novel in her hand. Standing right beside her was Alessia, holding out a plate of cakes the people of Siracusa call 'the eyes of Santa Lucia'. So they got their happy ending too. Not Santa Lucia, obviously, though martyrdom's probably not a bad way to go if you're a believer.

Gus and I love married life. Or perhaps we just love life with more intensity. Last summer, the evenings seemed longer and balmier, the roses more fragrant in London parks; in autumn, the air smelt smokier, the leaves looked more golden; in winter, sunlight reflecting off the City's glass towers lit up the shortest days. These recent fine spring mornings, the sky seems bluer, the birdsong louder and the blossom frothier than ever before.

The gift that cancer brings is a heightened sense of the beauty of the present, a bit like living in David Hockney's video-installation of the four seasons.

It's amazing what the human body can adapt to. Sometimes chemo makes you feel so terrible you can't remember what it was like to be well, or imagine ever feeling better. Then you have a break and suddenly it's a spring day, you're walking over Highbury Fields delighting in the greenness of the grass, and the crowds of yellow daffodils dancing in the breeze and you feel as happy as you've ever been.

You get into a routine: chemo, scan, break, scan, chemo, scan, break. Until one day it was chemo, scan, break, scan, lockdown.

I never thought there would come a time when I'd be impatient for my chemotherapy to start again.

One of the weird things about coronavirus is that cancer isn't special any more, which may not be altogether a bad thing, because cancer's awful, but so are many other diseases that kill you and don't get talked about with the same reverence. Now you're just someone with 'comorbidities'.

At least nobody bangs on about how you must be positive any more, because everyone knows when the hospital beds run out, no amount of positivity is going to put you first in the queue for a ventilator.

At least my treatment has started up again, because a lot of cancer care has been postponed.

At least Gus is able to live in Marcus's city flat, because Marcus and Keiko are working from their home in the country, and it wouldn't be sensible or safe for Gus to be with Covid patients all day, then come home to me and my compromised immune system.

Gus offered to give up work to be in a bubble with me, but the thing that you want most when you've got cancer is to be treated as normal. You may not be around for as long as you hoped, but you don't want to lose your identity while you're still here. And the last thing I was going to do was take a doctor away from the NHS in the crisis of a pandemic. I couldn't have lived with myself.

Doll insisted on coming to stay for the first couple of weeks. I think everyone thought the lockdown would be over much quicker than it was.

'You can't be on your own just sitting around waiting for chemo to begin again,' she said.

'But what about the kids?'

'They'll be safe with Dave.'

We passed the time watching box sets and chatting. In a way, there was no one I would rather have had there because we share so much past and she let me talk about the future without the terror in her eyes that Gus can never quite disguise.

'I wanted us to grow old together,' she said, one evening. 'And go on a cruise and be outrageous old biddies.'

'This is a bit like being on a cruise, isn't it?' I said. 'All cooped up in a cabin and unable to get off the ship?'

When it became clear that it wasn't going to be temporary, I made her return to her family.

'What will you do all day?' she asked.

'I've decided to try to write my second novel,' I told her. 'It'll give me something to do and there's no excuse for not sitting down at the computer now.'

When I was a child, I thought that the whole point of stories was that they took you to different worlds, but every creative writing teacher I've ever had has told me to write about what I know.

It was Nash who planted the seed for my first novel when

she talked about my story with Gus being a contemporary fairy tale. Then Sandy gave me the confidence to write it.

It ended with two people whose paths had crossed for many years meeting for the first time. When I wrote *The End* I honestly thought it was.

Then, a few months later, I remembered my Auntie Catriona saying to Mum that falling in love is only the beginning of the story. And I suddenly wanted to find out whether, being so different, and having spent all their formative years apart, it was even possible for my characters to live happily ever after.

Please don't make the mistake of thinking that this is pure autobiography with some names changed, as people always say in their acknowledgements. But if parts of it sound a bit far fetched, that might just be because truth is stranger than fiction.

Like, if there'd been an announcement last New Year that we needn't bother making resolutions because a curse had been put on the planet that was going to change it completely in three months, who would have believed it?

Like, who would have guessed that Hope would become a TikTok sensation after Jessy filmed her singing 'Pie Jesu' and posted it online?

I always thought there was something similar about Hope and Santa Lucia. Two millennia ago, it took two hundred years for news of the saint's mysterious story to go round the world. Hope's bizarre performance was disseminated by social media and within two weeks she had half a million devoted followers.

I think it was partly her name. Everyone needs a bit of Hope. Her angelic voice brought people comfort in a time of need. But she isn't a saint. None of us are. She's a person who has difficulty communicating, but touches the world with her singing.

Which is a miracle in itself, when you think about it.

The thing I've realised by writing about Gus and me is that, even when we were together, we were on different pages a lot of the time. Not just literally. So we kept on missing each other even after we met and fell in love.

The doorbell is buzzing. The neighbours downstairs have already ordered in their pizza this evening. It's a bit late for another delivery. I pick up the handset.

'Hello?'

'It's me!'

'OK, just a moment . . .'

I run all the way to through the apartment and out onto the roof terrace.

Gus is standing six floors below looking up. He's on his way to work. I can tell from the shape of his shoulders that he's rested and ready to go again. His face lights up when he sees me, then frowns as he asks, 'How was it today?'

'OK. Tired though.'

'I hope you get a good night.'

'Me too!' I say, brightly, though we both know that's impossible because the steroids give you a buzz that makes your body jittery with wakeful exhaustion all through the lonely, silent hours of darkness, until the cacophony of dawn birdsong finishes off any chance of sleep.

'I love you, Tess,' he calls.

'I love you, Gus.'

I lean over, reaching my hand towards him, like Rapunzel without the hair. Standing on tiptoe, he stretches his arm up as far as he can. Even though he's tall, he can't extend past the windows of the ground floor, but our longing is so powerful, I can feel it connecting us invisibly, like an electric current.

He blows me a kiss and I watch as he walks backwards,

still looking up at me, all the way down the street until, at the corner, he stands waving for a long time. Neither of us wants to be the one to turn away first, but I don't want to make him late for work, so I give a final, energetic wave, with both my arms, then go back inside, filled with the dreamy sensation of knowing I am loved that makes my face keep smiling through a blur of tears.

When my mother used to read me fairy tales, I think I always focused on the 'ever after' instead of the 'happily'.

The story of Gus and me has never been straightforward, but with him I have known happiness more blissful than I could have imagined.

I think he would say the same.

And nobody lives ever after, do they?

Acknowledgements

Publishing is a collaborative effort and I'm delighted that Orion Books adopts the sensible policy of crediting everyone involved in bringing this book to life. I am very grateful to you all. I'd like to add my particular thanks to Sam Eades whose insightful response to the manuscript and encouragement helped me so much. It is such a pleasure working with you. Thank you also to Sarah Benton. I left that lovely lunch, where we all met for the first time, walking on air!

As always, I am indebted to Mark Lucas, Niamh O'Grady, Nicki Kennedy, Jenny Robson and Katherine West for supporting and championing my work.

Writing novels is a lonely occupation and this one felt very solitary indeed as it was mostly written during lockdown. Thank you to all the quizzers: Liam, Benedict, Barbara, Sam, Jamie, Laura, Simon, Naomi, Jacob, Jake and Winnie da Clue, Susie and Les Lyonnaises and to our amazing quizmaster Connor for being Emcee at his very own virtual cabaret. Thank you to my brilliant friends: Lucy, Martha, Issy, Debra, Emily, Nicola, Kasia, Mark, Michael and Ajay, Sheree, Nick and Roz, Leah and David, Renée, Vanessa, Julia, Pat, Anne, Dee, Jane, Rod and Luke, and Linda, for all the walks, chats and laughter during those strange months of isolation and beyond.

Thank you Vadim Muntagirov and Marianela Nuñez for making me happy whenever I see you dance.

Thank you to everyone who works for the NHS under such unreasonable pressure. Thank you, Michael. I am particularly grateful to the doctors and nursing staff at Royal Bournemouth Hospital who saved my life on Christmas Day 2021. Thank you to everyone on ESCU Ward 15, especially Branca, Anna, Sandiya, Mercy, Stacy, and the exceptionally lovely Pink Ladies Hannah and Ellen, for your help and your kindness. Thank you to Jane, Jane and Emma for your support and patience. Thank you to Glyn, Vi, Irene and Mr Ghanbari at the Homerton Hospital for your continuing care.

Thank you, Rumi.

I could not have written this book without the love and support of my wonderful family who have been there with me steadfastly through some difficult times in recent years. A huge and heartfelt thank you to Pete, Becky, Giles, Nick and my beloved son Connor.

Credits

Kate Eberlen and Orion Fiction would like to thank everyone at Orion who worked on the publication of *Ever After* in the UK.

Editorial
Sam Eades
Sanah Ahmed

Copyeditor
Sophie Buchanan

Proofreader
Sally Partington

Audio
Paul Stark
Jake Alderson

Contracts
Anne Goddard
Humayra Ahmed
Ellie Bowker

Design
Charlotte Abrams-Simpson
Joanna Ridley
Nick Shah

Editorial Management
Charlie Panayiotou
Jane Hughes
Bartley Shaw
Tamara Morriss

Finance
Jasdip Nandra
Sue Baker

Marketing
Helena Fouracre

Production
Ruth Sharvell

Publicity
Frankie Banks

Operations
Jo Jacobs
Sharon Willis

Sales
Jen Wilson
Esther Waters
Victoria Laws
Rachael Hum
Anna Egelstaff
Frances Doyle
Georgina Cutler

Discover the first instalment of
Tess and Gus' love story in *Miss You*

Tess is in Florence for one last adventure with her best friend before university. Gus and his parents are also on holiday in Florence. And for one day, the paths of these two eighteen-year-olds will criss-cross before they each return to England.

Over the course of the next sixteen years, life and love will offer them very different challenges. Separated by distance and chance, there's no way the two of them are ever going to meet each other properly . . . is there?

'Witty, poignant and uplifting' Sophie Kinsella

'Just the thing for long summer nights' *Good Housekeeping*

Available to buy now from https://www.panmacmillan.com/authors/kate-eberlen/miss-you/9781509819959

Read on for an extract . . .

1

August 1997

TESS

In the kitchen at home, there was a plate that Mum bought on holiday in Tenerife with a hand-painted motto: *Today is the first day of the rest of your life.*

It had never registered with me any more than Dad's trophy for singing, or the New York snow dome my brother Kevin sent over one Christmas, but that last day of the holiday, I couldn't seem to get it out of my head.

When I woke up, the inside of the tent was glowing orange, like a pumpkin lantern. I inched the zipper door down carefully so as not to wake Doll, then stuck my face out into dazzling sunlight. The air was still a little bit shivery and I could hear the distant clank of bells. I wrote the word 'plangent' in my diary with an asterisk next to it so I could check it in the dictionary when I got home.

The view of Florence from the campsite, all terracotta domes and white marble towers shimmering against a flat blue sky, was so like it was supposed to be, I had this strange feeling of sadness, as if I was missing it already.

There were lots of things I wouldn't miss, like sleeping on the ground – after a few hours, the stones feel like they're

3

growing into your back – and getting dressed in a space less than three feet high, and walking all the way to the shower block, then remembering you've left the toilet roll in the tent. It's funny how when you get towards the end of a holiday, half of you never wants it to end and the other half is looking forward to the comforts of home.

We'd been Interrailing for a month, down through France, then into Italy, sleeping on stations, drinking beer with Dutch boys on campsites, struggling with sunburn in slow, sticky trains. Doll was into beaches and Bellinis; I was more maps and monuments, but we got along like we always had since we met on the first day at St Cuthbert's, aged four, and Maria Dolores O'Neill – I was the one who abbreviated it to Doll – asked, 'Do you want to be my best friend?'

We were different, but we complemented each other. Whenever I said that, Doll always said, 'You've got great skin!' or 'I really like those shoes,' and if I told her it wasn't that sort of compliment, she'd laugh, and say she knew, but I was never sure she did. You develop a kind of special language with people you're close to, don't you?

My memories of the other places we went to that holiday are like postcards: the floodlit amphitheatre in Verona against an ink-dark sky; the azure bay of Naples; the unexpectedly vibrant colours of the Sistine Chapel ceiling, but that last, carefree day we spent in Florence, the day before my life changed, I can retrace hour by hour, footstep by footstep almost.

Doll always took much longer than me getting ready in the mornings because she never went out without full make-up even then. I liked having time on my own, especially that morning because it was the day of my A-level results and I was trying to compose myself for hearing if I'd done well enough to get into university.

On the way up to the campsite the previous evening, I'd noticed the floodlit facade of a church high above the road, pretty and incongruous like a jewel box in a forest. In daylight, the basilica was much bigger than I'd imagined, and as I climbed the grand flights of baroque steps towards it, I had the peculiar thought that it would make the perfect setting for a wedding, which was unlike me because I'd never had a proper boyfriend then, let alone pictured myself in a long white dress.

From the terrace at the top, the view was so exhilarating, I felt an irrational urge to cry as I promised myself solemnly – like you do when you're eighteen – that I would one day return.

There was no one else around, but the heavy wooden door of the church opened when I gave it a push. It was so dark inside after the glare, my eyes took a little time to adjust to the gloom. The air was a few degrees cooler than the heat outside and it had that churchy smell of dust mingling with incense. Alone in God's house, I was acutely aware of the irreverent flap of my sandals as I walked up the steps to the raised chancel. I was staring at the giant, impassive face of Jesus, praying that my grades were going to be OK, when suddenly, magically, the apse filled with light.

Spinning round, I was startled to see a lanky guy about my own age, standing beside a box on the wall where you could put a coin in to turn the lights on. Damp brown hair swept back from his face, he was even more inappropriately dressed than me, in running shorts, a vest and trainers. There was a moment when we could have smiled at one another, or even said something, but we missed it, as we both self-consciously turned our attention to the huge dome of golden mosaic and the light went out again with a loud clunk, as decisively and unexpectedly as it had come on.

I glanced at my watch in the ensuing dimness, as if to imply that I would like to give the iconic image more serious consideration, perhaps even contribute my own minute of electricity, if I wasn't already running late. As I reached the door, I heard the clunk again, and, looking up at Christ's solemn, illuminated features, felt as if I'd disappointed Him.

Doll was fully coiffed and painted by the time I arrived back at the campsite.

'What was it like?' she asked.

'Byzantine, I think,' I said.

'Is that good?'

'Beautiful.'

After cappuccinos and custard buns – amazing how even campsite bar snacks are delicious in Italy – we packed up and decided to go straight down into town to the central post office where I could make an international call and get my results so that wouldn't be hanging over us all day. Even if the news was bad, I wanted to hear it. What I couldn't deal with was the limbo state of not knowing what the future held for me. So we walked down to the *centro storico*, with me chattering away about everything except the subject that was preoccupying me.

The fear was so loud in my head when I dialled our number, I felt as if I'd lost the ability to speak.

Mum answered after one ring.

'Hope's going to read your results to you,' she said.

'Mum!' I cried, but it was too late.

My little sister Hope was already on the line.

'Read your results to you,' she said.

'Go on then.'

'A, B, C . . .' she said slowly, like she was practising her alphabet.

'Isn't that marvellous?' said Mum.

'What?'

'You've an A for English, B for Art History and C for Religion and Philosophy.'

'You're kidding?' I'd been offered a place at University College London conditional on my getting two Bs and a C, so it was better than I needed.

I ducked my head out of the Perspex dome to give Doll the thumbs-up.

Down the line, Mum was cheering, then Hope joined in. I pictured the two of them standing in the kitchen beside the knick-knack shelf with the plate that said *Today is the first day of the rest of your life*.

Doll's suggestion for a celebration was to blow all the money we had left on a bottle of *spumante* at a pavement table on Piazza Signoria. She had more money than me from working part-time in the salon while she was doing her diploma and she had been hankering for another outside table ever since Venice, where we'd inadvertently spent a whole day's budget on a cappuccino in St Mark's Square. At eighteen, Doll already had a taste for glamour. But it was only ten o'clock in the morning, and I figured that even if we stretched it out, we would still have hours before our overnight train to Calais, and probably headaches. I'm practical like that.

'It's up to you,' said Doll, disappointed. 'It's your celebration.'

There were so many sights I wanted to see: the Uffizi, the Bargello, the Duomo, the Baptistery, Santa Maria Novella . . .

'You mean churches, don't you?' Doll wasn't going to be fooled by the Italian names.

Both of us were brought up Catholic, but at that point in our lives Doll saw church as something that stopped her having a lie-in on Sunday and I thought it was cool to describe myself as agnostic, although I still found myself quite often praying for things. For me, Italy's churches were principally places not so much of God but of culture. To be honest, I was pretentious, but I was allowed to be because I was about to become a student.

After leaving our rucksacks in Left Luggage at the station, we did a quick circuit of the Duomo, taking photographs of each other outside the golden Baptistery doors, then navigated a backstreet route towards Santa Croce, stopping at a tiny artisan *gelateria* that was opening up for the day. Ice cream in the morning satisfied Doll's craving for decadence. We chose three flavours each from cylindrical tubs arranged behind the glass counter like a giant paintbox.

For me, refreshing mandarin, lemon and pink grapefruit.

'Too breakfast-y,' said Doll, indulging herself with marsala, cherry and fondant chocolate, which she described as orgasmic and which sustained her good mood through an hour's worth of Giotto murals.

The fun thing about looking at art with Doll was her saying things like, 'He wasn't very good at feet, was he?' but when we emerged from the church, I could tell she'd had enough culture and the midday city heat felt oppressive, so I suggested we take a bus to the ancient hill town of Fiesole, which I had read about in the *Rough Guide*. It was a relief to stand by the bus window, getting the movement of air on our faces.

Fiesole's main square was stunningly peaceful after Florence's packed streets.

'Let's have a celebratory *menu turistico*,' I said, deciding to splurge the last little bit of money I'd been saving in case of emergencies.

We sat on the terrace of the restaurant, with Florence a miniature city in the distance, like the backdrop to a Leonardo painting.

'Any educational activities planned for this afternoon?' Doll asked, dabbing the corners of her mouth after demolishing a bowl of spaghetti *pomodoro*.

'There is a Roman theatre,' I admitted. 'But I'm fine going round on my own, honest . . .'

'Those bloody Romans got everywhere, didn't they?' said Doll, but she was happy enough to follow me there.

We were the only people visiting the site. Doll lay sunbathing on a stone tier of seats as I explored. She sat up and started clapping when I found my way onto the stage. I took a bow.

'Say something!' Doll called.

'Tomorrow and tomorrow and tomorrow!' I shouted.

'More!' shouted Doll, getting out her camera.

'Can't remember any more!'

I jumped down from the stage and made my way up the steep steps.

'Shall I take a picture of you?'

'Let's get one with both of us.'

With the camera positioned three steps up, Doll reckoned she could get us in the frame against the backdrop of Tuscan hills.

'What's the Italian for cheese?' she asked, setting the timer, before scurrying down to stand next to me for the click of the shutter.

In my photograph album, it looks like we are blowing kisses at the camera. The self-stick stuff has gone all yellow now, and the plastic covering is brittle, but the colours – white stone, blue sky, black-green cypresses – are just as sharp as I remember.

With invisible crickets chattering in the trees around us, we waited for the bus back to Florence in uncharacteristic silence.

Doll finally revealed what was on her mind. 'Do you think we'll still be friends?'

'What do you mean?' I pretended not to know what she was asking.

'When you're at university with people who know about books and history and stuff . . .'

'Don't be daft,' I said confidently, but the treacherous

thought had already crossed my mind that next year I would probably be holidaying with people who would want to look at the small collection of painted Greek vases in the site museum, or enjoy comparing the work of Michelangelo and Donatello, and the other Ninja Turtles (as Doll referred to them).

Today is the first day of the rest of your life.

There was a little twist of excitement and fear in my tummy whenever I allowed myself to think about the future.

Back in Florence, we made a small detour for another ice cream. Doll couldn't resist the chocolate again, this time with melon, and I selected pear which tasted like the essence of a hundred perfectly ripe Williams, with raspberry, as sharp and sweet as a childhood memory of summer.

The Ponte Vecchio was a little quieter than it had been at the start of the day, allowing us to look in the windows of the tiny jewellery shops. When Doll spotted a silver charm bracelet that was much cheaper than the rest of the merchandise, we ducked through the door and squeezed inside.

The proprietor held up the delicate chain with miniature replicas of the Duomo, the Ponte Vecchio, a Chianti bottle and Michelangelo's *David*.

'Is for child,' he said.

'Why don't I buy it for Hope?' Doll said, eager to find a reason to spend the rest of her money.

We were probably imagining, as we watched the man arrange the bracelet on tissue in a small cardboard box stamped with gold fleurs-de-lys, that this would be something my sister would keep safely in a special place and that, from time to time, we would all unwrap it together and gaze upon it reverently, like a precious heirloom.

Outside, the light had deserted the ancient buildings and the noise of the city had softened. The mellow jazz riff of a busker's clarinet wafted on the balmy air. At the centre of the bridge, we waited for a gap in the crowd so we could take photos of each other against the fading golden sky. It was weird to think of all the mantelpieces we would appear on in the background to other people's photos, from Tokyo to Tennessee.

'I've got two shots left,' Doll announced.

Scanning the crowd, my eyes settled on a face that was somehow familiar, but which I only managed to place when he frowned with confusion as I smiled at him. It was the boy I'd seen in San Miniato al Monte that morning. There was a reddish tinge to his hair in the last rays of sunshine, and he was now wearing a khaki polo shirt and chinos, and standing awkwardly beside a middle-aged couple who looked like they might be his parents.

I held the camera out to him. 'Would you mind?'

The perplexed look made me wonder if he was English, then, his pale, freckly complexion flushing with embarrassment, he said, 'Not at all!' in a voice Mum would have called 'nicely spoken'.

'Say cheese!'

'*Formaggio!*' Doll and I chorused.

In the photo, our eyes are closed, laughing at our own joke.

With a six-berth couchette to ourselves, we lay on the bottom bunks, passing a bottle of red wine between us and going over our memories of the holiday as the train trundled through the night. For me, it was views and sights.

'Remember the flowers on the Spanish Steps?'

'Flowers?'

'Were you even on the same holiday?'

For Doll, it was men.

'Remember that waiter's face in Piazza Navona when I said I liked eating fish?'

We now understood that the phrase had another meaning in Italian.

'Best meal?' said Doll.

'Prosciutto and peaches from the street market in Bologna. You?'

'That oniony anchovy pizza thing in Nice was delish . . .'

'*Pissaladière*,' I said.

'Behave!'

'Best day?'

'Capri,' said Doll. 'You?'

'I think today.'

'Best . . . ?'

Doll drifted off, but I couldn't sleep. Whenever I closed my eyes, I found myself in the little room I had reserved in the university halls of residence which, until now, I hadn't allowed my imagination to inhabit, excitedly placing my possessions on the shelves, my duvet cover on the bed, and Blu-Tacking up my new poster of Botticelli's *Primavera* which was rolling gently from side to side on the luggage rack above me. Which floor would I be on? Would I have a view over rooftops towards the Telecom Tower, like the one they'd shown us on Open Day? Or would I be on the street side of the building, with the tops of red double-decker buses crawling past my window and sudden shrieks of police sirens that made it feel like being in a movie?

The air in the compartment grew chilly as the train started its climb through the Alps. I covered Doll with her fleece. She murmured her thanks but did not wake, and I was glad because it felt special to have private time to myself, just me and my plans, travelling from one stage of my life to the next.

I must have fallen asleep in the small hours. I awoke with the rattle of a breakfast trolley. Doll was staring dismally at viscous raindrops chasing each other down the window as the train sped across the flat fields of Northern France.

'I'd forgotten about weather,' she said, handing me a plastic cup of sour coffee and a cellophane-wrapped croissant.

*

It wasn't that I was expecting bunting, or neighbours lining the street to welcome me back, but as I walked up Conifer Road after leaving Doll outside her house on Laburnum Drive, I couldn't help feeling disappointed that everything was exactly the same. Our council estate was built in the late sixties. It was probably the height of modernity then with its regular rectangular houses half pale brick, half white render, and communal lawns instead of front gardens. All the streets were named after trees, but apart from a few spindly flowering cherries, nobody had bothered to plant any. Some of the right-to-buy households had added a glazed porch at the front, or a UPVC conservatory to the through-room downstairs, but the houses all still looked like the little boxes in that song. With a month's distance, it was clear to me that I had outgrown the place.

Mum only had a rough idea of when I'd be getting back, but I was still slightly surprised that she and Hope were not positioned by the window or even sitting on the front lawn, waiting for me. It was a lovely evening. Maybe Mum had filled the paddling pool in the back garden? Perhaps there was too much splashing for them to hear the bell?

Eventually, a small, familiar shape appeared on the other side of the frosted glass.

'Who's there?' Hope called.

'It's me!'

'It's me!' she shouted.

It was never quite clear whether Hope was playing games or being pedantic.

'It's Tree!' I said. 'Come on, Hope, open the door!'

'It's Tree!'

I could tell Mum was responding from somewhere in the house but I couldn't hear what she was saying.

Hope knelt down to speak through the letter box at the bottom of the front door. 'I get chair from kitchen.'

'Use the one in the hall,' I instructed through the letter box.

'Mum said kitchen!'

'OK, OK . . .'

Why didn't Mum come down herself? I was suddenly weary and irritable.

Eventually, Hope managed to open the door.

'Where is Mum?' I asked. The house was slightly chilly inside and there was no warm smell of dinner on the air.

'Just getting up,' said Hope.

'Is she poorly?'

'Just tired.'

'Dad not home yet?'

'Pub, I 'spect,' said Hope.

I manoeuvred my rucksack off my back, then Mum was at the top of the stairs, but instead of rushing down delighted to see me, she picked her way carefully, holding the banister. I put it down to the slippers she had on under the washed-out pink tracksuit she wore for her aerobics class. She seemed distant, almost cross, and wouldn't catch my eye as she filled a kettle at the sink.

I looked at my watch. It was after eight o'clock. I'd forgotten it stayed lighter in the evenings in England. I started to think I should have found a phone box and rung home after getting off the ferry, but that didn't seem a serious enough offence for Mum to give me the silent treatment.

I noticed Mum's hair was unbrushed at the back. She had been in bed when I arrived. Just tired, Hope had said. She'd had four weeks of coping on her own.

'I can do that,' I offered, taking the kettle from her.

I felt the first whisper of alarm when I noticed the collection of dirty mugs in the kitchen sink. Mum must really be exhausted, because she always kept the place spotless.

'Where's Dad?' I asked.

'Down the pub, I expect,' said Mum.

14

'Why don't you go back upstairs and I'll bring you a cup?'

To my surprise, because nothing was ever too much trouble for Mum, she said, 'All right,' then added, as if she'd only just remembered I'd been away, 'How was your holiday?'

'Great! It was great!'

My face was aching with smiling at her and not getting anything back.

'The journey?'

'Fine!'

She was already on her way back upstairs.

When I took the tea up, my parents' bedroom door was open and I caught a glimpse of Mum's reflection in the dressing-table mirror before I entered the room. You know how sometimes you see people differently when they're not aware you're looking at them? She was lying with her eyes closed, as if some vital essence had drained from her, leaving her insubstantial, like an echo of herself. For a couple of seconds I stared, and then she stirred, suddenly noticing me standing there.

Her eyes, bright with anxiety, locked on mine, telegraphing, *Don't ask in front of Hope.* Then, seeing I was alone, closed again, relieved.

'Let's sit you up,' I said.

She leaned against me as I plumped up the pillows behind her, and her body felt light and fragile. Half an hour before, I'd been walking up the Crescent, hating how familiar and ordinary it was, and now everything was shifting around me like an earthquake and I desperately wanted it to go back to normal.

'I'm poorly, Tess,' she said, in answer to the question I was too scared to ask.

I waited for her to say, 'It's OK, though, because . . .' But she didn't.

'What sort of poorly?' I asked, giddy with panic.

Mum was diagnosed with breast cancer when she was pregnant with Hope. She hadn't had the chemo until after

15

Hope was born, but she'd recovered. She'd had to go regularly for a check-up but the last one, just a few months ago, had been clear.

'I've got cancer of the ovary and it's spread to my liver,' she said. 'I should have gone to the doctor before, but I thought it was a bit of indigestion.'

Downstairs, Hope was singing a familiar tune, but I couldn't work out what it was.

My brain was trying to picture Mum before I left. A bit tired, perhaps, and worried, I'd thought because of my exams. She was always there for me: in the kitchen at breakfast time, keeping Hope quiet as I raced through my notes; and when I came home, with a cup of tea and a listening ear if I wanted to talk, or if I didn't, just pottering around washing up or chopping vegetables, a quietly supportive presence.

How could I have been so selfish that I didn't notice? How could I have even gone on holiday?

'There was nothing you could do,' Mum said, reading my thoughts.

'But you were fine at your last scan!'

'That was in my breast.'

'And they don't check the rest of you?'

Mum put a finger to her lips.

Hope was on her way upstairs. The nursery rhyme was 'Goosey Goosey Gander', except she was singing 'Juicy Juicy Gander'.

'Upstairs, downstairs, in my lady chamber . . .'

We forced ourselves to smile as she came into the room.

'I'm hungry,' she said.

'OK!' I jumped up from the bed. 'I'll make your tea.'

If I'd needed further evidence how bad things were, it was the empty fridge. Although there was never a lot of money in our family, there was always food. I felt suddenly angry with my father. In our house the division of labour was very traditional: Dad was the breadwinner, Mum was the homemaker, but surely he could have stirred himself in these circumstances? I pictured him in the pub milking the self-pity, with his mates buying him pints. Dad was always moaning about the hand life had dealt him.

I found a can of Heinz spaghetti in the cupboard and put a slice of bread in the toaster.

Hope was staring at me, but my mind was so full with trying to take it all in, I couldn't think of anything to say to her.

The spaghetti began to bubble on the stove.

I slopped it onto the piece of toast, recalling the bowl of perfectly al-dente pasta we'd eaten in Fiesole the day before, with a sauce that tasted of a thousand tomatoes in one spoonful, and Florence in the distance, the backdrop to a Leonardo painting, so far away now, it felt like another life.

The dictionary confirmed that 'plangent' means resonant and mournful. It comes from the Latin *plangere*: to beat the breast in grief.

2

August 1997

GUS

I took up distance running after my brother died because it was an acceptable way of being alone. Other people's concern was almost the most difficult thing to deal with. If I said I was OK, they looked at me as if I was in denial; if I admitted I was finding things pretty difficult, there was no way for them to make it better. When I said I was training for a charity half-marathon to raise money for people with sports injuries, people nodded, satisfied, because Ross had been killed in a skiing accident, so it made sense.

At optimum speed, the rhythmic pounding of shoe on road delivered a kind of oblivion that had become addictive. It was what made me get out of bed every morning, even on holiday, although in Florence, the uneven cobbles and sudden, astonishing encounters with beauty, made it difficult to maintain a pace that made me forget where or who I was.

On the last day of the holiday, I ran along the Arno at dawn, crossing the river in alternate directions at each bridge, then looping back on myself to mirror the route, with the pale gleam of the sun in my eyes one way and its warmth on my back the other. With only an occasional road-sweeper for com-

18

pany, it felt as if I owned the place, or, perhaps, that it owned me. At the level of cardiovascular exertion that freed ideas to float across my mind, it occurred to me that I could come back to Florence one day, even live here, if I wanted. In this historic city, I could be a person with no history, the person I wanted to be, whoever that was. At eighteen, the thought was a revelation.

On my third crossing of the Ponte Vecchio, I slowed to a walking pace to cool down. There was no one else around. The glittering goldsmiths' wares were hidden behind sturdy wooden boards. There was nothing to indicate that I hadn't been transported back in time five hundred years. Yet somehow it felt less real than it had the previous evening, heaving with tourists. Like a deserted film set.

I suppose I'd hoped to find the girl there again. Not that I'd have known what to say to her any more than I had on the first two occasions. Handing back the camera, I hadn't even been brave enough to make eye contact, then, given a third chance, I'd blown that too.

Standing in the queue for ice cream beside the bridge, I'd felt a tap on my shoulder, and there she was again, smiling as if we'd known each other all our lives and were about to go on some amazing adventure together.

'There's this brilliant *gelato* place just down Via dei Neri where you can get about six for the price of one here!' she informed me.

'I don't think I could manage six!'

My attempt at wit had come out sounding pompous and dismissive. I wasn't very practised at talking to girls.

'Honest to God, you would from this place!'

Why don't you show me where it is? Great! Let's go there! None of the responses I'd like to have given had been available with my parents standing right beside me. Instead, I'd stared at her like a moron, with sentences jostling for position in my head as her smile faded from sparkling to slightly perplexed before she hurried off to catch up with her friend.

On the north side of the river, Florence was beginning to wake up to the mechanical clatter of shutters as bars opened up for the day. As I entered the Duomo square, the sun's rays lit up the cassata stripes of the Campanile and the air was suddenly full of bells. Florence was a kind of heaven on earth and I thought it would be impossible to be unhappy living here.

I joined my parents in the lobby of our hotel on their way in to breakfast.

'The loneliness of the long-distance runner!' my father remarked.

It was what he always said when he saw me after a run, as if it meant something, when it was actually just the title of a film he'd seen in his youth.

I always felt prickly with my parents, like a Pavlovian reaction to their company.

I knew, from overhearing conversations at school, that a proper Tuscan holiday meant renting a villa with a pool, if you didn't actually own one yourself, surrounded by olive groves and views of rolling hills. My father had instead booked us into this expensive hotel in the centre of Florence. I was never sure how the done thing got established, but I was aware from quite an early age that there was a done thing and that my father often got it slightly wrong. Not having been to a private school himself, but now able to afford to send his sons to one, he would turn up to sports days wearing a blazer and tie, whereas the cool dads, who went to the Cannes film festival, or held offshore accounts in the Cayman Islands, wore jeans, polo shirts and loafers with no socks, as if vying for a most-casually-dressed award. As a liberal-minded sixth-former, I upheld the right of anyone to dress as they wished; as his son, I was mortified.

'Who on earth wants cheese at this time in the morning?'

My father inspected the buffet table. He was the sort of man who made loud statements, as if inviting the room to agree with him.

'I think it's what Germans eat.' My mother spoke in a low voice so as not to be overheard.

'You never hear about the German rates of colonic cancer, do you?' Dad mused. 'All that smoked sausage too . . .'

'Where are you off to today?' I asked, as we returned to the table with laden plates.

Included in the price of the Treasures of Tuscany package were excursions to the other principal tourist cities of the region. Since having to stop the coach twice to throw up on the first trip to Assisi, I now spent the days in Florence alone, visiting the galleries and churches at my own pace, enjoying the wonderful feeling of weightlessness that came from getting away from my parents.

'Pisa,' my father said.

As someone who didn't quite believe in travel-sickness, he couldn't disguise his irritation at my failure to get full value from the holiday and the tour company's refusal to refund a proportion of the cost.

The city centre was filling with groups of tourists following dutifully behind the raised umbrellas of their guides, but it was easy enough to peel away down a shadowy side street. I'd walked so much in the past week, I had the map of Florence in my head. The covered market near San Lorenzo, its cool air infused with the smoky scent of delicatessen, was my first daily pilgrimage. Some of the stallholders recognized me now. At the fruit stall, the old man's practised thumb roamed over a pyramid of peaches to select a perfectly ripe fruit. At the *salumeria*, the friendly mamma paid serious attention to my search for a filling for my single bread roll, offering little slivers of different salamis for me to taste or sniff like fine wine. As it was my last day, I treated myself to *un'etto* of expensive San Daniele prosciutto. She carefully arranged the wafer-thin translucent slices in overlapping layers on a sheet of shiny paper.

'*Ultimo giorno,*' I told her, attempting a few Italian words. It's my last day.

'*Ma ritorno,*' I added – but I'll come back – as if voicing it would make my intention more real.

I had bought a sketchbook, covered in hand-printed Florentine paper, to take with me to the art galleries because drawing made me look more closely at the paintings and feel less self-conscious about it. Art had always been my best subject at school, if you considered it a subject, which my father didn't. The more I studied the art in Florence, the more I wished that I had summoned the courage to apply for Art History at university. It wasn't just the skilful application of paint to canvas or fresco, it was what the artist was thinking that fascinated me. Did they believe in the religious stories they made so human, with saints and apostles dressed like Florentine burghers, or were they just doing it to make a living?

I'd been steered towards Medicine, because it was 'in the family', as my sixth-form tutor put it, as if it was some kind of genetic mutation. As everyone always said, I could look at pictures in my spare time. Now, inspired by this city where art and science had flourished side by side, I wondered if there was even a way of combining the two. Perhaps I would come back to the Uffizi one day as a visiting professor in Anatomy? At least as a doctor, I'd have the means to return. There was no money in Art, my father always said. 'Even Van Gogh couldn't make a living out of it!'

I ate my *panino* sitting on the steps of the Palazzo Vecchio, occasionally tapping my foot to the music of a guitar-playing busker to make it look as if I was doing something. Time on my own seemed to pass very slowly and I was pathetically shy about striking up conversations with strangers. I wondered if I'd have been any better at it if my friend Marcus had been there. We were supposed to be Interrailing together, but he'd got off with a girl from our sister school at the end of school prom, and had naturally chosen sex in Ibiza over trailing round Europe with me. Neither of us had any real experience with girls and I think had both assumed that sex was something that wouldn't happen until university, so I had a grudging admiration for Marcus, but it had left me with the unwelcome decision to cancel our holiday or go it alone.

Around the same time, one of my father's patients, who'd broken a crown on a slice of panforte, expressed astonishment that my father had never been to Tuscany. The inferred criticism had stung Dad into action.

'What do you think?' he'd asked, pushing a brochure across the kitchen table one morning, as I was shovelling down cereal before cycling to my summer job at our town's new gastropub.

'Great idea!' It had been good to see him focusing on a plan again.

'Want to join us?'

'Really?' Somehow, through a mouthful of Weetabix, I made dread sound like surprised enthusiasm.

Being a dentist, Dad never expected much more than a slight nod in answer to his questions, so, by the time I arrived back from work, the holiday had been booked and paid for.

I'd told myself that it would be churlish not to accept my parents' generosity, but the truth was, I was a wuss.

Scanning the crowds of tourists taking photos with the replica statue of Michelangelo's *David*, I began to wonder if I would actually recognize the girl if I saw her again. She was tall, and her hair was longish and brownish, I thought. There wasn't anything particularly memorable about her features, except that when she smiled her face was suddenly full of mischief and intimacy, as if there was a thrilling secret that only she knew and was about to share only with you.

Via dei Neri was a narrow street winding towards the Piazza Santa Croce and I missed the *gelateria* on the way down. It was just a single door with a dark interior. For my first cone, I chose *nocciola* and *limone*, because that was what the Italian man in front of me ordered, the delicious creaminess of the hazelnut perfectly complemented by the refreshing citrus tang. I walked back down to Santa Croce eating it, then returned and ordered another, pistachio and melon, and loitered in the cool shade of the shop, glancing at each new customer in the hope of seeing the girl again.

In the heat of the afternoon, I made my way through the crowds on the Ponte Vecchio to the Boboli Gardens. The numbers of tourists dwindled the higher I climbed, and, on the top terrace, I found myself completely alone beside the ornamental lake. The sun was still very hot but invisible now behind a veil of humidity that muted the view of the city like the varnish of age over an old master. Distant thunder rolled around the hills and the air was thick with imminent rain. Opening my sketchbook, I recorded the smudgy outline of the Duomo.

Suddenly, a bright beam of light broke through the unnatural yellowish twilight, giving surreal definition to the trimmed box hedges, lighting up the greenish-blue water. As I raised my camera, a white heron, which I had perceived as a static element of the ornate marble fountain in the centre of the lake, took off, startling me. It flew across the water, the flapping of its wings the only sound or movement in the still air.

It occurred to me that I had not given Ross a thought since breakfast.

For a moment, I saw my brother's face glancing back at me through a cloud of thickly falling snow, his teeth white, the flakes settling on his dark, swept-back hair, his eyes hidden behind mirror ski goggles.

24

A fat raindrop splattered my drawing. I closed the pad and stood for a few moments with my face tilted towards the sky, enjoying a warm drenching, until a splinter of lightning reminded me that I was one of the tallest objects around, and should probably take cover. As I skeltered down the suddenly slippery marble steps, hordes of tourists were emerging from the gardens, shiny guidebooks held over their heads.

There was a feeling of camaraderie as we stood crowded together in the scant shelter of the Pitti Palace walls, one or other of us occasionally extending a bare arm to test the heaviness of the downpour and judge whether to make a dash for it or wait.

Beside me, three American girls about my age, with cumbersome rucksacks on their backs, were consulting their guidebook, trying to work out how to get to the campsite. I knew the route, having passed it on my way to Piazzale Michelangelo on my run the previous morning, but wasn't sure whether it would be polite or intrusive to show them. One of them was very pretty. I could feel myself going red even before I spoke.

'I couldn't help overhearing. Can I help?'

My voice sounded as if it were coming from another person, initially croaky, then far too loud and public school.

'You're English, aren't you?' the pretty one said. 'Your accent's SO cute!'

'Are you camping too?'

'No. I'm in a hotel,' I confessed, unable to think of anything cooler to say quickly enough.

'Why don't we all go for an *aperitivo*?' the loud one suggested.

'Actually, I'm meeting my parents for dinner.'

With the rain easing, I set off in a hurry, convinced they were laughing at me. Ross would have known exactly how to behave. Was charm something you were born with, or just a matter of practice?

The storm had driven the crowds from the Ponte Vecchio. I paused for a last look at the view, but the hills beyond the city walls were shrouded in low cloud and the green-and-white striped facade of San Miniato al Monte which I could see flood-lit at night from the pool on the roof of the hotel had disappeared.

The essential experiences for every visitor to Tuscany were listed at the front of the complimentary full-colour guidebook that had thumped through our letter box in a stiff white envelope with our tickets. Each evening, when we convened for dinner, my father recapped the day's activities, counting the completed targets on his fingers, like a conscientious Cub Scout ticking off badges achieved.

- SAN GIMIGNANO'S COBBLED STREETS?
  Wandered.
- TUSCANY'S TALLEST TOWER?
  Conquered.
- GIOTTO'S FAMOUS FRESCO CYCLE OF THE LIFE OF
  SAN FRANCESCO?
  Seen. (And that was enough religious paintings to last a lifetime!)
- THE EXCITEMENT OF THUNDERING HORSES' HOOVES
  IN SIENA'S PALIO SQUARE?
  Available only on two specific days of the year.
- A RELAXING APERITIF ON THE FAMOUS FAN-SHAPED PIAZZA?
  Consumed, despite the extortionate price of a gin and tonic.
  'How was Pisa?' I asked that evening, as we waited for menus in an expensive restaurant with beams and bare brick walls that gave it the feel of a medieval banqueting hall.

'Bigger than you'd think.' My father put on his reading specs although he already knew exactly what he was going to choose.

'The Leaning Tower was smaller than I thought it would be,' my mother said.

'They should sort out their queuing system,' my father announced, from which I gathered that they had not been able to climb the monument, and could not therefore deem it a mission accomplished.

- THE LEANING TOWER OF PISA.
  Photographed but unclimbed.

It was not an entirely satisfactory conclusion to the holiday.

'There are lots of other buildings,' said my mother.

'Cathedral and whatnot. Jam-packed with tourists, obviously.'

Nothing in their description gave me a reason to say that I'd like to go one day, and if I had, it would only have reminded my father of the wasted place on the coach, so I said nothing.

'Ah, yes, *buona sera* to you too,' said my father when the waiter arrived to take our order. 'We're going to have the Florentine beefsteak.'

The best place to sample this 'most famous typical dish' had been a project from the start of the holiday. Dad had sought the advice of the driver who met us at the airport on our first night and all the receptionists at the hotel. We were now sitting in the restaurant recommended by a majority of five to one.

Priced by the kilo, a *bistecca alla Fiorentina* was not just a meal, it was a spectacle performed on a raised platform within the dining area of the restaurant. First the rib of beef was held aloft by a chef in a tall white hat; a large knife was sharpened with swift, dramatic strokes; then a very thick slice of meat, a chop for a giant, was severed and weighed before being placed on a trolley and wheeled over to the table for approval. My father swelled with satisfaction as the other tables oohed and aahed obligingly at each stage of the ritual. I didn't begrudge him this small pleasure, but my insides squirmed with embarrassment.

'What did you get up to?' my father asked, as the meat was

trolleyed off to the kitchen and we had to talk to each other again.

'Walking, mainly. I went to the Boboli Gardens.'

Silence.

'I saw this heron, actually.'

'Heron? We're too far inland, aren't we? Sure it wasn't a stork?' said my father.

'It was kind of weird, because I thought it was part of the statue at first, then it just took off, as if the stone had come alive.'

My parents exchanged glances. 'Fey' was the word my mother sometimes used to describe me. 'Airy-fairy' or 'arty-farty' were my father's expressions. In the shorthand descriptions that parents give to their children, I was the one with my head in the clouds.

I made the mistake of extemporizing.

'It was the sort of thing that might make you think you'd seen a vision, you know . . . I mean, maybe all those visions of St Francis actually have a neurological explanation? Maybe there was something different about his brain . . .'

I realized, too late, that 'brain' was one of the words we didn't say any more. Certain words triggered inevitable associations. Over the last few months our family's spoken vocabulary had shrunk dramatically.

Now my parents were both staring into the middle distance.

My carelessness had got them thinking about the side of Ross's head, the thickness of the bandage unable to disguise the fact that there was a bit missing.

Had some of my brother's brain spilled out into the snow? I wondered. Had the rescue party covered it up with more snow? And when the snow melted in the spring, were there still fragments of skull on the mountain?

If this holiday was an attempt to move on, it hadn't been a great success. The last time we were on holiday, Ross was with us. A winter holiday, so very different from the sticky heat of Florence, but a family holiday nonetheless. When you remember holidays you think about the sights and the weather, but somehow you always forget the confinement of being together, meal after meal. Ross used to dominate the conversation, bantering with my father and joshing me while my mother gazed at him adoringly. Now, his absence made him seem almost more present.

You know that expression, 'the elephant in the room'? You're the elephant, Ross!

I thought he'd quite like that description. Occasionally, I found myself speaking to my brother in my head even though we hadn't had that kind of relationship when he was alive. I was surprised in retrospect how much we'd had in common just by virtue of being in the same family. Ross was the one person who would have understood how pitiful my parents were in their grief, and yet how annoying they still managed to be.

'You have to deal with reality,' said my father eventually. I wasn't sure whether it was intended as a reprimand to me or an instruction to himself. 'You have to get to grips with what's in front of you.'

What was in front of him now was the giant steak, charred and leaking blood onto the wooden board on which it was presented.

My father looked up at the waiter.

'We'd like Chef to cook it for us if that's not too much trouble!' he barked.

I pictured the chef's face as the waiter returned to the kitchen. During my summer job I'd learned that customers who sent their steaks back to be well done were even further down the hierarchy of contempt than pot washers.

When the steak was returned to us, it was pale brown all

the way through, as if it had been given ten minutes in a microwave.

My father doled out the leathery slices.

'How many for you, Angus?'

'Just one.'

'One?'

'Angus has never had a huge appetite,' my mother reminded him.

Ross had an enormous appetite. Was it over-sensitive of me to hear an unspoken comparison?

I was completely different to Ross. My brother was dark, handsome and built; I had inherited my mother's willowy height, and, although my hair wasn't orange like my father's, I had enough of his freckly complexion to be called a ginge at school.

Ross had been captain of the rugby and rowing teams and Head Boy; I enjoyed football and had never been considered for the prefect body. Ross's summer job after leaving school had been a lifeguard at the local open-air swimming pool. Being a lifesaver was something to boast about, unlike being a kitchen boy. Not that Ross ever actually saved a life, although plenty of girls pretended to be struggling in the hope of being man-handled by him. Ross had starred in his own version of *Baywatch*. In Guildford.

I was never sure whether the truth was that my parents weren't very good at disguising their obvious preference, or that I was in fact pretty mediocre compared to Ross. It wasn't some-thing you could talk about without sounding like a whinger, so I never did, except occasionally to Marcus, who knew what Ross was really like. Was it Ross's sporting prowess that had made the teachers at our school so willing to turn a blind eye to his other activities, we'd sometimes speculated, or had they too lived in fear of him? Perhaps Ross and his acolytes kept a record of punishable offences committed by the staff as well as the lower-school boys? I'd never know, because nobody said anything remotely critical about him now that he was dead.

We sat in silence, chewing our steak.

'I expect you're itching to get to uni . . .' my mother said.

Was my discomfort so obvious?

The truth was that although I was counting down the hours until the claustrophobia of the holiday would be over, I was also feeling pretty nervous about what was coming next. I thought I'd probably be OK at Medicine because I was good at Biology and interested in how people worked.

'Which makes you sound like an agony aunt!' Ross had needled, just the previous November, which now felt like a lifetime ago, because, in a way, it was.

In spite of his ridicule, or maybe because it had made me think harder, I'd performed well at the interview and been offered a place conditional on achieving three As at A level. But I'd always felt uneasy about following in my brother's footsteps. Over that Christmas holiday, I had actually made up my mind to ask if I could defer a year and use the time to decide if Medicine was what I really wanted to do.

Then the accident happened.

When I returned to school the deadline for acceptances was looming. My father had been so proud at the thought of both his sons becoming doctors. Doing Medicine, or at least, not *not* doing it, was the only small way I could begin to make it up to him.

Only the previous day, calling the school to get my A-level results, with my parents hovering in the hotel corridor just outside the door, a tiny part of me had still been hoping to be granted a reprieve. But my grades were good enough.

I realized I hadn't responded to my mother.

'Yes, really looking forward to it now,' I assured her.

At least there would be sex. If Ross's experience was anything to go by, medics were at it all the time.